Leo gazed at her He still didn't understand why she was here. She hadn't possessed enough honour to be faithful to him—why would she care whether he knew about his own child or not?

'I would have expected you to pass it off as this other man's,' he said abruptly.

Margo winced at that. 'Clearly you don't have a very high opinion of me.'

'And you think I should?'

'No.' She let out a little defeated sigh. 'No, I don't.'

'So why didn't you do that, Margo?' It was the first time he'd said her name since he'd seen her again, and it caused him a sudden, surprising flash of pain. He clenched his hands into fists, then deliberately flattened them out, resting them again on his desk.

'Because I am not—no matter what you think—completely without morals,' she replied with a bit of her old spirit. 'I want my child, and I want my child to know his or her father.' She took a deep breath. 'And, more than that. I want my child to have a loving, stable home. A home where she knows she's safe, where her parents are there, loving and protecting her. *Always*.' Her dark brown eyes seemed to glow with an inner fire, an utter conviction.

'And how,' Leo asked after a pause, 'do you suppose *that* is going to work?'

'That's the other thing I want,' Margo said, still holding his gaze, her eyes like burning coals in her pale face. 'I want you to marry me.'

The Marakaios Brides

Powerful Greeks meet their match!

Proud Greek blood flows through the veins of brothers
Antonios and Leonidas Marakaios. With determination
and ruthlessness they have built their family's empire
to global heights.

It has been their sole focus—
even to the exclusion of love.

But now two women look set to challenge their pride,
their passion and their marriage vows!

Read Antonios's story in:

The Marakaios Marriage

May 2015

And meet Leonidas in:

The Marakaios Baby

August 2015

THE MARAKAIOS BABY

BY
KATE HEWITT

Published in Great Britain 2015
by Mills & Boon, an imprint of Harlequin (UK) Limited,
Eton House, 18-24 Paradise Road, Richmond, Surrey, TW9 1SR

© 2015 Kate Hewitt

ISBN: 978-0-263-25074-9

Printed and bound in Spain
by CPI, Barcelona

After spending three years as a die-hard New Yorker, **Kate Hewitt** now lives in a small village in the English Lake District with her husband, their five children and a golden retriever. In addition to writing intensely emotional stories she loves reading, baking, and playing chess with her son— she has yet to win against him, but she continues to try.

Learn more about Kate at www.kate-hewitt.com

Visit the author profile page at millsandboon.co.uk for more titles

To Lauren,
Thank you for your many years of friendship. Love, K.

CHAPTER ONE

'WILL YOU MARRY ME?'

The question seemed to bounce off the walls and echo through the room as Marguerite Ferrars stared in shock at the face of the man who had asked the question—her lover, Leonidas Marakaios.

He gazed at her with a faint half-smile quirking his lips, his eyebrows slightly raised. In his hand he held a small black velvet box, and the solitaire diamond of who knew how many carats inside sparkled with quiet sophistication.

'Margo?'

His voice was lilting, teasing; he thought she was silent because she was so surprised. But, while that was true, she felt something else as well. Appalled. *Terrified.*

She'd never expected this—never thought that charismatic playboy Leo would think of *marriage.* A lifetime commitment, a life—and love—you could lose. And she knew the searing pain of losing someone—the way it left you breathless and gasping, waking up in the night, your face awash in tears, even years later...

The moment stretched on too long, and still she said nothing. She couldn't. Because she didn't dare say yes and yet no seemed just as impossible. Leo Marakaios was not a man who accepted refusal. Rejection.

She watched as a slight frown pulled his eyebrows together and he withdrew the hand holding the open velvet box to rest it in his lap.

'Leo…' she began finally, helplessly—because how could she tell this impossibly arrogant, handsome, charismatic man no? And yet she had to. Of course she had to.

'I didn't think this would be *that* much of a surprise,' he said, his voice holding only a remnant of lightness now.

She felt a surge of something close to anger, which was almost a relief. 'Didn't you? We've never had the kind of relationship that…'

'That what?' He arched an eyebrow, the gesture caught between wryness and disdain.

She could feel him withdrawing, and while she knew she should be glad, she felt only a deep, wrenching sorrow. This wasn't what she'd wanted. But she didn't—couldn't—want marriage either. Couldn't let someone matter that much.

'That…led somewhere,' she finished, and he closed the box with a snap, his expression turning so terribly cold.

'I see.'

Words stuck in her throat—the answer she knew she had to give yet somehow couldn't make herself say. 'Leo, we've never even talked about the future.'

'We've been together for two years,' he returned. 'I think it's reasonable to assume it was *going somewhere*.'

His voice held a deliberate edge, and his eyes were blazing silver fire. Or maybe ice, for he looked so cold now—even contemptuous. And moments ago he'd been asking to marry her. It almost seemed laughable.

'Together for two years,' Margo allowed, determined to stay reasonable, 'but we've hardly had what most people would call a "normal" relationship. We've met in strange cities, in restaurants and hotels—'

'Which is how you wanted it.'

'And how you wanted it too. It was an *affair*, Leo. A—a fling.'

'A two-year fling.'

She rose from her chair, agitated now, and paced in front of the picture window that overlooked the Île de la Cité. It was so strange and unsettling to have Leo here in her apartment, her sanctuary, when he'd never come to her home before. Restaurants and hotels, yes—anonymous places for emotionless no-strings sex…that was what they'd *agreed*. That was all she could let herself have.

The risk of trying for more was simply too great. She knew what it was like to lose everything—even your own soul. She couldn't go through that again. She *wouldn't*.

Not even for Leo.

'You seem upset,' Leo remarked tonelessly.

'I just didn't expect this.'

'As it happens, neither did I.'

He rose from where he'd been sitting, on the damask settee she'd upholstered herself, his tall, rangy figure seeming to fill the cosy space of her sitting room. He looked wrong here, somehow, amidst all her things—her throw pillows and porcelain ornaments; he was too big, too dark, too powerful…like a tiger pacing the cage of a kitten.

'I thought most women wanted to get married,' he remarked.

She turned on him then, another surge of anger making her feel strong. 'What a ridiculous, sexist assumption! And I, in any case, am *not* "most women".'

'No,' Leo agreed silkily. 'You're not.'

His eyes blazed with intent then—an intent that made Margo's breath catch in her chest.

The sexual chemistry between them had been instantaneous—electric. She remembered catching sight of him in a hotel bar in Milan two years ago. She'd been nursing a single glass of white wine while she went over her notes for the next day's meeting. He'd strolled over to the bar and slid onto the stool next to hers, and the little hairs on the back of her neck had prickled. She'd felt as if she were finally coming alive.

She'd gone back with him to his room that night. It had been so unlike her—she'd always kept herself apart, her heart on ice. In her twenty-nine years she'd had only two lovers before Leo, both of them lamentably forgettable. Neither of those men had affected her the way Leo did—and not just physically.

From that first night he'd reached a place inside her she'd thought numb, dead. He'd brought her back to life. And while she'd known it was dangerous she'd stayed with him, because the thought of *not* being with Leo was worse.

Except now that was a reality. She'd thought an affair with Leo would be safe, that he would never ask more of her than she was prepared to give. But here he was asking for marriage, a lifetime, and her response was bone-deep terror.

Which was why she could not accept his proposal.

Except she had a terrible and yet thrilling certainty that he had a different proposal in mind now, as he came towards her, his gaze turning hooded and sleepy even though that lithe, powerful body she knew almost as well as her own was taut with suppressed energy and tension.

She licked her lips, felt the insistent thud of her heart, the stirring of blood in her veins. Even now her body yearned for him.

'Leo...'

'You surprise me, Margo.'

She gave a little shake of her head. 'You're the one who surprised *me*.'

'Clearly. But I thought you'd be pleased. Don't you want to get married?'

He sounded so reasonable, but she saw a certain calculation in his eyes, and he ran one hand up and down her bare arm, so gooseflesh broke out in the wake of his touch.

'No.'

'Why not?'

His easy, interested tone jarred with the fingers he continued to run up and down her arm, and with that sleepy, knowing gaze.

'I'm a career woman, Leo—'

'You can be a *married* career woman, Margo. This is the twenty-first century, after all.'

'Oh? And how would that work, exactly? You live in central Greece—the middle of nowhere. How am I supposed to work from there?'

For a second she thought she saw a gleam of something like triumph in his eyes, but then it sparked out and he gave a negligent shrug of his shoulders. 'You could commute. The flight from Athens to Paris is only a few hours.'

'Commute? Are you serious?'

'We could work something out, Margo, if that's all that's stopping you.'

There was a note of challenge in his voice, and she realised then what he was doing. Leonidas Marakaios was a powerful and persuasive man. He was CEO of the Marakaios Enterprises, a company that had started with a few olive groves and a cold press and was now a multibillion dollar company—a man of the world who was used to getting what he wanted. And he wanted her. So here he was, breaking down her defences, discarding her arguments. And the trouble was she was so weak, so tempted, that it might actually work.

She turned away from him to take a few steadying

breaths without him seeing how unsettled she was. In the darkness of the window she could see her reflection: a too pale face, wide eyes, and a tumble of long dark brown hair that fell nearly to her waist.

When Leo had shown up twenty minutes ago she'd been in yoga pants and a faded tee shirt, her face without a lick of make-up, her hair down. She'd been silently appalled. She'd always been careful that he saw only the woman she wanted him to—the woman the world saw: sexy, chic, professional, a little bit distant, a little bit cool. All their meetings had been stage-managed affairs; she'd swept into a restaurant or hotel room in full make-up, a sexy little negligee in her bag, insouciant and secure.

He'd never seen her like this: vulnerable, without the mask of make-up, the armour of designer clothes. He'd never seen her agitated and uncertain, her *savoir-faire* slipping from her fingers.

'Margo,' Leo said quietly. 'Tell me the real reason.'

Another quick breath, buoying inside her lungs. 'I told you, Leo. I don't want marriage or what it entails. The whole housewife routine bores me to death.' She made her voice cold—careless, even.

Steeling herself, she turned around to face him and nearly flinched at the careful consideration in his eyes. She had a horrible feeling she wasn't fooling him at all.

'I just said you don't need to be a housewife. Do you think I want to change you completely?'

'You don't even know me, Leo, not really.'

He took a step towards her, and again she saw that intent in his eyes, felt an answering flare inside her. She had, she realised, just given him a challenge.

'Are you sure about that?'

'I'm not talking about sex.'

'What don't I know, then?' He spread his hands wide, his eyebrows raised. 'Tell me.'

'It's not that simple.'

'Because you don't want it to be. I *know* you, Margo. I know your feet get cold in the middle of the night and you tuck them between my legs to keep them warm. I know you like marshmallows even though you pretend you don't eat any sweets.'

She almost laughed at that. 'How do you know about the marshmallows?' Her dirty little secret, when it seemed as if every other woman in Paris was stick-thin and ate only lettuce leaves and drank black coffee.

'I found a little bag of them in your handbag once.'

'You shouldn't have been looking through my things.'

'I was fetching your reading glasses for you, if you remember.'

She shook her head—an instinctive response, because all those little details that he'd lobbed at her like well-aimed missiles were making her realise how intimate her relationship with Leo really had been. She'd thought she'd kept her distance, armoured herself—the elegant Marguerite Ferrars, keeping their assignations in anonymous places. But in truth reality had seeped through. Emotion had too, as well as affection, with the glasses and the marshmallows and the cold feet. Little signs of how close they'd become, how much he'd begun to mean to her.

And she saw all too clearly how he would chip away at her defences now—how he would seduce her with knowing words and touches until she'd say yes. Of course she'd say yes. Because she was already more than halfway to loving him.

For a second—no more—Margo thought about actually accepting his proposal. Living a life she'd never thought to have, had made herself never want. A life of happiness but also of terrible risk. Risk of loss, of hurt, of heartbreak. Of coming apart so she'd never put the pieces of her soul back together again.

Reality returned in a cold rush and she shook her head. 'No, Leo.'

That faint smile had returned, although his eyes looked hard. 'Just like that?'

'Just like that.'

'You don't think I—*we*—deserve more explanation?'

'Not particularly.' She'd made her voice indifferent, maybe too much, because anger flashed in his eyes, turning the silver to grey.

He cocked his head, his gaze sweeping slowly over her. 'I think you're hiding something from me.'

She gave a scoffing laugh. 'You would.'

'What is that supposed to mean?'

'You can't believe I'm actually turning you down, can you?' The words tumbled out of her, fuelled by both anger and fear. 'You—the Lothario who has had half the single women in Europe.'

'I wouldn't go quite that far. Forty per cent, maybe.'

There was the charm, almost causing her to lose that needed edge of fury, to smile. 'No woman has ever resisted you.'

'You didn't,' he pointed out, with what Margo knew was deceptive mildness.

'Because I wanted a fling,' she declared defiantly. 'Sex without strings.'

'We never actually said—'

'Oh, but we did, Leo. Don't you remember that first conversation? We set out the rules right then.'

She saw a glimmer of acknowledgement in his eyes, and his mouth hardened into a thin line.

It had been an elaborate dance of words, their talk of

business concerns and obligations, veiled references to other places, other people—every careful remark setting out just what their affair would and wouldn't be. Both of them, Margo had thought, had been clear about their desire for a commitment-free relationship.

'I didn't think you wanted to get married,' she said.

Leo shrugged. 'I decided I did.'

'But you didn't at the beginning, when we met. You weren't interested then.' She'd felt his innate sense of distance and caution, the same as her own. They had, she'd thought, been speaking the same language, giving the code words for no commitment, no love, no fairytales.

'People change, Margo. I'm thirty-two. You're twenty-nine. Of course I'd think of settling down...starting a family.'

Something clanged hard inside her; she felt as if someone had pulled the chair out from under her and she'd fallen right onto the floor.

'Well, then, that's where we differ, Leo,' she stated, her voice thankfully cool. 'I don't want children.'

His eyebrows drew together at that. 'Ever?'

'Ever.'

He stared at her for a long, considering moment. 'You're scared.'

'Stop telling me what I feel,' she snapped, raising her voice to hide its tremble. 'And get over yourself. I'm not scared. I just don't want what you want. I don't want to marry you.' She took a breath, and then plunged on recklessly. 'I don't love you.'

He tensed slightly, almost as if her words had hurt him, and then he shrugged. 'I don't love *you*. But there are better bases for a marriage than that ephemeral emotion.'

'Such as?'

'Common goals—'

'How romantic you are,' she mocked.

'Did you want more romance? Would that have made a difference?'

'No!'

'Then I'm glad I didn't wine and dine you at Gavroche, as I was considering, and propose in front of a crowd.'

He spoke lightly enough, and yet she still heard an edge to his voice.

'So am I,' she answered, and held her ground as he took a step towards her. She could feel the heat rolling off him, felt herself instinctively sway towards him. She stopped herself, holding herself rigid, refusing to yield even in that small way.

'So this is it?' he said softly, his voice no more than a breath that feathered her face. His silvery gaze roved over her, seeming to steal right inside her. 'This is goodbye?'

'Yes.' She spoke firmly, but he must have seen something in her face, for he cupped her cheek, ran a thumb over her parted lips.

'You're so very sure?' he whispered, and she forced herself to stare at him, not to show anything in her face.

'Yes.'

He dropped his hand from her face to her breast, cupping its fullness, running his thumb over the taut peak. She shuddered; she couldn't help it. He'd always affected her that way, right from the beginning. A single, simple touch lit a flame inside her.

'You don't seem sure,' he murmured.

'We have chemistry, Leo, that's all.' She forced the words out past the desire that was sweeping through her, leaving nothing but need in its wake.

'Chemistry is a powerful thing.'

He slid his hand down to her waist, his fingers splaying across her hip. Sensation leapt to life inside her, low down, sparks shooting through her belly.

'It's not enough,' she said through gritted teeth.

She ached for him to move his hand lower, to touch her with the knowing expertise her body had once revelled in. Still she didn't move, and neither did Leo.

'Not enough?' he queried softly. 'So you want love, then?'

'Not with you.'

He stilled, and she made herself go on—say the words she knew would hurt them both and turn him from her for ever. She had to…she couldn't risk him breaking down any more of her defences. She couldn't risk, full stop.

'I don't love you, Leo, and I never will. Frankly, you were just a fling—something to while away the time. I never intended for it to be *serious*.' She let out a laugh, sharp and high, as Leo pulled back his hand from her hip. 'Honestly—a *proposal*?' She made herself continue. 'It's almost funny… Because I'd actually been planning to end it when we met in Rome next week.' She took a quick breath and went on recklessly. 'The truth is, I'm seeing someone else.'

He stared at her for a long, taut moment. A muscle flickered in his jaw, but that was all. 'How long?' he finally asked, the two words bitten off and spat out.

She shrugged. 'A couple of months.'

'*Months*—?'

'I didn't think we were exclusive.'

'I've always been faithful to you,' he said in a low voice.

'I never asked you to be,' she replied with another shrug.

She could hardly believe she was actually fooling him— didn't he see how she trembled? And yet she knew he was taken in. She saw it in the way everything in him had gone dangerously still.

Then a cold little smile played about his mouth.

'Well, then, this really is goodbye,' he said, and before she could answer he pulled her towards him and kissed her.

She hadn't been expecting it, the sudden press of his mouth on hers, knowing and sure, a delicious onslaught that had her insides flaring white-hot even as her mind scrambled frantically to resist.

But Leo had always been impossible to resist, and never more so than now, when he was utterly, ruthlessly determined to make her respond to him. His tongue slid inside her mouth as his hands spanned her waist, fitting her to his muscled body perfectly.

She kissed him back, gave herself up to the rush of sensations that left her dizzy with longing. The feel of Leo's hands on her body was so intense it almost hurt— like touching a raw nerve. He slid his hands under her tee shirt, discarding the flimsy bit of cotton with ease. And then her yoga pants were gone too. She kicked them off, needing to be naked, too enflamed by desire to feel either exposed or ashamed as she stood before him, utterly bare, her breath coming in pants and gulps.

Leo stood in front of her and slowly unbuttoned his shirt. She saw a predatory gleam in his eyes, but even that could not cool her desire. Was this his revenge? His punishment? Or simply his proof that she desired him still? Whatever it was, she'd take it. She'd welcome it. Because she knew it would be the last time she'd hold him in her arms, feel him inside her.

He shrugged his shirt off. The crisp white cotton slid off his shoulders, revealing his taut six-pack abs, the sprinkling of dark hair that veed towards his trousers. With a snick of leather he undid his belt and then kicked off his trousers, and he too was naked.

He came towards her, taking her in his arms in a way

that was possessive rather than sensual. When he kissed her she felt branded. Perhaps she always would.

He backed her towards the window, so her back was against the cold glass, and then without a single murmur or caress he drove inside her.

Even so she was ready for him, her body expanding to fit around his length. She wrapped her legs around his waist and pulled him inside her even more deeply, her head thrown back against the glass so she felt suspended between this world and the next, caught in a single moment of memory and desire.

The tension and pressure built inside her, a tornado that took over her senses, and at its dizzying peak Leo took her face in his hands and looked her straight in the eyes.

'You won't forget me,' he said, and it was a declaration of certainty, a curse, because she knew he was right.

Then, as her climax crashed over her, he shuddered into her and withdrew, leaving her trembling and weak-kneed against the window. She watched, dazed and numb, as he dressed silently. She could not form a single sentence, not even a word.

She watched him walk to the door. He didn't speak, didn't even look back. The door closed with a quiet, final-sounding click. Slowly she sank to the floor, clutching her knees to her chest as the aftershocks of her climax still shuddered through her.

Leo was gone.

CHAPTER TWO

Leo strode from Margo's apartment, his body still shuddering from their lovemaking—but no, he couldn't call it that. *Never* that.

With one abrupt movement he lobbed the little velvet box into the nearest bin. A foolish waste, perhaps, but he couldn't bear to look at that wretched ring for another moment. He couldn't stand the thought of it even being in his pocket.

He drew a deep breath and raked a hand through his hair, willing back the emotion that had nearly overwhelmed him in Margo's apartment. All of it. She was out of his life. He need never think of her again.

It wasn't as if he'd loved her, he reminded himself. Margo had been right about that. He had liked her, yes, and they'd certainly shared an explosive sexual chemistry. She'd seemed the obvious choice when he'd decided it was time he married.

Six months ago, just after their mother's death, his brother Antonios had resigned as CEO of Marakaios Enterprises and Leo had taken his place. It was what Leo had wanted his whole life, what he had striven for as a young man, working for the father who had never even noticed him. Who had chosen Antonios instead of him, again and again.

But he was over that; he'd made peace with Antonios, and his father had been dead for ten years. His mother too was gone now, and all of it together had made him want to marry, to start a family, create his own dynasty.

But Margo doesn't even want children.

Why hadn't he known that? Why hadn't he realised she was so faithless, so unscrupulous? *Theos*, she'd been *cheating* on him. He could hardly credit it; they'd seen each other every week or two at least, and their encounters had always been intense. But she had no reason to lie about such a thing.

And when he thought of how he'd asked her to marry him, how he'd tried to convince her, persuade her with gentle reason and understanding because he hadn't been able to believe she didn't want him… Leo closed his eyes, cringing with the shame of it.

Well, no more. He wouldn't marry. Or if he did it would simply be for a child. He would not engage his emotions, would not seek anything greater than the most basic of physical transactions. And he would never see Margo again, Margo of the cold feet and the marshmallows…

His face twisted with regret before he ironed out his features and strode on into the night.

Margo's stomach lurched for the third time that morning and she pressed one hand against her middle, closing her eyes and taking a deep breath. This stomach bug was both insistent and annoying. She'd been feeling nauseous for over a week, although she'd thankfully never actually been sick.

'Are you all right?'

Margo looked up to see Sophie, her colleague and fellow buyer at Paris's exclusive department store Achat, frowning at her.

They'd worked together for six years, starting as interns, Sophie with her freshly minted college degree and Margo doing it the hard way, having worked on the shop floor since she was sixteen. They'd both moved up to being assistants, and now they were buyers in their own right. Margo was in charge of the home department; Sophie covered accessories. Both of them were completely dedicated to their jobs.

'I'm fine. I've just been feeling a little sick lately.'

Sophie raised her eyebrows, a teasing smile playing about her mouth. 'If it was anyone but you I'd be worried.'

'What is *that* supposed to mean?' Margo asked, a note of irritability creeping into her voice. She had been out of sorts for a month now, ever since Leo had left her alone and aching.

It was for the best—it had to be—but she couldn't keep herself from feeling the hurt. The emptiness.

'I mean,' Sophie answered, 'that I'd think you were pregnant. But you can't be.'

'Of course I'm not,' Margo answered sharply.

Sophie knew her stance on relationships and children: one night over a bottle of wine they'd each confided their intention to have single, solitary, *safe* lives. At least that was how Margo had viewed it; she suspected Sophie just wanted to play the field.

'I'm on the mini-pill,' she stated, and Sophie raised her eyebrows.

'You haven't forgotten to take it, then?'

'No, never.'

Margo frowned at her computer screen and the image there of a selection of silk throw pillows, handcrafted in Turkey, that she was considering for Achat's exclusive range. Her mind was racing back to that night a month ago, when she and Leo had had their memorable farewell.

But she'd taken a pill that morning, and one the next day. She hadn't missed anything.

'Well, then, it's probably just a stomach bug,' Sophie said dismissively.

Margo barely heard her.

The next morning she'd taken it a bit later, she recalled. She hadn't been able to sleep after Leo had left, her mind seething and her body aching, so she'd taken a herbal sleeping tablet some time in the middle of the night. It had knocked her out, which had been a blessing at the time, and she had slept for eight hours, waking around eleven, which was only three hours after she normally took the pill...

She couldn't be pregnant.

But what if those few hours had made a difference? Allowed enough of a window...?

She let out a laugh, then, a trembling, near-hysterical sound that had Sophie looking up from her laptop across their shared open-plan office.

'Margo...?'

She shook her head. 'Just thinking how ridiculous your suggestion was.'

And then she turned back to her computer and worked steadily until lunchtime, refusing to give her friend's teasing suggestion a single second of thought.

Her mind was filled with a static-like white noise even as she focused on the Turkish pillows of hand-dyed silk, and at lunchtime she left her desk and hurried down the Champs-Élysées, walking ten blocks to a chemist that wasn't too close to Achat's offices.

She paced the length of the shop, making sure no one who knew her was inside, and then quickly bought a pregnancy test without meeting the cashier's eye. She stuck the paper bag in her handbag and hurried out of the shop.

Back at the office, she went into the bathroom, grateful that it was empty, and stared at her reflection, taking comfort from the elegant, composed face in the mirror. Her mask. Her armour. For work she wore nothing more than some eyeliner and red lipstick, a bit of powder. Her hair was in its usual sleek chignon and she wore a black pencil skirt and a silver-grey silk blouse.

The shade suddenly reminded her of the colour of Leo's eyes.

But she couldn't think about Leo now.

Taking a deep breath, she fumbled in her bag for the test and then locked herself in one of the stalls. She read the directions through twice, needing to be thorough, to focus on the details rather than the big picture that had been emerging ever since Sophie had made her suggestion.

Then she took the test and waited the requisite three minutes, staring at the face of her watch the whole time. As the second hand ticked to twelve for the third time she turned the test over—and stared down at two blazing pink lines.

Positive.

She was pregnant…with Leo's baby.

For a moment she couldn't think, couldn't breathe, couldn't even see. She doubled over as the world swam and darkened all around her. Then she took a few shallow breaths and straightened. She wrapped the test in a paper towel and shoved it deep in the bin, washed her hands and retouched her make-up. She would not think about this yet. She couldn't.

She went back to her office, ignoring a curious look from Sophie, and sat at her desk and worked non-stop until six. She took phone calls, she attended a meeting, she even chatted and joked a little with colleagues.

But all the time she could hear the buzzing in her head. She felt as if she were watching herself from a distance, applauding how effortlessly she was handling it all. Except she wasn't really…because inside she could feel the beginnings of panic ice over her mind and her belly.

She was pregnant with Leo's baby.

'Do you want to go for a drink?' Sophie asked as Margo rose to gather her things at six.

'I don't think…' Margo began, intending to put Sophie off, but then she hesitated.

She couldn't bear the thought of returning to her apartment and spending the evening alone—not with this bomb of knowledge still ticking inside of her, waiting to detonate.

'Why not?' she amended as lightly as she could, and slipped on her blazer.

It was a warm evening in early September, and the office buildings of Paris's centre were emptying out onto the wide boulevard of the Champs-Élysées. They walked to a wine bar on a narrow side street, one of their favourites, and sat outside at a rickety table so they could watch the world go by.

'Red or white?' Sophie asked as she moved to go inside and order their wine from the bar.

Margo hesitated, and then shook her head. 'I'll just have a glass of sparkling water. My stomach is still a little queasy.'

Sophie stared at her for a moment and Margo held the stare. She'd come out with Sophie tonight to avoid being home alone with this new knowledge, this new *life* inside her, but she wasn't ready to tell her friend yet.

'Very well,' Sophie said, and went inside.

Margo sat back in her chair and blindly watched people stream by, heading home or to a bar like this—people with plans, with jobs and busy lives…

Hours ago she'd been just like them—at least on the surface. To the world she presented an image of the confident, sophisticated career woman who had everything she wanted. She'd always known it was nothing more than a flimsy façade, but no one else had.

And now the façade was about to crumble. Because she was pregnant. Pregnant with a baby…a child of her own…

Instinctively her hand crept to her still flat stomach. She imagined the little life nestled inside her, the size of a grain of rice and yet with a brain and a beating heart. *A baby…*

'So what's going on?' Sophie asked as she returned to the table and handed Margo her glass of water.

Quickly Margo dropped her hand from her middle. 'What do you mean?'

'You've been acting strange all afternoon. Almost as if you were in a daze.'

'I've been working.'

Sophie just gave her a look; she knew her too well for Margo to dissemble. She took a sip of water to stall for time.

'Is everything all right?' Sophie asked quietly, abandoning her usual flippancy for a sincerity that made Margo's eyes sting.

She didn't have many friends. She had acquaintances and colleagues, people on the periphery of her life, but no one had ever been at its centre. She hadn't allowed anyone to be, because loneliness was safer. And maybe it was all she deserved.

If you'd married Leo he would have been there.

But she couldn't think that way because she'd made her choice. She couldn't change her mind now, couldn't wonder or wish for something else.

'Margo?' Sophie prompted, real concern wrinkling her forehead.

Margo took a deep breath. 'Actually…I really am pregnant.' She hadn't been planning on admitting it, but now that she had it was such a relief to share the burden, even if Sophie looked as dazed and shocked as she'd felt a few hours ago.

'Seriously? But…'

'I took a test at lunchtime.'

Sophie shook her head slowly. 'I didn't even know you were seeing anyone seriously.'

'I wasn't. It was…casual. He lives in Greece.'

'And…? Have you told him?'

Margo let out a trembling laugh. 'Sophie, I told you, I just found out at lunchtime.'

'Right.' Sophie sat back in her seat and took a sip of wine. 'So you're still processing it, I suppose?'

Margo passed a hand over her forehead. Telling Sophie had made her pregnancy seem more real, and she felt a bit shaky as a result. 'I don't think I've even started.'

'Well,' Sophie said, 'I didn't think you wanted children.'

'I didn't. Don't.'

Sophie raised an eyebrow and Margo realised her hand had strayed once more to her middle. She let out another uncertain laugh and dropped it.

'I don't know what I want,' she said quietly, and felt everything inside her lurch at this admission.

'What about the father, this Greek guy? How long had you been with him?'

'We were together for two years—'

'Two *years*?' Sophie's jaw dropped. 'Why didn't you ever *tell* me, Margo?'

'I…' Why *hadn't* she told Sophie about Leo? Because, she supposed, she had been afraid to allow Leo to seem that important to her, and yet she was afraid it had happened anyway. 'It was just a fling,' she said lamely.

Sophie laughed in disbelief. 'Quite a long-term fling.'

'Yes, I suppose… In any case, our…relationship is

finished. Completely.' Margo stared down at her glass of water. 'It didn't end well.'

'If you're thinking of keeping the baby, he should still know,' Sophie pointed out.

Margo couldn't keep herself from wincing. How on earth could she tell Leo now? Considering what she'd said to him the last time they'd been together, he might not even believe the baby was his.

'I can't think about all this just yet,' she said. 'It's too much. I have time.'

'If you're *not* going to keep it,' Sophie replied warningly, 'the sooner you decide the better. For your own sake.'

'Yes…'

A termination, she supposed, might seem like the obvious answer. And yet the most fundamental part of herself resisted the possibility, shrank away from it in horror.

She hadn't expected that. She hadn't expected pregnancy to awaken anything in her but dread and fear. And yet she couldn't deny the faint stirrings of hope, as ephemeral as a will-o'-the-wisp, that had gathered inside her. A *baby*. A second chance.

'You do have *some* time,' Sophie allowed, reaching over to pat her hand. 'Don't make any rash decisions, in any case.'

'I won't,' Margo promised, but already her mind was spinning, spinning. If she actually decided to keep the baby she would have to tell Leo. And how on earth would *that* work? Would he believe her? Would he want to be involved?

She left Sophie an hour later and took the Metro back to her apartment on the top floor of an eighteenth-century townhouse on the Île de la Cité. As she stepped into the little foyer, with its marble table and antique umbrella stand, she felt some of the tension leave her body, uncramp her shoulders. This was her home, her haven, lovingly created over the years and the only real one she'd ever known.

She ran a bubble bath in the claw-foot tub and sank gratefully into its warmth, closing her eyes and trying to empty her mind for a few moments. But thoughts crept stealthily back in. *A baby.* How would she manage with her job? Childcare in Paris was expensive, and she was entitled to only sixteen weeks of maternity leave. Even though she made a decent salary she didn't think she'd be able to keep her apartment *and* pay for the full-time childcare she'd need.

But far more concerning, far more terrifying than the financial implications of having a child, were the emotional ones. A baby…a human being she would be entirely responsible for, a person who would be utterly dependent on her…

A person she could love. A person she could lose. *Again.*

And then, of course, there was Leo. She didn't even know if he would see her or listen to anything she had to say. And if he did…would he want to be involved in her child's life? And if so…how much? How would they come to a custody arrangement? And was that what she wanted for her son or daughter? Some awful to-ing and fro-ing between parents who as good as hated each other?

Exhaustion crashed over her and she rose from the tub. She couldn't think about all this yet. She certainly couldn't come to any decisions.

As the days and then the weeks slipped past Margo knew she had to decide soon. Sophie had stopped asking her what she was going to do, but at work she could see the silent question in her friend's eyes and knew she was concerned.

And then the sickness really hit. The faint nausea that

had been plaguing her for a few weeks suddenly turned into something else entirely, something horrendous that left her barely able to get out of bed, and unable to keep anything down.

Lying alone in her bed, unable to do anything but crawl to the toilet, she realised how alone she was. She had so few friends in the city. Sophie wanted to help, but as a single working woman her resources and time were limited.

Margo knew all too well how short a step it was to destitution, to tragedy, when you were on your own. When there was no family, no safety net. If she was going to keep this baby she couldn't do it on her own. She couldn't risk it.

After suffering for a week, she managed to drag herself to the doctor for some anti-nausea medication.

'The good news,' the doctor told her cheerfully, 'is that nausea usually means a healthy pregnancy. That baby is here to stay.'

Margo stared at him, his words reverberating through her. He had no idea, of course, how conflicted she was about this child. Except in that moment she realised she wasn't conflicted at all. This baby was a gift—a gift she'd never expected to receive. And she knew then—realised she'd known all along—that of course she was keeping her child.

And of course she would have to tell Leo.

CHAPTER THREE

'SOMEONE'S HERE TO see you, sir.'

Leo glanced up from his laptop at his assistant Elena, who stood in the doorway of his office on the Marakaios estate. He'd been going over some figures for a new deal with a large North American restaurant chain, and it took a few seconds for Elena's words to penetrate.

'Someone? Who is it, Elena?'

'A woman. She wouldn't give her name, but she said it was urgent.'

Leo frowned. His office was on the family compound in central Greece—the middle of nowhere, as Margo had so acerbically reminded him. He didn't get unexpected visitors to his office here. *Ever.*

'Well, why on earth wouldn't she give her name?' he asked as he pushed back from his chair.

'I don't know. But she's well-dressed and well-spoken. I thought perhaps...'

Elena trailed off, blushing, and Leo took her meaning. She'd thought this woman might be one of his lovers. Only he hadn't taken a lover in months—not since he'd last seen Margo.

And he very much doubted *Margo* had come all the way to Greece to see him.

Leo's mouth twisted cynically at the thought. It had

been over four months since he'd seen her—over four months since he'd walked out of her apartment with that ring in his pocket. Four months since he'd let himself think of her. That part of his life was over.

'Whoever this woman is, Elena, I find it decidedly odd that she wouldn't give her name.'

'She seemed very insistent…'

With a sigh, Leo strode to the door. 'I'll see her, then,' he said, and walked briskly out of his office.

It wasn't until he reached the foyer and saw the woman standing there amidst the leather sofas and sleek coffee tables that his step slowed. His heart seemed to still. And an icy anger came over him like a frozen shell.

He folded his arms. 'If I'd known it was you I would have told Elena to send you away.'

'Please, Leo…' Margo said quietly.

She looked awful—gaunt, with dark shadows under her eyes. She wore a black wool coat that made her ivory skin look pale…too pale.

Leo frowned. 'What do you want?'

'To talk to you.' She glanced at Elena, who had gone back to her desk and was ostentatiously busying herself, but was of course listening to every word. 'Privately.'

Leo opened his mouth to tell her they had nothing to say to one another, but then he paused. He didn't want to have this conversation in public—didn't want anyone, even his assistant, to know his private affairs.

With a terse nod he indicated the corridor. 'Come to my office, then,' he said, and without waiting for her to follow he turned and strode back the way he had come.

He watched as Margo came in and carefully closed the door behind her. She looked bruised and exhausted, as if a breath of wind would knock her right over.

'You don't look very well,' he said flatly.

She turned to him with the ghost of a smile. 'I don't feel very well. Do you mind if I sit down?'

He indicated one of the two chairs in front of his desk and she sank into it with a sigh of weary relief.

'Well?' Leo asked, biting off the single syllable. 'What do you want?'

She looked up at him, and he felt a ripple of uneasy shock at the resignation in her eyes. It was so different from the way he'd usually seen her—all elegant polish and sassy sophistication. This was a different Margo... one with a layer stripped away.

'Leo,' she said quietly, 'I'm pregnant.'

He blinked, the words taking him totally by surprise.

She said nothing, waiting for his reply.

'And how does this concern *me*?' he asked coolly.

She held his iron gaze. 'The baby is yours.'

'And you know that *how*? Do I need to remind you of what you told me four months ago?'

'No.' She hesitated, her gaze moving away from his. 'The other...man...he can't be the father,' she said at last.

A rage so fierce it felt like an earthquake shaking his insides took hold of him. *'Don't,'* he said in a voice like a whip-crack, 'talk to me of him. *Ever.*'

'This baby is yours, Leo.'

'You can't know that.'

She sighed, leaning her head back against the chair. 'I *do* know it,' she said wearily. 'Utterly. But if you like I'll have a paternity test done. I can prove it beyond a doubt.'

He stared at her, shaken more than he wanted to admit or reveal that she sounded so certain. 'I thought you didn't want children,' he said, after a long, taut moment.

'I didn't,' she answered.

'Then I'm surprised you didn't just deal with this on your own,' he snapped.

She put a hand to her throat, the gesture making her seem even more fragile. Vulnerable.

'Is that what you would have wanted?'

'No.' He realised he meant it utterly. A child...*his* child, if she wasn't lying. Yet how could he trust a word she said? 'Why have you come here and told me?' he asked instead. 'Do you want money?'

'No, not particularly.'

He laughed at that—a cold, sharp sound. 'Not *particularly*?'

'I admit having this child will be hard for me financially. But I didn't come here to ask for a hand-out. I came because I thought you should know. You'd want to know.'

He sank into his chair, the reality of it crashing over him as he raked his hands through his hair. '*Theos*, Margo. This is a lot to take in.'

'I know. I've had three months to process it—'

'You've known for that long and you are only telling me *now*?'

Colour touched her cheeks faintly. 'I've been very ill. Extreme morning sickness, apparently.'

'Are you taking medication?' he asked sharply, and she nodded.

'It helps a little.' She sighed and shifted in her seat. 'The truth is, Leo, I didn't know how you would respond, or if you'd even see me. And I wanted to tell you in person. But with being so sick I couldn't face travelling all this way until now.'

He nodded. It all sounded so very reasonable and yet he still felt angry. He should have known. He should have had the choice to be involved from the beginning. And now...?

'If this is indeed my child,' he told her, laying his hands flat on the desk, 'there is no question of my not being involved.'

'I know.'

'And I don't mean some weekend arrangement,' Leo continued, knowing he meant it even though he was still reeling from her news. 'I won't be the kind of father who sees his child only on a Saturday afternoon.'

'No,' Margo agreed quietly. 'I don't want that either.'

'Don't you?'

He gazed at her narrowly for a moment. He still didn't understand why she was here. She hadn't possessed enough honour to be faithful to him, so why would she care whether he knew about his own child or not?

'I would have expected you to have had a termination,' he said abruptly. 'Or, if you wanted the child, to pass it off as this other man's.'

She winced at that. 'Clearly you don't have a very high opinion of me.'

'And you think I should?'

'No.' She let out a little defeated sigh. 'No, I don't.'

'So why didn't you do either of those things, Margo?'

It was the first time he'd said her name since he'd seen her again, and it caused him a sudden, surprising flash of pain. He clenched his hands into fists, then deliberately flattened them out, resting them again on his desk.

'Because I am not, no matter what you think, completely without morals,' she replied with a bit of her old spirit. 'I want my child, and I want my child to know its father.' She took a deep breath. 'And more than that I want my child to have a loving, stable home. A home where it knows it's safe, where its parents are, loving and protecting. *Always.*'

Her dark brown eyes seemed to glow with an inner fire, an utter conviction.

'And how,' Leo asked after a pause, 'do you suppose *that* is going to work?'

'That's the other thing I want,' Margo said, still holding his gaze, her eyes like burning coals in her pale face. 'I want you to marry me.'

In another situation, another life, Margo might have laughed at the way Leo's expression slackened with surprise. He hadn't been expecting that—and why would he? The last time he'd seen her she'd sent him away with a scornful rejection, told him lies of infidelity that she'd known would make him hate her. And here she was now, with a proposal of her own.

'You must,' Leo said, his voice like ice, 'be joking.'

'Do you think I'd come all the way to Greece just to make a joke?' Margo asked quietly.

Leo stood up, the movement abrupt. He paced in front of the window that overlooked the Marakaios olive groves, now stark and bare in winter, which produced Greece's finest olive oil.

'Your *proposal*,' he said, his teeth clenched and the word a sneer, 'is offensive.'

'I mean it sincerely—'

He cut her off, his voice now low and pulsating with fury. 'The last time I saw you, you told me you didn't want marriage or children.'

She gestured to the gently swelling bump that was just barely visible under her coat. 'Things have changed.'

'Not that much. Not for *me*.'

'Don't you want to know your own child?'

'Who says I won't? Who says I won't sue for custody?'

Her stomach plunged with fear at that, but she forced herself to stay calm.

'And do you think that would be in the best interest of our baby, Leo?'

He sat back down in his chair, raking his hands through

his hair. With his head lowered she could see the strangely vulnerable nape of his neck, the momentary slump of his shoulders, and everything in her ached.

'I'm sorry, Leo, for springing this on you,' she said quietly. 'I've thought long and hard over these last few months about what is best for our baby, and I've come to the conclusion that it's to live in a stable home with two parents.'

It hadn't been an easy decision to make, but Margo's own sorry history made her wary of going it alone as her mother had. Just like her, her mother had had no friends, no family, no safety net. And she'd lost everything.

Margo would not subject her child to the same risk.

He lifted his head, his eyes flashing although the set of his mouth was grim, bleak. 'Even two parents who don't love each other? Who have absolutely no reason whatsoever to respect or trust each other?'

She flinched slightly. 'I respect you, Leo.'

'You've had a funny way of showing it, then.'

She should tell him, Margo knew, that she'd made up the other man. Any hope of a marriage that was amicable at least was impossible with that perceived betrayal between them. But she was afraid Leo wouldn't believe her if she told him now, and even if he did believe her he would want to know why she had told such an outrageous and damaging lie. The answer to that question was to admit her own fear, and that was something she was not ready to do.

'I know you don't respect *me*,' she said.

She clenched her hands in her lap and fought another wave of nausea. The sickness had eased a bit in the last few weeks, but she still felt as if she had to drag herself through each day.

'I know you don't trust me. I hope that maybe, in time, I can win back both your respect and your trust. But this marriage would be for the sake of our child, Leo. To give our baby the opportunity of a stable home. And even if we don't love each other we'll both love this child.'

'So you're willing to enter a cold, loveless union, all for the sake of a baby you professed to not even want?'

Another deep breath and she met his gaze without a flinch. 'Yes.'

'I don't believe you.'

'Why would I be here, then?' she asked quietly.

'You want something. Are you in trouble? Did this other man throw you over? Do you need money?'

'I told you before, I'm not asking for a hand-out.'

'You also said,' Leo reminded her ruthlessly, 'that having this baby would be a struggle financially.'

'A struggle, yes, but not impossible. I could do it. I've thought about doing it,' she continued, determined to make him believe her, even if he didn't—*couldn't*—understand her motives. 'I thought very hard about raising this child on my own and not even telling you I was pregnant.'

'And yet you now want me to *trust* you?'

'I *didn't* choose to do that, Leo,' Margo said, her voice rising. She strove to level it; giving in to temper now would not help her cause. 'I knew that you needed to know, and that our child needed more. Two parents. Stability, safety—'

'You don't think you could give this child those things on your own?'

'No. Not for certain. I don't...I don't have a lot of friends, and no family. This baby needs more than just me. He or she needs a father.'

'If I *am* the father.'

'Please...'

She closed her eyes, waves of both nausea and fatigue crashing over here. Coming all this way, dealing with the plane and the rental car and the endless travel, had completely exhausted her.

She summoned what little strength she had left and made herself continue. 'Let's not argue. I want to marry you for the sake of our child. I'm not expecting you to love me or even like me after—after what I did, but I do hope we might act amicably towards each other for the sake of the baby. As for...' She dropped her gaze, unable to look him in the eye. 'As for the usual benefits of a marriage... I'd understand if you chose to look elsewhere.'

Leo was silent and Margo risked a look up, wondering if he'd taken her meaning.

'Am I to understand,' he asked, his voice toneless, 'that you are giving me permission to violate my marriage vows?'

'It would be a marriage of convenience—'

'But still a marriage.'

'I'm trying to make this more amenable to you—'

'To sweeten the deal?' He cut across her, his voice hard. 'It still tastes rancid to me.'

'Please, Leo...' She swallowed, hating the fact that she had to beg.

Maybe he was right. Perhaps she should go back to Paris, raise the baby on her own. Leo could be the sort of weekend father he claimed he didn't want to be. Plenty of couples did it—why not them?

Because she was afraid of going it alone. Because she wanted more for her child. So much more than she'd had.

'You ask so *nicely*,' Leo said, his eyes glittering now.

He was furious with her, even after so many months apart. She wondered if his anger could ever be appeased. Perhaps if she told him the truth...if only he would believe it.

'I'm willing to live in Greece,' she continued, deciding she might as well say it all.

'Even in the "middle of nowhere"?'

'I'd leave my job at Achat. I'd want to stay home with the baby for the first few years, at least.'

'I thought the whole "housewife routine" bored you to death?'

Once again he was throwing her words back in her face, and she couldn't blame him. 'It's different now.'

'So you're saying you *want* those things? That life?'

He sounded incredulous—contemptuous, even—and bile surged in her stomach again. She swallowed past the metallic taste in her mouth. 'I'm saying that I am willing,' she answered. 'It's a sacrifice I'm prepared to make.'

'So I'd be marrying a martyr? What an appealing thought.'

'You'd be making a sacrifice too,' Margo replied. 'I understand that.'

'I still don't understand you,' Leo answered.

'Why is it so hard to believe I'd be willing to do this?' Margo demanded. She could take only so much of his sneering disbelief. 'Most women would.'

'And yet,' Leo reminded her softly, 'you *aren't* "most women".'

She closed her eyes, felt herself sway.

She heard Leo's sharply indrawn breath. 'Margo, are you all right?'

His voice was rough, although with impatience or anxiety she couldn't tell.

She forced her eyes open.

'I'm just very tired, and still quite nauseous,' she said levelly. 'Obviously you need time to think about my—my proposal.' Not the word she'd wished to use, and Leo's mouth twisted cynically when she said it. There had been too many proposals already. 'If you could let me know when you've decided…'

'Are you actually intending to return to France?' Leo asked sharply. 'You're in no condition to travel.'

'I'll spend the night at a local hotel,' she answered, 'and fly out of Athens tomorrow.'

'No.' Leo's gaze was cold and implacable as he gave his order. 'You'll stay here. I'll give you my answer tomorrow.'

Which made her feel like Scheherazade, wondering if she was to be beheaded in the morning. Not the way she would have wanted to think about her marriage, but she'd reconciled herself, or thought she had, to what life with Leo would be like. She'd told herself it was worth it, that anything was worth it if she could give her baby a stable, loving home.

Even if you and Leo will never love each other?

Some sacrifices, she reminded herself grimly, were necessary. And maybe it would be better this way. Without the complication and risk of loving someone, you could never be hurt. Hopefully.

She rose from her chair, blinking back dizziness. Even so Leo must have seen something in her expression, for he reached forward and steadied her elbow with his hand. It was the first time he'd touched her in three months, since he'd made love to her against the window and then walked away.

'I'm fine,' she said, and shook off his hand. 'Just a little dizzy when I stand up, that's all.'

'I'll arrange for someone to show you to the guest suite,' Leo said.

He was frowning, although over her dizziness or the whole situation she didn't know. Couldn't think. He was right: she really wasn't in a fit state to travel.

She stood, swaying slightly, as Leo made arrangements on his phone. Then he ended the call and gave her one last, hard look.

'I'll see you tomorrow,' he said, and Margo knew it was a dismissal.

CHAPTER FOUR

A BABY. HE WAS going to be a father… If the child was truly his. Leo knocked back his third whisky and stared grimly out at the starless night. It had been eight hours since Margo had confronted him in his office, and he was still reeling.

He hadn't seen her in all that time. Elena had taken her to the house, and then his personal staff had seen to her comforts. He'd called his housekeeper Maria to check on her, and she'd told him that Margo had gone to her room and slept for most of the afternoon. He'd requested that a dinner tray be taken up to her, but Maria had told him it hadn't been touched.

Anxiety touched with anger gnawed at his gut. If the child was his, he wanted to make sure Margo was staying healthy. Hell, even if the child *wasn't* his, he had a responsibility towards any person under his roof. And he hadn't liked how pale and ill Margo had looked, as if the very life force had been sucked right out of her.

Restlessly Leo rose from the leather club chair where he'd been sitting in the study that had once been his father's, and then his brother Antonios's. And now it was his. Six months into his leadership of Marakaios Enterprises and he still burned with the determination to take the company to a new level, to wield the power his father and brother had denied him for so long.

A lifetime of being pushed to the sidelines, being kept in the dark, had taken its toll. He didn't trust anyone—and especially not Margo. But if the child was his…then why *not* the cold marriage of convenience she'd suggested? It was what he'd determined he'd wanted after she'd turned him down. No messy emotion, no desperate searching for love. He just hadn't expected Margo to be his convenient bride.

Grimly Leo turned back to the whisky bottle. What she'd suggested made sense, and yet everything in him resisted it. To live with a woman who had been unfaithful, who had *rejected* him, and who was now viewing their marriage as the altar upon which she'd sacrifice herself, her hopes and dreams… It was a bitter pill to swallow—and yet what was the alternative? To come to some unsatisfactory custody arrangement and not be nearly as involved in his child's life as he wanted?

If the child was his.

If it was then Leo knew he had to be involved. He wanted to be the kind of father his own father hadn't been to him. Loving, interested, open. And he wanted a family—a child, a wife. Why not Margo? He could control his feelings for her. He had no interest in loving her any more.

He could make this marriage work.

Margo had thought she wouldn't be able to sleep, but she was so tired that she'd fallen into a deep and thankfully dreamless sleep the moment her head had hit the pillow, after Leo's housekeeper had shown her to her room.

When she awoke it was dark and the room was chilly, the curtains open to the night sky. Margo rolled over in bed, feeling disorientated and muzzy-headed, as if she were suffering from jet lag or a hangover, or both. She heard a knock on the door, an urgent *rat-a-tat-tat* that made her think it was not the first knock.

She rose from the bed, pushing her hair out of her face, and went to answer the door.

The housekeeper Maria stood there, with a tray of food. The salad, bread, and lentil soup looked and smelled delicious, but Margo's stomach roiled all the same. She didn't think she could manage a mouthful.

'*Efharisto*,' she murmured, and reached out to take the tray.

But Maria would have none of it. She shook her head and bustled into the room, setting the tray on a table in the corner. Bemused, Margo watched as she drew the curtains across the windows and remade the bed, plumping the pillows. She turned on a few table lamps that were scattered about the room and then looked around, seemingly satisfied with how cosy she'd made it in just a few minutes.

'*Efharisto*,' Margo said again, and Maria nodded towards the food.

'*Fae*,' she commanded, and while Margo didn't recognise the word she could guess what it meant. *Eat*.

She gave the housekeeper a weak smile and with another nod Maria left the room.

Margo walked over to the tray and took a spoonful of soup, but, warm and nourishing as it was, her stomach roiled again and she left it.

Now that the cobwebs were clearing from her brain she remembered every excruciating detail of her conversation with Leo. His disbelief and his contempt, his suspicion and anger. And now she was stuck here, waiting to see if he would marry her.

Shaking her head at her own stubborn folly, she crawled back into the bed and pulled the covers over herself. She wouldn't back out of her offer. She cared too much about this child inside her—this child she'd never expected to have, never dared want.

This child she would sacrifice anything for to ensure it had a better childhood, a better life, than she had had. To keep her, or him, safe.

She slept again and when she woke it was dawn, with the first grey light of morning creeping through a crack in the closed curtains. She dozed for a little while longer and then finally got up and went to shower, to prepare herself to meet with Leo and hear his answer—whatever it was.

At eight o'clock Maria knocked on the door and brought in a breakfast tray. Margo didn't know whether to feel like a pampered princess or a prisoner. At some point, she realised, Maria must have removed the untouched tray from the night before. She must have been sleeping at the time.

'*Efharisto*,' she said again, and Maria gave her a stern look.

'*Fae.*'

'Yes—I mean, *ne*.' Margo smiled apologetically. 'I can't keep much down, I'm afraid.'

Maria clucked at that, but Margo didn't think the older woman understood her. She bustled about a bit more, pouring coffee and juice, taking the lids off jam and butter dishes. Finally she left and Margo gazed in dismay at the lavish breakfast Maria had left. The smell of the coffee made her stomach lurch.

For the housekeeper's sake she tried to eat some yogurt with honey, but after two spoonsful she left it aside and then paced the room, wondering if she should go in search of Leo or wait for him to summon her.

She'd paced for several minutes, restless and anxious, until she realised she was being ridiculous. Had she lost all her spirit since coming here? She might be tired and unwell, and afraid of Leo's response, but she'd faced far worse obstacles than this and survived. Her strength in the face of adversity was something she clung to and prided herself on.

Determinedly she strode to the door and flung it open—only to stop in her tracks when she saw Leo standing there, looking devastatingly handsome in a crisp white shirt and grey trousers, his ink-dark hair still damp and spiky from a shower. He also looked decidedly nonplussed.

'Going somewhere?' he enquired.

'Looking for you, actually,' she replied crisply. 'I'd like your answer, Leo, because I need to get back to Paris. My flight is at two o'clock this afternoon.'

'Cancel it,' he returned. 'You won't be returning to Paris. Not right now, at any rate.'

She stared at him, as nonplussed as he'd been. 'Excuse me?'

His eyes flashed and his mouth thinned. 'Which part of what I said didn't you understand?'

Margo gritted her teeth. Yesterday she might have donned a hair shirt and beaten her chest in grief and repentance, but clearly that hadn't been enough for Leo. She didn't think she could endure a lifetime of snide remarks, all for a crime she hadn't even committed.

Except you told him you did.

'Perhaps,' she suggested, with only a hint of sharpness, 'we could discuss our future plans in a bit more detail?'

'Fine. I was coming to get you, anyway. We can go down to my study.'

'Fine.'

Silently she followed him down the terracotta-tiled corridor to the sweeping double staircase that led to the villa's soaring entrance hall. Yesterday she'd been too over-whelmed and exhausted to take in any of her surroundings, but today she was keenly aware that this grand place was, in all likelihood, her new home. It seemed, based on what Leo had said about cancelling her flight, that he was going to agree to marry her.

And from the plunging sensation in her stomach she knew she wasn't sure how she felt about that.

He led her to a wood-panelled study overlooking the villa's extensive gardens. This late in November they were stark and bare, but Margo could imagine how lush and lovely they would be come spring. Would she walk with her baby out there? Bring a blanket and lie on the grass, look up at the clouds while the baby gurgled and grabbed its feet?

'Let me cut to the chase,' Leo said, and Margo was jolted out of her pleasant daydream to the current cold reality.

He stood behind a huge desk of carved mahogany, his hands braced on the back of a chair, his expression implacable.

In the two years they'd been together she'd seen his lazy, knowing smiles, his hooded sleepy gazes. She'd seen him light and laughing, and dangerously, sensually intent. But she hadn't seen him like this—looking at her as if she were a difficult business client.

Well, if he could be businesslike, then so could she. She straightened and gave him a brisk nod. 'Please do.'

'I will marry you—but only on certain conditions.'

Margo took a deep breath and let it out evenly. 'Which are?'

'First, we drive to Athens this afternoon and you undergo a paternity test.'

It was no more than she'd expected, although the fact that he believed the baby might not be his still stung. This, at least, was easy to comply with. 'Very well.'

'Second, you resign from your job immediately and come and live with me here in Greece.'

So he wanted complete control of her and their child? She couldn't say she was really surprised. 'Fine.'

'Third, you agree to have a local doctor of my choosing provide you with medical care.'

Her temper finally started to fray. 'I think I'm capable of finding my own doctor, Leo.'

'Are you?' He arched an eyebrow, coldly sceptical. 'Because you came here looking dreadful.'

'Thanks very much, but my looks have nothing to do with my medical care or lack of it,' Margo snapped.

How much of this was she supposed to take? Maybe, she thought with a surge of reckless fury, the answer was none of it. She'd come to Leo as a supplicant, truly believing that their child should know his or her father. Trusting that she was making the right decision in seeking to provide the kind of stable home life she'd never had…no matter what the sacrifice to her.

If Leo was going to snipe at her constantly, was that really an environment she wanted to raise her child in? The kind of relationship she wanted her son or daughter to emulate?

But the alternative was too bleak to consider. Raise her baby alone, a single mother without a safety net. No parents, no relatives, no one who could help or support her besides a few friends like Sophie, who didn't even want children themselves. One wrong choice or an accident away from destitution, from losing everything. *Again*.

'Leo,' she said, keeping her voice even, 'if you're going to snipe at me about everything this whole negotiation process will be very unpleasant.'

Leo's mouth hardened. 'I'm just trying to be clear.'

'You are. Abundantly.'

A muscle flickered in his jaw. His gaze was the colour

of a sea in winter, slate-grey and utterly icy. 'I'm not finished with my conditions.'

'Fine,' she said wearily. 'What are the rest of your conditions?'

'You don't work while you're pregnant—or while our
child is small. I want my child to have a mother who is
fully present and available.'

'I've already said I would give up my job for a few
years,' she reminded him. 'And anyway, considering I'll
be stuck in the middle of Greece, a career is hardly an op-
tion for me at the moment.'

'Our marriage might be made for convenience,' Leo
continued relentlessly, 'but it won't be *that* convenient.
When you are healthy, and recovered from the birth of
our child, I want you in my bed.'

Her stomach plunged again, with that weird mixture of
anticipation and dread. 'I thought you could hardly stand
the sight of me?' she said after a second's pause. Her voice
sounded husky.

'We have chemistry,' Leo answered. 'Why should I look
elsewhere when I have a woman to see to my needs right
there at home?'

'Are you *trying* to be as offensive as possible?'

'Just stating facts,' Leo answered in a bland voice. 'And
here's another fact: if you ever cheat on me again I will
divorce you. Immediately. And I will gain complete custody of our child.'

Margo stared at him for a moment, saw the steely glint
of challenge in his eyes, the hard set of his mouth.

Her hands clenched into fists at her sides. 'No.'

'No? You mean you can't even *pretend* you're going to
be faithful?'

'I'll be faithful to you, Leo,' Margo said, her voice very
even despite the maelstrom of fury and pain she felt whirl-

ing through her. 'But if you ever threaten to take my child away from me again I will leave you and I will never come back. I will go where you will never find me, and you will never see either of us again—' She broke off, her nails digging into her palms, her chest heaving.

'That's a lot of nevers,' Leo remarked tonelessly.

'You started it.'

'I wonder why you are so fierce and protective,' he answered, his silvery gaze sweeping slowly over her, 'when you made it abundantly clear the last time we met that you didn't even *want* children.'

'People change.'

'And yet I wonder if you really have?'

She shook her head, her anger subsiding, replaced only by weariness. She sank onto one of the chairs in front of his desk. 'Are there any other conditions?'

'None we need to discuss at present.'

She looked up. 'Good. Then I have a few of my own.'

She almost laughed at the look of shock that blazed across his features. Did he think her so weak and spineless that she would accept all his conditions without naming her own? Or perhaps he was simply that confident of his own strong position.

She thought of his threat—no, his *promise* to claim full custody if she was unfaithful, or even if he just thought she was unfaithful. His position was strong and hers was weak, because she knew her threat to leave him and go where he could never find her was just that: a threat. Empty. Meaningless.

Leo would always find her.

'So what are your conditions?' he asked, folding his arms.

'First, that you never threaten me again.' She glared at him and he gazed back, unsmiling.

'What you call "threat" I call statement of fact.'

'Nevertheless.'

He shrugged. 'What are the others?'

Margo almost dug her heels in and argued the point, but she was so very, very tired. 'I have sole care of our child. No nannies or nurses.'

He inclined his head in acknowledgement. 'You'll have no argument from me. I said I wanted you to be present and available.'

'Even though you don't respect or trust me?' Margo couldn't help but jibe.

Leo pressed his lips together, and then bit out, 'I trust you to be a good mother to our child.'

And despite all his sneers and orders it touched her that he thought that. Because the truth was she wasn't sure she thought it herself. She *wanted* to be a good mother, God knew, but she certainly hadn't had the best example. And she had too many regrets when it came to loving a child. Losing a child.

'What else?' Leo asked.

'Any decisions regarding our child's welfare are made jointly. I won't have you laying down the law when it comes to our baby.'

His jaw set. 'It seems reasonable to discuss things,' he said after a pause.

Margo cast around for more conditions, but she couldn't think of anything. This was all so unknown, so unbelievable. She had no idea what her marriage, her *life* would look like. *But at least it would be safe.* Her baby would be safe.

'Good,' she said finally, with a nod. 'Then I have no more conditions…at present.'

'I'm glad we've come to an agreement,' Leo answered, inclining his head. 'We'll leave for Athens this afternoon.'

'I will have to return to France at some point,' Margo warned him. 'I have to give notice and deal with my apartment.'

She swallowed, the realisation of all she was leaving behind hitting her with sudden force, making her breathless. The career she was so proud of. The friends she'd made. The home she'd created for herself—her sanctuary and haven, the only place she felt she could be herself. All of it gone.

But it's worth it. It has to be worth it.

'When you are fit to travel,' Leo said, his tone implying that *he* would be the one to make the decision, 'you may return to France and deal with your job and apartment.'

His imperious tone, as if he were giving her permission, grated on Margo's already raw nerves. 'Who do you think you are,' she demanded, 'to order me about in such a way? I *chose* to come here, Leo—'

'I'll tell you who I am,' Leo cut across her, his voice quiet and deadly. 'I'm your husband.'

'Not yet,' Margo answered, her voice just as quiet, just as deadly. 'And at the rate you're going maybe not ever.'

He took a step towards her, his eyes narrowing to silver slits. 'Do you *really* think,' he asked, 'that I'd let you go now you are carrying my child? *If* it is my child.'

'Oh, enough with that, Leo—'

'We'll know the truth by tomorrow,' he answered. 'And then we'll be married.'

CHAPTER FIVE

THEY DIDN'T SPEAK during the three-hour drive to Athens. His hands clenched on the wheel, Leo slid a covert, sideways glance towards Margo. She sat very still, one hand resting on the handle of the door, her face pale and composed.

She seemed a little better than she had yesterday, but she still looked tired and washed out. She wore a sweater dress of magenta wool that clung to her shape, making him realise just how much weight she'd lost—although he could still see the gentle swell of her small baby bump. *His* baby.

He was, of course, going to insist on the paternity test, and yet Leo felt in his gut that the baby was his. Margo wouldn't have agreed to everything so readily if she'd had any doubt. Which made him wonder how she could be so certain.

He hadn't given much thought to the other man in Margo's life; he'd simply shut the door on the whole idea and tried not to think of her—or him—at all. Now, however, he wondered—and he realised they needed to address it.

'This other man,' he said abruptly. 'Are you still with him?'

She turned to him, the ghost of a sad smile curving her lips. 'Do you think I'd be here if I was?'

'I have no idea.'

She let out a small sigh. 'No, Leo. We're not together.'

'When did you break it off?'

She didn't answer and his hands clenched harder on the steering wheel, his knuckles turning white.

'Well, Margo? It's not that hard a question. I need to know if this guy is going to resurface in our lives, because I assure you—'

'Oh, this is ridiculous,' she said, and closed her eyes. 'Leo, there *is* no other man. There never was.'

He turned sharply to stare at her. Her eyes were still closed; she was leaning her head back against the seat. 'You expect me to believe that?'

'Not really, but it's the truth.'

'Why did you lie to me before, then?' he demanded.

Again she didn't answer, and he wondered if she were scrambling for some plausible excuse.

'Because,' she finally said softly, her eyes still closed, 'I knew it was the one thing that would send you away for good.'

Leo blinked, stung by this almost as much as he'd been by her alleged infidelity. 'You mean my proposal of marriage was so abhorrent to you that you needed to *lie* to get rid of me?'

'You're putting it in the worst possible light, but, yes, I suppose that's true.'

The sheer rejection of it, as brutal as his father's had been, left him speechless.

He stared straight ahead, flexing his hands on the steering wheel. 'And yet here we are, about to get married.'

She opened her eyes and gazed at him bleakly. 'Yes. Here we are.'

'I don't understand you, Margo.'

'I know.'

'If, four months ago, the idea of marrying me was so

disagreeable, why did you come back? Plenty of children live with single or divorced parents. You could have managed. I wouldn't have forced you to marry me. We could have come to a custody arrangement.' He hesitated, and then continued. 'We still could.'

'Is that what you want?'

'I don't know.' He shook his head, thoughts whirling through his mind like leaves in an autumn wind. Margo's rejection of him hurt more than he wanted to admit. And yet…she'd come back. She'd chosen to be here. They could still find a way ahead, for the sake of their child.

And the truth is, you still want her.

Underneath his anger the old desire burned just as bright, just as fierce.

'Leo…there's no reason we can't be amicable with each other, is there?'

She laid her hand on his arm, her fingers long and slender, the touch as light as a butterfly and yet still seeming to reach right inside him and clench a fist around his heart.

'We can be friends,' she continued. 'A convenient marriage doesn't have to be a cold one.'

Friends—when she'd either cheated on him or lied in the worst possible way in order to avoid marrying him? Friends—when she clearly viewed marriage to him as a *sacrifice*? The desire he'd felt was no more than that: desire. Lust.

He pulled his arm away. 'I don't think so,' he answered coolly. 'I think it's best if we keep this businesslike.'

She turned her head towards the window. 'And will we be "businesslike" in bed?'

'We've never had a problem with that aspect of our relationship,' Leo answered. He'd keep his physical feelings for Margo separate from any potential emotional complications. 'And we won't once we're married.'

They were on the outskirts of Athens now, with the raised mount of the Acropolis visible on the horizon. They didn't speak until they'd reached Leo's apartment in Kolonaki.

Margo had never been to Leo's city home before. Now she walked around the elegant rooms that took up the top floor of a nineteenth-century townhouse. The living room and dining room had been knocked together to create a large open space scattered with black and white leather sofas and tables of chrome and glass.

A huge canvas of wavy green lines and white splotches was the only colour in the whole room. She stood in front of it, wondering if this was the kind of modern art Leo liked. It had probably cost a fortune, and it looked as if it had been painted by a five-year-old.

'A masterpiece made by my nephew Timon,' he said as he came to stand beside her.

'I didn't know you had a nephew.'

There was, she realised, so much she didn't know about him. She knew what he liked in bed, and what kind of food he liked to order in, and that he preferred classical music to jazz. She knew he shaved with an old-fashioned straight razor and that the only cologne he wore was a splash of citrus-scented aftershave. She knew what a woman would know of a lover, but not of someone she loved. Not of a husband.

'Yes, my sister's son.'

'Is he an aspiring artist, then?' she asked, with a nod to the canvas.

'I suppose you could say that. He's three.'

Margo let out a surprised laugh. 'And I was just thinking this painting looked like it was done by a five-year-old and had probably cost a fortune.'

'Luckily for me, it cost nothing. My interior designer wanted me to spend a hundred thousand euros on some modern atrocity and I said my nephew could do something better. He did.' He glanced briefly at the huge canvas. 'I quite like it, actually. It's meant to be the olive groves, when the trees blossom in spring.'

'I like it too,' Margo answered. 'Especially now that I know it's done by your nephew.'

For a moment, no more, it felt like the way things had used to be, or even better. Easy, relaxed… A faint smile curved Leo's mouth as he stared at the painting, and Margo felt her wilting spirits lift as hope that they might in fact be able to have an amicable marriage after all unfurled inside her.

Then Leo turned away.

'I've put your things in the guest bedroom. You can re-fresh yourself and then we'll go to the doctor.'

The guest bedroom was as sumptuous as the rest of the apartment, with a huge king-sized bed covered in a cream silk duvet and an en-suite bathroom with a sunken marble tub. Margo was tempted to run a bath and have a soak, but she knew Leo would be waiting, watching her every move, and the thought made her too uptight to relax, even in a bubble bath.

She washed her face and hands instead, and put on a little make-up, no more than concealer to cover the dark shadows under her eyes, and a little blusher and lipstick to give her face some colour.

'Have you eaten today?' Leo called through the closed door. 'Maria told me you didn't have supper last night, nor breakfast this morning.'

So Maria was her keeper and his spy? Margo tried not to let it rankle. 'I can't manage much food,' she answered. She took a quick breath and opened the door.

Leo stood there, scowling.

'You need to keep up your strength.'

'I would if I could, Leo, but I can't keep anything down.'

'I thought the medication you were prescribed helps?'

'It does,' Margo answered. 'But I still have to be careful.' She tried for a smile. 'I've eaten a lot of melba toast. It's the one thing my stomach can stand.'

'Melba toast?' he repeated.

Margo shrugged. 'My doctor said I should start to feel better soon.'

'I don't even know how far along you are.'

'Seventeen weeks. The baby is due in the end of April.'

He looked startled by that news, and Margo wondered if the actuality of a baby—a living person coming into their lives—had just become more real to him.

But all he said was, 'We should go.'

'I'll just get my coat.'

Leo insisted on driving to the doctor's, even though it was only a few blocks away.

'You look as if a breath of wind could knock you over,' he informed her, and Margo told herself he was actually being considerate, even if it came across, as did everything else, as both a command and a criticism.

The doctor's office was plush and well-appointed, and they were seen immediately. Margo perched on top of the examination table, feeling shy and rather exposed with Leo in the room, standing in the corner, practically glowering.

The doctor, a neat-looking woman with a coil of dark hair and a brisk, efficient manner, took them both in with a single glance. 'Would you prefer to be seen alone?' she asked Margo in clipped English.

Leo looked taken aback. Clearly he'd expected the doctor he'd chosen to leap to do his bidding, just as everyone else did.

'No,' Margo answered, 'but maybe you could sit down?' She raised her eyebrows at Leo, who took a seat without a word.

'Now, let's see.' The woman, who had introduced herself as Dr Tallos, flipped through the forms Margo had filled out in the waiting room. 'You believe you're seventeen weeks along? Have you had an ultrasound?'

'Not yet. I was scheduled for one at twenty weeks.'

'Well, we can do one now, just to make sure everything's all right,' Dr Tallos said briskly. 'If you'd like?'

A tremor of both fear and excitement rippled through Margo. 'Yes, all right.'

'Let's get that done first, then, shall we?'

'What about the paternity test?' Leo asked, and the doctor shot him a narrowed look while Margo flushed at the obvious implication.

'We can establish paternity by a simple blood test. I'll draw blood from both of you after we've established the baby is healthy.' She raised her eyebrows at him, her expression and voice both decidedly cool. 'If that's all right with you?'

A blush touched Leo's cheeks and Margo almost felt sorry for him. The doctor didn't know their convoluted history.

'That's fine,' he said, and sat back in his chair.

A nurse wheeled in a machine with a screen and wires, and Margo lay back on the examination table.

'Do you mind?' Dr Tallos asked, and lifted her dress all the way up to right underneath her breasts, pulling her tights down to reveal the soft white swell of her belly.

Now she felt really exposed, lying there like a beached whale with her belly on view. She couldn't so much as sneak a glance at Leo, but she felt his presence, his tension.

'This will be a little cold,' Dr Tallos murmured, and squirted a clear gel onto Margo's bare stomach.

It wasn't just cold, it was icy, and she shivered.

'Here we go.' She started pressing a wand into Margo's belly, hard enough to make her wince.

'That's hurting her,' Leo said sharply, and both Margo and Dr Tallos turned to him in surprise.

'It's a bit uncomfortable,' the doctor said, 'but I promise you it's not hurting anyone.'

Leo didn't look convinced, and Margo said quietly, 'I'm all right, Leo.'

'There we are,' Dr Tallos announced, and they all turned to look at the fuzzy shape on the screen.

Margo blinked, trying to connect what looked like nothing more than a few blobby circles into a shape that resembled a baby.

Then Dr Tallos started pointing things out on the screen. 'There's the head, and the stomach, and you can see fingers and toes—look.'

And almost as if by magic Margo could see it: the curled up bud of her baby unfurling as he—or she—stretched out arms, kicked tiny legs.

'Kicking up a storm,' Dr Tallos said cheerfully. 'Do you feel anything?'

Margo shook her head. 'Not yet.'

'Well, don't worry, you're sure to in the next few weeks. And there's the heart, beating away.' She pointed to the flickering image on the screen, pulsing with life. 'Let me turn up the volume and you can hear it.'

She twirled a knob on the ultrasound machine and all at once the room was filled with a sound like the galloping of a horse, an insistent swoosh that had both Leo and Margo's jaws dropping in amazement.

'I've never heard such a sound,' Leo said softly.

He looked gobsmacked, as if someone had hit him on the head, and Margo knew how he felt. That rushing sound had knocked her for six too. It was so *real*.

'Baby is measuring seventeen weeks, just as you said,' Dr Tallos continued as she pressed some keys to take measurements. 'Everything looks well. It's a bit early to tell the sex, but we'll schedule a more comprehensive ultrasound for twenty weeks. Now…' She flicked off the machine and removed the wand from Margo's stomach before handing her a paper towel to wipe off the gel. 'I'll give you a moment to clean yourself and we'll do the blood test.' She turned to Leo with raised eyebrows. 'I'm assuming that's still required?'

He hesitated, and Margo jumped in. 'Yes, it's required,' she said. She would not have Leo casting any more aspersions or doubt.

Fifteen minutes later they'd left the doctor's office, with their promise to call with the results of the paternity test tomorrow.

It was strange, walking along the city street together, crossing the wide boulevard lined with cafés and upscale boutiques.

'Wait just a moment,' Leo said, and ducked into a gourmet deli.

Margo waited on the pavement, the brisk December wind buffeting her.

He came out a few minutes later, a paper bag in hand. 'Melba toast,' he said, and Margo, quite suddenly, felt near to tears. 'Margo, what is it?' he asked.

She sniffed and shook her head. 'Nothing. I'm just emotional because I'm pregnant. And being at the doctor's office…hearing the heartbeat…'

Leo frowned. 'That was a good thing, was it not?'

'Yes. Yes, of course it was.'

And yet hearing that heartbeat had also terrified her—because what if it stopped? What if the next time she had an ultrasound she heard nothing but yawning, endless silence? She was used to expecting, and experiencing, the worst. She couldn't bear for it to happen again, and yet she still braced herself for it.

'Here.' Leo opened the bag of melba toast and handed her a piece. 'Eat something. You'll feel better.'

But his kindness only made her feel worse; it opened her up so she felt broken and jagged inside. She'd told him she'd wanted an amicable marriage, but now she wondered if Leo's coldness, even his snideness, would have been easier to handle. These little kindnesses hurt her, made her realise how much they'd both given up—and all because she hadn't felt strong or brave enough to risk the real thing.

But it was too late for regrets, she reminded herself as she took a piece of toast and munched obediently. And it was better this way. If she kept telling herself that perhaps she'd start to believe it.

Leo watched as Margo ate a piece of toast, her shoulders hunched against the winter wind, her face pale and composed now, although he could still see the sheen of tears in her dark eyes, turning them luminous and twisting his gut.

He didn't want her to cry. He had been angry and alarmed when he'd thought the doctor had hurt her during the ultrasound. He felt worse now, seeing her near tears. He still had feelings for Margo—feelings he had neither expected nor wanted to have. *Feelings which had led him to agreeing to this marriage.*

For the last four months he'd refused even to think of her. She'd been as good as dead to him. And since she'd come back into his life twenty-four hours ago he'd made sure to keep both his distance and his composure. But he hadn't been keeping either. He saw that now. He'd been fooling himself—punishing her with snide or sarcastic comments because it was easier than grabbing her by the shoulders and demanding to know why she'd left him. Or maybe just kissing her senseless.

Who cared what her reasons had been? She was here now.

And she rejected you once. Why shouldn't she again?

But he didn't need to punish her any more. Perhaps he never should have, if she really was telling the truth when she said there hadn't been anyone else. He could at least be amicable. Amicable and no more.

'We should get back,' he said. 'You look like you need a rest. And I need to arrange the wedding details.'

Margo's step faltered. 'The wedding? Already?'

'We'll marry tomorrow afternoon in a civil service here in Athens. Pending the paternity results, of course.' Margo looked dazed by that news, but he continued, an edge to his voice. 'Surely, considering our circumstances, you don't expect the whole church and white dress affair?'

Fire flashed in her eyes. 'Are you *really* so old-fashioned and chauvinistic?'

'How is that *either* of those things?' Leo demanded. 'We're getting married for the sake of this child, Margo—not because we love each other or even want to be with each other.'

He was saying it for his own sake as well as hers, and somehow that just made him even more furious. 'A church wedding would be a mockery.'

'And a white dress would too, I suppose?'

'This isn't some criticism of you,' Leo answered. 'It's simply a statement of fact and what our marriage really is. What it will be.'

'Fine,' Margo answered, her eyes still flashing. 'Fine,' she said again and, dropping the remnants of her toast in the bin, she walked past him towards the car.

CHAPTER SIX

SHE COULDN'T SLEEP. Margo had tossed and turned in the guest bedroom for several hours before she'd finally given up trying. It wasn't the bed—it was one of the most comfortable she'd ever slept in. And it wasn't that she wasn't tired, because she still felt exhausted. Even so her mind seethed with half-formed questions and thoughts, and they spun around in her brain until she decided to make herself some herbal tea in an attempt to help her sleep.

She reached for her dressing gown and the box of ginger tea she'd brought with her; it was one of the few things she could stomach. Tiptoeing out of her bedroom, not wanting to disturb Leo, she made her way to the kitchen.

The rest of the day had passed uneventfully enough: she'd had a nap and a bath while Leo had worked in his study. And at around dinnertime he'd knocked on her door and told her he was planning to order food in, asked her what she'd like.

It had reminded Margo painfully of the weekends they'd spent together in this hotel or that, drinking champagne and eating takeaway, making love. Weekends stolen from reality, and yet so precious to her. Weekends when she'd felt carefree and alive in a way she never had before—or since.

She'd thought those weekends had kept her safe, kept

her from being emotionally engaged. Emotionally vulnerable.

Now she knew she'd been a fool. And she was still being a fool, because every moment she spent with Leo made her feel more raw. More afraid.

The meal they'd shared tonight had been utterly different from those earlier ones. They'd sat at either end of a huge dining room table, a modern-looking thing of carved ebony, and Margo had picked at her plain pasta while Leo had eaten souvlaki and answered emails on his smartphone. Neither of them had spoken.

This, then, was her future. Silent meals and endless tension.

Would it have been different if she'd said yes to Leo's proposal? Or would they have ended up here anyway, because they'd never loved each other? At least, Leo hadn't loved *her*. And what she'd felt for Leo had been only the beginnings of something, a tender shoot that had been plucked from the barren soil of her heart before it could take root and grow.

She hadn't let herself truly love Leo because loving someone meant opening yourself up to pain, heartache and loss. She'd learned long ago that people left you. Her mother, her foster parents, her sister. *Oh, God, her sister.*

Margo closed her eyes and willed back the rush of memory and pain.

Leo wouldn't leave her. He had too much honour for that. And as for this child… She pressed a hand to her middle and closed her eyes. *Stay safe, little one*, she prayed silently. *Stay strong.*

She made a cup of ginger tea, cradling the warm mug in her hands, and curled up on a window seat in the living room. The huge bay window overlooked Kolonaki's wide boulevards and narrow side streets, now illuminated only by a few streetlights and a thin crescent moon high above. In the distance she could see the Acropolis, its ancient buildings lit at night, a beacon for the city.

She took a sip of tea and tried to settle her swirling thoughts, but they were like leaves in a storm and the moment she tried to snatch at one another blew away. She closed her eyes and leaned against the window frame, tried instead to think of nothing at all.

'Is everything all right?'

Margo opened her eyes to see Leo standing in the doorway, dressed only in a pair of navy silk pyjama bottoms that rested low on his trim hips. The sight of his bare chest, all sleek rippled muscle, the sprinkling of dark hair veeing down to the waistband of his pyjamas, made her heart lurch and the breath stop in her lungs. She knew how hot and satiny his skin could be. She remembered the feel of that crisp hair against her seeking fingers. She knew the intimate feel of his whole body pressed against hers, chest to breasts, hips bumping, legs tangled.

She stared at him, willing herself to speak, not to want. 'I couldn't sleep,' she finally managed, her voice coming out in little more than a croak. 'I made some tea to help me settle. I'm sorry if I disturbed you.'

'I couldn't sleep either,' he said, and to her shock he came to sit down beside her on the window seat, his hip nudging her toes. 'Why couldn't you sleep?' he asked quietly.

'Why couldn't *you*?' Answering his question with one of her own was easier than admitting all the fears and worries that were tumbling through her mind.

'It's a lot to process,' Leo said after a moment. 'A baby, marriage… Just over twenty-four hours ago I wasn't anticipating either.'

'No, I suppose I've had more time to deal with it.'

He glanced down at her bare feet and then wrapped one warm hand around her foot. Everything in Margo jolted hard, almost painfully, at the feel of his strong hand curled around the sensitive arch of her foot, his fingers touching her toes.

'Your feet are cold,' he said, and drew them towards him, tucking them under his leg just as he had so many times before, when they'd been together.

Margo simply sat there, rigid with shock, with both of her feet tucked under his legs, everything in her aching.

'When you found out you were pregnant…' Leo asked slowly. 'How did it happen? How did you feel?'

Margo tensed, wondering if this was some kind of trap. Was he attempting to remind her once again of how non-maternal she'd been? Because she knew that. Of course she knew that, and it fed her fear.

'Why do you ask?'

'I just want to know. I feel like I've missed a big part of this.'

'I'm only four months along, Leo,' Margo said, but she relaxed slightly because she believed him. This wasn't a trap. Not with the sincerity she heard in his voice and her feet tucked under his legs.

'I had no idea at the start,' she began. 'I was on the pill, as you know. I didn't even miss taking one.'

'Then how did you get pregnant?'

'The day after…' She swallowed, felt a blush heat her cheeks and hoped Leo couldn't see in the dark. 'The day after I saw you I slept in. I took the pill three hours later than I normally would.'

'And that was enough to keep it from working?'

With a self-conscious laugh she patted her little bump. 'Apparently the mini-pill has to be taken at exactly the same time every day—although I didn't know things were quite that strict until it was too late.'

'You must have been shocked.'

'I was in a complete daze. I…I didn't know what I was going to do.' She hesitated in making that admission, afraid that Leo would use it against her, but he just nodded.

'That's understandable.'

'So for a while I didn't do anything. And then I felt so sick I *couldn't* do anything but drag myself through each day. When I went to the doctor to get some medication for my nausea he said something—just a throwaway comment about how such sickness usually meant the baby was healthy. "Here to stay," is what he said. And I knew that he was speaking the truth. That this baby was here to stay…that my inertia had been out of—well, out of fear,' she said.

Suddenly she realised just how much she was revealing. But she hadn't talked about this to anyone, and it felt good to unburden herself a little. Or even a lot.

'Fear?' Leo frowned. 'What are you afraid of?'

So many things. 'Of what the future would look like,' Margo answered, knowing she was hedging. 'Of how it would work. And of how you would take the news—what it would mean.'

'And so you decided to ask me to marry you?' Leo said. 'I still don't understand *that*, Margo.'

She swallowed, her throat feeling tight and sore. 'I grew up without a father,' she said after a brief pause. 'I didn't want the same for my child.'

He was silent for a moment. Then, 'I don't actually know anything about your childhood.'

And there was a very good reason for that. 'We didn't share many confidences, really, during our…' She trailed off.

'Our fling?' Leo filled in tonelessly.

'Yes.'

Even though her toes were still tucked under his warm thigh she felt a coolness in the air, tension tauten between them. It was a timely reminder of just what they'd had together…and what they had now.

'You want this baby,' Leo said slowly, a statement.

He lifted his head to look her straight in the face, and even in the darkness she could see the serious, intent look on his face, although she didn't know what it meant.

'Yes, I do.'

'You've changed in that, then?'

She took a deep breath and nodded. 'Yes.'

'Why?'

She stared at him, knowing he deserved to know at least this much. 'I didn't want children before because I was afraid,' she said slowly. 'Afraid of loving someone…and losing them. Or of getting it wrong. Parenting is a huge responsibility, Leo. The biggest.'

'But one you feel ready to take on now?'

'With your help.'

Except she didn't feel ready, not remotely. She felt inadequate and afraid and guilty. Because she wasn't sure she deserved another chance with someone's life.

'I *will* help you, Margo,' Leo said. 'We can do this. Together.'

She smiled even as she blinked back tears. She wanted to believe him. She almost did.

'I hope the tea helps you sleep,' he said, nodding towards her cup.

Margo knew he was about to leave and realised she didn't want him to.

'Leo…thank you,' she said, her voice both hurried and soft.

He stopped and turned to look at her in surprise. 'What are you thanking me for?'

'For…for being kind.'

He let out a huff of sound—almost a laugh. 'I don't think I've actually been very kind to you, Margo.'

'I know you were angry. I know you thought I'd cheated on you—maybe you still do. But even so you've agreed to marry me, and you've—you've shown concern for my welfare. I do appreciate that.'

He gazed at her for a long, fathomless moment before rising from the window seat. 'That's not very much, really.'

'I'm still grateful.'

It seemed as if he were going to say something else, something important, and Margo caught her breath… waited.

But all he said was, 'Get some sleep,' before returning to the darkness of his bedroom.

Leo stretched out on his bed and stared up at the ceiling, as far from sleep as he'd ever been. So much had happened today, tender little moments that had left him feeling uneasy and raw. It would be easy, he realised, to let himself care about Margo again. Let himself fall in love with her.

Let himself be rejected. Again.

Whatever had kept Margo from being with him before, it was still there. He didn't know what it was—the conversation he'd just had with her had left him wondering, uncertain. He'd seen a new vulnerability and fear underneath Margo's glossy, confident sophistication, and it had shocked him. It had made him realise there was depth and sadness to the woman with whom he'd had a passionate affair. The woman he was going to marry tomorrow.

The results of the paternity test were nothing more than a formality; he knew the baby was his. He knew Margo knew it. And with a baby and a marriage they could, in time, begin to build something together. Maybe not a grand passion or love, but something good and real and strong.

Then he reminded himself with slamming force of how she'd refused to marry him just four months ago, when they'd still been having their *fling*. She still clearly viewed their marriage as a sacrifice. How could he build on *that*— and, even if he could, why would he want to?

He'd had enough of trying to win people's trust or affection. For his entire childhood he'd been desperate for his father to notice him, love him. But Evangelos Marakaios had only cared about his business, and about handing it to his oldest son. In his mind Leo had been nothing more than spare—unneeded, irrelevant.

When his father had died Leo had hoped that his older brother Antonios would include him more in the family business, that they would have a partnership. But Antonios had cut him off even more than his father had, making him nothing more than a frontman, the eye candy to bring in new business without actually having any serious responsibility.

All that had changed six months ago, when Antonios had finally told Leo the truth. Evangelos had been borrowing against the company, making shoddy and sometimes illegal investments and running everything into debt. He'd hidden it from everyone except Antonios, confessing all when he'd been on his deathbed. Antonios had spent the next ten years hiding it from Leo.

He'd finally told the truth when prompted by his wife Lindsay and by Leo's own furious demands. And, while Leo had been glad to finally learn the truth, the knowledge didn't erase ten years of hurt, of anger, of being intentionally misled. His father and his brother, two of the people most important to him, had lied to him. They hadn't trusted him, and nothing they'd done had made Leo believe they loved him.

After so many years of trying to make them do both, he was far from eager to try the same with his soon-to-be wife.

He let out a weary sigh and closed his eyes, willed sleep to come. Enough thinking about Margo and what might have been. All he could do was take one day at a time and guard his heart. Make this marriage what they'd both agreed it would be: businesslike and convenient, and, yes, amicable. But nothing more.

Never anything more.

CHAPTER SEVEN

IF BRIDES WERE meant to look radiant on their wedding day, Margo thought, she fell lamentably short. She still had the exhausted, washed-out look she'd been sporting since the nausea had first hit, and she was, according to Leo's plan, going to get married this afternoon.

Sighing, she dragged a brush through her dark hair and wondered which of the two outfits she'd brought would be better to get married in—a sweater dress or jeans?

She didn't actually want the whole white wedding affair that Leo had mocked yesterday, but even so it felt pathetic and sad to be married like this, in the clothes she'd travelled in, looking like death barely warmed over.

With a sigh, she pulled her hair back into a neat ponytail and went in search of Leo.

She found him in the dining alcove of the kitchen, where the wide windows overlooked the small garden at the back of the townhouse. He'd made breakfast: toast and coffee, yogurt and fruit.

'I know you probably can't manage anything,' he said, gesturing to all the food, 'but I thought I'd make it just in case.'

'Thank you,' Margo murmured and sat down.

She spooned a little fruit and yogurt into a bowl and stirred honey into the centre.

Leo rose from the table and a few seconds later brought back a mug of ginger tea.

Margo blinked in surprise. 'How—?'

'You left the box of sachets in the kitchen. It seems like something you can keep down.'

'Just about the only thing.'

'Don't forget melba toast.'

'Right.'

She took a sip of tea and tried to still her swirling thoughts. Leo's consideration made her feel both restless and uneasy. It would have been easier to deal with his businesslike briskness, even his coldness, but this kindness… it reached right inside her. It made her ache with both regret and longing.

'Why are you doing this, Leo?' she asked.

'Doing what?'

'This.' She gestured to the breakfast dishes. 'You're being so…considerate.'

He gave her the ghost of a smile. 'Is that a bad thing?'

'No, but…'

'I don't want to fight all the time, Margo. That's not good for either of us, or our child.' He hesitated and then said, 'The doctor's office called this morning with the results of the paternity test.'

So that was the reason for his kindness and consideration. 'So now you know.'

'And you knew all along.'

'I told you there wasn't anyone else, Leo.'

'I believe you.'

He didn't look particularly pleased, though, and Margo wondered if the truth had hurt him as much as her lie had. Could he ever understand the desperate fear that had driven her to act as she had? She didn't even want him to.

'The marriage ceremony is at the town hall, at two

o'clock,' he said after a pause. 'We can drive back to the estate afterwards.'

'All right.'

'We need two witnesses for the ceremony,' he contin-ued. 'I thought I'd ask two of my staff from the Athens office.'

'Fine.'

It wasn't the way she'd ever anticipated getting married —a cold ceremony in a bureaucrat's office in a country she didn't know—but then she'd never anticipated marry-ing at all. She'd expected to live her life alone, the way she had since she was twelve and she'd lost everyone. *She'd lost Annelise.*

Leo glanced at the rumpled sweater dress she'd worn two days in a row. 'Do you have something to wear to the wedding?'

'I wasn't planning to get married today,' she reminded him. 'I have this or jeans.'

He frowned and took a sip of coffee. 'Then we'll go shopping this morning for something suitable. If you feel up to it?'

She almost asked him why they should bother, but then just nodded instead. Leo had said arguing would be un-pleasant for both of them, and she agreed. She would do her part in keeping things civil, even if his kindness had a strange way of hurting her.

Half an hour later they were strolling down Voukour-estiou Street, home to many designer boutiques. Leo led her into the first one, a soaring space of airy lightness, with a white leather sofa where shoppers could rest and a few select garments hanging from silver wires suspended from the ceiling.

Margo glanced at the elegant gowns in bemusement, for she had no idea what kind of dress she was supposed to get married in. But this was a business arrangement, so a business outfit seemed appropriate. She saw a pale grey suit at the back of the boutique and nodded to it.

'How about that one?'

Leo frowned. 'That doesn't look much like a wedding dress.'

'This isn't much of a wedding,' she answered.

His frown deepened. 'We might be marrying in a civil ceremony, but it is still very much a wedding. We will still very much be married.'

He nodded towards a dress of cream silk with an empire waist and a frothy skirt glittering with beaded crystals.

'How about that one?'

It was a feminine, frou-frou kind of dress—so unlike her usual tailored wardrobe. Margo hesitated, because while it wasn't something she would normally wear, she *did* like it. It was different. It wasn't armour.

She gave a quick nod. 'All right. I'll try it on.'

Moments later she stared at herself in the mirror, surprised at how the dress softened her. The warm cream of the material actually brought a bit of colour to her face, and complemented her dark hair and eyes. The sales assistant had brought her a matching pair of shoes—slim heels with a small diamante on each toe. They went perfectly with the dress.

'Well?' Leo called.

'You're not supposed to see it before the ceremony,' Margo called back. 'But I think it will do.'

At the cash desk she offered to pay for it, but Leo silenced her with a single look as he handed over his credit card. He'd been the same when they were dating: he'd paid for all their meals and hotels, despite Margo's insistence that she could pay her way. She hadn't minded, because she'd still felt safe. Still kept him at a distance.

This felt different. This was a wedding dress—the start of a new life that would be utterly intertwined with Leo's.

'We should go back to the apartment,' he said as he accepted the dress, now swathed in a designer hanging bag. 'You should rest before the ceremony.'

A few hours later Margo's stomach was seething with a whole different kind of nausea, now caused by nervousness. She'd showered and put on her new dress and heels, coiled her hair into its usual elegant chignon. The dress's high waist hid her small baby bump, for which she was grateful. She'd rather not have some sanctimonious city official looking at her disapprovingly.

'Are you ready?' Leo called, and she gave her reflection one last, swift look.

In less than an hour she would be married. She would have made vows that would bind her to Leo for ever.

'I'm coming,' she called, and walked out of the bedroom.

Leo's eyes widened as he took in her appearance, and then he gave one nod. 'You look very nice.'

It was a rather 'milquetoast' compliment, but Margo saw the way colour touched his cheekbones. She felt awareness—physical awareness—sweep through her in an electrifying wave.

'You look nice too,' she said, which was a serious understatement.

In a dark grey suit and silvery-grey tie he looked amazing. The colour of his tie made his eyes look even more silver, seeming to blaze in his swarthy face, and his dark hair was brushed back, the strong lines of his cheekbones and jaw emphasised by the cut of his suit.

'We should drive to the town hall,' he said. 'And then

we can leave directly from there. I need to get back to the estate to work.'

Margo nodded. No matter how incredible Leo looked, this marriage was still no more than a business arrangement. 'I'll get my bag.'

They drove in silence to the town hall, with tension stretching and snapping between them, or at least that was how it felt to Margo. She knew the civil marriage ceremony would be short and simple, but she would still be making promises to Leo. To herself. To their baby. Promises she intended to keep. Which made her heart race and her hands go clammy. There would be no going back from this.

The town hall in Athens was an impressive building in the centre of the city; the marriage ceremony was to be held in a small room on a top floor, with only a few people in attendance. The two staff from Leo's office greeted him with bland faces, although Margo imagined they had to be curious as to why their CEO was getting married in such a quick and pragmatic way. Thank goodness her bump wasn't visible, although of course it would be soon enough.

The official cleared his throat and began, and within a few minutes it was over. Margo had barely had to say a word.

Leo slid a ring of white gold on her finger; she stared down at it in surprise.

'When did you…?'

'I had it couriered,' he answered, and for some reason it hurt her—the thought that someone else had bought her wedding ring.

It was stupid, of course, but then she'd been so emotional lately. In any case, Margo knew she'd have to get used to these little things and remind herself that they weren't slights. She hadn't wanted romance, so she shouldn't expect it. Its absence surely shouldn't hurt her.

Just like the fact that he hadn't kissed her shouldn't hurt. It was simply the way it was. And so they walked out of the town hall into the bright winter sunshine, and then to the car.

They drove out of Athens as husband and wife, with not one word or person to mark the occasion.

Leo drove in silence for nearly an hour, his mind seething with thoughts he didn't want to articulate. The ceremony had been both simple and brief, which was how he'd expected and wanted it to be, and yet somehow he felt as if he were disappointing Margo. Disappointing himself.

It had hardly seemed appropriate to have a big church wedding, and yet… It had been a very small ceremony for a big step such as they were taking.

He glanced at the ring she'd slid onto his finger, her fingers seeming so fragile and cold on his. *Married.* He was a husband now, with responsibilities to his wife and child. Responsibilities he'd bear gladly, and yet he still felt their weight.

And one of those responsibilities was introducing Margo to his family. He hadn't considered the ramifications of marrying quickly and bringing Margo back to his villa immediately after. He'd simply wanted to control the situation, to have it on his terms.

Now he realised two of his sisters, Xanthe and Ava, who lived on the estate with him, would be wide-eyed and speculating when he brought back his sudden and obviously pregnant bride.

His older brother Antonios had done virtually the same thing—coming back from a business trip to North America with his unexpected bride, Lindsay. Antonios's iron will had assured Lindsay was made welcome, but even so Leo had seen how hard it had been on her, for a variety of reasons. And she hadn't even been pregnant.

He didn't want the same rocky start for Margo.

Flexing his hands on the steering wheel, he glanced at her, looking so pale and weary. 'My sisters will be at the estate when we return,' he began, and she turned to him sharply.

'Sisters? I didn't even know you *had* sisters.'

'Three, and one brother.'

'Your brother I know about. He was CEO before you?'

'Yes.' He'd told her that much at least, although he hadn't even hinted at the strains and sins that had marred their relationship. 'Two of my sisters live on the estate. They will want to meet you.'

'They weren't there before when I came?'

'No, they were visiting Parthenope, my third sister. She lives with her family near Patras.'

'Timon's mother?'

'Yes.'

Margo expelled a shaky breath. 'And what about your parents?'

'They're both dead.'

'I'm sorry.' She glanced at him, her eyes dark. 'When?'

'My father ten years ago, and my mother six months ago.'

Her eyes widened. 'When we were together?'

'Yes.'

He hadn't told her. There was so much he hadn't told her. And for the first time Leo acknowledged how Margo had had a point, claiming their relationship hadn't been going anywhere. He'd kept inside its careful parameters as much as she had. It was only when he'd become CEO that he'd decided he should marry and have an heir, and Margo had seemed the obvious choice. The right choice.

And now it had all happened just as he'd wanted...and yet not at all as he'd expected.

'They won't be pleased, will they?' Margo said after a moment. 'To welcome a surprise sister-in-law, and one who's pregnant?'

'They'll be surprised,' Leo allowed.

Margo let out a huff of laughter. 'I should say so. Did they even know you were—that we were—?'

'No.' He shifted in his seat. 'I never told anyone about us.'

She eyed him curiously. 'And yet you asked me to marry you?'

'I know.' He hesitated, and then continued a bit stiffly, 'I realise now how surprising my proposal must have been. Regardless of how you felt about it, it had to have been a shock.'

'It was.' She took a breath. 'Why...why did you ask me, Leo? If you didn't love me?'

'It felt like the right time to get married. I'd just been made CEO and I was conscious of needing an heir, stability. And as we were already together...'

'It was convenient?'

She let out another huff of sound, although whether it was a laugh or something else Leo couldn't tell.

'Well, that's what it is now. *Convenient.*'

'In any case,' Leo continued, 'I want to make sure my family accepts you as mistress of the household. You'll have my full support—'

'I don't want to displace anyone.'

'As my wife, you will have a role—'

'I know.' She leaned her head back against the seat and closed her eyes. 'I know. And I will rise to that particular challenge, I promise you. Just...just give me some time—please?'

'What about *your* family?' he asked, deciding it was wiser, or at least safer, to leave the topic of his own family for now. 'Is there anyone you want to tell? You could invite them to come—'

'No,' she cut across him flatly, her face turned to the window. 'There's no one.'

'Your parents?' Belatedly he remembered she'd said she'd grown up without a father. 'Your mother, at least?'

'I haven't seen her since I was twelve.'

'Really?'

Perhaps he shouldn't have been shocked. In the last few days he'd sensed a sorrow, even a darkness, in Margo's past that he'd never noticed before, perhaps because she'd been careful to hide it.

'Why not?'

She twitched her shoulders in a shrug. 'She wasn't a very good mother.'

It was clear she didn't want to talk about it, and Leo decided not to press. There had been enough emotional upheavals today.

'I'm sorry,' he said, and she bowed her head, a few tendrils of hair escaping her ponytail to rest against her cheek.

'So am I,' she said, and she sounded so sad that Leo felt an answering emotion rise in him in an unstoppable tide.

For a moment he considered pulling the car over, pulling her into his arms. Making her feel better.

But then she raised her head, set her jaw, and that moment passed almost as if it had never happened at all.

They didn't speak until they reached Amfissa.

CHAPTER EIGHT

MARGO FORCED HERSELF to relax as Leo turned the car up the sweeping drive that led to the Marakaios estate. She'd seen it all before, of course, when she'd driven up here in her rental car just two days ago. But then it had just been a house, grand and imposing; now it was her home.

As he pulled the car up to the front of the sprawling villa she noticed the other buildings surrounding it. The Marakaios estate was actually a complex, almost a little city.

'What are all the other buildings?'

'The office, a guesthouse, staff housing, a private villa where I used to live before I moved to the main house.'

'When was that?'

'When I became CEO.'

Which seemed to have been a life-changing moment, with his moving and then thinking of marrying.

'Why did your brother step down?'

'He wanted to move into investments,' Leo said, and the terseness of his reply made Margo wonder if there were more to it than that. She really knew so little about this man, her *husband*. So little about his life, his family.

And some of his family were coming out of the house right now: two tall, dark-haired women with the same striking good looks as Leo. Margo was intimidated by them already, and they hadn't even seen her yet, or her bump.

As Leo climbed out of the car the first one addressed him in a torrent of Greek, her hands on her hips. Distantly Margo considered that perhaps she should learn her husband's native language. Lessons, at least, would fill her empty days until the baby was born.

Leo came round to open the passenger door as his other sister joined them, unleashing her own incomprehensible diatribe. Leo didn't answer, just extended a hand to Margo.

She rose from the seat, still in her wedding dress, and as she stood the material caught on the door and tugged tight, outlining her small bump. Both sisters stopped abruptly and sucked in their breaths.

'*Kalispera*,' Margo said, and pinned on a bright and utterly false smile.

One of the sisters turned to Leo and began speaking again in rapid Greek. He held up a hand to silence her. 'Speak English, please, Xanthe. You're perfectly capable of it. My wife does not speak Greek.'

'Your *wife*—' Xanthe said, and her mouth dropped open.

She looked, Margo thought, appalled.

'Yes. My wife. We married today and, as you can see, we are expecting our first child in a few months.' He placed a hand on Margo's lower back, propelling her forward. 'Xanthe, Ava—please meet Margo Ferrars, Margo Marakaios now.'

She smiled weakly.

'Margo—my sisters.'

'I'm pleased to meet you,' she said, and they both nodded stiffly. Margo couldn't really blame them for the lack of welcome; they were clearly completely shocked. Still, it stung.

'Come inside,' Leo said, and drew her past his sisters into the villa.

Maria bustled up to them as soon as they stepped inside the door, and Leo spoke to her in Greek before turning to Margo with a grimace of apology. 'Maria doesn't speak English, but I've told her we're married.'

Margo nodded. She couldn't tell a thing from the house-keeper's expression, but she felt too overwhelmed and exhausted to care. It had been an incredibly long day, and she didn't have the energy to deal with any of these strangers.

'Leo,' she said, 'I'm tired, and I'd like to rest.'

It was only a little past seven, yet even so Margo knew she couldn't face an evening with Leo's family. Was she neglecting her responsibilities, even her vows, so soon? So be it. Tomorrow she would try to be the Stepford Wife he seemed to want. Today she needed to recover.

'Of course. I'll show you to your bedroom.'

Margo felt the silent stares boring into her back as she followed Leo up to the bedrooms. He went down a different corridor than before, and then ushered her into a sumptuous room decorated in pale blue and ivory.

'This is your bedroom. I have an adjoining one.' He gestured to a wood-panelled door in the corner, by the window.

So they wouldn't be sharing a bedroom. Margo didn't know how she felt about that, and in her exhausted state didn't feel like probing the tangle of her own emotions.

'Thank you,' she murmured, and took a few steps into the bedroom.

'You must let Maria know if you would like anything,' Leo said. 'And I'll be right next door if you need something in the night...'

She swallowed painfully. A lump had risen in her throat and it was hard to speak around it. It was their wedding night and they would be sleeping apart. She knew she shouldn't expect, much less want anything else.

'I'll be fine,' she said, and he nodded, one hand on the doorknob, seeming reluctant to leave her.

But he did, and Margo sank onto the bed and dropped her head into her hands. She felt more alone, more isolated, than she had in a long, long while—and considering the lonely course of her life, the loss of both her mother and Annelise, that was saying something.

She missed her apartment desperately, with its cosy, familiar furnishings, its sense of safety. She missed her life, the job that had given her security and purpose, her friends like Sophie, who might not have known that much about her but had still been *friends*.

She should text Sophie and tell her everything that had happened… But Margo didn't think she had it in her to weather Sophie's undoubtedly stunned and concerned response. No, she'd sleep. And maybe in the morning it would all look a little bit better.

At least their wedding night, wretched as it was, would be over.

Leo sat alone in his bedroom and stared moodily out of the window. He'd endured a barrage of questions from his sisters, who had wanted to know how he'd met Margo and why he'd married her.

'You might have noticed she's carrying my child,' he'd said tersely.

Xanthe had rolled her eyes. 'It's the twenty-first century, Leo. Illegitimacy isn't the stigma it once was.'

'I'm a traditional man.'

But he hadn't simply married Margo because she was pregnant with his baby, he acknowledged now. That might have been the impetus, but the truth was he'd wanted to marry her. He'd wanted her four months ago and he wanted her now.

And now it was his wedding night, and he was sitting here alone, drinking his second whisky, when what he really wanted was to take Margo into his arms and feel her softness against him…

Muttering a curse, Leo finished his whisky in one burning swallow. It was going to be a long, long night.

When Margo woke up the next morning she felt a lump of dread in her middle, as heavy as a stone, at the thought of facing the day and Leo's sisters, his staff…facing this whole strange world that she was now a part of.

She lay in bed and blinked up at the ceiling as wintry sunlight filtered through the curtains and illuminated the room's luxurious furnishings. For a girl who had been a breath away from growing up on the streets, she really had landed in a soft place indeed.

Resolutely Margo swung her legs over the side of the bed. After the usual moment of dizziness passed, she rose. She might not be looking forward to today, but she would meet it. She'd certainly faced far worse. And no matter how uncertain of her or unfriendly Leo's sisters might be, this was her new life. She had to accept it. Embrace it, even.

With that in mind, Margo put on her last remaining outfit, jeans and a jumper, and headed downstairs.

She could hear Leo's sisters' voices from the dining room as she came downstairs. They spoke in Greek, but Margo didn't need to know the language to understand the gist of what they were saying. Agitation, hurt and anger were audible in their tones.

She took a deep breath, squared her shoulders, and entered the room. '*Kalimera.*' Her knowledge of Greek extended only to greetings and saying thank you, but she hoped she was at least showing them she was trying.

Xanthe and Ava fell silent, forcing smiles to their lips. Margo sat at the opposite end of the table from Leo and busied herself with putting a napkin on her lap. She could see yogurt, fresh fruit and pastries on the table, and coffee, tea and juice on the sideboard. She wasn't very hungry but, wanting something to do, began to fill her plate.

'Good morning,' Leo answered her in English, and from the corner of her eye Margo saw him give a pointed look to his sisters. 'Did you sleep well?'

Margo felt a ripple of surprise from his sisters, and knew they were wondering why Leo should ask such a question. It would soon be clear to everyone that they had not shared a bedroom.

Leo must have realised it too, for his mouth tightened and he took a sip of coffee.

'I slept very well, thank you,' Margo said quietly.

They sounded like polite strangers. His sisters' eyes were on stalks.

'I thought perhaps after breakfast I could show you around the estate a bit,' Leo continued, his tone stiff now with formality. 'If you feel up to it?'

'That would be good.'

They sounded as if they were ironing out the details of a business merger—which was, Margo supposed, essentially what they were doing. If Leo wanted their marriage to be businesslike, then she supposed he wouldn't mind his sisters knowing it.

'Leo hasn't told us anything about you,' Xanthe said after a few moments of strained silence, when all Margo did was toy with her food and stare at her plate. 'Where are you from?'

She looked up and met Xanthe's speculative gaze with what she hoped was a friendly smile. 'I lived in Paris.'

'I love Paris!'

Ava jumped in quickly, and Margo wondered if the sisters would actually be welcoming towards her after all.

'It must have been very hard to leave.'

Margo glanced at Leo, whose face was as bland as ever. 'A bit,' she allowed, 'but I have other things to think about now.'

She rested one hand on her small bump, which unintentionally but effectively silenced all conversation. Both Xanthe and Ava excused themselves a few minutes later, leaving Leo and Margo alone with about an acre of polished mahogany between them.

'I'm sorry things seem a bit awkward,' Leo said after a moment. 'They'll come to accept you in time.'

'Maybe,' Margo allowed. 'I don't suppose it really matters.'

'Doesn't it? This is your home now, Margo. My family is your family. I want you to feel a part of things. I want you to *be* a part of things.'

'I know.' She toyed with a piece of melon and then laid down her fork. 'I'll hold up my end of the bargain, Leo.'

To her surprise he threw his napkin down and rose from the table. 'I don't want to talk about bargains,' he said. 'Let me know when you are ready to begin the tour. I'll be in my study.'

Mystified, Margo watched him stride out of the dining room. She'd annoyed him, obviously, but she didn't know how or why. Sighing, feeling the day stretching out in front of her would be very long indeed, she ate a bit of yogurt and nibbled on a pastry before rising herself and going to find Leo.

He'd told her he would be in the study, but she couldn't remember where it was—although she certainly recalled the interview she'd had in there just two days ago. She pressed a hand to her forehead, amazed at how much had changed in such a short time. Her whole life had been up-ended.

After opening and closing a few doors that led to various impressive reception rooms, she finally found the study. Leo sat behind the desk, one hand driving through his hair, rumpling it in a way that would have made him seem endearing if he hadn't had such a scowl on his face.

Margo knocked on the already open door and Leo looked up. His face cleared, but only just.

'Did you eat something?'

'A bit. I'm fine.'

He hesitated, then said, 'Things will get better. As you settle in.'

'I hope so. Although I'm not sure what you want sometimes, Leo. You almost seemed angry back there, talking about our marriage as a bargain, and yet *you're* the one who said you wanted to keep it businesslike.' The words spilled out of her, even though she hadn't intended to say them.

'I know,' Leo said, and drummed his fingers on the desktop.

Margo waited for him to elaborate but he didn't.

'I just want us to be on the same page,' she said quietly. 'Whatever page that is.'

'I think it will take time to decide what page that is,' he said finally. 'But in the meantime we can deal with practical matters.' He nodded towards her jeans and jumper. 'You need clothes and toiletries. We can order some things online, or go into Amfissa—'

'I'd like to get my things from Paris,' Margo answered. 'I'll need to speak to people at work, put my apartment on the market.'

'There's no need to sell your apartment. I can certainly afford to keep it, and it might be nice for us to have a permanent place in Paris.'

She blinked, surprised by his generosity. It was a far cry from the conditions he'd given her the last time they'd been in this room. 'Are you—are you sure?'

'Yes. Why shouldn't we keep it?' He stared at her for a moment and then said, his voice gaining an edge, 'Not *everything* about our marriage has to be a sacrifice, Margo.'

'I didn't mean it like that—'

'No? Sometimes when you look at me you seem as if you're steeling yourself.' He rose from the desk, shrugging on his suit jacket. 'It seems strange that it is so difficult for you to spend time with me now when we had two years together. But perhaps when you said you were planning to end it you spoke the truth, whether there was another man or not.'

He spoke with such bland indifference that it took Margo a few seconds for his meaning to penetrate. 'Leo, I thought it was you who didn't want to spend time with *me*. You've been angry with me for months, and I understand why—'

'I'm not angry.'

'No? If I look like I'm steeling myself,' Margo said, her heart starting to beat hard at this sudden, unexpected honesty, 'it's because I'm bracing myself for whatever mood you're in—whatever you're going to say. Sometimes… sometimes it feels like you're still punishing me for leaving you.'

He stared at her for a long moment, his eyes like shards of ice in his fathomless face. Margo waited, her breath held.

'I'm not punishing you,' he said at last. 'Not any more. I admit when you first came here…when I believed you'd been unfaithful…I may have been acting out of anger, or even spite.' He sighed, the sound weary. 'A petty, useless emotion if ever there was one. But I don't want to act like that any more. We need to move on, Margo, and make this marriage something we can both live with.'

'Which is?'

'That I don't know yet. But hopefully we'll find out in time.' He moved past her towards the door. 'Now, let me show you the rest of the villa.'

She followed him through the house as he showed her various rooms: a formal living room and a smaller, cosier TV room, the large dining room where they'd had breakfast, and another less formal room for family meals. A music room, a library, a second kitchen for parties… Margo started to feel overwhelmed. The house was huge. And Leo wanted *her* to be its mistress.

'What exactly do you want me to do, Leo?' she asked as they left the second kitchen.

He turned to her with a frown. 'What do you mean?'

'I mean what are my responsibilities? You mentioned that you wanted me to be in charge of your household…'

'I only meant that as a courtesy to you and your position here. I don't expect you to have *duties*.'

Which made her feel more confused than ever. 'I don't understand…'

'Margo, we're married. You're the—'

'Mistress of the house? The chatelaine? Yes, I understand that.'

'You can do as much or as little as you like. If you want to consult with Maria about meals, or housekeeping, or anything, you're more than welcome. If you want to redecorate, go ahead. I'm trying to give you freedom, not a burden.'

'Thank you,' Margo said after a moment, because she didn't know what else to say.

She might have established her career in acquiring household items for a large department store, but even so she wasn't about to bring her skills to bear here. She doubted his sisters would appreciate her changing so much as a cushion. As for meals... Her cooking skills had always been limited. She couldn't imagine planning meals for everyone.

And yet...

This was her life. She needed to own it.

'Do Xanthe and Ava both eat in the main house?' she asked. 'Will we have meals with them every day?'

'They come and go. Neither of them really work, although Xanthe does a little PR for Marakaios Enterprises. Ava travels to Athens frequently. I suspect she's seeing someone there, but she's quite close-mouthed on the subject.'

So she'd have both women underfoot...watching and judging her. Margo pressed a hand to her middle to suppress the lurch of queasiness that prospect gave her.

Leo, of course, noticed.

'Are you well?'

'I'm fine, Leo. I'm actually feeling a bit better today than yesterday.' A good night's sleep and no more travelling had helped in that regard. 'But I do need some more clothes and things.'

'I can take you into Amfissa this afternoon for some supplies. And, if you'd like to make a list, I'll arrange for whatever possessions you want to be sent here from your apartment in Paris.'

'All right,' Margo said. And although she didn't like the thought of some stranger rifling through her things she had the sense to know that another long trip would exhaust her, and she appreciated Leo's kindness.

He took her upstairs, where he pointed out Xanthe and Ava's bedrooms, in a separate wing from theirs. And then he hesitated before opening the door to a slightly smaller bedroom next to hers.

'I thought, when the times comes, this could be the nursery.'

She glanced at the beautiful yet bland room, decorated in pale greens and creams.

'You can completely redecorate it, of course. Have you…?' He cleared his throat. 'Have you given some thought as to whether you'd like to know if it's a boy or girl?'

Shock rippled through her at the question; it raised a host of images and possibilities in her mind. Pink frilled dresses or blue romper suits. And whatever this child was—boy or girl—*they* would be the parents. Together they'd be raising this person, putting this tiny being at the centre of their shared lives.

'I don't think I've let myself,' she said slowly.

'What do you mean?'

She swallowed, not wanting to admit how fearful she was, about so many things. How even now she was terrified of losing this child, of something going terribly wrong.

'So far I've just wanted to make sure the baby is healthy,' she said. 'Do *you* want to find out?'

'I haven't thought about it,' Leo answered, rubbing his jaw. 'But I think…yes. If you do. It could help us prepare. Make it more real.'

Again she thought of the swooshing sound of the baby's heartbeat, the reality of this life inside her, so small and vulnerable, so *important*. 'Yes, I suppose it would.'

'Dr Tallos has recommended a local obstetrician,' he said. 'You're meant to have an ultrasound in three weeks.'

'Just before Christmas.'

And what a wonderful Christmas present that would be—the promise of a healthy baby, boy or girl.

Something must have shown in her face, for Leo stopped to look at her seriously, and then took her chin in his hand, his touch light, his gaze searching.

'Margo, what is it?'

'What do you mean?'

'You seem…afraid.'

Her throat tightened and she tried to smile. 'I just don't want anything to go wrong with the baby.'

'Why do you think something might?'

Because she knew what it was like to lose someone precious. One day Annelise had been there—soft and smiling and warm, with her button-black eyes and her round cherubic cheeks—and the next she'd been gone. There had been nothing left but emptiness and heartbreak.

'Margo…' Leo said again, and he sounded alarmed.

She knew she must have an awful expression on her face.

She stepped back, away from his hand. 'I'm a first-time mother,' she reminded him as lightly as she could. 'I'm bound to be nervous.'

But judging by Leo's frown she didn't think she'd fooled him into believing that was all it was.

CHAPTER NINE

A WEEK PASSED and Margo started to think she and Leo were finding that same page. Things had settled, more or less, into a routine: Leo worked most of the day and Margo drifted. She didn't mind it for now, because with her nausea and her exhaustion drifting through each day was about all she could manage.

But as the days passed, and her nausea thankfully started to abate, she knew she needed to find some focus. Some purpose.

Xanthe and Ava had thawed towards her a little, which made life less tense if not exactly easy. And her things had arrived from Paris. Besides her clothes and toiletries she'd requested that some of her personal items—paintings and ornaments and books—be shipped to Greece. It felt both comforting and strange to arrange her things in the bedroom that still didn't feel like hers. They were dotted around the yawning space like buoys bobbing in an unfamiliar sea.

Still, life marched on, and Margo knew she needed to march with it.

She drove into Amfissa one afternoon and wandered the streets, window-shopping. She went into a shop that sold nursery furniture and gazed in wonder at the array of cradles and buggies—at a whole arsenal of parental tools with which *she* would one day need to be equipped.

When she came back down the sweeping drive that led to the main villa of the Marakaios estate Leo came out of the house, standing on the portico as he glowered at her.

She hadn't even cut the engine before he was striding over to the driver's side and opening door.

'Where were you—?'

'In Amfissa. I told Maria.' She'd managed to learn enough Greek, and Maria knew enough English, to communicate with the housekeeper.

'By yourself?'

Leo sounded incredulous and Margo only just kept from rolling her eyes.

'Leo, I'm a grown woman—'

'You're also pregnant—'

'Pregnancy is not a disease.'

'You've been suffering from extreme morning sickness, Margo, and I've seen how dizzy you can get. What if something had happened?'

She quelled the lurch of alarm she felt at that thought. Just when she'd been coming to grips with her own fear Leo had managed to rake it all up again.

'I can't just stay in the villa, Leo, like some knocked-up Rapunzel in her tower. I'll go mad.'

She heard a snort of laughter from behind her and turned around.

'Knocked-up Rapunzel?' Leo repeated, a smile tugging at his mouth. 'That presents quite an image.'

Margo smiled back. She'd missed this kind of banter so much. The jokes and the teasing…the *lightness*. She needed it to combat the darkness she felt so often in herself. 'Well, that's how I feel. And I don't even have tons of beautiful blonde hair to compensate.'

'Your hair is beautiful,' Leo said.

And just like that he dropped the banter, replacing it with an intent sincerity that made Margo's heart judder.

'I always enjoyed watching you when you unpinned it in the evening.'

All at once she had an image of Leo, gazing at her as she reached up to undo the chignon she normally kept her waist-length hair in. She pictured the hotel room, the candlelight casting flickering shadows across the wide bed. The moment's intimacy and expectation, the sheer eroticism of it…

It felt like a lifetime ago—and yet it also felt very real. She could remember exactly how it had felt when her hair had cascaded down her back and Leo had reached for her, taken her into his arms and pushed the heavy mass aside to kiss the tender nape of her neck…

She swallowed hard, not sure if she wanted to revel in the moment spinning out between them or move past it.

In the end Leo chose for her.

'I understand you needing to get out. But your mobile phone doesn't even work here—'

'Then perhaps I should get a new one. I can't be a prisoner, Leo.'

'I don't want you to be. I'll order you a phone today. I should have done it before. I'm sorry.'

She nodded wordlessly, still caught in the thrall of that moment, that memory.

'I was thinking,' Leo said abruptly, 'we should have a party. To welcome you properly and introduce you to the community. If you feel up to it.'

'I'm feeling much better. I'd like that.' Maybe a party would help her to meet people and finally start feeling a part of things.

* * *

Somewhat to Margo's surprise, Xanthe and Ava were excited about the party. They set a date, and contacted caterers, and sent out invitations to everyone in the local community.

And they took Margo shopping.

She resisted at first, because the thought of the two women fluttering around her like butterflies while she tried on dresses was alarming, to say the least. But they insisted and she finally gave in, driving with them into Amfissa one afternoon a few days before the party.

'You're not quite ready for maternity wear,' Ava said, casting a critical eye over Margo's neat bump. 'How far along are you, anyway?'

'Just over eighteen weeks,' Margo said.

The nausea had almost completely gone, and she was starting to feel a little more energetic and look a little less gaunt.

'You're so *thin*,' Xanthe said, envy audible in her voice. 'It seems like all Parisian women are thin. Do you ever eat?'

'Not lately,' Margo admitted, 'but normally, yes.'

Suddenly she thought of the mini-marshmallows she'd kept in her bag—her secret vice—and how Leo had known about them.

'You're smiling like a cat who just ate the cream,' Ava noted.

Margo shook her head. 'Just…remembering something.'

Which made the sisters exchange knowing looks.

And then Xanthe asked abruptly, 'So what is going on between you and Leo? Because obviously…' she gestured towards Margo's bump '…you've been together, but…' She trailed off as Ava gave her a quelling look.

Margo sighed. She'd come to realise that Ava and Xanthe were good-natured and well-intentioned, if a little interfering. They deserved the truth, or at least as much as she could tell them without betraying Leo's confidences.

'We were together. But things had…started to cool off. And then I became pregnant.'

'Accidentally?' Xanthe asked with wide eyes.

Ava snorted. 'Of course accidentally, *ilithia*.'

Margo recognised the Greek word for idiot; this wasn't the first time Ava had used it towards her younger sister and Leo, amused, had told her what it meant.

Ava turned to Margo. 'So you told Leo about the baby?'

'Yes. I never thought I'd have children, but—'

'Why not?' Xanthe interjected.

Margo hesitated. 'I suppose because I was focused on my career.' Which was no more than a half-truth. It was because she was afraid of loving and losing someone again—so desperately afraid.

Her hand crept to the comforting swell of her bump and Ava noticed the revealing gesture.

'Come on, let's try and find some dresses,' she said, and Margo was glad for the change in subject.

She spent a surprisingly enjoyable afternoon with both sisters once she'd got used to Xanthe's nosiness and Ava's bustling, bossy manner. She realised they were both fun to be around, and she could tell they actually cared about her. It almost felt like being part of a family—something she hadn't experienced since she'd been twelve years old, and even then not so much…

They finally all agreed on a dress of deep magenta that brought colour to Margo's face and complemented her dark eyes and hair. Its empire waist and swirling skirt drew attention away from her bump without hiding it completely.

'Understated, elegant, and just a little bit sexy,' Ava declared in satisfaction. 'Perfect. Leo will love it.'

And with a little thrill Margo realised she *wanted* Leo

to love it. She wanted to be beautiful to him again. A dangerous desire, perhaps, but still, caught in the happy glow of their shared afternoon, Margo didn't try and suppress it. Leo was her husband, after all. Why shouldn't she want him to find her attractive, desirable?

The night of the party, as she stood in front of the full-length mirror in her bedroom and gazed at her reflection, she wondered again just what Leo would think of her in this dress. She'd done her hair in its usual chignon but styled it a bit more loosely, so a few tendrils escaped to frame her face. She'd taken care with her make-up, making her eyes look bigger and darker with eyeliner and mascara, choosing a berry-red lipstick that matched her dress.

She looked, Margo thought, a bit more like her old self—the old Margo, who'd armed herself with make-up and designer clothes and stiletto heels. And yet she looked…softer, somehow. Her face was rounder, her bump was visible, and she didn't feel quite as guarded as she normally did.

Maybe living here in Greece with people all around her was softening her slowly. Changing her just a little. It was so different from the isolation she'd known for so long.

A knock sounded on the door that joined her bedroom to Leo's. He used it on occasion, to come and say goodnight to her, or talk with her about various matters. He always knocked first—always kept things formal and brief.

Now Margo cleared her throat before calling for him to enter.

'Are you—?'

He stopped as he caught sight of her, and Margo's breath dried in her throat as she looked at him. He wore a tuxedo, something she'd never actually seen him in before, and the crisp white shirt and black jacket was the perfect foil for his swarthy skin and ink-dark hair. The strong, clean lines of his jaw and cheekbones made Margo ache to touch him. And when she saw the blaze of desire in his eyes she felt as if a Roman candle had lit up inside her, fizzing and firing away.

'I was going to ask you if you were ready,' Leo said, his voice turning husky, 'but you obviously are. You look beautiful, Margo. Utterly enchanting.'

Colour touched her cheeks, and when she spoke her voice was almost as husky as his own. 'Thank you. You look…incredible.'

She blushed even more at this admission, and Leo's mouth quirked in a small smile. Margo could feel the tension snapping between them, but for once it was a good, exciting kind of tension. Sexual tension.

'Shall we?' he asked, and held out his hand.

Nodding, Margo took it.

Even though they'd been living as man and wife for a couple of weeks, they'd hardly ever touched. In this charged atmosphere the feel of his fingers sliding along her hand and then curling over her fingers made heat pool deep in Margo's belly.

Leo drew her out of the room and down the stairs towards the guests who were already arriving and milling in the foyer; the extra staff hired for the night circulated with trays of champagne and canapés.

The pooling desire she'd felt was replaced by a sudden lurch of nerves at the sight of all the people waiting to meet her, and maybe to judge her.

Leo gently squeezed her fingers. 'Chin up,' he said softly. 'You look beautiful and you are amazing.'

She glanced at him swiftly, surprise slicing through her at the obvious sincerity in his tone. What was happening between them? This certainly didn't feel businesslike.

But before she could say anything, or even think about

it any further, he was drawing her down the stairs and to-wards the crowd.

It had been a long time since Margo had socialised; morning sickness had kept her from doing anything but the bare minimum. Now, however, wearing a gorgeous dress, feeling beautiful and even cherished on Leo's arm, she felt some of her old sparkle return. And people, she found, were happy to welcome her.

A few glanced askance at her baby bump, but she suspected that most had already heard and come to terms with the new, unexpected addition to the Marakaios family. As Leo's wife, she was accepted by the people unequivocally, and it made her both relieved and grateful.

She felt even more so when Leo held his flute of champagne aloft and proposed a toast. 'To my lovely bride, Margo,' he said, his clear, deep voice carrying throughout the whole villa. 'May you welcome her and come to love her as I do.'

Margo smiled and raised her own glass of sparkling water, but his words caused a jolt of shock to run through her. *Love her*. He didn't, of course. She knew that. And yet for the first time she wondered what it would feel like if he did. If she loved *him*. If they had a proper marriage— real and deep and lasting.

A moot question, of course, because even if she wanted to risk her heart by loving Leo there was no guarantee that he would love her back. There were no guarantees at all— which was why it was better this way. They'd reached a level of amicability that was pleasant without being dangerous. She shouldn't want or seek more.

By the end of the evening her feet, in the black suede stilettos she'd had brought from Paris, were starting to ache, and she was definitely starting to wilt. Leo seemed to notice the exact moment she felt ready to call it a night, for in one swift movement he came to her side, putting his arm around her waist.

'You look tired. Why don't we retire?'

'I don't want to seem rude…'

'Greeks love a party. They will stay here till dawn unless I kick them out.'

Her mouth twitched in a smile and she let herself lean slightly into Leo's arm. Not enough for him to notice, or for it to matter. Just enough to feel the heavy, comforting security of it. To feel safe.

'So, are you going to boot them to the door?'

'I'll leave that to the staff. I'm going to come upstairs with you.'

And even though she knew he didn't mean it in *that* way, she still felt a shivery thrill run through her.

To her surprise, Leo didn't leave her at her bedroom door as he usually did at night, but came into the room behind her. Margo hadn't expected that, and she'd already started to undo her hair—the pins had been sticking into her skull all evening.

Suddenly self-conscious, she lowered her arms—and then froze at the sound of Leo's husky voice.

'Don't stop.'

In an aching rush she remembered how he'd told her he liked to watch her unpin her hair. It felt even more intimate, even more erotic, now that she knew he liked it. Slowly, her heart starting to thud, she reached up and took the pins out of her hair one by one.

Leo didn't say anything, but she could hear him breathing…feel the very air between them tauten. The pins now removed, she gave her head a little shake and her hair came tumbling down her shoulders, all the way to her waist.

Leo gazed at her, his eyes blazing, and Margo stared back, every sense in her straining, her heart thudding hard.

'Margo…'

She heard a world of yearning in his voice and it made her tremble. She pressed a hand to her middle to stay the nerves that leapt like fish in her belly—and then realised they weren't nerves at all.

'*Oh…*'

'What?' Leo came towards her quickly, his voice sharp with concern. 'What is it?'

'I think…' Margo pressed her hand against her bump, a smile dawning across her face. 'I think I felt the baby kick.'

'You *did*?' Leo sounded incredulous, amazed, as if he'd never heard of such a thing.

Margo let out a little laugh as she felt that same insistent pulse of life. 'Yes! I just felt it again!' She looked up at him, beaming, as amazed as he was. 'It feels so *funny*. There's actually a person inside me!'

He laughed then, and so did she, and then he reached out a hand—before staying it. 'May I?' he asked.

Margo nodded. She reached for his hand, pressing it to her bump, her hand on top of his. 'Wait,' she whispered, and they both stood there, still and transfixed, barely breathing.

It seemed an age, but then finally it came again: that funny little inward thump.

Leo let out an incredulous laugh. '*Theos*, I felt it! I really felt it.'

She looked up at him, still beaming, but the wide smile slid right off her face as she saw Leo's own joyful incredulity turn into something else. Something sensual.

The breath rushed from her lungs as he reached out one hand and slid it through her hair so his fingers curved around the nape of neck, warm and sure and seeking. He drew her slowly towards him and she came, one palm resting flat against his chest so she could feel the thud of his heart, as insistent as her own.

And then he kissed her, as she knew he would, his lips brushing hers once, twice, in a silent question. Without waiting for an answer—an answer she'd have given with every part of her body—he went deep, his tongue sliding into her mouth as he pulled her more closely to him, fitting their bodies together as much as her bump would allow.

The feel of his lips on hers…his hands on her body… his touch made every sense she had flare painfully alive as need scorched through her. She slid her hands up to clutch at his lapels and opened her mouth to his kiss, his tongue, felt the raw passion inside her kindle to roaring flame.

And then the baby kicked again—that determined little pulse—and Margo froze. Her thoughts caught up with the sensations rushing through her and that little kick reminded her just why they were here in the first place. The only reason they were here.

Leo, as attuned as ever to her emotions, broke off the kiss and stepped back. Margo couldn't tell a single thing from his expression. His gaze dropped to her bump and she wondered if he too were reminding himself of the real and only reason they'd got married.

The silence stretched on, and Margo could not think how to break it. Her emotions felt like a maelstrom, whirling inside her; she couldn't separate one from the other, couldn't articulate how she felt about anything.

In the end Leo broke it with a single word. 'Goodnight,' he said quietly, and then walked to the door that joined their bedrooms.

Margo was still standing in the centre of the room, one hand pressed to her bump, another to her kiss-swollen lips, as she heard the door click softly shut.

CHAPTER TEN

LEO PACED THE length of his bedroom and willed the blood in his veins to stop surging with the furious demand to taste Margo again. To bury himself inside her.

He let out a shuddering breath and sank onto the bed, dropping his head into his hands. *He'd come so close...*

But then she'd frozen, and he'd felt her emotional if not her physical withdrawal. No matter how sizzling their chemistry had once been, Margo had still chosen to reject him. And the way she'd stilled beneath his touch had felt like another rejection.

His hands clenched in his hair and he considered opening the door between their bedrooms and demanding his marital rights. They were husband and wife, and he knew Margo desired him—whether she wanted to or not. She was feeling better and the pregnancy was healthy—why shouldn't they enjoy each other?

But, no. He would not share Margo's bed until she wanted him to be there. Utterly.

And yet the evening had started so promisingly. He'd loved seeing Margo at the party, looking bright and beautiful, as much her old self as ever, reminding him of how interesting and articulate and sophisticated she really was. And when she'd drawn his hand to her bump and he'd felt their child kick... It had been the most intimate thing Leo had ever experienced.

The kiss had felt like a natural extension of that intimacy. He couldn't have kept himself from it if he'd tried—which he hadn't.

So what had gone wrong? What had spooked Margo?

Then, with a wince, Leo remembered the toast he'd given at the party. *'May you welcome her and come to love her as I do.'* He hadn't thought of the words before he'd said them; they'd simply flowed out of him, sounding so very sincere. But he'd assured Margo he didn't love her—just as she didn't love him. Had his toast frightened her off?

Had he meant those words?

It was a question he strove to dismiss. Things had become muddied with Margo. Their business arrangement was morphing into something more amicable and pleasant. And yet...*love*?

No. No, he wouldn't go there. He'd suffered enough rejection in his life—starting with his father's determination to exclude his second son. He didn't need more of it from a woman who had already made it clear what she wanted from this marriage.

The same thing he wanted. The *only* thing he'd let himself want. A safe, stable life for the child they had created.

The next morning Margo came into the breakfast room and hesitated in the doorway. Leo saw uncertainty flash across her features and forced himself to stay amicable, yet a little cool. They'd had breakfast together every morning since they'd been here and today would be no different.

'Good morning.' He rose from the table to pour the ginger tea he'd requested Maria to brew every breakfast time. 'Did you sleep well?'

'Yes, thank you.'

Margo sat across from him and spread out her napkin on her lap. Leo thought she looked paler than usual, with dark smudges under her eyes.

She must have caught him looking for she smiled ruefully and said, 'Actually, not really.'

'I'm sorry to hear that.' He handed her the tea and then returned to his seat before snapping open his newspaper. 'It's always hard to sleep after a party, I find.'

Such bland, meaningless conversation—and yet it provided a necessary kind of protection, a return to the way things needed to be.

'It wasn't because of the party, Leo,' Margo said.

He glanced up from the paper and saw her give him a direct look that stripped away his stupidly bland attempts at conversation, saw right into his soul.

'It was because of our kiss.'

Our kiss. Memories raced across his brain, jumpstarted his libido.

He took a sip of coffee and answered evenly. 'Yet you were the one who stopped it.'

'Actually, *you* were,' she answered.

'Semantics,' he returned. 'You were the one who stopped responding, Margo.'

'I know.' She looked down at her plate, her long, slender fingers toying with her fork, her face hidden.

'Why did you, as a matter of interest?' Leo asked, half amazed that he was asking the question. Did he really want to know the answer? 'It wasn't because you weren't interested. I could feel your desire, Margo. You wanted me.'

'I know,' she said softly. 'Whatever you think…whatever you believe…I've never stopped wanting you, Leo.'

'Ah, yes, of course,' he drawled sardonically. 'It's *loving* me you have a problem with.' *Damn it*. He had *not* meant to say that.

She looked up, her gaze swift and searching. 'But you don't love me, either.'

'No.' So why did he feel so exposed, so *hurt*? He let out a short, impatient huff of breath. 'I'm not sure why we're even having this conversation.'

'Because I think we're both trying to navigate this relationship,' Margo answered quietly. 'This marriage. And I'm not sure I know how to be businesslike with my husband.'

'You seem to be managing fine.'

'Maybe, but when you came into my room last night… when you felt the baby kick…it made me realise that we're actually going to be parents.' She let out a self-conscious laugh and continued, 'I knew it before, of course, but for a moment I had this image of us together with a child— giving it a bath, teaching it to ride a bike. Boy or girl, this baby is ours and we'll both love him or her. I know that. And I don't know where being businesslike fits in with that. With a family. The kind of family I want…that I've always wanted—' She broke off, averting her face.

Leo stared at her. 'Yet you're the one who has said you don't wish to be married, who viewed this marriage as a sacrifice,' he reminded her. Reminded *himself.* As much as he wanted to, he couldn't get past that. The real feelings, or lack of them, that she'd shown when he had proposed.

'I said that because I thought you'd hate me after what I said before,' Margo said. 'About there being someone else.'

'And why *did* you say that?' Leo challenged in a hard voice. 'Why did you choose to lie in such an abominable way?'

'I told you before. Because it was the only way I could think of to—to make you leave me.'

Everything in him had crystallised, gone brittle. 'Yes,

I remember. And why did you want me to leave you so much, Margo?'

She was silent—so terribly, damnably silent.

Leo reached for his fork and knife. 'I see,' he said quietly, and he was afraid he saw all too well. The brutal rejection of it, of *him*, was inescapable.

Margo had come to breakfast after a restless, sleepless night, determined to talk to Leo and, more than that, to come to an agreement. An arrangement. Even though the details remained vague in her head. She didn't want to be businesslike any more—didn't want this polite stepping around each other.

Yet what was the alternative? How did you engage your heart and mind and maybe even your soul without risking everything?

And she knew she wasn't ready to do that. She hadn't even been able to tell Leo that the real reason why she'd refused his marriage proposal was that she'd been so very afraid. Annelise… Her mother… The foster parents who had decided she wasn't what they wanted… So many had turned away, and she knew she couldn't take it if Leo did. Not if she'd given him her heart—fragile, trampled on thing that it was.

But her silence had led to this terrible strain, with Leo having turned back to his newspaper, his expression remote and shuttered.

'What are you doing today?' she blurted, and he looked up from the paper, not even a flicker of interest or emotion on those perfectly chiselled features.

'Working in the office, as usual.'

'I should probably arrange to go to Paris soon. I still need to finish things at Achat.'

'If you feel well enough,' he said, sounding uninterested. 'I don't see a problem with that.'

Margo stared at him, her heart sinking right down to her toes. She didn't want this. She'd come down this morning wanting to try to make things better, and she'd only made them worse.

'Leo, you gave me a tour of the villa, but I haven't seen the rest of the estate or the olive groves. Do you think you'd have time today to show me?'

There. That was her peace offering—her attempt at building some kind of bridge. She just hoped Leo would take the first step onto its flimsy surface.

He gazed at her, his eyes narrowed, and then gave a brief nod and folded up his newspaper. 'I suppose… I'll come back to the villa after lunch.'

Margo spent as much time getting ready for her tour of the olive groves as if it were a first date. Not that she'd had many of those. Both her short-lived and frankly disappointing relationships prior to Leo had made her wonder if she was even capable of a real, loving relationship. She certainly didn't have a lot of experience of them.

It was cold out, at just a little less than two weeks before Christmas, and Margo struggled to fit into her jeans. She couldn't zip them all the way up, and the button was a lost cause. She wore a tunic top of aquamarine cashmere that fell nearly to her knees and fitted snugly round her bump while hiding the undone zip and buttons.

She left her hair loose, which she rarely did, and put on a bit of eyeliner and lipstick. She didn't necessarily want to look as if she was trying too hard, but she definitely wanted Leo to notice.

Unfortunately he didn't say a word when she met him in the foyer, and Margo suppressed the flicker of disappointment she felt at his silence. Had she really expected him to compliment her? She was wearing *jeans*, for heaven's sake. Still, she noticed that Leo seemed terser than usual as they headed out into the bright, frosty afternoon.

'There isn't actually all that much to see in the olive groves at this time of year,' he remarked as they walked along the gravel road that went past his office and led to a pair of wrought-iron gates. 'The trees are bare, and they won't begin to bud until March.'

'I still want to see,' Margo said, trying to keep her tone upbeat. 'This is my home now, after all. I don't know the first thing about olive trees or oil or *any* of it.'

'You don't need to learn.'

So he really was rebuffing her.

'I *want* to learn, Leo. You told me you wanted me to be a part of things. That's what I'm trying to do.'

He stared at her, as inscrutable as ever, and she decided to try a different tack.

'Tell me about your childhood. Did you grow up playing hide-and-seek in these groves?'

They'd stepped through the gates and were now walking among the trees, the trunks twisted and gnarled, the branches stark and bare.

'A bit,' Leo answered. 'I grew up here, certainly.'

'Did you like it?' she asked, for she sensed more than reticence in Leo's reply, and wondered at his memories.

'I loved the olive trees,' he said after a moment. 'The white waxy blossoms, the dusty scent in summer, the nuttiness of the oil…' He shook his head. 'I probably sound ridiculous, but I love it all. I always have.'

So why, Margo wondered, did he sound so regretful? So *bitter*?

'It's a good thing you're in the olive oil business,' she said, and Leo gave her a rather tight smile.

'Yes.'

'Why,' Margo asked after a moment, as they walked between the bare trees, 'do I feel as if you're not telling me everything?'

'What do you mean?'

She shrugged, half afraid to press, yet wanting to know more about him. Wanting to keep building this bridge, flimsy as it seemed. 'When you talk about the trees, the business, you sound...tense.' She hesitated and then added, 'Almost angry.'

Leo was silent for a long moment, and the only sound was the wind soughing through the trees and making the branches rattle. 'I suppose,' he said finally, 'that's because I am. Or was, at least. I think I'm getting over it. I hope so, anyway.'

Leo's face gave nothing away, and yet Margo knew instinctively this was a big admission for him to make. 'Why, Leo?' she asked quietly. 'What happened?'

He sighed, shrugging and shaking his head at the same time. 'Just complicated family politics.'

'Tell me.'

He hesitated, then said, 'My grandfather started the business from scratch. He was a dustman before he scraped together enough drachmas to buy a bit of property, and he built it from there. We've always been so proud of how we came from nothing. How we built this empire with our own hands. First my grandfather, and then my father...'

He trailed off, frowning, and Margo dared to fill in, 'And now you?'

'Yes. But it didn't happen as seamlessly as that.'

'Your brother...?'

'Yes, my brother.' His face tightened. 'Antonios was my father's favourite. The oldest child and his heir...I suppose it was understandable.'

'It's *never* understandable,' Margo countered. 'If we have more children I won't favour one more than the other.'

He gave her a swift, blazing look. 'Do you *want* more children, Margo?'

'I…' She swallowed hard. More children to love. *More children to lose.* And yet a proper family—the kind of family she'd always longed for but had been afraid to have. Was afraid she didn't deserve. 'I don't know.'

He kept staring at her, his gaze searching and yet not seeming to find any answers, for eventually he looked away and resumed his story.

'Well, understandable or not, Antonios was the favourite. I didn't accept that, though. I tried—*Theos*—how I tried to make my father love me. Trust me—'

He broke off then, and Margo ached to comfort him. But she didn't, because everything about Leo was brittle and tense, and she had a terrible feeling—a fear—that he would shake her off if she tried to hug him as she wanted to.

'To make a long story short,' he continued finally, his voice brusque, 'he never did. He had a heart attack and he sent for Antonios—told him the truth about the business. He'd been involved in dodgy dealings for years, trying to make back the money he'd lost on bad investments. He was a hair's breadth away from losing everything. He made Antonios swear not to tell anyone…not even me.'

'And *did* he tell you?' Margo asked.

Leo shook his head. 'Not for ten years. Ten years of my not understanding, feeling cut off and kept in the dark. Well…' he shrugged and then dug his hands into his pockets '…I don't suppose I should have been very surprised. My father never trusted me with anything—why would he with the truth?'

'But your brother…?'

'Antonios didn't either. Not until I pushed and pushed

for him to say something—and then I think he only did because of Lindsay, his wife. She wanted an end to all the secrets, all the acrimony.'

'And *has* there been an end to it?' Margo asked.

'I…I don't know. We get along—more or less. Antonios resigned as CEO, as you know, and is happier working in investment management.'

'Are *you* happy?' Margo asked, and the question hung there, suspended, encompassing so much more than just the business.

'I don't know,' Leo said again, and he turned to look at her, his face more open and honest and vulnerable than she'd ever seen it before—even when he'd asked her to marry him. 'I don't know,' he said again, and it seemed like more than an admission. It seemed like a revelation… to both of them.

They started walking again, back towards the gates, neither of them speaking. This time, however, the silence didn't feel strained, Margo thought, more expectant. Although what she—or Leo—was waiting for, she had no idea.

The gates loomed ahead of them and Margo had the strange sensation that once they passed through them things would change. The spell of intimacy and honesty that had been cast over them amidst the trees would be broken.

She turned to tell Leo something of this—something of herself—but before she could say anything her foot caught on a twisted root and she pitched forward. The moment felt as if it lasted for ever, and yet no time at all, no time to try to right herself, or even to break her fall with her hands.

She fell hard onto her front, her belly slamming into the ground, her face and hands and knees scraped and stinging.

'*Margo*—' Leo's voice was sharp with alarm and even fear as he knelt at her side.

She got onto her hands and her knees, her heart thudding from the fall.

Leo put a hand on her shoulder. 'Are you all right? Let me look at you.'

Slowly, wincing from the bruises and scrapes, she eased back into a sitting position, the ground hard and cold beneath her.

'I think I'm okay,' she said, and pressed one hand to her belly, her fingers curving around her bump, willing the baby to give a little comforting kick in response to the silent question her hand was asking.

Then she caught Leo staring at her; his face was pale, his eyes wide, and he leaned forward, grabbing her arm.

'What—?' she began, but Leo was already sliding his phone out of his pocket and dialling 112, which she knew was the number in Greece for the emergency medical services. 'Leo, I'm okay,' she said.

And that was when she felt a sticky wetness between her thighs, and when she looked down she saw blood spreading across the hard earth.

CHAPTER ELEVEN

'No!' MARGO'S VOICE was hoarse as she stared at the blood on the ground, and then she let out a harsh, keening cry that tore at Leo's heart. '*No.* Leo—no, no, *no*—' Her voice caught and she struggled for a moment, every breath an effort as panic swamped her.

'I have an emergency medical situation,' he snapped into the phone. 'I need an ambulance at the Marakaios estate immediately.'

He tossed the phone aside and reached for Margo. She was rocking back and forth, her arms wrapped around her middle, her whole body trembling.

'Margo, breathe,' he commanded. 'Nice and even. It's going to be okay.'

She took a few hitched breaths, her shoulders shaking, and then finally managed to speak. 'Don't lie to me, Leo,' she said raggedly. 'Don't ever lie to me. It's *not* going to be okay. You can't know that.'

'You're bleeding,' he acknowledged steadily, 'but that doesn't mean anything is wrong with the baby.'

But Margo seemed barely to hear him. She shook her head, tears streaking down her face. 'This can't happen,' she whispered to herself. 'This *can't* happen. I won't let this happen again.'

Again? Leo's mind snagged on the word, but now was hardly the time to ask her what she meant.

'An ambulance will be here in a few minutes. I'm going to move you so it can reach you more easily.'

Gently he scooped her up into his arms and carried her out of the olive grove. He could see the blood staining her jeans and coat and his stomach roiled with fear. Margo had been right. He couldn't know if it was going to be okay.

Soon an ambulance came screeching and wailing up the drive. Leo saw his sisters and Maria crowd onto the villa's portico as he carried Margo towards the vehicle. A paramedic came out to help her onto a stretcher.

'Leo!' Xanthe cried, and he shook his head.

'I'll call you,' he promised, and then climbed into the ambulance with Margo.

She looked so vulnerable, lying there on the stretcher, her eyes huge and dark in her pale face, and she scrabbled for his hand, her fingers fragile and icy in his as the paramedic took her vitals and then asked Leo what had happened.

Leo gave the details as clearly and evenly as he could; he could feel Margo clinging to his hand, her breath coming in little pants as she tried to control her panic.

Dear God, he prayed, *let nothing have happened to the baby.*

The next half-hour was a blur as the ambulance took them to the hospital in Amfissa, and then to an examination room in the A&E. A doctor, brisk and purposeful, came in with an ultrasound machine while Margo lay on the examination couch.

'The first thing to do,' the doctor said in Greek, 'is a scan, so I can see what's going on.'

Leo translated for Margo and she nodded frantically, still clutching his hand.

The next few minutes, as the doctor set up the machine, seemed to last for ever. Leo watched as she spread cold, clear gel on Margo's belly and then pressed the wand against her bump. The silence that stretched on for several seconds was the worst thing he'd ever heard, and Margo gave a soft, broken little cry before turning her head away from the ultrasound screen. Tears snaked silently down her cheeks, and Leo felt the sting of tears in his own eyes.

This couldn't be happening.

'There it is,' the doctor said in Greek, and Leo stared in stunned disbelief as she pointed to the screen and the tiny heartbeat, still going strong.

'*Margo*—'

'She has a partial placenta praevia,' the doctor said, and Leo tried to listen as she explained how the placenta was covering the cervix and the fall had aggravated it, which had caused the bleeding.

He could barely take it in, however—all he could do was stare at that wonderful little pulsing assurance of life.

'Margo…' he said again and, touching her cheek, he turned her face to the screen.

She blinked, tears still slipping down her face, as she stared in confusion at the screen.

'It's okay,' he said softly. 'It really is okay.'

Smiling, the doctor turned up the volume, and that wonderful, whooshing, galloping sound of the baby's heartbeat filled the room. Leo thought Margo would be relieved, that she might even smile or laugh, but as she heard the sound of the heartbeat her face crumpled and she collapsed into sobs, her shoulders shaking with their force.

Leo didn't think past his overwhelming need to comfort her. He leaned over and put his arms around and she buried her face in his shoulder as her whole body shook and trembled.

Quietly the doctor turned the machine off and wiped the gel from Margo's bump. 'She should stay overnight— just for observation,' she told Leo. 'Tomorrow we can do another scan to see how the bleeding looks and if the placenta has moved any more.'

Leo nodded wordlessly. He'd have to process all that later; the only thing he could think about now was Margo.

Eventually she eased back from him and wiped the tears from her face, managing the wobbliest of smiles. A nurse came to transfer her to a room, and Leo called his sisters while Margo showered and changed into a hospital gown. When he came back into the room she was lying in bed, her hair brushed and her face washed, but her eyes still looked puffy and red from crying.

He sat on the edge of her bed and took her hand. 'The doctor said you have a partial placenta praevia,' he said. 'To be honest, I can't remember what that means, exactly, but I'll arrange for a doctor who speaks English to talk to you about it.'

'I know what it means,' Margo said.

She sounded exhausted, emotionally spent, and Leo squeezed her fingers. 'The important thing is the baby is okay.'

'Yes. For now.'

She bit her lip, and Leo saw her eyes glisten with the sheen of new tears.

'There's no reason to be afraid, Margo—'

'Oh, Leo, there's every reason.' She leaned her head back against the starchy white pillow and closed her eyes. '*Every* reason.'

'I don't understand…'

He thought once more of how she'd said she didn't want this to happen *again*. He wanted to ask her what she'd meant, but he knew Margo was feeling too fragile now for such an emotional conversation.

'Is there something you're not telling me?' he asked instead, needing to know that much.

She opened her eyes and shook her head. 'Nothing that really matters.'

'Then why—?'

'I'm just so afraid.' She bit her lip. 'I'm *always* so afraid. That's why I didn't want to have children.'

He stared at her in confusion, trying to understand what she meant. He thought of when he'd met her in that hotel bar, looking sassy and smart in a black wrap cocktail dress, her long legs encased in sheer tights, a stiletto dangling from one slim foot. She'd looked like the most fearless person he'd ever met, and she'd always seemed that way to him: breezing into hotel rooms, giving him a naughty smile, shrugging out of her dress with confidence and ease.

He'd liked that about her, had enjoyed her sense of confidence. But now he wondered. Since Margo had come back into his life he'd wondered what she'd been hiding, what secrets she had. Had that breezy confidence all been an *act*?

'You don't need to be afraid,' he said, squeezing her fingers.

But, withdrawing her hand from his, Margo just turned away and said nothing.

Frustration bit hard but he forced himself not to demand answers or explanations. Once again he was being kept in the dark about something. It felt like another kind of rejection, because Margo obviously didn't trust him with whatever truth she was keeping from him. But he wouldn't press. He wouldn't beg.

Reluctantly he eased himself off the bed. 'Is there anything I can get you?' he asked. 'Something to drink or eat? Or something from the villa? Your own pyjamas or clothes?'

She was still looking away from him, her hair brushing her cheek. 'No, thank you.'

He hated how formal she was being, even though that morning he'd decided that was just how he wanted it. Things had changed. Both their conversation in the olive grove and the terrifying events afterwards had changed him. And they'd changed Margo too—but not in a way he liked or wanted.

Everything about her, from her brittle voice to the way she wouldn't look at him, made him think she wanted him to go. But he wasn't going to leave her here alone, whatever she wanted, so he settled himself into a chair opposite the bed and waited.

Neither of them spoke for a very long time, and eventually Margo drifted off to sleep.

When Margo awoke the room was dark, and panic doused her in an icy wave. She struggled upright, one hand going to her middle, curving over the reassuring bump even as the remnants of the nightmare she'd been having clung to her consciousness.

'Leo—'

'I'm here.'

In the darkness she couldn't see him, but she felt his hand come and close over hers. Even so she couldn't stop shivering.

'I had the most awful dream.' Her voice choked and her throat closed. She'd dreamed about Annelise—something she hadn't done in a very long time. 'It was so terrible—'

'It was just a dream, Margo,' Leo said, his voice soft and steady. 'It wasn't real. Everything's all right. The baby's all right.'

She nodded and gulped, wanting, *needing* to believe him and yet not quite able to do so. The dream had been real once upon a time. She'd relived the worst memory she had in her nightmare, and she was so afraid of it happening again. But Leo couldn't understand that because she hadn't told him.

'Don't leave me,' she whispered, and he squeezed her hand.

'I won't.'

But she needed more than just his reassurance; she craved the comfort of his touch. 'Leo…' she began, and then, thrusting any awkwardness aside, she blurted, 'Would you hold me?'

Leo didn't answer, and Margo braced herself for his refusal—because they didn't have that kind of relationship. That kind of marriage.

Then wordlessly he rose from the chair and peeled back the covers on her bed. He kicked off his shoes and slid into the narrow bed next to her, pulled her carefully into his arms.

Margo wrapped herself around him, burying her face in his neck, breathing in the clean, comforting scent of him. She'd needed this—needed him—more than she could ever have put into words.

He didn't say anything, just held her, one hand stroking her hair, until she felt the icy panic that had frozen her insides start to recede, the nightmare begin to fade. Her breathing evened out and her body relaxed into his embrace.

Lying there, safe in his arms, she felt a creeping sense of guilt for how much she'd kept from him. He'd been her rock since she'd fallen in the olive grove—he'd never left her, never wavered for an instant, offering her unconditional encouragement and support.

The realisation brought a lump to Margo's throat and she pressed her face more snugly against the hollow of his neck, breathing him in more deeply...

She must have fallen asleep again, for when she woke up the pale grey light of early dawn was filtering through the curtains and Leo was still in her bed.

Margo eased back to look at him. His eyes were closed, his thick, dark lashes fanned out on his cheeks. His jaw was rough with morning stubble, which made his lips look all the more lush and mobile and eminently kissable.

He was still in his clothes from yesterday, his shirt unbuttoned at the throat, his tie tossed on a chair. Margo felt as if a fist had wrapped around her heart and squeezed.

Then the door to the room opened and a nurse wheeled a machine in. 'Time to take your vitals,' she said cheerfully, and Margo blinked in surprise.

'You speak English?'

'Yes, Kyrie Marakaios requested that someone who could speak English attend to you. Or French, he said. But no one spoke good enough French.' She gave a little smile and a shrug, and then took out a blood pressure cuff and wrapped it around Margo's arm.

Leo had woken up and was now easing himself to a sitting position, wincing slightly at the stiffness in his body from spending a night fully clothed on a hospital bed. His hair was rumpled and he blinked sleep out of his eyes before turning to Margo.

'Are you all right?' he asked quietly.

She nodded. The fear that had gripped her so tightly yesterday had now eased a little, thanks to Leo.

He rose from the bed and while the nurse took Margo's blood pressure and temperature he left the room in search of coffee and a shave.

'The doctor will visit in a little while, for another ultrasound,' the nurse told her. 'And in the meantime you can have breakfast.'

Margo nodded, and a few minutes later Leo returned with two cups—one of coffee and another of ginger tea.

'Where on earth did you get *that*?' Margo asked as he handed her the cup.

'I make sure to always have some on me. Just in case.'

'You're so thoughtful,' she said, almost wonderingly.

Leo laughed ruefully. 'Don't sound so surprised!'

'I *am* surprised,' she admitted. 'There haven't…there haven't been that many people in my life who have been thoughtful.'

Leo frowned and Margo looked away. She wasn't ready to tell him any more than that, but she could tell he had questions. Questions he wanted answers to.

Before he could ask anything the door opened again, and a smiling woman brought in a breakfast tray.

After breakfast the doctor came with the ultrasound machine, and they both silently held their breath as she set it up—until the image of their baby came onto the screen, still kicking up a storm.

'Oh, I can feel that!' Margo exclaimed, one hand pressed to her bump. 'I hadn't felt anything since I fell, but I felt that.'

'This little one doesn't like being poked,' said the doctor, who also spoke English, with a smile. 'Everything looks fine. You'll have your twenty-week scan in a few days, and we'll check on the placenta praevia then.' Smiling, the woman put the machine away and Margo pulled down her shirt. 'You're free to go.'

It wasn't until she was dressed and they were back in the car, heading towards the estate, that Leo turned to her, his expression serious.

'Margo, we need to talk…'

Her body went tense and she turned to stare blindly out of the window.

'What are you not telling me?' Leo asked, his voice quiet but insistent. 'Because there's something.'

'It doesn't matter.'

'It *does* matter. It matters because in the hospital you were terrified—'

'Of course I was!' She turned to look at him. 'Leo, I was afraid I was losing my baby.'

'*Our* baby,' he corrected quietly, and Margo bit her lip. 'Don't shut me out, Margo.'

She turned back to the window without replying, and they drove in silence all the way back to the Marakaios estate.

CHAPTER TWELVE

WHEN THEY ARRIVED at the villa Leo helped Margo out of the car, one hand on her elbow as he guided her inside.

Xanthe, Ava and Maria all met them in the foyer.

'You're all right?' Ava asked, her face pinched with anxiety.

'Yes—and, more importantly, the baby is all right,' Margo said, and smiled when Maria muttered a prayer of thanksgiving and crossed herself.

'I'm going to get Margo upstairs,' Leo cut across his sisters' anxious chatter. 'It's been an incredibly long twenty-four hours, and I don't think either of us slept well last night.'

Actually, Margo had slept better than she had in months, wrapped in Leo's arms. But she could imagine Leo had spent a considerably less comfortable night, cramming his large body onto the narrow bed, still in his suit.

They went upstairs, and as Margo came into her bedroom she breathed a sigh of relief. She wanted to crawl into the big, soft bed and stay there for about a million hours—good night's sleep or not.

Behind her, she heard Leo close the door. 'I need to shower and change,' he said, 'and I imagine you'd like to freshen up. And then we'll talk.'

His tone was implacable, leaving no room for arguments. Still, Margo tried. 'I'm very tired, Leo—'

'There will be plenty of time for you to rest today. But I won't let you put me off, Margo.' He hesitated, seeming to want to say more, but then simply turned and left the room.

Margo went into the bathroom, stepping into the huge two-person shower with its marble sides and gold fixtures. As the water streamed over her body she had a sudden image of Leo joining her there. They'd showered together a few times during their stolen weekends away, but that felt like a lifetime ago. She felt like a different person from the insouciant, carefree career woman she'd been back then, embarking on a no-strings affair.

But then she *was* a different person—because that carefree woman had been nothing more than a part she'd played, a mask she'd worn. She hadn't dared try to be anything else. Anything deeper or more lasting.

In just a few minutes Leo was going to demand answers, and if she was brave enough she would drop that mask for ever and tell him everything. She knew he deserved to know.

She rested her head against the cool marble, willing herself to be strong enough for that kind of hard honesty.

A few minutes later she was dressed in a pair of loose yoga pants and a soft hoodie, curled up on the window seat that overlooked the villa's gardens, the grass now coated with a thick rime of frost.

Leo tapped once on the door that joined their bedrooms before poking his head in and then coming through completely. His hair was damp from his shower, and he wore a soft grey tee shirt and faded jeans that were moulded perfectly to his muscular legs. Wordlessly he walked over and joined Margo on the window seat.

Neither of them spoke for a long moment; the only

sound was the wind rattling the bare branches of the trees outside.

Finally Margo spoke, and each word felt laborious, even painful. 'I'm not who you think I am.'

'Who do you *think* I think you are?' Leo asked quietly.

'The woman you met in that bar. That glamorous, confident, sexy woman.' She let out a shaky laugh. 'Not that I'm trying to be arrogant, but that's how I wanted to be... to seem.'

Leo was silent for a moment, then finally he asked, 'Who are you, then?'

'A street rat from Marseilles.' She glanced at him, expecting to see if not disgust then at least surprise. But Leo looked completely unfazed.

'How did a "street rat from Marseilles" end up as a confident career woman in Paris?' he asked after a moment.

'Luck and hard work, I suppose.' She tucked her hair behind her ears and gazed out at the wintry afternoon. 'But I've always felt like a street rat inside.'

'That doesn't mean you *are*, Margo. I don't think anyone feels like the person they present to the world all the time.'

She pretended to look shocked. 'You mean you *don't* feel like an arrogant, all-powerful CEO all the time?'

He smiled and gave a little shrug. 'Well, obviously I'm the exception.'

She laughed at that, and then shook her head. 'Oh, Leo.' She let out a weary sigh, a sound of sadness. 'If you knew about my childhood...'

'Then tell me,' he said.

And although his voice was soft she knew it was a command. A command she should obey, because she'd already come to the decision that she needed to tell him the truth. But truth was a hard, hard thing.

'I grew up one step away from the street,' she began

slowly. 'And sometimes not even that. My mother was a drug addict. Crystal meth—although I didn't realise that until later. But it…the drug…controlled her life.'

Now, surely, he would look shocked. But when Margo looked at him his expression was still calm, although his mouth had pulled down at the corners with sympathy.

'I'm sorry.'

'So am I.' She let out a wobbly laugh that trembled into a half-sob. 'Oh, God, so am I.'

'Was she able to care for you?'

'No, not really, and sometimes not at all. At the beginning, yes. Before she became an addict. At least I think she did. I survived, anyway. But my father left when I was four—I only have a few fuzzy memories of him.'

'That must have been hard.'

'Yes.'

The few fuzzy memories she had were precious—of a man who'd pulled her into a bear hug and swung her in the air. *Why* had he left? It was a question that had tormented her for years. How could a man walk away from his family? Had she not been lovable enough?

'After he left my mother went very much downhill.'

She lapsed into silence then, because she did not want to tell him how grim it had been. The sheltered housing, the stints in various homeless shelters, the weeks when she'd been taken away from her mother and sent from one foster home to another. Some of them had been good, some of them mediocre, and some of them had been very bad. But always, in the end, she'd been brought back for her mother to try again, having promised she'd stay clean, and for a few days, sometimes a few weeks, she had.

Life during those periods had been normal, if fragile, and sometimes Margo would begin to believe it was going to be okay this time. Then she'd come home from school to find her mother strung out, or manically high, the promises all broken, and the whole cycle would start once more.

Until Annelise. But she really didn't want to talk about Annelise.

'Margo?' Leo prompted softly. 'Tell me more. If she couldn't care for you, how did you survive?'

She shrugged. 'Sometimes not very well. I was in and out of foster homes my whole childhood. When I was old enough I learned to take care of myself.'

'And how old was that?' Leo asked in a low voice.

'Seven…eight? I could use the gas ring in our bedsit and I could make basic meals. I got myself to school most days. I managed.'

'Oh, Margo.' He shook his head, reached for her hand. 'Why didn't you tell me this before?'

'I don't talk about my childhood to anyone,' she said, her voice thickening. 'Ever. It's too awful. And in any case, Leo, we didn't have that kind of relationship.'

His fingers tightened on hers. 'Do we now?'

Her heart lurched at the thought. 'I…I don't know.'

Which was what he had said to her yesterday morning. So much uncertainty, for both of them, and yet here she was confessing. Trying.

'Tell me more about your childhood,' Leo said after a moment.

She closed her eyes briefly. 'I could go into details, but I'm sure you can guess. It…it wasn't pretty, Leo.'

'I know that.' He was silent for a moment, his fingers still entwined with hers. 'But there's something more, isn't there? Something you're not telling me?'

'Yes.' She took a deep breath. 'When I was eleven, my mother had a baby. My half-sister. There was no father ever in the picture.' Another breath to keep herself going. 'Her name was Annelise.'

'Was?' Leo said softly, his fingers tightening on hers. 'What happened to her?'

'She…she died.'

She closed her eyes against the memories, but they came anyway. Annelise cuddled up to her in her bed, one chubby hand resting on her chest. Annelise toddling towards her with a big toothy grin, hands outstretched as she called Margo 'Go-Go'. Annelise with her arms wrapped around her neck, her cheek pressed to Go-Go's.

'I'm so sorry, Margo.'

'My mother was lucky not to have Annelise taken away from her right at the beginning,' she said, the words just barely squeezed out. 'With her history. But we'd flown under the radar for a couple of years by then. I was managing to get myself to school, and my mother seemed like she could control her addiction.'

She held up a hand to stop Leo saying anything, although he hadn't even opened his mouth.

'Which is ridiculous, I know, because of course an addiction can't be controlled. But she…she functioned, at least, and then when she found out she was pregnant she cleaned herself up for a while—enough for Annelise to be born and brought home.'

'And then?'

'As soon as Annelise was home she lost interest. I didn't mind, because I took care of her. I *loved* taking care of her.'

'But you had school—'

'I stopped going to school. I had to, for Annelise's sake. I told them we were moving, and nobody bothered to check. It was easy. Honestly, if you don't want to be noticed by the authorities it can be remarkably easy.'

'And so you stayed home and took care of Annelise?' Leo was silent for a moment. 'What did you do for money?'

'We got a little bit from the government. And my mother

would sometimes…' She hesitated, not wanting to admit just what her mother had done to score her drugs, but Leo must have guessed because his mouth tightened.

'She found a way to get money?' he surmised.

She nodded. 'Yes.' And then, because now that she'd started the truth-telling she felt she needed to say it all, she blurted, 'She sold herself. To men. For money.'

Leo nodded, his jaw tense, and Margo wondered what he thought of her now. In and out of foster homes, her mother a prostitute… She hated him knowing it.

'So what happened to you and Annelise?'

'I was her mother,' she whispered. 'I did everything for her. *Everything.*' She blinked rapidly and managed, 'She called me Go-Go.'

She stared down at her lap, at their entwined hands. And she thought of Annelise—her soft baby's hair, her gurgle of laughter.

How, after seventeen years, could it still hurt so much?

'How did she die?' Leo asked quietly.

'The flu. *The flu.*' Her voice choked and a tear slipped down her cheek. 'She just had a fever at first. I was taking care of her. I gave her some medicine and had her sleep in my bed, but…' She drew in a gasping breath. 'The fever spiked, and I was so scared, but I knew if I took her to hospital the authorities would get involved and they might take her away. I couldn't bear that, so I just bathed her in cool water and gave her more medicine.'

'And then…?' Leo asked softly.

'And then she started having convulsions. I begged my mother to take her to hospital then, but she…she wasn't herself.' She'd been high on drugs, barely aware of her children. 'So I took her myself. I carried her to the hospital in my arms. When I got there a nurse took her from me. She…she was already dead.'

She bowed her head, the memory and the pain and the guilt rushing through her.

'It was my fault, Leo. My fault she died.'

She'd never said those words aloud—never even admitted her guilt to herself. And saying it now made her feel both empty and unbearably full at the same time. She bowed her head and tried to will back the tears.

'Oh, Margo.' Leo's arms came around her and he pulled her towards him, her cheek against his chest. 'I'm so, so sorry.'

He didn't speak for a moment and she simply rested there, listening to the steady thud of his heart, letting the grief subside.

'It *wasn't* your fault, you know. You were twelve. You never should have had to bear that kind of responsibility.'

'I wasn't a child. And it *was* my fault. If I'd gone to the hospital earlier they could have given her antibiotics. Brought her fever down. Maybe she'd have been taken away, but she'd still be alive.' She spoke flatly, dully, knowing it was the truth and that nothing Leo could say would change it.

'What happened after that?' he asked after a moment. His arms were still around her, her cheek still against his chest.

'I was put into foster care—a few different families.'

She spoke diffidently, not wanting to admit all the terrible details. The foster mother who had dragged her by the hair into the bathroom because she'd said Margo was dirty. The family who had left her, at fourteen years old, in front of the council offices with nothing but a cardboard suitcase because they hadn't wanted her any more.

'It was tough for a few years,' she allowed. 'I missed Annelise so much… I acted out. I was hard to deal with.' And so people had chosen *not* to deal with her.

'When I was sixteen,' she continued after a moment, 'I finally calmed down. I stayed with a family for a year. They were good to me. They helped me find a job, saw me settled.'

'Are you still in touch with them?'

'No. It wasn't that kind of a relationship. They had a lot of different foster kids. I was just one of many. We wrote letters for a while, but…' She gave a little shrug. 'I am grateful to them. And really,' she continued quickly, 'I don't blame anyone except myself. The people who fostered me all tried their hardest. They didn't *have* to take children in. They were doing their best. And I really was difficult. I can't blame anyone but myself for that.'

'But you were a *child*,' Leo protested, 'in an incredibly difficult situation.'

'Yes, but I was mature for my age. I'd had to be. I could have…controlled myself.' Except she hadn't wanted to. She'd been wild with grief, wanting and needing to strike out. To hurt someone as she'd been hurting.

'And this is why you're so afraid now of something happening to the baby?' Leo said slowly. 'Because of what happened to Annelise?'

She nodded. 'I know it's not rational, but everyone I know has left me at one time or another. And Annelise… losing Annelise was by far the worst. I don't think I could survive something like that again, Leo. I really don't think I could.'

'You won't have to.'

'But you can't know—'

'I don't have a crystal ball to predict the future, no.' Leo took her chin his hand, turning her face so he could look her in the eye. 'But do you believe me, Margo, when I tell you I will do everything in my power—absolutely everything—to keep you and our child safe and healthy? I won't let you down, I swear to you. You can trust me.'

'Thank you,' she whispered, and although she didn't know if she had the strength to believe him she was still glad he'd said it.

Then, simply because it felt right, she leaned forward, closing the small space between them, and brushed her lips with his. It was barely more than a peck—a kiss that wasn't sexual or even romantic, but something else entirely. Something deeper and more tender.

Leo stilled under her touch, and then he eased back, his expression serious. 'Thank you for telling me. For trusting me that much.'

'I'm sorry I didn't before.'

'Like you said, we didn't have that kind of relationship.'

And did they now? Margo still didn't know. She didn't know what she was capable of, or what Leo wanted.

'You should rest,' Leo said as he stood up from the window seat. 'It's been a very long couple of days.'

'Yes…'

But she didn't feel tired, and after he'd left she paced the room restlessly, her mind starting to seethe with doubt and worry. She'd just unloaded a huge amount of emotional baggage onto Leo. When they'd struck their business deal he hadn't expected to have to cope with all that. What if he decided she was too much work? Or if he withdrew emotionally rather than deal with all the neurotic fears Margo had just confessed? Going back to being business-like would be even harder and more painful now she'd confessed so much.

Tired with the circling questions she knew she couldn't answer, she decided to keep busy instead of simply pacing and worrying. She went to the adjoining bedroom that was meant to be a nursery and started sketching ideas to transform it into a space for a baby.

It had been weeks since she'd exercised her mind or her creativity, and it felt good to think about something other than the current anxieties that revolved around Leo and the baby. To remember that she'd had a career, one she'd enjoyed, and could still put to use, if only in this small way.

And as she sketched and planned she felt her uncertainties fall away, as if she were shedding an old skin, and she knew that she wanted to move forward from the past, from the pain. She wanted to move forward with Leo and have a real marriage. A loving one.

If she dared.

CHAPTER THIRTEEN

IN THE DAYS after Margo told him about her childhood Leo found himself going over what she'd said and connecting the dots that before had seemed no more than a scattered, random design of inexplicable behaviour.

Now he was starting to understand why Margo had decided to marry for the sake of their child.

After a childhood like hers, he could see how the stability of a family life was something she would want to provide for her child…even if they didn't love each other.

Except that basis was one Leo realised he could no longer assume. *Did* he love Margo? *Could* he love her? He certainly admired her resilience and her strength of spirit, her devotion to their unborn child. He was still deeply attracted to her, God knew. And if he let himself…if he stopped guarding his heart the way he suspected Margo was guarding hers…

Could this businesslike marriage become something more? Did he even want that? Margo had rejected him once. He understood why now, but it didn't mean she wouldn't do it again.

Things at least had become easier between them, and more relaxed: they shared most meals and chatted about ordinary things, and Margo had shown him her preliminary designs for the nursery, which he'd admired.

They were rebuilding the friendship they'd had before his marriage proposal, and this time it was so much deeper, so much more real.

One morning at breakfast Leo told her that Antonios and his wife Lindsay would be coming after Christmas for a short visit.

'Are you looking forward to that?' she asked, her dark, knowing gaze sweeping over him.

'Yes, I think I am,' Leo answered slowly.

He hadn't seen his brother since right after his mother's funeral, when Antonios and Lindsay had moved to New York and Leo had taken the reins of Marakaios Enterprises. He and Antonios had made peace with each other, but it was an uneasy one, and although they'd emailed and talked on the telephone since then Leo didn't know how it would feel to be in the same room, to rake over the same memories.

'It will be nice to meet some more of your family,' Margo said, breaking into his thoughts. 'Sorry I can't return the favour.'

She spoke lightly, but he saw the darkness in her eyes, knew she was testing him, trying to see how he felt about what she'd told him now that he'd had time to process it. Accept it.

And what he felt, Leo knew, was sadness for Margo. Regret that he hadn't known sooner. And a deep desire to make it better for her.

'We have all the family we need right here,' he said, and she blinked several times before smiling rather shyly.

'What a lovely thing to say, Leo.'

'It's true.'

'It's still lovely.'

That afternoon they headed into Amfissa for Margo's twenty-week scan. The last time they'd come to the hospital they'd been in an ambulance, filled with panic and fear. Leo saw the vestiges of both on Margo's face as he drove into the hospital car park and knew she was remembering. Hell, he was too.

The panic didn't leave Margo's face or Leo's gut until they were in the examination room and they could see their baby kicking on the screen.

The technician spent a long time taking measurements, checking the heart and lungs, fingers and toes. Leo held Margo's hand the whole time.

'Everything looks fine,' she said, and they both sagged a bit with relief. 'The placenta is starting to move, so hopefully the praevia will clear up before delivery. But we'll keep an eye on it. If it doesn't move completely by thirty weeks we'll have to talk about a scheduled Caesarean section.'

Margo nodded, her face pale. Leo knew she would do whatever it took to keep their baby safe and healthy, although such an operation was hardly ideal.

'Do you want to know the sex?' the technician asked. 'Because I can tell you. But only if you want to know.'

Leo and Margo looked at each other, apprehensive and excited.

'Could you write it down?' Leo asked. 'And put it in an envelope? Then we can open it together.'

'On Christmas Day,' Margo agreed, clearly getting into the spirit of the thing. 'A Christmas present to both of us.'

He smiled at her, and she smiled back, and Leo felt a kind of giddy excitement at the thought of knowing—and of knowing together.

Margo was determined to have a wonderful Christmas. The Christmases of her childhood had been unmarked, simply another day to survive. As an adult she'd decorated her apartment, and she and Sophie had exchanged presents, but that was as far as the celebrations had gone. Now, with a home and family of her own, she wanted to go all-out.

Leo told her that they'd never made much of Christmas either, when he was a child. In the Greek Orthodox church Easter was by far the greater holiday. Besides eating a grand meal on Christmas Day, and exchanging presents on January the sixth, Christmas passed by most Greek households virtually unnoticed.

'But I think we have much to celebrate this year,' he said, 'so I wouldn't mind changing things.'

So Margo did.

She wanted to keep the Greek spirit of things, and tried her hand at different Christmassy Greek treats: *melomakarona*, honey-dipped cookies stuffed with nuts, and *kourambiedes*, cookies dusted with powdered sugar. She and Maria made loaves of *christopsomo*—a round loaf decorated on the top with a cross, one of which adorned just about every Christmas table in Greece.

She gathered evergreen and pine boughs from around the estate and decorated the mantels and banisters; soon the whole villa smelled like a forest.

Leo brought in a Christmas tree and Margo made dough ornaments with Timon when Parthenope came to visit, enjoying the time with her husband's nephew and imagining how one day it would be her own child at her side.

It still seemed too good to be true, too wonderful to trust that it would actually happen. But with each day that passed she felt her faith in the future grow stronger…even as she wondered about herself and Leo.

Things were better, certainly, and far from businesslike. But they hadn't actually talked about the future, or what they felt for each other, and Margo wasn't brave enough to be the first one to confess that her feelings were growing and turning to love. She hardly wanted to admit it to herself, afraid that the fragile happiness they'd found would shatter into a million pieces…just as it had before.

In any case, there was still much to enjoy.

They all went into Amfissa on Christmas Eve for a midnight service. The Byzantine *kalandas* were different from the traditional songs and hymns Margo knew, but she liked them all the same.

Afterwards Ava and Xanthe retired to their rooms, and once she and Leo were alone in the sitting room, a fire crackling in the hearth and the Christmas tree glowing with fairy lights, Leo took an envelope out of his pocket.

'Shall we?'

'It's not Christmas yet,' Margo protested, even as she felt a tremulous thrill of excitement.

'It's after midnight.' Leo sat cross-legged on the thick rug in front of the fire and patted the space next to him. 'We'll open it together, so we can see at the same time.'

'All right,' Margo said, and a little bit awkwardly, because of her growing bump, sat next to him on the rug.

Wordlessly they opened the envelope, their fingers brushing as they withdrew the single slip of paper and read the single sentence in English the technician had written there.

It's a…boy!

'A boy…' Margo repeated wonderingly.

She felt jolted, almost unsettled. She'd been excited to find out the sex of their baby, but now that she knew it, it made things more real and less real at the same time.

She put both hands to her bump. 'A son. We're going

to have *a son*.' She glanced at Leo, who looked as gob-smacked as she felt. 'Are you happy?'

'I'm…overjoyed.' He put one hand over hers, on top of her bump. 'What about you?'

'Yes. It's strange, but it seems so hard to believe.'

'I know what you mean. But you're not…you're not disappointed?'

'Disappointed? Why would I be?'

'Because…because of Annelise.'

Just the name caused a little ripple of pain to go through her, but no more than that. Her hands curved more possessively around her bump. 'A baby girl wouldn't have replaced Annelise, Leo.'

'I know. Nothing can replace her. But it might have eased things, a bit.'

'No, it's better this way. A whole new start, for all of us.'

She caught her breath, her heart starting to thud as she realised just how much she meant that. How much she wanted it.

And Leo must have understood that, because Margo saw his eyes darken and his gaze move to her mouth.

'Margo…' he said, and then he kissed her. Softly, one hand cradling her face, the other still resting on her bump.

It was the most perfect moment, the most intimate and tender thing she'd ever experienced.

Then Leo broke away. 'I want you,' he said bluntly, and the simply stated fact caused a tremor to run through her. 'I want you very badly. But only…only if you want me.'

The vulnerability on his face made her ache. Those awful words she'd flung at him so many months ago still had the power to hurt.

She raised her hand to his cheek, cradling his face just as he'd cradled hers. 'I want you, Leo. I want you very much.'

'And it's safe…?'

'The doctor said it was.' She gave a small smile. 'And we don't need to worry about birth control.'

He laughed softly and kissed her again, this time holding nothing back, his tongue and lips causing a symphony of sensation inside her as beautiful and wondrous as any *kalanda* they'd sung that night.

'We could go upstairs,' Leo whispered, and he moved from her lips to her shoulder, kissing the curve of her neck as his hand found the warm swell of her breast, one thumb running over its already taut and aching peak.

Letting out a shudder of longing, Margo glanced at the crackling fire, the Christmas tree sparkling with lights. The house stretched all around them, quiet and dark.

'No, let's stay here,' she whispered, and began to unbutton Leo's shirt.

It felt like a wedding night, with the lights and the fire and the quiet sacredness of what they were doing.

Leo stilled under her touch as she finished unbuttoning his shirt and then slid the crisp cotton from his shoulders, revelling in the feel of his skin, so hot and satiny, under her fingers. She pressed a kiss to his collarbone, needing to feel that hot, smooth skin under her lips. Leo let out a groan as she touched her tongue to his skin, tasted salt.

'You will undo me before we've even begun…'

She looked up, mischief in her eyes. 'Would that be a bad thing?'

'A very bad thing—because I want to savour every moment.'

Smiling, he undid the tie on her jersey wrap dress and it fell open. Margo felt only a little self-conscious in her bra and pants, with the swell of her bump visible and making her shape so different from the last time they'd been together like this.

Yet they'd *never*, she realised, been together like this. So intimate. So tender. So honest.

Leo slid the dress off her shoulders and then rested one hand on her bump, his skin warm on hers. 'You are so very beautiful.'

'Even pregnant?'

'Especially pregnant. Knowing you are carrying my child makes you impossible to resist.'

He bent down and pressed a kiss to her bump, and then gently he laid her back on the rug, its soft bristles tickling her bare back as he stretched out beside her.

Margo gazed up at him, everything about her open and trusting as Leo pressed a kiss to her mouth and then worked his way lower, kissing her breasts and her bump, and then all the way down to her thighs. Margo gasped as he kissed her *there*, spreading her legs wide so he could have greater access, making her feel even more vulnerable...

And yet she didn't mind. She felt treasured rather than exposed, and she wanted Leo to feel the same way.

'My turn now,' she said with a little grin, and Leo arched an eyebrow as she pushed him onto his back.

'If you insist,' he said—and then let out a groan as Margo began to kiss him, taking her time, savouring the salty tang of his skin.

She kissed her way down his chest and Leo's hands tangled in her hair as she moved lower, his breath coming out in a hiss as she freed his arousal from his boxer shorts, sliding one hand up its smooth, hot length before taking it into her mouth.

'*Margo...*' His breath ended on a cry as his hips arched upwards.

Margo watched him with hot eyes, his own desire making hers ratchet higher.

Then Leo reached for her, pulling her up towards him

so she was straddling his hips. She sank onto his shaft with a sigh of relief that turned into a moan of pleasure as he began to move, his hands tightly gripping her hips so she moved with him in an exquisite rhythm.

The firelight cast shadows over their bodies as they moved together, climbing higher and higher towards that barely attainable peak. Logs shifted and cracked, sparks scattered, and Margo cried out as she finally reached the apex, drawing Leo even more tightly into her body as she threw her head back and her climax shuddered through her.

Afterwards they lay tangled together on the rug, warm and sated, their breathing only just starting to slow.

'Thank goodness Maria didn't come down for a glass of warm milk…' Leo said.

Margo stiffened. 'She wouldn't—?'

'She is known to on occasion. It helps her sleep.' He kissed the top of her head. 'But don't worry. No one came. Except you, that is.'

She laughed softly and snuggled up against him. 'And you.'

'Most certainly. And *that*, I have to say, was a long time to wait.'

'There wasn't…?' She hesitated, not wanting to spoil the mood but needing to know. 'There wasn't anyone else? Since…?'

'No one,' Leo told her firmly. 'No one but you for over two years now, Margo.'

'And there was no one but you for me, Leo. You *do* believe me?'

'Yes.'

He spoke with such certainty that she relaxed once more into his embrace. Just asking the question had made her tense.

They lay there in a comfortable silence, as the sweat cooled on their bodies and the fire cast its shadows, and Margo felt completely, wonderfully content. This, she thought, was what a true, loving marriage could and should be. If only it could last...

CHAPTER FOURTEEN

A FEW DAYS after Christmas Antonios and Lindsay came to the villa, all the way from New York. Margo had spent hours getting ready: supervising the preparations for meals, tweaking the decorations, and finally seeing to her outfit. She was nervous about meeting Leo's brother and his wife—both for her sake and his.

Their relationship had been growing stronger in the last few days, but it still felt fragile. They hadn't said those three important words, and Margo quaked inwardly to think of actually committing herself in that way to Leo, of making her frail hopes real and spoken. Of losing it all.

She'd known the worst to happen so many times; she couldn't help but expect it now.

With Antonios's upcoming arrival, Leo had withdrawn a bit, spending more time in the office, coming to bed late at night. At least they now shared a bed. They hadn't discussed it; Leo had simply joined Margo there on Christmas Eve, after they'd made love. And he'd continued to join her every night, much to her relief and joy.

The night before she'd turned to him, smoothed a thumb over the furrow in his forehead. 'Tell me what's going on,' she'd said quietly.

Leo had twitched under her caress. 'Nothing's going on.'

'Are you worried about seeing Antonios again?'

'I'm not worried.'

'But there's something. You haven't been yourself, Leo—'

'I'm fine.'

He'd rolled onto his side, away from her, and Margo had sunk back against the pillows, more hurt than she'd wanted to admit even to herself.

'Leave it alone,' he'd muttered, and they'd gone to sleep in silence.

Now she stood on the portico, shivering slightly in the wintry breeze, as Antonios and Lindsay's hired car came up the estate's sweeping drive. Leo joined her on the step, his expression inscrutable as the car came to a stop in front of them.

Margo had felt a distance between them this morning; apparently their new relationship didn't extend to the kind of honesty and intimacy she'd been looking for last night. Lesson learned.

Lindsay got out first, waving her welcome. She was beautiful in a pale, almost ethereal way, and she smiled at Margo. Leo had told her a few days ago that Lindsay suffered from social anxiety, but with Antonios's help was able to manage it. Margo wanted to make things as easy for her new sister-in-law as possible and she started forward, smiling her own welcome.

'I'm so very glad to meet you.'

'And I you. Although I haven't heard that much about you.' Lindsay gave Leo a teasing look, and he smiled back tightly.

Margo knew Lindsay had no idea about their complicated history; she certainly wasn't going to mention it now—not when she was wondering yet again just what *was* between her and Leo.

'Come inside,' she said, drawing Lindsay up the steps towards the villa. 'It's freezing out.'

Although Antonios was only just getting out of the car Margo could still feel the tension emanating from both of the brothers. Better, she decided, for them to have their reunion in private. Leo had already shown her he didn't want her involved.

Lindsay came behind her into the villa, stopping to admire the garlands of greenery looped over the banisters and along the doorways. 'Oh, but it's beautiful! Did *you* do this?'

'Yes, I wanted a proper Christmas,' Margo said, feeling rather shy.

Lindsay beamed at her. 'I love it. I wish I could make our apartment back in New York look half as nice. I'm hopeless with decorating and things like that. Hopeless with almost everything except for numbers.'

'I doubt that.'

Leo had told her that Lindsay was a brilliant mathematician, and was currently teaching at a university in New York City. Looking at her sister-in-law, Margo couldn't help but feel a bit intimidated. Lindsay might have social anxiety, but she hid it remarkably well. Margo was the one who felt and no doubt *looked* anxious…about so many things.

Xanthe, Ava and Parthenope came into the room, greeting Lindsay with warm hugs, reminding Margo that she was still on a somewhat fragile footing with Leo's sisters. It would come right in time, she told herself, and sat down on a settee while Maria came in with coffee for everyone. Just as things would with Leo. She had to trust that—had to believe that things would work out this time.

But that was easier said than done.

Eventually the three women finished their greetings and catch-up and turned to Margo.

'Leo is a dark horse,' Lindsay said teasingly. 'I didn't even know he was seeing someone.'

Margo's insides tensed. 'He likes to keep things quiet, I suppose,' she said.

'You're one to talk, Lindsay,' Xanthe said, grinning. 'Antonios showed up with *you* with no warning whatsoever!'

'That's true,' Lindsay agreed with a laugh.

Desperate to direct the spotlight away from herself, Margo said, 'That sounds like there's a story to be told.'

Lindsay agreed, and then told Margo how she and Antonios had met and married in New York City all within a week.

'When you know, you know, right?' she said, with a smile that Margo suspected was meant to create solidarity but only made everything inside her shrink with apprehension.

Lindsay made it sound as if everything was obvious and easy when you were in love, but Margo still felt so much uncertainty, so much fear. She wanted to embrace this new life, and yet still she was holding back, and Leo was too. Perhaps they always would.

It was certainly hard for *her*. Everyone had let her down at one point or another. No one had been there for her when she'd needed it. It was so difficult to let go of that history—not to make it affect her choices even now. Difficult not to brace herself for when Leo would fail her, or say he'd had enough, or just walk away. Everyone else had—why wouldn't he?

Antonios and Leo finally came into the sitting room. Margo shot Leo a swift, searching look, but she couldn't tell anything from his face and she wondered what had passed between the two brothers.

The conversation moved on to Parthenope's family, and little Timon's antics. Margo sat back and let it all wash over her; it felt good to be part of a family—even if she was just sitting and listening to everyone else. She caught Leo's eye and he smiled at her, and the uncertainty that had been knotting her stomach eased a little.

It was going to be okay. She would believe that. At least she would try.

Leo sat on the settee across from Margo, barely listening to everyone's chatter. The stilted conversation he'd had with Antonios out on the steps replayed in his mind.

It had been strange and unsettling to see his brother again, standing there in front of their childhood home, remembering the death of both of their parents, a decade of hostility and suspicion between them… Leo had felt himself tense, his hands ball into instinctive fists. He'd seen from the set of Antonios's jaw and his narrowed eyes that he felt the same.

They could clear the air, they could forgive the past, they could say they were moving on, but the reality was that memories still clung. They still held power. And if he couldn't move past things with Antonios, how could he with Margo?

He wanted to tell her he loved her, wanted to trust that what they had was real and lasting. But the memory of her last rejection still had the power to hurt. To make him stay silent. They'd had just over a month together…a few intense moments. Nothing, he acknowledged, that actually constituted a real, loving, trusting relationship.

'How's marriage?' Antonios had asked as they'd stood outside in wintry silence.

'Fine.'

'I didn't know you were seeing anyone.'

'It's not as if we keep each other up to date on our personal lives,' Leo had answered. He'd meant to sound light, but it had come out terse and dismissive instead. 'You're one to talk, anyway,' he'd added, trying for a joke, but it had fallen flat.

Antonios had just nodded, his jaw bunched, and they hadn't spoken again until they were settled in the sitting room with everyone else—and then only about innocuous matters.

Leo's gaze kept straying to Margo. She was listening to everyone, but he thought she looked tense, maybe even unhappy, and he wished they could be alone. Wished he could be sure of her feelings...and of his own.

'Is everything all right between you and Antonios?' Margo asked as they got ready for bed that evening.

They hadn't spoken much during the day, busy as they'd both been with their guests. Margo, Leo noticed now, looked pale and tired, with lines of strain around her eyes.

'As well as they can be, I suppose,' he said as he stretched out on the bed.

Leo still kept his clothes in the adjoining room, but he'd brought a few things into Margo's bedroom: his books, his reading glasses, his pyjamas. Small yet intimate things that spoke of building a life together. But lying there he felt as if his presence in Margo's life, in her bed, was transient.

Margo took down her hair, and Leo felt a frisson of sensual pleasure as he watched her raise her slender arms, anticipating the sudden tumble of dark, wavy hair down to her waist.

'What does that mean?' she asked as she reached for the satin nightdress she wore to bed and quickly undressed.

Leo had tantalising glimpses of her breasts and thighs, milky-pale and soft-looking, before she shrugged the nightdress on and slid under the covers, pillows propped behind her as she looked at him and waited for his answer.

'We have ten years of hard history,' Leo said slowly. 'Even though we've talked about it and tried to put it behind us, I don't think it's that easy or simple.'

'No,' Margo agreed quietly. 'It isn't.'

He knew she was thinking of her own past hurts. As much as she might want to, could she move on from her appalling childhood and the many wrongs that had been done to her? Could *they* move on from the hurt they'd caused each other?

He wasn't about to ask those questions. They spoke of his own past, his own uncertainty and fear. He'd spent his childhood trying to prove himself to his father—wanting Evangelos to love him, and receiving only rejection.

And it was those experiences that kept him silent now.

'Do you think things will get better in time?' Margo asked, her gaze serious and intent on him.

For a second Leo thought she was asking about things with them. Then he realised she meant Antonios.

'Maybe,' he said with a shrug.

He didn't sound hopeful.

Wanting to end the discussion, he reached for her, wrapping a thick tendril of hair around his wrist as he pulled her gently towards him. She came with a smile, her features softened and suffused with desire, their bodies bumping up against one another as Leo brushed a kiss across her mouth.

They'd made love many times in the days since Christmas Eve. Their chemistry had always been explosive, right from the beginning, but in the last week it had become even more intimate and arousing.

Margo let out a soft little sigh as she brought her arms up around his neck, her body yielding to his in a way that made Leo's head spin and desire spiral dizzily inside him. He slid his hand from her shoulder to her waist to her hip, loving the silky feel of her skin, the ripe fullness of her breasts and hips.

She twitched slightly beneath his caress and he stilled his hand. 'What is it?'

'Just the normal fears of a pregnant woman,' she said with an uncertain little laugh. 'I feel fat.'

'Fat? *Fat?* Margo, you are not remotely fat. You are fecund and beautiful and glowing. I like your body more, I think, than before you were carrying our baby.'

'You do *not*!'

'You doubt me?' he said in a mock growl, and she let out another laugh, this one breathless with anticipation.

'I do.'

'Then perhaps I should prove to you just how beautiful you are,' Leo said, and bent his head to her breasts, taking his time to give each one his full, lascivious attention.

Margo let out a sigh of pleasure, her hands tangling in his hair, and Leo lifted his head.

'Does that satisfy you?' he demanded, and she gazed at him with a mischievous smile.

'Not…quite.'

'I see I'll have to prove it to you some more.'

'You just might.'

Laughing softly, he slid a hand between her thighs. 'I can do a lot of proving,' he murmured, 'if that's your wish.'

'It is,' Margo whispered back, her hips arching upwards. And then they lost themselves to their shared pleasure.

The next day Leo and Antonios repaired to the office, to discuss matters relating to Marakaios Enterprises, and Lindsay sought out Margo up in the soon-to-be nursery, where she was comparing fabric swatches.

'Hello,' she said, poking her head around the door, and Margo gave a self-conscious smile before welcoming her in.

'Sorry, I'm not trying to hide away.' She rubbed her lower back while motioning to the swatches. 'Just trying to make a decision about fabric. It can take ages for it to come in once you place an order.'

'I wouldn't know,' Lindsay answered with a laugh. 'But Leo mentioned you worked in decorating before…?'

'I was a buyer for a department store in Paris. Home furnishings.' It occurred to her this must seem like a rather useless job to a brilliant mathematician, but Lindsay appeared genuinely interested.

'Do you miss it? When Antonios and I lived here I missed my old life a lot more than I thought I would. My old job…'

Margo was intrigued to think that Lindsay and Antonios's marriage hadn't always been as perfect as it now seemed.

'I don't *miss* it exactly,' she answered slowly. 'But I miss feeling productive and useful sometimes.'

Lindsay nodded in sympathy before saying in a rush, 'Look, I think I may have put my foot in it yesterday, which isn't all that surprising, considering how bad I am at social situations. But when I mentioned not knowing that you and Leo were dating…' She swallowed, a blush staining her pale cheeks. 'Well, it's none of my business whether you were dating or not. I didn't mean to make you feel awkward.'

'But you noticed that you *did*?' Margo answered with an uncertain laugh.

'I'm sorry.'

'No, don't be. It was a perfectly innocent question. And the truth is my relationship with Leo is…complicated.'

'I can relate to that.'

'Can you?' Margo glanced at her sister-in-law with open curiosity. 'Because from where I'm standing you and Antonios seem to have the fairytale.'

'Oh, don't say that!' Lindsay cried, and Margo raised her eyebrows. 'It used to seem like a fairytale,' she explained. 'Meeting the way we did in New York. Antonios sweeping me straight off my feet.' Lindsay sighed and shook her head. 'But life isn't a fairytale, you know? Reality sets in. And when it did for Antonios and me, it was hard.'

'How so?'

'Did Leo tell you about my social anxiety?'

'A bit…'

'As soon as we were married Antonios whisked me off here and put me in charge of the household. He thought he was honouring me, but in truth it just terrified me. I've had social anxiety since I was a child—talking in front of crowds, being the centre of attention…it all makes me start to panic. And when I landed here…with all of Antonios's sisters as well as his mother looking at me, measuring me…it was hard.'

'But his sisters love you now,' Margo remarked.

Lindsay smiled wryly. 'That doesn't mean they weren't taken aback when Antonios showed up with me out of the blue.'

'The same way Leo showed up with me,' Margo admitted with a laugh. 'Poor girls. They've had an awful lot of shocks.'

'So why *did* you and Leo marry, if you don't mind me asking? *Were* you dating…?' Lindsay's blush deepened. 'Sorry, I'm being inexcusably nosy. But, if you don't mind me saying so, you remind me a little bit of me when I came here. A little overwhelmed…a little lost.'

'Do I?' Margo could hear how stiff and stilted her voice

sounded and busied herself organising the swatches of fabric, just to give herself a little time to order her thoughts.

'Am I wrong?' Lindsay asked quietly.

'Not exactly. Coming here as Leo's wife was overwhelming—especially considering the circumstances.' She glanced down at her bump and Lindsay nodded her understanding. 'I don't have a lot of experience with big families or houses. I've pretty much been on my own my whole life.'

'As have I,' Lindsay said quietly.

Margo looked at her in surprise. 'We seem to have quite a bit in common.'

'Not least being married to difficult Marakaios men.'

They both laughed at that, and then Margo said seriously, 'But Antonios seems to dote on you.'

'Antonios can be stubborn and set in his ways. He tends not to see another person's perspective unless it's pointed out to him. *Repeatedly*.' Lindsay softened this observation with a smile and added, 'But I'm utterly in love with him, and he with me, and that makes all the difference.'

'Yes, I'm sure it does,' Margo murmured.

She thought of how she and Leo had made love last night, spending the whole night sleeping in each other's arms. Was that love? It seemed like it, on the surface, but the fact remained that she still felt wary and guarded, and she thought Leo did too. They were both still holding back, both afraid to commit fully to their marriage... Or maybe Leo just didn't want to. Maybe what they had was enough—was all he wanted.

And yet she knew she wanted more. She wanted the fairytale.

CHAPTER FIFTEEN

A MONTH PASSED in wintry days spent with Margo decorating the nursery and managing the household, getting to know Leo's sisters—and getting to know Leo.

They spent far more time together now than they ever had in their two years of dirty weekends and meals out. They chatted about everything—from politics to music and books, to places they'd like to visit. He was becoming as good a friend as he was a lover.

And yet she still felt that reticence in him, and in herself. They still hadn't said *I love you*, hadn't discussed anything about the future. Leo still hadn't moved his things into her bedroom.

As the weeks passed Margo wondered if this wasn't actually a *good* thing. If Leo kept a little distance, then she could too. Maybe they could enjoy each other's company and bodies and still stay safe. Still not risk getting hurt.

Yet she knew that for a lie when she thought about the possibility of losing Leo. She would be utterly devastated.

At the end of January Leo came into the house, where she'd been browsing through a catalogue of baby toys, and asked if she'd come to the office with him.

'The office? Why?'

'I need your opinion on something.'

Surprised and a bit bemused, she walked with him across the estate to the long, low-lying building that overlooked the olive groves.

'What do you think of these?' he asked, and gestured to a box of olive-based bath supplies.

Frowning a little, Margo examined the items, noting the pleasingly thick glass bottles, the nutty smell of the olives.

'They feel expensive,' she offered. 'Although they smell a bit more like cooking oil than something you'd want to put in your bath.'

He nodded. 'I was afraid of that. I want to develop a new range of bath products to supply the Adair chain of hotels, but I don't think these are up to scratch.'

'A little olive oil goes a long way, I suppose,' Margo answered with a smile.

'I could use your expertise here,' Leo said. 'If you're willing to give it. Someone with a good eye for design and good taste to offer an opinion about our merchandise.'

Margo just stared.

'Not a full-time job, necessarily,' he continued. 'I know with the baby coming you wouldn't want that. But you have a lot of talent and expertise to offer, Margo, and I don't want to squander it.'

And so she started going into the office two days a week—to review the different products Marakaios Enterprises was offering and strategise the best way to market them. She enjoyed the work—and even more so because it meant she and Leo were working together…a true partnership.

Leo glanced across the breakfast table and smiled to see Margo balancing her teacup on top of her bump. Her hair was loose and dark about her face, her expression thoughtful as she read a journal about decorative art. They'd been married for only two months but they were already acting like an old married couple, reading their separate periodicals over breakfast.

Not that Leo minded. He loved these mornings with Margo, even when they weren't talking to each other. Just being in her presence, seeing her smile or watching the way her eyes darkened intently as she listened to him, made him happy.

Several weeks ago Margo had asked him if he was happy and Leo hadn't been able to answer. Now he knew he could. Yes, he was happy with Margo. He was happy—and in love—with his wife.

Just acknowledging that fact to himself gave him a little fizz of anticipation, as well as a twist of apprehension. He wanted to tell her how he felt, *all* he felt, and yet he held back. No time felt right. What if she told him she didn't love him back? What if she wasn't capable of it? He understood why she'd kept herself from love and life before, but it wouldn't make it any easier to accept now.

Rejection, Leo thought bleakly, was still rejection.

'How would you like to go to Paris?' he asked now, and she looked up from her journal, her eyes widening in surprise.

'Paris? Why?'

'I have a little business there. We could make it pleasure too, though. We could check on your apartment and see the city together. Visit some of our old haunts.'

'That sounds good,' Margo said slowly, almost as if she didn't trust that he'd want to go to Paris with her. 'It would be great to check in with Achat too. I gave my notice, obviously, but it would be good to have a proper goodbye. I worked there a long time.'

'Very well. Shall I make the arrangements? We could leave tomorrow.'

Margo nodded, her gaze still moving over him, and Leo looked away. He didn't want anything in his face to reveal the surprise he was planning for her.

They left early the next morning, driving to Athens and then flying on to Paris; they were in Margo's apartment on the Île de la Cité by mid-afternoon.

Leo stood on the threshold of the living room and gazed at the picture window overlooking Paris, the twin towers of Notre-Dame visible in the distance.

He'd asked Margo to marry him here. He'd felt the painful sting of rejection, the bitter and furious hurt that had led to the baby boy now nestled inside her waiting to be born. So much had changed, and yet for a moment he felt mired by the past.

He didn't actually know what Margo wanted. Once, six months ago, he'd thought he did. He'd asked her to marry him, feeling confident of her answer.

Looking back, he knew that his confidence had in fact been arrogance. Margo had given him no hint that she'd wanted a ring on her finger. Everything about her—her bold, sassy, sensual confidence, her easy acceptance of their arrangement—had indicated otherwise. And yet she'd admitted that the persona she'd adopted was nothing more than a mask.

So did the *real* Margo, the lovely, thoughtful, interesting woman he'd come to know beneath that mask, want what he wanted now?

'Leo…' She came up behind him and rested her hands lightly on his shoulders.

Leo blinked back the memories before turning around to face her and slip his arms around her waist.

'We'll always have Paris,' he quipped, and though she smiled he saw her eyes were troubled.

'Will we?' she asked softly, sadly, and too late Leo realised how that had sounded.

They would always have Paris and the memories they'd made here…whether they wanted them or not.

Margo tried to banish the disquiet that fluttered through as she saw Leo's eyebrows draw together in a faint frown. She'd been nervous about coming back to Paris, to the city where they'd met so often during their affair, and the very room where Margo had rejected him. She didn't think she'd imagined the suddenly shuttered look on Leo's face as he'd come into her apartment, and she had a terrible feeling he was remembering how he'd proposed to her here and what her answer had been.

Now, however, he smiled, his face clearing, and looked around her sitting room. 'Do you know, before I came here I would have thought you'd have some modern, sleek penthouse? All chrome and leather and modern art.'

'You mean like your bachelor pad in Athens? I prefer a homier place to live.'

'Which is why you were a buyer of home furnishings, I suppose?'

She nodded and he strolled around the apartment, noting the squashy velveteen sofa, the Impressionist prints, the porcelain ornaments and figurines. She'd had a lot of her things sent to Greece, but there were certainly enough left for Leo to examine and make her feel oddly exposed.

'How did you get into the buying business, anyway?' he asked as he picked up a carved wooden figurine of a mother holding her infant.

It had been whittled from one piece of wood and the result was a sinuous, fluid sculpture in which it was impossible to tell where the mother finished and the child began. Margo had always loved it, but never had it seemed so revealing of her life, her secret desires and heartache.

'I got a job with Achat, working on a sales counter, when I was sixteen. From there I moved up through the ranks,' she said. 'I've never actually worked anywhere else.'

'And you wanted to go into the buying side of things? Home furnishings in particular?'

'Yes, that was what I always liked.'

The bedsits and sheltered housing, the homeless shelters and foster placements that had comprised her childhood homes had never felt like proper places to grow up. Safe or loving places. And she had, Margo knew, been trying to create that for herself—through her job and in her own apartment.

Somehow she had a feeling Leo knew that too.

He put the figurine down and turned to her. 'You have a beautiful home here,' he said. 'You have a real talent for making a space feel cosy and welcoming.'

'Thank you.'

'If there are any more things you'd like to take to Greece I can arrange for them to be shipped.'

'I'll look around tomorrow and box things up.'

He smiled and reached for her again. Margo snuggled into him, grateful for the feel of his arms around her, making her feel safe. *For now.*

While Margo went to Achat to say her goodbyes Leo attended to his business in the city. He'd been acting a bit mysteriously, which had made Margo wonder what he was doing or planning, but she told herself not to be nervous and just to wait and see.

In any case, her arrival at Achat put Leo out of her mind for a little while, as she was caught up in reunions with different acquaintances, a bittersweet meeting with her boss, who wished she could stay, and then a catch-up with Sophie.

They left the office for a café with deep velvet chairs and spindly little tables a few blocks from Achat. Sophie ordered them both bowl-sized cups of hot chocolate with lashings of whipped cream.

'A celebration,' she proclaimed, 'since things seem to have turned out all right for you.'

'How do you know they have?' Margo challenged as she took a sip of the deliciously rich hot chocolate.

'You haven't sent me any panicked texts,' Sophie answered, 'and, more importantly, you look *happy*, Margo. Happier than I think I've ever seen you.'

'I *am* happy…' Margo said quietly.

Sophie arched an eyebrow. 'Why do you sound so uncertain, then?'

'Because happiness can be so fleeting.' She took a deep breath. 'And Leo hasn't actually told me he loves me.'

'Have you told *him*?'

'No…'

'Well, then.'

When Margo had first been pregnant Sophie had heard the full story of Leo's proposal and Margo's rejection.

'Can you really blame him for not going first?' she asked, and Margo sighed.

'Not really.'

'So why *haven't* you told him you love him?'

'Because I'm afraid that's not what he wants to hear. Because we're both holding back.'

'Then stop,' Sophie suggested with a smile.

'It's not that simple,' Margo said. 'It's…' She hesitated, thoughts and fears swirling around in her mind. 'I feel like if I try for too much—if I do anything to jeopardise what we have—it will all topple like a child's tower of bricks because it's not strong enough to stand...'

'Stand what?' Sophie asked gently.

'*Anything*. Anything bad.' Margo swallowed. 'I know I'm afraid, and that I'm letting my fear control my actions. I understand that, Sophie, trust me.'

'But it's keeping you from doing something about it.'

'I think I'd rather just hold on to what we have and be happy with it than try for more and lose,' Margo confessed quietly. 'If that makes me a coward, so be it.'

Sophie eyed her sceptically. 'As long as you *are* happy,' she said after a moment.

Margo didn't answer.

Sophie's words still pinged around in her head as she headed back to her apartment. *Was* she happy? *Could* this be enough?

Maybe Sophie was right, and Leo was holding back simply because *she* was. Maybe if she made the first move and told him she loved him he would tell her back.

They were going out to dinner tonight. Leo had made the arrangements, although he hadn't told Margo where. But they'd be alone, and it might even be romantic, and it would be a perfect opportunity for Margo to tell Leo the truth.

To tell him she loved him.

She spent a long time getting ready that evening. First she had a long soak in the tub, and then she did her nails, hair and make-up before donning a new maternity dress of soft black jersey.

It had a daring V-neck that made the most of her pregnancy-enhanced assets and draped lovingly over her bump before swirling about her knees. She'd put her hair up for the simple pleasure of being able to take it down again in

Leo's presence later that night, and had slipped her feet into her favourite pair of black suede stiletto heels.

And now she waited—because Leo still wasn't home.

He'd been due back at seven to collect Margo for their date, but as the minutes ticked by Margo's unease grew. It figured that the one night she'd decided to tell Leo how she felt he'd be AWOL. It almost seemed like a sign, a portent of things to come. Or rather not to come.

At seven forty-five she texted Leo. At eight she took off her heels and her earrings—both had been starting to hurt—and curled up on her bed.

Her phone rang at eight-fifteen.

'Margo, I'm so sorry—'

'What happened?' Her voice was quiet and yet filled with hurt.

'I had a meeting with Adair Hotels. It's an important deal and the meeting ran long. I didn't even realise the time…'

'It's okay,' she said. And it *was* okay. At least it should have been okay. It would have been okay if she hadn't built this evening up in her own mind.

Maybe she'd built *everything* up in her own mind.

In that moment she felt as if she couldn't trust anything or anyone, least of all herself. It was nothing more than a missed dinner, and yet it was so much more. It was everything.

'When will you be back?' she asked, and Leo sighed.

'I don't know. Late. Talks are still ongoing, and we'll most likely go out for drinks afterwards.' He hesitated and then said, 'Don't wait up.'

And somehow that stung too.

She was being ridiculous, over-emotional, overreacting. She knew that. And yet she still hung up on Leo without replying.

* * *

Leo stared at the phone, the beep of Margo disconnecting the call still echoing through his ear. Had she actually just hung up on him? Simply because he'd missed dinner?

He let out a long sigh and tossed his phone on the desk. He felt as if something big had happened, something momentous, and damned if he knew what it was.

But then he hadn't known what was going on for a while. For the last month he and Margo had been existing in an emotional stasis which he suspected suited them both fine. Neither of them had been ready to take their relationship up to that next level. To say they loved each other... to bare the truth of their hearts.

At least *he* hadn't. Maybe Margo had nothing to say... nothing to bare.

'Leo?' One of his staff poked his head through the doorway, eyebrows raised. 'Are you ready?'

Leo nodded. This deal was too important for him to become distracted about Margo.

And yet as he went back into the conference room he couldn't stop thinking about her. About the hurt he'd heard in her voice and the way she'd hung up on him. About all the painful truths she'd shared about her childhood and all the things he hadn't said.

He lasted an hour before he called the meeting to a halt.

'I'm sorry, gentlemen, but we can resume tomorrow. I need to get home to my wife.'

After she'd hung up on Leo, Margo peeled off her dress and ran a bath. Perhaps a nice long soak in the tub would help alleviate her misery—or at least give her a little perspective. It was one missed dinner...one little argument. It didn't have to mean anything.

Sighing, Margo slipped into the water and closed her

eyes. She felt as if she couldn't shift the misery that had taken up residence in her chest, as if a stone were pressing down on her.

At first Margo thought the pain in her belly was simply the weight of that disappointment and heartache, but then the twinges intensified and she realised she was feeling actual physical pain. Something was wrong.

She pressed her hands to her bump, realising she hadn't felt a kick in a while—a few hours at least. She'd become used to feeling those lovely flutters. Now she felt another knifing pain through her stomach, and then a sudden gush of fluid, and she watched in dawning shock and horror as the water around her bloomed red.

CHAPTER SIXTEEN

THE APARTMENT WAS quiet and empty when Leo came into the foyer just after nine o'clock.

'Margo?'

He tossed his keys on the table, a sudden panic icing inside him. Had she left? Left *him*? He realised in that moment that he'd been bracing himself for such a thing, perhaps from the moment they'd married. Waiting for another rejection.

'Margo?' he called again, but the only answer was the ringing silence that seemed to reverberate through the empty rooms of the apartment.

He poked his head through the doorway of her bedroom, and saw how the lamplight cast a golden pool onto the empty bed. Her dress and shoes were discarded and crumpled on the floor and the bathroom door was ajar, light spilling from within. All was silent.

He was about to turn back when he heard a sound from the bathroom—the slosh of water. He froze for a millisecond, and then in three strides crossed to the bathroom, threw open the door, and saw Margo lying in a tub full of rose-tinted water, her head lolling back, her face drained of colour.

'Margo—' Her name was a cry, a plea, a prayer. Leo

fumbled for his phone even as he reached for her, drew her out of the tub. 'Margo…' he whispered.

She glanced up at him, her face with a waxy sheen, her eyes luminous.

'I've lost the baby, haven't I?'

'I don't know—' He stopped, for she'd slumped in his arms, unconscious.

Margo came to, lying on a stretcher. Two paramedics were wheeling her to an ambulance, and panic clutched at her so hard she could barely speak.

'My baby—'

One of them reassured her that they were taking her to a hospital, and Leo reached for her hand. His hand felt cold, as cold as hers. He was scared, she realised. He knew the worst was happening.

The worst *always* happened.

Just hours ago she'd been buoying up her courage to tell Leo she loved him. Now everything had fallen apart. Nothing could be the same. Her relationship with Leo had been expedient at its core; without this child kicking in her womb there was no need for a marriage.

And yet she couldn't think about losing Leo on top of losing the baby; it was too much to bear. So she forced her mind to go blank, and after a few seconds her panic was replaced by a numb, frozen feeling—a feeling she'd thought she'd never have to experience again.

It was the way she'd felt when she'd realised Annelise was gone. It was the only way she'd known how to cope. And yet she hadn't coped at all. And she didn't think she could cope now—except by remaining frozen. Numb.

She felt distant from the whole scene—as if she were floating above the ambulance, watching as the paramedics sat next to her, taking her vitals.

'Blood pressure is dropping steadily.'

She barely felt a flicker of anything as they searched for the baby's heartbeat. They found it, but from the paramedics' mutterings it was clearly weak.

'Baby appears to be in distress.'

In distress. It seemed such a little term for so terrible a moment.

'Margo…Margo.' Leo was holding her hand, his face close to hers. 'It's going to be okay. *Agapi mou*, I promise—'

My love. The words didn't move her now, didn't matter at all. 'You can't promise anything,' she said, and turned her face away.

The next few minutes passed in a blur as the ambulance arrived, siren wailing, at a hospital on the other side of the Île de la Cité—one of Paris's oldest hospitals, a beautiful building Margo had walked by many times but never been inside.

Now she was rushed into a room on the emergency ward, and doctors surrounded her as they took her vitals yet again. She could see Leo standing outside, demanding to be allowed in. A doctor was arguing with him.

Margo felt herself sliding into unconsciousness, one hand cradling her bump—the only connection she had to the baby she was afraid she'd never meet.

'Madame Marakaios?'

A doctor touched her arm, bringing her back to wakefulness.

'You have had a placental abruption. Do you know what that is?'

'Is my baby dying?' Margo asked. Her voice sounded slurred.

'We need to perform an emergency Caesarean section as your baby is in distress. Do you give your consent?'

'But I'm only twenty-seven weeks…'

'It is your child's only chance, *madame*,' the doctor said, and wordlessly Margo nodded.

What else could she do?

They began to prep her for surgery and Margo lay there, tears silently snaking down her face; it appeared she wasn't that frozen after all.

And yet neither was she surprised. Wasn't this what happened? You let people in, you loved them, and they left you. Her baby. *Leo.*

The last thought Margo had as she was put under anaesthetic was that maybe it would have been better not to have trusted or loved at all.

CHAPTER SEVENTEEN

LEO PACED THE waiting room restlessly, his hands bunched into fists. He hadn't been allowed inside the operating room and he felt furious and helpless and desperately afraid. He couldn't lose their son. He couldn't lose Margo.

He wished more than ever that he'd had the courage to tell her he loved her. Three little words and yet he'd held back. He'd held back in so many ways, not wanting to risk rejection or hurt, and all he could do now was call himself a fool. A frightened fool for not speaking the truth of his heart to his wife.

If Margo made it through this, he vowed he would tell her. He would tell her everything he felt.

'Monsieur Marakaios?' A doctor still in his surgical scrubs came through the steel double doors.

Leo's jaw bunched and he sprang forward. 'You have news? Is my wife—?'

'Your wife and son are all right,' the man said quietly, 'although weak.'

'Weak—?'

'Your wife lost a great deal of blood. She is stable, but she will have a few weeks of recovery ahead of her.'

'And the baby? My son?' A lump formed in his throat as he waited for the doctor to respond.

'He's in the Neonatal Intensive Care Unit,' the doctor

answered. 'He's very small, and his lungs aren't mature. He'll need to stay in hospital for some weeks at least.'

Leo nodded jerkily; he didn't trust himself to speak for a moment. When he had his emotions under control, he managed, 'Please—I'd like to see my wife.'

Margo had been moved to a private room on the ward, and was lying in bed, her eyes closed.

'Margo?' he said softly, and touched her hand.

She opened her eyes and stared at him for a long moment, and then she turned her head away from him.

Leo felt tears sting his eyes. 'Margo, it's okay. You're all right and our son is all right.'

'He's alive, you mean,' she said flatly.

Leo blinked. 'Yes, alive. Small, and his lungs aren't mature, but he's stable—'

'You can't know that.'

'The doctor just said—'

She shook her head.

Leo frowned and touched her hand. 'Margo, it's going to be okay.'

She withdrew her hand from his. 'Stop making promises you can't keep, Leo.'

Helplessly Leo stared at her, not knowing what to say or do. 'I know it's been frightening—'

'You don't know *anything*!' She cut across him, her voice choking on a sob. 'You don't know what it's like to lose everything again.'

'But you didn't—we didn't—'

'I want you to go.' She closed her eyes, tears leaking from under her lids and making silvery tracks down her cheeks. 'Please—please go.'

It went against every instinct he had to leave Margo alone in this moment. He wanted to tell her how he loved her, and yet she couldn't even bear to look at him. How had this happened?

'Margo—' he began, only to realise from the way her breathing had evened out that she was asleep. He touched her cheek, wanting her to know even in sleep how he felt, and then quietly left the room.

'It's difficult to say what's going to happen,' the doctor told Leo when he went to ask for more details about his son's condition. 'Of course there have been terrific strides made in the care of premature babies. But I don't like to give any promises at this stage, because premature infants' immune systems aren't fully developed and neither are their lungs. It's very easy for them to catch an infection and have it become serious.'

Leo nodded, his throat tight. He'd just tried to promise Margo it was going to be okay. But she was right: he couldn't promise anything. And he didn't know if their marriage, fragile as it was, would survive this.

He stood outside the neonatal ICU and watched his impossibly small son flail tiny red fists. He was covered in tubes to help him breathe, eat, live. It made Leo ache with a fierce love—and a desperate fear.

Eventually he went back to see Margo. She was awake and sitting up in bed, and while the sight of her lifted his spirits, the expression on her face did not.

'The doctor says the next few weeks will be crucial,' Leo said.

Margo nodded; she looked almost indifferent to this news.

'He'll have to stay in hospital for a while—at least a month.'

Another nod.

'He can't be taken out of the ICU,' Leo ventured, 'and

we can't hold him yet, but I could wheel you up there so you can at least see him?'

Margo stared at him for a moment before she answered quietly, 'I don't think so.'

Leo stared at her in shock. 'Margo—'

'I told you before, I'd like to be alone.'

She turned away from him and he stared at her helplessly.

'Margo, please. Tell me what's going on.'

'Nothing is going on. I've just realised.' She drew a quick, sharp breath. 'I can't do this. I thought I could—I wanted to—but I can't.'

'Can't do what?'

'This.' She gestured with one limp hand to the space between them. 'Marriage. Motherhood. Any of it. I can't let myself love someone and have them taken away again. I just...*can't.*'

'Margo, I won't leave you—'

'Maybe not physically,' she allowed. 'You have too much honour for that. But you told me yourself you didn't love me—'

'That was months ago—'

'And nothing's changed, has it?' She lifted her resolute gaze to his in weary challenge. 'Nothing's changed,' she repeated.

Leo wondered if she was saying that nothing had changed for *her*. She didn't love *him*.

For a second he remained silent, and a second was all Margo needed for affirmation.

She nodded. 'I thought so. We only had a couple of months together, Leo. They were lovely, I suppose, but that's all they were.'

'No.' Finally he found his voice, along with his resolve.

'*No*, Margo. I don't accept that. I won't let you torpedo our marriage simply because you're afraid.'

'Of *course* I'm afraid,' she snapped, her voice rising in anger. 'Do you even know what it's like to lose someone—?'

'I lost both my parents,' Leo answered. 'So, yes, I do.'

'Yes, of course you do,' she acknowledged. 'But a *child*. A child *I* was responsible for—a child who looked to *me* for love and care and food and everything—' Her voice broke and her shoulders began to shake with sobs.

'Margo…Margo…' Leo crooned softly and, sitting on the edge of the bed, gently put his arms around her.

She stilled, unable to move away from him but still trying to keep herself distant. Safe. But safety, Leo realised, was Margo knowing how he truly felt.

'I love you,' he said, and then, in case she still doubted him, he said it again. 'I love you. And that will never change. No matter what happens. *No matter what.*'

To his surprise and dismay her shoulders shook harder.

She pulled away from him, wiping the tears from her face. 'Oh, Leo. I don't deserve you.'

'*Deserve?* What does this have to do with deserving?'

'It's *my* fault Annelise died. Maybe it's my fault our son is in such danger. I might have done something… I don't deserve…'

'Margo, hush.' Tenderly he wiped the tears from her cheeks. 'You must stop blaming yourself for what happened.'

She'd been tortured by both guilt and grief for years, and he longed to release her.

'What happened to Annelise could have happened to any child, any mother. And you were only a child yourself. As for our son…you've been so careful during this pregnancy. I've seen you. Nothing is your fault.'

She shook her head but he continued.

'You must let the past go and forgive yourself. You must look to your future—*our* future—and our son's future. Because I love you, and I wish I'd told you before. I wish you'd known how much I loved you when you went into surgery. I wish you'd had that to hold on to.'

She blinked up at him, searching his face. 'Do you mean it, Leo?' she asked quietly. 'Do you really mean it?'

'With all my heart.'

'I haven't even said how I feel.'

'If you don't love me,' he answered steadily, 'it's all right. I can wait—'

'But I *do* love you.' She cut him off. 'I was going to tell you tonight, when we had dinner—'

'Nothing turned out quite as we expected, did it?' he said, and pressed a kiss to her palm. 'But now we've told each other, and we have our son, and I will do everything in my power to keep you safe and secure and—'

'I believe you!' With a trembling laugh she pressed the palm he'd just kissed against his lips. 'You don't have to convince me.'

'I want to spend a lifetime convincing you.'

Tears sparkled on her lashes. 'And our little boy…?'

'Why don't you come and see him?'

Margo's heart was beating with thuds so hard they made her feel sick as Leo wheeled her up to the ICU. He parked the wheelchair in front of the glass and Margo stared at the row of plastic cradles, the tubes and the wires, the tiny beings fighting so hard for life.

And then she saw the words *'Enfant Marakaios'* and everything in her clenched hard. Her son. Hers and Leo's.

'Oh, Leo,' she whispered, and reached for his hand.

They stared silently at the baby they'd made, now waving his fists angrily.

'He's got a lot of spirit—or so the doctor says,' Leo said shakily. 'He'll fight hard.'

Margo felt a hot rush of shame that she'd considered, even for a moment, protecting herself against the pain of loving this little boy. Of loving Leo. She'd spent a lifetime apart, atoning for her sins, trying to keep her shattered heart safe. But Leo, with his kindness and understanding and love, had put her back together again. Had made her want to try. To fight, and fight hard—just as their son was.

'I'm sorry—' she began, but Leo shook his head.

'No, don't be sorry. Just enjoy this moment. Enjoy our family.'

'Our little man,' Margo whispered, and then looked up at Leo.

He smiled down at her, his eyes bright with tears. Her family, Margo thought, right here.

There were no certainties—not for anyone. No guarantees of a happily-ever-after, no promises that life would flow smoothly. Life was a rough river, full of choppy currents, and the only thing she could do was grab on to those she loved and hold on. Hold on for ever.

And, clinging to Leo's hand, that was just what she was going to do.

EPILOGUE

'WHERE ARE WE GOING?' Margo asked as they stepped out onto the pavement in front of her apartment.

It was three months since their son had been born, and he was coming home from the hospital tomorrow. To celebrate, Leo was taking her out to dinner.

It had been a long, harrowing three months.

Annas—the name meant 'a gift given by God'—had had several lung infections that had terrified both Leo and Margo at the time, and twice it had been touch and go. Margo had felt more fear then than she ever had before, and yet with Leo's support and strength she'd met every challenge head-on, determined to believe in her son, to imbue him with all the strength and love she felt.

And he was healthy now—weighing just over five pounds, and more precious to Leo and Margo than they ever could have known.

Leo hailed a cab, and as the car pulled to the kerb he leaned over the window to give directions. He'd been making a big secret of their destination, which made Margo smile.

When the cab pulled up to the Eiffel Tower she looked at him in surprise. 'Sightseeing…?'

'In a way,' he answered, and drew her by the hand from

the cab to the base of the tower, where a man stood by the elevator that surged up its centre, waiting for them.

'*Bon soir*, Monsieur Marakios,' he said as he ushered them into the lift.

Margo looked at Leo with narrowed eyes. 'What is going on?'

'You'll see.'

They stepped out onto the first floor of the tower, saw the city stretched all around them. The platform was completely empty, as was the upscale café.

'What…?' Margo began, and Leo explained.

'I reserved it for us.'

'The whole tower?'

'The whole tower.'

'You can't do that—'

'I can,' he answered, and Margo let out an incredulous laugh.

'No wonder you've been looking so pleased with yourself.' She moved into the café, where the elegant space was strung with fairy lights, and a table for two flickered with candlelight in the centre of the restaurant. 'Oh, Leo, it's amazing.'

'I'm glad you think so.' He pulled her to him to kiss her lightly on the lips. 'Truth be told, I was afraid you might think it all a bit much.'

'No, it's wonderful. It's perfect.'

The sheer romance of it left her breathless, overwhelmed, and very near tears. They'd come through so much together, and she loved him more than ever. More than she'd ever thought possible.

'I can't believe you hired the whole of the Eiffel Tower,' she said with a shaky laugh as Leo guided her to a chair and spread a napkin in her lap.

A waiter came unobtrusively to pour wine and serve a

first course of oysters on crushed ice before quietly disappearing.

'Some might say that it is a *bit* over the top,' she teased, and Leo grinned.

'Well, I wanted to do it right this time.'

'This time?'

He took a sip of wine, his expression turning serious and making everything in Margo clench hard in anticipation.

'When I proposed again.'

'Proposed? Leo, we're already married.'

'We had a civil service, yes.'

'You want to have another marriage ceremony?'

'No, I don't want to have another ceremony. The one we had was real and binding. But I want to do it right this time—to make a proposal we can both remember.'

'You don't—'

'I know. But I want to. Because I love you that much.'

'I love you, too. So much.'

'So…' With a self-conscious smile Leo rose from his chair and then dropped to one knee. Margo let out another shaky laugh as he took her hand in his. 'Margo Marakaios—I love you more than life itself. I love the woman you are, the wife you are, the mother you are. Every part of you leaves me awash in amazement and admiration.'

'Oh, Leo—' Margo began, but he silenced her with a swift shake of his head.

'I mean it—every word. You are strong and brave and—'

'But I've been so afraid for so much of my life!'

'And you've overcome it. Overcome so much tragedy and pain. That's strength, Margo. That's courage.'

She pressed a hand to his cheek. 'You're strong too, Leo. You're my rock.'

'And yet I lived in fear too. Fear of rejection. Whether

it was by my father or brother or you. You've helped me to move past that, Margo. Helped me to realise just how important love is. Loving *you* is.'

'I'm glad,' she whispered.

He withdrew a black velvet box. 'Then will you accept my ring?'

'Yes!' She glanced down at the sapphire flanked by two diamonds. 'It's beautiful…'

'Each stone symbolises a person in our family. Annas, you and me.' He slid it onto her finger. 'So, Margo Marakaios, will you marry me?'

She laughed—a sound of pure joy. 'I already have.'

'Phew!' Leaning forward, Leo brushed her lips with his as the city twinkled and sparkled all around them. 'Thank goodness for that…'

* * * * *

Mel's hand was enclosed in his and she was standing close to him now. So close that if she pressed forward she would bind herself against the strong column of his body.

She longed to feel that sheathed muscled strength against the pliant wand of her own body, to lift her mouth to his and wind her fingers up to the base of his neck and draw that sculpted mouth down upon hers...

It shook her, the intensity of her urge to do so. Like a slow-motion film running inside her head, she felt her brain try to reason its way out of it. Out of the urge to reach for him, to kiss him...

It had been so, so long since she had kissed a man—any man at all. And longer still since she had given rein to the physical impulse of intimacy. And now here she was, gazing up at a man who was the most achingly seductive she'd ever encountered, wanting only to feel his mouth on hers, his arms around her.

As if he heard her body call to him Nikos bent his head to catch her lips. His mouth was as soft as velvet. As sensuous as silk.

Dissolving her completely.

Julia James lives in England, and adores the peaceful verdant countryside and the wild shores of Cornwall. She also loves the Mediterranean—so rich in myth and history, with its sunbaked landscapes and olive groves, ancient ruins and azure seas. 'The perfect setting for romance!' she says. 'Rivalled only by the lush tropical heat of the Caribbean—palms swaying by a silver sand beach lapped by turquoise waters…what more could lovers want?'

Books by Julia James

Mills & Boon® Modern™ Romance

The Forbidden Touch of Sanguardo
Securing the Greek's Legacy
Painted the Other Woman
The Dark Side of Desire
The Theotokis Inheritance
From Dirt to Diamonds
Buttoned-Up Secretary, British Boss
Forbidden or For Bedding?
The Master of Highbridge Manor
Penniless and Purchased
The Boselli Bride
The Playboy of Pengarroth Hall
The British Billionaire's Innocent
The Greek's Million-Dollar Baby Bargain

Visit the author profile page at
millsandboon.co.uk for more titles

CAPTIVATED
BY THE GREEK

BY
JULIA JAMES

MILLS
BOON

Published in Great Britain 2015
by Mills & Boon, an imprint of Harlequin (UK) Limited,
Eton House, 18-24 Paradise Road, Richmond, Surrey, TW9 1SR

© 2015 Julia James

ISBN: 978-0-263-25074-9

Harlequin (UK) Limited's policy is to use papers that are natural, renewable and recyclable products and made from wood grown in sustainable forests. The logging and manufacturing processes conform to the legal environmental regulations of the country of origin.

Printed and bound in Spain
by CPI, Barcelona

CAPTIVATED
BY THE GREEK

For carers everywhere—you are all saints!

CHAPTER ONE

NIKOS PARAKIS TWISTED his wrist slightly to glance at his watch and frowned. If he wanted to make his appointment in the City he was going to have to skip lunch. No way could he fit in a midday meal now, having delayed leaving his Holland Park apartment—his base in the UK—in order to catch a lengthy teleconference with Russian clients. He'd also, on this early summer's day, wanted to get some fresh air and brief exercise, so had dismissed his driver and intended to pick up a taxi on the far side of the park, in Kensington High Street.

As he gained the wide tree-lined pavement he felt a stab of hunger. He definitely needed refuelling.

On impulse, he plunged across the road and headed for what appeared to be some kind of takeaway food shop. He was no food snob, despite the wealth of the Parakis banking dynasty at his disposal, and a sandwich was a sandwich—wherever it came from.

The moment he stepped inside, however, he almost changed his mind. Fast food outlets specialising in pre-packed sandwiches had come a long way in thirty years, but this was one of the old-fashioned ones where sandwiches were handmade on the spot, to order, constructed out of the array of ingredients contained in plastic tubs behind the counter.

Damn, he thought, irritated, he really didn't have time for this.

But he was here now, and it would have to do.

'Have you anything ready-made?' he asked, addressing the person behind the counter. He didn't mean to sound brusque, but he was hungry and in a hurry.

The server, who had her back to him, went on buttering a slice of bread. Nikos felt irritation kick again.

'She's making mine first, mate,' said a voice nearby, and he saw that there was a shabbily dressed, grizzled-looking old man seated on a chair by the chilled drinks cabinet. 'You'll 'ave ter wait.'

Nikos's mouth pressed tight, and he moved his annoyed regard back to the figure behind the counter. Without turning, the server spoke.

'Be with you in a sec,' she said, apparently to Nikos, and started to pile ham onto the buttered slice before wrapping the sandwich in a paper serviette and turning to hand it to the man. She pushed a cup of milky tea towards him, too.

'Ta, luv,' the man said, moving to stand closer to Nikos than he felt entirely comfortable with.

Whenever the man had last bathed, it hadn't been recently. Nor had he shaved. Moreover, there was a discernible smell of stale alcohol about him.

The man closed grimy fingers around the wrapped sandwich, picked up the mug in a shaky grip and looked at Nikos.

'Any spare change, guv?' he asked hopefully.

'No,' said Nikos, and turned back to the server, who was now wiping the sandwich preparation surface clean.

The old man shuffled out.

The server's voice followed him. 'Stay off the booze, Joe—it's killing you.'

'Any day now, luv, any day...' the man assured her.

He shuffled out and was gone, lunch provided. Presumably for free, Nikos supposed, having seen no money change hands for the transaction. But his interest in the matter was zero, and with the server finally free to pay him attention, he repeated his original question about the availability of ready-made sandwiches—this time most definitely impatiently.

'No,' replied the server, turning around and busying herself with the tea urn.

Her tone of voice had changed. If Nikos could have been bothered to care—which he didn't, in the slightest—he might have said she sounded annoyed.

'Then whatever's quickest.'

He glanced at his watch again, and frowned. This was ridiculous—he was wasting time instead of saving it!

'What would you like?'

The server's pointless question made his frown deepen.

'I said whatever's quickest,' he repeated.

'That,' came the reply, 'would be bread and butter.'

Nikos dropped his wrist and levelled his gaze right at her. There was no mistaking the antagonism in her tone. Or the open irritation in his as he answered.

'Ham,' he bit out.

'On white or brown? Baguette or sliced?'

'Whatever's quickest.' How many times did he have to *say* that?

'That would be white sliced.'

'White sliced, then.'

'Just ham?'

'Yes.' Anything more complicated and he'd be there all day.

She turned away and busied herself at the preparation surface behind her. Nikos drummed his fingers on the counter. Realising he was thirsty, he twisted round to help himself to a bottle of mineral water from the chilled drinks cabinet against the wall.

As he put it on the counter the server turned round, sandwich prepared and wrapped in a paper serviette. She glanced at the bottle and Nikos could see she was mentally calculating the combined price.

'Three pounds forty-five,' she said.

He had his wallet out already, taking out a note.

'That's a *fifty*,' she said, as if she'd never seen one before.

Perhaps she never had, thought Nikos acidly. He said nothing, just went on holding it out for her.

'Haven't you anything smaller?' she demanded.

'No.'

With a rasp of irritation she snatched it from him and opened the till. There was some audible clinking and rustling, and a moment later she was clunking his change down on the countertop. It consisted of silver to make it up to a fiver, a single twenty-pound note and twenty-five individual pound coins.

Then she raised her gaze to Nikos and glared at him.

And for the first time Nikos looked at her.

Looked at her—and *saw* her.

He stilled completely. Somewhere inside his head a voice was telling him to stop staring, to pick up the ludicrous heap of coins and pocket the note and get the hell out of there. Get a taxi, get to his meeting, get on with the rest of his life and forget he'd ever been hungry enough to step into some two-bit sandwich bar patronised by alcoholic down-and-outs.

But the voice went totally and entirely unheeded.

Right now only one part of his brain was functioning. The part that was firing in instant, total intensity with the most visceral masculine response he had ever experienced in his life.

Thee mou, but she was absolutely beautiful.

There was no other word for her. In an instant Nikos took in a face that was sculpted to perfection: high cheekbones, contoured jawline, straight nose not a millimetre too long or too short, wide-set eyes of startling blue, and a mouth… Ah, a mouth whose natural lushness was as inviting as a honey-drenched dessert…

How the hell didn't I notice her straight away?

But the question searing through him was irrelevant. Everything right now was irrelevant except his desire—his need—to keep drinking her in. Taking in the incredible impact her stunning looks were having on him. His eyes narrowed in their instinctive, potent perusal of her features, and he felt his response course through him.

He was not a man who had been deprived of the company of beautiful women in his thirty-odd years. As the heir to the Parakis banking dynasty he'd become accustomed to having the hottest girls making a beeline for him. And he knew that it wasn't just the Parakis millions that drew them in. Nature, for whatever capricious reason, had bestowed upon him a six-foot frame—which he kept in peak condition with rigorous and ruthless physical exercise—and looks that, without vanity, he knew women liked. Liked a lot.

The combination had proved highly successful, and his private life was plentifully supplied by any number of keen and eager females only too happy to be seen on his arm, or to keep him company in bed. Given that, therefore, it would have been perverse of him not to have chosen those females who were of the very highest calibre when it came to their appearance.

And this woman, who had drawn his attention so rivetingly, was most definitely of that elite calibre.

His gaze worked over her, and as it did so another realisation struck him. She wasn't wearing a trace of make-up and her hair—blonde, from what little he could see of it—was concealed under some kind of baseball cap. As for her figure—although she appeared to be tall—she was clad in a baggy T-shirt that bore the legend 'Sarrie's Sarnies' and did less than nothing for her.

Hell, if she looked this good stuck in this dump, dressed in grunge, what would she look like dressed in designer labels?

For a moment—just a moment—he felt an overriding desire to put that to the test.

Then, in the next second, he crashed and burned.

'If you want a piece of meat, try a butcher's shop!'

The server's harsh voice cut right through Nikos's riveted attention to her physical attributes.

A frown of incomprehension—and annoyance— pulled his brows together.

'What?' he demanded.

Her face was set. Absently Nikos noted how looking angry actually made her even more stunning. Her cerulean eyes flashed like sapphires.

'Don't give me that,' she snapped. 'Now, take your change, *and* your damn sandwich, and go!'

It was Nikos's turn to experience anger. His face hardened. 'Your rudeness to a customer,' he said freezingly, 'is totally unacceptable. Were you one of *my* employees you would be dismissed instantly for taking such an attitude to those whose custom pays your wages.'

For answer, she put the palms of her hands on the counter—Nikos found himself noting how well shaped they were—and braced herself.

'And if I worked for *you*—which, thank God, I don't—I would be suing *you* for sexual harassment!' she bit back. Her eyes narrowed to slits. '*That's* what I meant by wanting "meat", sunshine!'

Nikos's expression changed. The hardness was still in his eyes, but there was something else, too. A glint that, had the stunning but inexplicably bolshie female facing him been one of his acquaintances, she would have known sent a crystal-clear message.

'Since when is it illegal to admire a woman's beauty?' he riposted silkily.

To prove his point he let his gaze wash over her again. Inside him, the visceral reaction she'd aroused so powerfully warred with the irritation he'd felt ever since his hunger had hit him—an irritation that her hostility and rudeness had elevated to outright anger. He wasn't sure which emotion was predominant. What he *was* sure of, though, was that right now his overpowering desire was to rattle her cage...

'If you *want* to go round ogling women like *meat*, then you should damn well wear sunglasses and spare us the ordeal,' she shot back.

Nikos felt yet another emotion spark through him. Almost unconsciously, he found himself starting to enjoy himself.

One arched eyebrow quirked tauntingly. 'Ordeal?' he asked limpidly.

And then, quite deliberately, he let his gaze soften. No longer assessing. More...caressing. Letting her see clearly that women who received his approbation most definitely did not regard it as an *ordeal*...

And before his eyes, to his intense satisfaction, he saw a wave of colour suffuse her clear, translucent skin. Her cheeks grew stained and her gaze dropped.

'Go away,' she said. Her voice was tight. 'Just...*go away*!'

He gave a low laugh. *Game, set and match—thank you very much.* He didn't need any further confirmation to know that he'd just effortlessly breached her defences...got right past that bolshie anger barrier and hit home, sweet home.

With a sweeping gesture he scooped the pile of coins into his pocket, together with the solitary twenty-pound note, then picked up his ham sandwich and the bottle of water.

'Have a nice day,' he said flippantly, and strolled out of the sandwich shop.

His irritation was gone completely.

As he emerged he saw the down-and-out, Joe, leaning against a nearby lamppost, wolfing down the sandwich he had been given. On impulse, Nikos reached into his jacket pocket, jingling with all the pound coins she'd landed him with.

He scooped up a handful and proffered them. 'You asked about spare change,' he said to the man, who was eyeing him.

'Ta, guv,' said the man, and took the handful eagerly, his bloodshot eyes gleaming.

His grimy hands were shaking, and Nikos felt a pang of pity go through him.

'She's right, you know,' he heard himself telling the man. 'The booze *is* killing you.'

The bloodshot eyes met his. They were not gleaming now. There was desolation in them.

'I know, mate...'

He pulled his gaze away and then he was off again, shuffling down the street, pocketing the money, shoulders hunched in defeat. For a moment Nikos's eyes stayed on him. Then he saw a taxi cab approaching along the High Street, with its 'For Hire' sign illuminated. He flagged it down and flung himself into the back seat, starting to wolf down his ham sandwich.

His own words to the down-and-out echoed in his head. *'She's right, you know...'*

His jaw tightened. Damn—she was, too. And not just about that wretched alcoholic.

Finishing his sandwich, he lifted his mobile phone from his inside pocket and pressed the speed-dial key for his London PA. She answered immediately, and Nikos gave her his instructions.

'Janine, I need to have some flowers delivered...'

Mel stood, palms still pressed into the surface of the counter, and glared after the tall retreating figure. She was mad—totally hopping mad. She hadn't been this angry since she couldn't remember when.

Damn the arrogance of the man!

She could feel her jaw still clenching. She hadn't liked him the moment he'd walked into the shop. The way he'd spoken—not even waiting for her to turn around to him, just making his demands as if she was some kind of servant. Underling. Minion. *Lackey*. The insulting words marched through her head.

She'd tried for her customary politeness while she was finishing Joe's sandwich, but then she'd caught the way the damn man had looked at Joe—as if he was a bad smell. Well, yes, he was—but that wasn't the point. The point was that Joe was in a bad way, and for heaven's sake *anyone* would have felt pity for the guy, surely? Especially—and now her jaw clenched even more—especially a man whom life had so obviously *not* treated anything *like* as grimly as it had poor old Joe.

That had put her back up straight away. And from then on it had just got worse.

The whole monosyllabic exchange about what kind of sandwich he'd wanted replayed itself in her head, followed by—oh yes—his dropping a fifty-pound note down in payment. Mel's mouth tightened in satisfaction. Well, it had given her particular pleasure to dump all those pound coins on him by way of change.

Boy, it had riled him—she had seen that immediately. Trouble was…and now her expression changed yet again, to a mix of anger and something else quite entirely…he had had that comeback on her…

Right through her body she could feel the heat flush. It was running right through her—through every vein, right out to the tips of her fingers—as though someone has tipped hot water into her. And to her own mortification she even felt glorious heat pooling in her core, felt her breasts start to tingle with traitorous reaction.

Oh, damn! Damn, damn, damn!

Yet she couldn't stop herself. Couldn't stop the memory—instant, vivid and overpowering—of the way he'd looked at her. Looked *right* at her. Looked her over…

Meat, she said desperately to herself. *As if you were a piece of meat—that's how he looked at you. Just as you told him.*

She fought to call back the burst of satisfaction she'd felt when she'd rapped that out at him, but it was impossible. All that was possible now was to go on feeling the wonderful flush of heat coursing through her. She fought it down as best she could, willing it to leave her—to leave her alone—just as she'd told him to go, just *go away…*

She shut her eyes, sighing heavily—hopelessly. *OK— OK*, she reasoned, *so face it.* However rude, arrogant and obnoxious he was, he was also—yup, she had to admit it—absolutely, totally and completely drop-dead *devastating.*

She'd registered it instantly—it would have been impossible not to—the minute she'd turned round with Joe's sandwich to see just who it was who'd spoken to her in such a brusque, demanding fashion. Registered it, but had promptly busied herself in making Joe's tea, pinning her eyes on pouring it out and ladling sugar into it the way Joe needed it.

But she'd been conscious of that first glimpse of Mr Drop-dead Devastating burning a hole in her retina— burning its way into her brain—so that all she'd wanted to do was lift her gaze and let it do what it had been trying to do with an urgency she still bewailed and berated.

Which was simply to stare and stare and stare…

At *everything* about him.

His height…his lean, fit body, sheathed in that hand-tailored suit that had fitted him like a glove, reaching across wide shoulders and moulding his broad chest just as the expanse of pristine white shirt had.

But it wasn't his designer suit or even his lean physique that was dominating her senses now.

It was his eyes. Eyes that were night-dark and like tempered steel in a face that was constructed in some particular way that outdid every male she'd ever seen— on-screen or off. Chiselled jaw, strong nose, tough-looking cheekbones, winged brows and always, *always*, those ludicrously long-lashed, gold-flecked eyes that were lethal weapons entirely on their own.

That was what she'd wanted to gaze at, and that was what had been searing through her head all through their snarling exchange.

And then, as if a switch had been thrown, he'd suddenly changed the subject...

More heat coursed through her as the physical memory of how he'd looked at her hit her again. Turning the blatant focus of his male reaction on her like a laser beam. One that had burned right through her.

The slow wash of his gaze had poured over her like warm, molten honey—like a silken touch to her skin. It had felt as though he were caressing her, as if she could actually feel his hands shaping her body, his mouth lowering to hers to taste, to tease...to arouse.

All that in a single sensual glance...

And then, when she'd been helpless—pathetically, abjectly helpless—to do anything other than tell him— beg him—to leave, what had he done? He'd *laughed*! Laughed at her—knowing perfectly well how he'd got the better of her, how he'd made a cringing mockery of her defiance.

The colour in her cheeks turned to hectic spots as anger burned out that shaming blush he'd conjured in her.

Damn him!

Fuming, she went on staring blindly out through the shop door. She could no longer see him. With a final damning adjuration to herself to stop thinking of him, and everything about him, she whirled around to get on with her work.

Washing up had never been so noisy, nor slicing bread so vicious.

CHAPTER TWO

'DID YOU HAVE those flowers delivered?'

It was the first question Nikos found himself asking as he returned to his London office after his meeting that afternoon. He did not doubt that his PA had complied, for she was efficiency itself—and she was used to despatching flowers to the numerous assorted females that featured in his life when he was in the UK.

But not usually to females who worked in sandwich bars...

Mouthy, contrary females who gave him a hard time...

Possessed of looks so stunning he still could not get them out of his head...

He gave a shake of his head, clearing the memory and settling himself down at his desk. There really was no point thinking about the blonde any more. Let alone speculating, as he found himself wanting to do, on just what she might look like if she were dressed in an outfit that adorned her extraordinary beauty.

How much more beautiful could she look?

The question rippled through his mind, and in its wake came a ripple of something that was not idle speculation but desire...

With her hair loosened, a gown draping her slen-

*der yet rounded figure, her sapphire eyes luminous
and long-lashed...*

He cut the image. She'd been a fleeting fiery encounter and nothing more.

No, he thought decisively, switching on his PC, he'd sent flowers to atone for his rudeness—provoking though *she'd* been—and he would leave it at that. He had women enough to choose from—no need to add another one.

He flicked open his diary to see what was coming up in the remainder of his sojourn in London. His father, chairman of the family-run Athens-based investment bank, left that city reluctantly these days, and Nikos found himself doing nearly all the foreign travel that running the bank required.

A frown moved fleetingly across his brow. At least here in London he was spared his father's wandering into the office to make one of his habitual complaints about Nikos's mother. The moment Nikos got back to Athens, though, he knew there would be a litany of complaints awaiting him, while his father indulged himself and offloaded. Then—predictably—the next time he saw his mother a reciprocal litany would be pressed upon him...

With a sigh of exasperation he pushed his interminably warring parents out of his head space. There was never going to be an end to their virulent verbal attacks on each other, their incessant sniping and backbiting. It had gone on for as long as Nikos could remember, and he was more than fed up with it.

Briskly, he ran an eye down the diary page and then frowned again—for quite a different reason this time. *Damn.*

His frown deepened. How had he got himself involved in *that*? A black-tie charity bash at the Viscari St James Hotel this coming Friday evening.

In itself, that would not have been a problem. What *was* a problem, though, was that he could see from the diary that the evening included Fiona Pellingham. Right now that woman was *not* someone he wanted to encounter.

A high-flying mergers-and-acquisitions expert at a leading business consultancy, Fiona had taken an obvious shine to Nikos during a business meeting on his last visit to London, and had made it strikingly clear to him that she'd very much like to make an acquisition of *him* for herself.

But for all her striking brunette looks and svelte figure she was, as Nikos had immediately realised, the possessive type, and she would want a great deal more from him than the passing affair that was all he ever indulged in when it came to women. And that meant that the last thing he wanted to do was to give her an opportunity to pursue her obvious interest in him.

He frowned again. The problem was, even if he didn't go to this charity bash she'd somehow put into his diary, Fiona would probably find another way to pursue him. Plague him with yet more invitations and excuses to meet up with him. What he needed was to put her off completely. Convince her he was unavailable romantically.

What he needed was a handy, convenient female he could take along with him on Friday to keep Fiona at bay. But just who would fit that bill? For a moment his mind was totally, absolutely blank. Then, in the proverbial light-bulb moment, he knew exactly who he wanted to take. And the knowledge made him sit back abruptly and hear the question shaping itself inside his head.

Well, after all, why not? You did want to know just how much more beautiful she could look if she were dressed for the evening...

This would be a chance to find out—why not take it?

A slow smile started to curve his mouth.

Mel was staring at the cluttered table in the back room behind the sandwich bar. She didn't see the clutter—all she saw was the huge bouquet that sat in its own cellophane container of water, its opulent blooms as large as her fists. A bouquet that was so over-the-top it was ridiculous. Her eyes were stormy.

Who the hell did he think he was?

Except that she knew the answer to that, because his name came at the end of the message on the card in the envelope pinned to the cellophane.

Hope these make amends and improve your mood.

It was signed 'Nikos Parakis.'

Her brows lowered. So he was Greek. It made sense, now she thought about it, because although his English accent had been perfect, his clipped public-school vowels a perfect match with the rest of his 'Mr Rich' look, nevertheless his complexion had a distinctly Mediterranean hue to it, and his hair was as dark as a raven's wing.

Even as she thought about it his image sprang into her vision again—and with it the expression in those dark, long-lashed eyes that had looked her over, assessing her, clearly liking what he saw...

As if he was finding me worthy of his attentions!

She bristled all over again, fulminating as she glared at the hapless bouquet of lilies. Their heady scent filled the small space, obliterating the smell of food that always permeated the room from the sandwich bar beyond. The scent made her feel light-headed. Its strength was almost overpowering, sending coils of fragrance into her lungs. Exotic, perfumed…sensuous.

As sensuous as his gaze had been.

That betraying heat started to flush up inside her again, and with a growl of anger at her own imbecility she wheeled about. She had no idea where she was going to put the ridiculously over-the-top bouquet, but right now she had work to do.

She was manning the sandwich bar on her own because Sarrie himself was on holiday. She didn't mind because he was paying her extra, and every penny was bankable.

As she returned to her post behind the counter, checking what was left of the day's ingredients and lifting out a tub of sliced tomatoes from the fridge, she deliberately busied herself running over her mental accounts. It stopped her thinking about that ridiculous bouquet—and the infuriating man who'd sent it to her.

OK, so where was she in her savings? She ran the figures through her head, feeling a familiar sense of satisfaction and reassurance as she did so. She'd worked flat-out these last twelve months, and now she was almost, *almost* at the point of setting off on her dream.

To travel. To leave the UK and see the world! To make a reality of all the places she'd only ever read about. Europe, the Med, even the USA—and maybe even further…South America, the Far East and Australia.

She'd never been abroad in her life.

A sigh escaped her. She shouldn't feel deprived because she hadn't travelled abroad. Gramps hadn't liked 'abroad.' He hadn't liked foreign travel. The south coast had been about as far as he'd been prepared to go.

'Nothing wrong with Bognor,' he'd used to tell her. 'Or Brighton. Or Bournemouth.'

So that was where they'd gone for their annual summer holiday every year until she was a teenager. And for many years it had been fine—she'd loved the beach, even on her own with no brothers or sisters to play with. She'd had her grandfather, who'd raised her ever since his daughter and son-in-law had been killed in the same motorway pile-up that had killed his wife.

Looking back with adult eyes, she knew that having his five-year-old granddaughter to care for after the wholesale slaughter of the rest of his family had been her grandfather's salvation. And he, in return, had become her rock—the centre of her world, the only person in the entire universe who loved her.

When she'd finished with school and started a Business Studies degree course at a nearby college, she'd opted to continue to live at home, in the familiar semidetached house in the north London suburb she'd grown up in.

'I'd be daft to move out, Gramps. Student accommodation costs a fortune, and most of the flats are complete dumps.'

Though she'd meant it, she'd also known that her grandfather had been relieved that she'd stayed at home with him.

It hadn't cramped her social life to be living at home still, and she'd revelled in student life like any eighteen-year-old, enjoying her fair share of dating. It hadn't been until she'd met Jak in her second year that things had become serious. He'd taken her seriously, too, seeing past her dazzling looks to the person within, and soon they'd become an item.

Had she been in love with him? She'd discovered the answer to that at the end of their studies. Not enough to dedicate her life to him the way he'd wanted her to.

'I've got a job with the charity I applied for—out in Africa. I'm going to be teaching English, building schools, digging wells. It's what I've always dreamed of.' He'd paused, looking at Mel straight on. 'Will you come with me? Support me in my work? Make your life with me?'

It had been the question she'd known was coming— the question she'd only been able to answer one way. Whether or not she'd wanted to join Jak in his life's work, it had been impossible anyway.

'I can't,' she'd said. 'I can't leave Gramps.'

Because by then that was what it had come down to. In the three years of her being a student her grandfather had aged—had crossed that invisible but irreversible boundary from being the person who had raised her and looked after her to being someone who now looked to her to look after *him*. The years had brought heart problems—angina and mini-strokes—but far worse than his growing physical frailty had been the mental frailty that had come with it. Mel had known with sadness and a sinking heart that he had become more and more dependent on her.

She hadn't been able to leave him. How could she have deserted him, the grandfather she loved so much? How could she have abandoned him when he'd needed her? She had only been able to wait, putting her own life on hold and devoting herself to the one relative she'd possessed: the grandfather who loved her.

The months had turned into years—three whole years—until finally he'd left her in the only way that a frail, ill old man could leave his granddaughter.

She'd wept—but not only from grief. There had been relief, too—she knew that. Relief for him, that at last he was freed from his failing body, his faltering mind. And relief, too, for herself.

She hadn't been able to deny, though it had hurt to think it, that now, after his death, she was freed of all responsibility. Her grandfather had escaped the travails of life and by doing so had given Mel her own life back—given back to her what she wanted most of all to claim.

Her freedom.

Freedom to do what she had long dreamt of doing. To travel! To travel as she'd never had the opportunity to do—to travel wherever the wind blew her, wherever took her fancy. See the world.

But to do that she needed money. Money she'd been unable to earn for herself when she'd become her grandfather's carer. Yes, she had some money, because her grandfather had left her his savings—but that would be needed, as a safe nest egg, for when she finally returned to the UK to settle down and build a career for herself. So to fund her longed-for travels she was working all the hours she could—Sarrie's Sarnies by day, and waitressing in a nearby restaurant by night.

And soon—oh, *very* soon—she'd be off and away. Picking up a cheap last-minute flight and heading wherever the spirit took her until the money ran out, when she'd come back home to settle down.

If she ever did come back…

Maybe I'll never come back. Maybe I'll stay footloose all my life. Never be tied down again by anything or anyone! Free as a bird!

Devoted as she had been to her grandfather, after years of caring for him such freedom was a heady prospect.

So, too, was the looking forward to another element of youth that she had set aside till now.

Romance.

Since Jak had gone to Africa and she'd stayed behind to look after her grandfather romance had been impossible. In the early days she'd managed to go on a couple of dates, but as her grandfather's health had worsened those moments had become less and less. But now... Oh, now romance could blossom again—and she'd welcome it with open arms.

She knew exactly what she wanted at this juncture of her life. Nothing intense or serious, as her relationship with Jak had been. Nothing long-term, as he had hoped things would be between them. No, for now all she craved was the heady buzz of eyes meeting across a crowded room, mutual desire acknowledged and fulfilled—frothy, carefree, self-indulgent fun. *That* was what she longed for now.

Her mouth curved in a cynical smile and her eyes sparked. Well, that attitude should make her popular. Men were habitually wary of women who wanted more from them—they were the ones who didn't like clingy women, who didn't want to be tied down. Who liked to enjoy their pick of women as and when they fancied.

The cynical smile deepened. She'd bet money that Nikos Parakis was a man like that. Looking her over the way he had...

As she started to serve a new customer who'd just walked in she shook her head clear of the memory. She had better things to do than speculate about the love life of Nikos Parakis—or speculate about anything to do with him at all.

Soon his extravagantly OTT flowers would fade, and so would her memory of the intemperate encounter between them today. And eventually so would the disturbingly vivid memory of the physical impact he'd made on her, with his dark, devastating looks. And that, she said to herself firmly, would be that.

'What kind of sandwich would you like?' she asked brightly of her customer, and got on with her job.

'Pull over just there,' Nikos instructed his driver, who duly slid the sleek top-of-the-range BMW to the side of the road to let his employer get out.

Emerging, Nikos glanced along the pavement, observing for a moment or two the comings and goings at the sandwich bar and wondering whether he was being a complete idiot for doing what he was about to do.

He'd reflected on the decision on the way here from the Parakis offices, changing his mind several times. The idea that had struck him the day before when faced with the prospect of enduring an evening of Fiona Pellingham trying to corner him had stayed with him, and he'd reviewed it from all angles several times. But he'd found that whenever he'd lined up all his objections—she was a complete stranger, she was bolshie, she might not even possess an evening gown suitable for the highly upmarket Viscari St James—they'd promptly all collapsed under the one overwhelming reason he *wanted* her to accompany him on Friday evening.

Which was the fact that he could not get her out of his head.

And he could think of nothing else except wanting to see her again.

The same overwhelming urge possessed him again now—to feast his eyes on her, drink her in and feel, yet again, that incredible visceral kick he'd got from her. Anticipation rose pleasurably through him.

He glanced at his watch. It was near the end of the working day so she should be shutting up shop soon— these old-fashioned sandwich bars did not stay open in the evening. He strolled towards the entrance, pushed the door open with the flat of his palm and walked in. There was only one other customer inside, and Nikos could see he was handing over his money, taking his wrapped sandwich with him.

Serving him was the blonde, bolshie, bad-attitude total stunner.

Instantly Nikos's eyes went straight to her and stayed there, riveted.

Yes! The affirmation of all that he'd remembered about the impact she'd had on him surged through Nikos. She was as fantastic now as she had been then. Face, figure—the whole package. Burning right into his retinas, all over again.

Oh, yes, definitely—most definitely—this was the right decision to have made.

'Here's your change,' he heard her say to her customer as he paused just inside the door. Her voice was cheerful, her expression smiling.

No sign, Nikos noted with caustic observation, of the bolshiness she'd targeted *him* with. But what he was noticing more was the way that her quick smile only enhanced the perfection of her features, lending her mouth a sinuous curve and warming her sapphire eyes. He could feel his pulse give a discernible kick at the sight of her smile, even though it wasn't directed at him.

What will it feel like when she smiles at me? he wondered to himself. But he knew the answer already.

Good—that was what it would feel like.

And more than good. *Inviting...*

But just as this pleasurable thought was shaping in his brain he saw her eyes glance towards the latest person to come in—himself—and immediately her expression changed. She waited only before her customer had quit the shop before launching her attack.

'What are *you* doing here?' she demanded.

Nikos strolled forward, and it gave him particular satisfaction to see her take a half-step back, defensively. It meant she felt the need to raise her defences about him—and *that* meant, he knew with every masculine instinct, that she was vulnerable to him—vulnerable to the effect he was having on her. The effect he *wanted* to have on her.

He had seen it in her eyes, in the way they had suddenly been veiled—but not soon enough to conceal the betraying leap of emotion within.

It was an emotion that was as old as time, and one he'd seen before when he'd deliberately let his gaze wash over her, making his own reaction to her beauty as tangible as a caress...

And, veiled though it had been, it told him all he needed to know. That in spite of her outward bristling towards him, behind that layer of defence, she was reacting to him as strongly, as powerfully, as he was to her.

And once again he felt satisfaction spread through him at the knowledge that she was as reactive to him as he was to her—as powerfully attracted to him as he was to her—oh, yes, most definitely.

His eyes flickered over her again. He felt an overwhelming urge to drink her in, to remind himself of just what it was she had that so drew him to her. That extraordinary beauty she possessed was undimmed, even in these workaday surroundings and even clad as she was in that unprepossessing T-shirt. She had made not the slightest adornment to her natural beauty by way of make-up or styling her hair—most of which was still concealed under that unlovely baseball cap.

'I wanted to see you again,' he told her, coming up to the counter.

She stood her ground—he could see her doing it—but her figure had stiffened.

'Why?' she countered, making her expression stony.

He ignored her question. 'Did you get my flowers?' he asked. He kept his voice casual, kept his own eyes veiled now—for the time being.

'Yes.' The single-word answer was tight and…unappreciative.

An eyebrow quirked. 'They were not to your taste?'

Her chin lifted. 'I bet you don't even know what they are. I bet you just told your secretary to send them.'

His mouth indented. 'I suspect they will be lilies,' he answered. 'My PA likes lilies.'

'Well, send them to *her* next time!' was the immediate retort.

'But my PA,' he returned, entering into the spirit of their sparring, 'was not the one I needed to apologise to. And besides…' his dark eyes glinted '…*she* wasn't the one whose mood needed improving.'

It was deliberate baiting—and unwise, considering he wanted her to accept his invitation for the evening, but he couldn't resist the enjoyment of sparring with her and it got him his reward. That coruscating sapphire flash of her eyes—making her beautiful eyes even more outstanding.

'Well, they *didn't* improve my mood,' she snapped back. 'And you standing there doesn't either. So if that's all you came here to say, then consider it said.'

'It isn't,' said Nikos. His expression changed as he abandoned the sparring and became suddenly more businesslike. 'I have an invitation to put to you.'

For a moment she looked stupefied. Then, hard on the heels of that, deeply suspicious. 'What?'

'I would like,' Nikos informed her, 'to invite you to a charity gala this Friday night.'

'What?' The word came again, and an even more stupefied look.

'Allow me to elaborate,' said Nikos, and proceeded to do so.

His veiled eyes were watching for her reaction. Despite her overt hostility he could see that she was listening. Could see, too, that she was trying not to look at him. Trying to keep her eyes blank.

Trying—and failing.

She's aware of me, responsive to me—she's fighting it, but it's there all the same.

It flickered like electricity between them as he went on.

'I find,' he told her, keeping his tone bland and neutral, so as not to set her hackles rising again, 'that at short notice I am without a "plus one" for this Friday evening—a charity gala to which I am committed.' He looked at her straight on. 'Therefore I would be highly gratified if you would agree to be that "plus one" for the occasion. I'm sure you would find it enjoyable—it's at the Viscari St James Hotel, which I hope you will agree is a memorable venue.'

He paused minutely, then allowed his mouth to indent into a swift smile.

'Please say you'll come.'

Her expression was a study, and he enjoyed watching it. Stupefaction mixed with deep, deep suspicion. And even deeper scepticism.

'And of course, Mr Parakis, you have absolutely no one else you could possibly invite except a complete stranger—someone you told to her face you'd sack if she were unfortunate enough to be one of your hapless minions!' she finally shot at him, her head going back and her eyes sparking.

He was unfazed. 'Indeed,' he replied shamelessly. 'So, if you would be kind enough to take pity on my predicament and help me in my hour of need, my gratitude would know no bounds…'

A very unladylike snort escaped her. 'Yeah, right,' she managed to say derisively.

'It's quite true,' he answered limpidly. 'I *would* be extremely grateful.'

'And I'd be a complete mug to believe you,' she shot back.

Nikos's expression changed again. 'Why? What is the problem here for you?' His eyes rested on her, conveying a message older than time. 'Do you not know how extraordinarily beautiful you are? How any man would be privileged to have you at his side—?'

He saw the colour run out over her sculpted cheekbones. Saw her swallow.

'Will you not let me invite you?' he said again. There was the slightest husk in his voice. It was there without his volition.

Mixed emotions crossed her face. 'No,' she said finally—emphatically.

His eyebrows rose. 'Why not?' he asked outright.

Hers snapped together. 'Because I don't like you—that's why!'

He gave a half-laugh, discovering he was enjoying her bluntness. 'We got off to a bad start—I admit that freely. I was hungry and short-tempered, and you gave me a hard time and I resented it.'

'You spoke to me like I was beneath you,' she shot at him. 'And you looked down your nose at Joe—wouldn't give him a penny even though you're obviously rolling in it!' She cast a pointed look at him. 'Your wallet was stuffed with fifties!'

'Did you expect me to hand a fifty over to him?' he protested. 'And for your information I gave him a handful of all those pound coins you dumped on me.'

Mel's expression changed. '*What?* Oh, God, he'll have just gone off and spent it on booze.' Her eyes narrowed. 'Did you really give him money?'

'Ask him next time he comes in for a free sandwich,' said Nikos drily. 'So...' his voice changed '...are you going to take pity on me and accept my invitation?'

She was wavering—he could tell that with every male instinct. *She wants to accept, but her pride is holding her back.*

'You know,' he said temperately as her internal conflict played out in her betraying gaze, 'I really am quite safe. And very respectable, too. As is the Viscari St James Hotel and the charity gala.'

'You're a complete stranger.'

'No, I'm not. You know who I am—you addressed me by name just now,' Nikos countered.

'Only because you put your name on the card with those flowers—and *they* were an insult anyway.'

'How so?' Nikos's astonishment was open.

The sapphire flash that made her beauty even more

outstanding came again. 'You can't even see it, can you?' she returned. 'Sending me a ludicrously over-the-top bouquet and then having the gall to tell me to improve my mood—like you hadn't caused my bad mood in the first place. It was just so…so *patronising*!'

'Patronising? I don't see why.'

Mel's screwed her face up. Emotion was running like a flash flood through her. She was trying to cope with seeing him right in front of her again, just when she'd been starting to put the whole encounter of the previous day behind her, and trying urgently to suppress her reaction to seeing him again. Trying *not* to betray just what an impact he was having on her—how her eyes wanted to gaze at him, take in that sable hair, the incredible planes and contours of his face—and trying not to let herself fall head first into those dark eyes of his…

She was trying to use anger to keep him at bay—but he kept challenging it, eroding it. Throwing at her that ludicrous invitation which had stopped her dead in her tracks—an invitation which was as over-the-top as that vast bouquet had been.

'Yes,' she insisted, 'patronising. Mr Rich and Lordly sending flowers to Poor Little Shop Girl!'

There was a moment's silence. Then Nikos spoke. 'I did not mean it that way.' He took a breath. 'I told you—I sent them with the intention of making amends once I realised I had been rude to you—in more ways than one.'

He avoided spelling out what he was referring to, but he knew she was thinking about it for he could see a streak of colour heading out across her cheekbones again.

'But if you want me to apologise for sending the flowers as well, then—'

She cut across him. 'No, it's all right,' she said. She tried not to sound truculent. OK, so he hadn't meant to come across as patronising. Fine. She could be OK with that. She could be OK with him apologising to her. And she could be fine with him giving money to Joe, even if he *would* just go and spend it all on alcohol.

But what she *couldn't* be fine with was what he was asking her.

To go out with him. Go out with a man who set her pulse racing, who seemed to be able to slam right past every defence she put up against him—a man she wanted to gaze at as shamelessly, blatantly, as he had looked at her.

What's he doing to me? And how? And why am I being like this? Why can't I just tell him to go so I can shut the shop and never see him again and just get on with my life?

And why don't I want to do that?

But she knew why—and it was in every atom of Nikos Parakis, standing there across the counter, asking her why she didn't want to go out with him.

'Look, Mr Parakis, I don't know what this is about— I really don't. You set eyes on me for the second time in your life and suddenly you're asking me out for the evening? It's weird—bizarre.'

'Let me be totally upfront with you about why I'm asking *you*, in particular, to come with me on Friday evening,' he answered.

His eyes were resting on her, but not with any expression in them that made her either angry, suspicious or, worst of all, vulnerable to his overwhelming sexual allure.

'I'm in an awkward situation,' he said bluntly. 'Whilst in London I find myself committed to this charity gala tomorrow night, at the Viscari St James. Unfortunately, also present will be a woman whom I know through business and who is, alas, harbouring possessive intentions towards me which I cannot reciprocate.'

Was there an edge in his voice? Mel wondered. But he was continuing.

'I do not wish to spend the evening fending her off, let alone giving her cause to think that her hopes might be fulfilled. But I don't wish to wound or offend her either, and nor do I wish to sour any future business dealings. I need a…graceful but persuasive way to deflect her. Arriving with my own "plus one" would, I hope, achieve that. However, the lady in hot pursuit of me knows perfectly well that I am currently unattached— hence my need to discover a sufficiently convincing partner for the evening to thwart her hopes.'

His expression changed again.

'All of which accounts for my notion that inviting a fantastically beautiful complete stranger as my "plus one" would be the ideal answer to my predicament,' he finished, keeping his gaze steady on Mel's face.

He paused. His eyes rested on her with an unreadable expression that Mel could not match.

'You fit the bill perfectly,' he said. And now, suddenly, his expression was not unreadable at all…

As she felt the unveiled impact of his gaze Mel heard her breath catch, felt emotion swing into her as if it had been blown in on the wind from an opened door. He was offering her an experience she'd never had in her life—a glittering evening out with the most breathtakingly attractive man she'd ever seen.

So why not? What are you waiting for? Why hesitate for a moment?

She thought of all the reasons she shouldn't go—he

might be the most ridiculously good-looking and most ludicrously attractive man she'd ever seen, but he was also the most infuriating and arrogant and self-satisfied man she'd ever met.

But he's apologised, and his self-satisfaction comes with a sense of humour about it, and he's given me a cogent reason for his out-of-the-blue invitation...

But he was a complete stranger and could be anyone.

I know his name—and, anyway, he's talking about a posh charity bash at a swanky West End hotel, not an orgy in an opium den...

But she had nothing suitable to wear for such a thing as a posh charity bash at a swanky West End hotel.

Yes, I have—I've got that second-hand designer evening gown I bought in a charity shop that was dead cheap because it had a stain on it. I can cover the stain with a corsage...and I can make the corsage from that over-the-top bunch of lilies he's just sent...

But she ought to be working—she made good tips on a Friday night at the restaurant.

Well, I can work an extra shift on Sunday lunchtime instead, when Sarrie's is closed...

One by one she could hear herself demolishing her own objections against accepting Nikos Parakis's invitation. Heard herself urging on the one overwhelming reason for accepting it.

A little thrill went through her.

She was about to start a new life—her *own* life. She would be free of obligations to anyone else. Free to do what she wanted and go where she wanted. Free to indulge herself finally!

And when it came to indulgence what could be more self-indulgent than a gorgeous, irresistible man like the one standing in front of her? It was just too, too tempting to turn down.

If anything could herald her new life's arrival with the sound of trumpets it must surely be this. So why not grab the opportunity with both hands?

Why not?

'Well,' she heard him say, one eyebrow quirked expectantly, 'what's the verdict? Do we have a deal?'

Her eyelids dipped briefly over her eyes and she felt a smile start to form at her mouth.

'OK, then,' she said. 'Yes, we have a deal.'

CHAPTER THREE

MEL TWISTED AS best she could, but it was no good. She couldn't possibly see her full length reflection in the tiny mirror she'd got propped up on top of the filing cabinet where Sarrie kept the accounts.

Well, it didn't matter. She knew the dress suited her because she'd loved it from the moment she'd first seen it in the charity shop. It was the prize piece in the collection she'd been scouring charity shops for over the last year, putting together a cut-price but stylish wardrobe for her foreign travels.

The dress was silk, but in very fine plissé folds, which made it ideal for travelling as she could just twist it into a roll for packing. The colour suited her perfectly, she knew, because the pale blue was shot with a deeper hyacinth-blue, with a touch of lilac to it that set off her eyes. And its simple folds suited her preference for unfussy, 'no bling' styles.

With the reassurance of its designer label she knew she could go anywhere in it—even the Viscari St James. She'd looked up the hotel on Sarrie's PC and had whistled. It had a cachet that was way, way beyond any place she'd ever set foot in. But that was hardly surprising—for the internet had also revealed to her that Nikos Parakis was the scion of the Parakis banking dynasty—a

Greek-based outfit that seemed to be rolling in it to the tune of *zillions*.

And he came slumming along into a humble sandwich bar! she thought with mordant humour. No wonder he'd been so outraged at her lack of awed deference.

But, to his credit, he had at least apologised, and she'd draw a line under it. Now, she realised, she was simply looking forward to seeing him again. Would they still spar with each other?

She found a smile quirking her lips at the prospect... And, of course, at the prospect of feasting her eyes on the paean to male gorgeousness that was the very, *very* gorgeous Nikos Parakis.

Eyes glinting in anticipation of the treat that she knew this evening would be, she picked up the little satin clutch bag that went with her dress. Time to get going. Nikos had told her a car would collect her, and it was nearly the specified pickup time now.

She stepped outside on to the pavement, carefully locking up as she went and dropping the keys into her clutch, aware of a sleek, chauffeured car humming quietly and expensively at the kerb. She headed purposefully towards it, getting used to the unaccustomed feel of high heels and long skirts and her hair being loosened from its usual workaday tied-back plait.

As she approached the car the driver got out, tipping his cap to her in salutation, and from the very male expression in his eyes she knew she looked good enough for the evening ahead.

And for the man who was making it possible.

A little flutter of happy anticipation went through her as she got gracefully into the car when the door was held open for her. It had been so, so long since she'd gone out at all for the evening—and never like this, in such luxury and elegance.

The flutter came again, and she settled back happily to enjoy the chauffeured car, with its soft leather seats, its wide footwell lined with dove-grey carpet, and its fittings all in polished marquetry, as she was driven to her glamorous destination—and to the breathtakingly devastating man who awaited her there.

Her wonderful new life of freedom was just beginning, and this gorgeous, *gorgeous* man was just the person to start it off for her.

Nikos strolled up to the bar and placed his order. He did not sit down—merely propped one forearm on the gleaming mahogany surface, rested his foot on the brass rail and glanced around. The resplendent Edwardian-style bar just off the equally resplendent lobby at the Viscari St James was a popular watering hole for the well heeled. Many, like him, were in tuxedos, gathering for the evening's main function—the charity gala.

His mood, as he glanced around, was mixed. Happy anticipation filled him—his driver had phoned a while ago to inform him that he was en route, and soon—very soon—he was going to see just how even more fantastically beautiful his date for the evening looked in evening dress.

But he also felt a momentary doubt assail him. Would she possess the kind of attire that was appropriate for the Viscari? Perhaps he should have offered to help in that department? Then he quashed the thought—he was pretty sure that any such offer, however well intentioned, would have got shot down as 'patronising'. No, if having nothing to wear had been a problem she'd have said so.

He barely had time to take a first mellowing sip of his dry martini, directing another sweeping glance around the room, before he stilled.

She was walking into the bar area.

His eyes went to her immediately—it was impossible for them not to. Dimly, he was aware that he was far from being the only male whose eyes had gone straight to her. *Thee mou*, but she could turn heads!

And as for any concerns that she might not possess the kind of dress that was suited to a venue like the Viscari St James...they evaporated like a drop of water on a hot stove.

She looked stunning—*beyond* stunning.

Finally he could see just what nature had bestowed upon her, now untrammelled and unconcealed by her workaday appearance as it had been so far.

She was tall and slender, but with curves that went in and out in all the right places that were perfectly enhanced by the elegant fall of the ankle-length gown she was wearing. Its style and colour were perfect for her—a blending of delicate shades of blue and lilac. Her shoulders were swathed in soft folds of the multi-hued material, and the décolletage was draped but not low-cut. A creamy white corsage nestled in the drapery, and Nikos's mouth gave a quirk of amusement. He was pretty sure the corsage originated from the bouquet of lilies he'd had sent to her.

As for her hair—finally he could see what he'd wanted to see of it, freed from that obnoxious baseball cap. It was everything he could have wanted, loosened and swept back from her face, caught to one side with a mother of pearl comb before curving around one shoulder in a long, lush golden fall.

And her face— *Ah...* Nikos thought, satisfaction running through him with an even greater intensity. He had thought her stunningly beautiful when she'd had not a scrap of make-up on, but now, with her luminous eyes deepened, their lashes lengthened, her cheekbones delineated and her mouth, like a ripe damson...

He stepped forward, his smile deepening.

She saw him immediately—he could tell. Could tell, too, that the impact he was making on her was everything he'd wanted. His sense of satisfaction intensified again.

Her eyes widened with telltale revelation as she made her way towards him. And as she came up to him for the first time Nikos could detect a dent in her air of self-assured composure. Two spots of colour burned briefly but revealingly in her sculpted cheeks.

His eyes were warm upon her. 'You look fantastic,' he breathed.

His compliment drew a new expression from her face.

'I rather thought that was the idea,' Mel said.

Her voice was dry. But she needed it to be. She needed it to be because as her eyes had alighted upon Nikos Parakis she had felt a kick go through her that she had not intended to feel. If he'd looked drop-dead gorgeous before, in his handmade suit, now, in a handmade tux, he looked ten times more deadly.

And as for the sensation going through her now, as his dark gold-flecked eyes worked over her... She could feel awareness shooting through her, sky-high. Urgently she sought to quell it, to stay composed and unruffled.

Nikos's smile deepened. 'What can I get you to drink?' he asked.

'Sparkling mineral water is fine, thank you,' she managed to get out, without sounding too breathless.

He glanced at her. 'Do you not drink alcohol?'

'Oh, yes,' she replied, more easily now, glad to find her voice sounding a little more normal. 'But I assume there will be wine with dinner, so I don't want to make a start on it yet.'

'Very wise,' Nikos murmured, and relayed her order to the barman.

Then he turned his attention back to his date for the evening. A date, he suddenly realised with a sense of confusion, whose name he had absolutely no idea of!

Up to now, in his head, she'd simply been the stunning blonde in the sandwich shop. He blinked for a moment. Then, to his relief, he realised that of *course* he knew her name. It had been emblazoned on that unlovely T-shirt she'd been wearing in the sandwich bar.

The barman placed a glass of iced sparking water on the counter. Nikos picked it up and handed it to her. 'There you go, Sarrie,' he said, with a smile.

She took it, but stared at him. 'Sarrie…?' she echoed.

Nikos frowned slightly. 'You prefer not to be called that?' he checked.

She gave him a look. 'Well, no, actually—because it's not my name. *Sarrie*,' she elucidated, giving him another look—one that reminded him of their first sparking encounter, 'is the name of the guy who owns the sandwich bar—hence "Sarrie's Sarnies." *My* name,' she informed him, 'is Mel.'

She paused minutely.

'Do you require a surname? Or is that a complete irrelevance because after all,' she said lightly, 'our acquaintance is going to be terminated after tonight?'

Nikos found himself frowning. *Was* their acquaintance gong to be terminated after tonight? Was that what he intended?

Do I want this to be the only time I spend with her?

Did he really want this incredible, fantastic-looking, stunningly gorgeous blonde who was making his senses reel to be with him only for one single evening?

As his eyes flickered over her he knew what his body wanted him to answer—oh, yes, indeed! No doubt about that in the slightest. But it wasn't just his body responding to the overwhelming physical attraction he felt for this fantastically beautiful woman.

What was she like as a person? As an individual? Oh, he knew she could stand up to him—stand her ground and spark verbal fire with him—but how much more was there to her than that?

Time to find out...

He smiled a warm, encompassing smile. 'Mel,' he asked her, 'don't you realise yet that I want to know a lot more about you than just your surname?'

To his distinct satisfaction he saw once again that telltale colour run fleetingly over her sculpted cheekbones. He let his gaze have the effect he wanted, and then deliberately let it soften as he relaxed against the burnished mahogany surface of the bar.

Her colour was still heightened when she answered him. 'Well, it's Cooper—just in case you should need to know. Like when you introduce me to this woman you want me to keep at bay for you.'

There was an acerbic tinge to her voice, but Nikos ignored it.

I would want her here tonight even if Fiona Pellingham were a hundred miles away.

The knowledge was sure in his head—the certainty of it absolute. Mel Cooper—so fiery and so fantastically beautiful—was a woman he wanted to know more about. *Much* more.

'So, tell me, Mel Cooper,' he said, 'first of all how do you come to be working in an establishment rejoicing in the name of "Sarrie's Sarnies"?'

Deliberately he kept his tone light, with mild humour in it. He could see her recovering her composure. The slight stain of colour ebbed. She took a sip of water from her glass. Her voice, when she spoke, had lost its acerbic tone and he was glad.

'Sarrie Silva is the uncle of a friend of mine, and he offered me the job,' she explained. 'The pay isn't bad, and I actually enjoy the work.' No need to tell him that in comparison with looking after her grandfather day in and day out for years *any* kind of alternative work was bliss. 'And best of all he lets me use the back room as a bedroom, so I effectively live there.'

Nikos's eyebrows rose. 'You *live* in the back room of a sandwich bar?'

'Yes, it's rent-free—and in London that counts for a hell of a lot,' Mel answered feelingly.

'How long have you been living like that?' Nikos asked.

'Nearly a year now. Ever since I had to move out of my childhood home.'

Nikos frowned. 'Why did you have to do that?'

'It was after my grandfather died. I'd…looked after him…' She could hear her voice twist, feel her throat tighten, feel the familiar grief at his loss ache within her, and hurried on. 'When I lost him…' the twist in her voice was more pronounced, though she tried to cover it '…I decided I'd rather rent out the house, because that would give me some steady income.'

'But you became homeless?' Nikos objected.

She gave a quick shake of her head, smiling now. 'That

didn't matter, because it was only ever going to be temporary. I'll be off abroad soon,' she explained.

She said it deliberately. It had occurred to her as she spoke that it would be prudent to make it clear to Nikos Parakis that she was going to be out of London very soon. His words to her after she'd made that jibe at him just now echoed in her head.

'Don't you realise yet that I want to know a lot more about you than just your surname?'

Echoed dangerously...

Dangerously because all she wanted to do was enjoy this evening, enjoy the lavish luxury of her surroundings and keep as tight a lid as possible on the totally predictable effect Nikos Parakis was having on her female sensibilities.

Definitely time to make it clear that she was not hanging about in London for long. This evening was nothing more than an unexpected and most important a one-off treat—one she would enjoy, make the most of, and then consign to memory. And Nikos Parakis with it.

His dark eyebrows had come together when she'd mentioned going abroad.

'Where are you thinking of travelling to?' he asked.

'No idea,' she replied insouciantly, taking a sip of her water. 'Spain, probably—wherever I can get a cheap flight to.'

He looked slightly startled. 'You have no destination in mind?'

'Not really. I just want to travel—that's all. So any place is as good as another.' Her voice changed. 'Wherever I go it will be an adventure.'

Nikos took another sip of his martini. 'Where have you travelled so far in your life?' he asked.

'Nowhere. That's the whole point,' Mel replied.

There was emotion in her voice—Nikos could hear it. He could also see the enthusiasm in her face…the excitement. Could see, too, how it made her eyes sparkle, lighting up her face. Enhancing her stunning beauty.

It was a beauty, he knew, from all his long-honed masculine experience, that would cause total havoc amongst the entire male population of the world once she was out in it. Probably too much havoc…

'Are you going with friends?' he asked.

Behind his innocuous question he knew another one lurked. *Are you going with a boyfriend…?*

But of course she wasn't. If she were, she wouldn't have accepted his invitation tonight, would she?

The knowledge that she was unattached gave him satisfaction. More satisfaction than her answer to his question.

Mel shook her head. 'No, just solo. I'm sure I'll make friends as I go.'

'Well, be careful,' he found himself warning her. 'There are parts of the world where solo travellers—let alone female ones—are not advised to go.'

Her mouth tightened. 'I can look after myself.'

Nikos's expression was wry. 'Yes, I know,' he said, his voice dry. 'You can go twelve rounds verbally—no problem. But…' He held up a hand. 'All the same, stick to tourist areas—that's my advice.'

For a moment it looked as if she was going to argue the point, for he could see the warlike sparkle in her eyes. Then it subsided.

'OK, OK…' Mel temporised. 'I'll hire a bodyguard and lug him around with me—I get the picture,' she said, in a deliberately resigned voice.

'An excellent idea,' Nikos murmured, humour in his eyes. 'I can recommend a first-class firm offering the kind of close personal protection which I have, on occasion, engaged myself.'

Mel's expression changed. 'Good grief—are you serious?'

Nikos nodded. 'There are some…let us say *restless* places in the world, where it is advisable to have someone riding shotgun beside you.'

Her eyes widened. 'Why do you go to such places?'

'I do business there,' he answered drily. Then, at the questioning and indeed wary look in her eyes, he went on swiftly. 'And, no, before your fervid imagination carries you away, I am *not* an arms dealer. I am a very boring and tediously respectable banker,' he informed her.

'Yes, I know,' she admitted. 'I looked you up. Just in case,' she said dulcetly. 'Though of course,' she went on, allowing herself a provocative glance at him, 'I didn't think bankers *were* very respectable these days…' She paused, quirking an eyebrow questioningly. 'Or should that be *respected*?'

'Ouch!' said Nikos. He took another mouthful of his martini. 'Given the sorry economic state of the world, and the role that reckless lending by the banks has played in that, I can appreciate your scepticism. *However*,' he stressed, 'what banks *should* be doing— what I strive to do myself—is *aid* business recovery. Primarily for the Parakis Bank in Greece, which has been so badly hit by recession, but also in other parts of the world, as well.'

She was looking at him with an interested expression—no dumb blonde, it seemed—and the knowledge gladdened him.

He went on with his explication. 'The Parakis Bank is an investment bank, and we have always strived for genuine partnership with our clients—which means we take a financial hit if they lose money. It also means we have to choose clients very carefully—reckless, over-ambitious companies run by greedy, lazy people who want only to enrich themselves are not on our books. I look for clients who have a passion for the sector they are in, who understand the global trends in their markets and know where opportunities lie—who have worked hard to build their businesses so far, and who simply need a loan to get them to the next level, which is what we provide, to our mutual benefit.'

He smiled at her.

'So, have I convinced you that not all bankers are evil incarnate?' His voice was infused with wry humour.

Mel looked at him. 'It *sounds* persuasive,' she conceded.

'And are you persuadable?' he pressed.

His stance had changed subtly, and so had his tone. She heard it and broke eye contact, making herself glance away briefly, then looking back again. There was a subtext going on, she knew. One that had nothing to do with the banking industry.

She flashed a smile at him. Deliberately coruscating. Deliberately calling him on his challenge.

'Sometimes,' she said.

She let the ambiguity hang in the air. He wanted subtext—she could do subtext. Or so he could think if he wanted. Which it seemed he did. She saw long eyelashes dip over his dark expressive eyes.

'How very reassuring,' he murmured, and again Mel knew the subject was not banking or finance.

She made a face, abandoning her pose of ambiguity.

'Well, you knew that anyway, didn't you? I mean, you persuaded me to turn up here tonight,' she exclaimed, in a half-exasperated tone.

'And how incredibly glad I am that I did,' he answered, his voice openly warm. 'Or I would have missed out on having the most beautiful woman in London on my arm and being the envy of every male here.'

There was humour in his voice, too, and Mel gave a laughing shake of her head at the over-the-top compliment.

'Yeah, yeah...' she said with good humour, playing down his over-the-top compliment. Even as she spoke, though, she could feel a little thrill of gratification go through her that he had given it.

She drained the last of her mineral water and replaced the glass on the bar. 'So...' she changed the subject '...do we actually get to eat tonight? It might sound weird, considering I work in a sandwich shop, but I never get time for lunch and I'm totally starving.'

'Excellent,' said Nikos. 'The food here is outstanding—even when you're dining *en masse* as we shall be doing—so a hearty appetite is a distinct advantage.' He threw an assessing glance at her slender figure. 'I do hope you're not the type of woman who considers two lettuce leaves a feast?'

Mel laughed again. 'Not tonight, I promise you,' she assured him.

'Excellent,' he said again. 'In which case, shall we go through? I see people are beginning to make a move.'

He set his own empty martini glass on the bar and with the slightest flourish proffered his arm to Mel with a very small bow.

'Sounds good,' she said, and hooked her hand over his sleeve. 'Lead me to the food!'

Long lashes swept over dark, dark eyes, not quite hiding the glint within. 'I am yours to command,' Nikos murmured, and started to escort her forward.

Mel cocked her head at him. 'You might live to regret that rash offer,' she riposted, a smile audible in her voice.

Deep within the dark eyes that glint came again. 'I regret nothing about you whatsoever, Mel, I do assure you,' was his murmured answer.

She gave a low laugh and felt in excellent humour, for tonight was turning out to be even more enjoyable than she'd hoped it would be—and it wasn't because of the fancy venue and the chance to dress up to the nines, much as she appreciated both of those factors.

No, it was the man at her side who was giving her that buzz—as if she'd already drunk a glass of champagne and it was fizzing in her veins. The man whose strong arm was beneath her lightly resting hand, whose tall figure was at her side, and whose long-lashed, dark glinting glance was making her heart beat that enticingly bit faster...

Careful! a voice in her head was whispering, low, but urgent. *You're only with him for a single evening—remember that! So enjoy the next few hours, enjoy Nikos Parakis—his gorgeous looks, the sparky fun you're having with him—then walk away and put it in the memory box.*

She heard the voice—listened to it and knew it was telling her the truth. But as she walked out of the bar on Nikos Parakis's arm she could still feel her heart beating just that bit faster than it had ever done before...

CHAPTER FOUR

'OH, MY WORD!' Mel's exclamation was instantaneous and audible.

'Impressive, isn't it?' murmured Nikos.

'And then some.'

Mel was gazing around her at the ballroom of the hotel, now filling up with other guests taking their places for the evening. The room was quite a sight, its opulent *fin de siècle* Edwardian decor of gilding and gold satin drapery enhanced tonight by an array of damask-covered tables, each adorned with its own candelabrum and floral arrangement, as well as the glitter of crystal and silver.

Nikos led her forward. It felt good to have her on his arm. Good for multiple reasons. The main one, he reminded himself, was that having a fantastic-looking female on his arm was exactly what he'd planned for this evening to keep Fiona Pellingham at bay. But he was also increasingly aware, with every minute he was spending in Mel's company, that even without the other woman's presence here tonight, he would still want Mel with him.

Thee mou, what man wouldn't want this golden-haired goddess at his side? What man wouldn't desire her…?

'I think that's our table—just over there,' he murmured, pulling his thoughts to heel, indicating their places with a slight nod.

As they approached he realised that one of the several guests already seated was the woman whose presence had inspired him to make his choice of partner for this evening. Fiona Pellingham had turned her dark brunette head towards him and was levelling her dusky gaze at him with an intensity that made him even more glad of Mel at his side.

'That's her, isn't it?' he heard Mel say out of the corner of her mouth in a low voice. 'The pesky female who's got the unrequited hots for you?'

'Alas, yes,' Nikos replied. 'And it would seem,' he went on, his voice low, too, 'that she has taken exception to your presence.'

Fiona's gaze was, indeed, gimlet-eyed, and Nikos could see that his arrival with Mel on his arm was *not* what the other woman had wanted to see.

'What a pity,' Mel returned.

There was a sweet acidity in her voice now, and Nikos glanced at her.

'Don't let her put you down.' he said, with sudden warning in his voice.

A shaft of concern went through him. Fiona Pellingham was a high-flying career professional in a top job—and she hadn't got there by being sweetness and light to others…especially to other women.

But his concern was unnecessary.

'I wouldn't dream of it,' Mel assured him sweetly, and Nikos was instantly reminded of just how unput-downable Mel could be. He should know!

As they joined their table the other men present got to their feet and Nikos greeted them. He knew one or two professionally, and Fiona introduced the others. His greeting to Fiona was urbane—and hers, he noted observantly, was unruffled: a manner that did not go with the assessing expression in her eyes when they turned to the fabulous blonde beauty on Nikos's arm as he introduced his dinner partner.

'Hi,' said Mel casually, with a dazzling smile.

With not the slightest sign of apprehension she settled herself down at the table in one of the two remaining spaces. Nikos took his place beside her, opposite Fiona. He could see that the other males present were taking in Mel's fantastic looks, despite the presence of their own partners.

A waiter glided up to the table and started the business of pouring wine and water, while another circled with bread rolls.

Mel shook out the stiff linen napkin at her place and draped it over her lap. Then she dug into the basket of warm bread rolls and helped herself.

'I skipped lunch,' she said cheerfully, and reached for the butter dish, where tiny pats of butter floated in iced water.

She busied herself tearing the bread roll in half and applying butter to it while all around her the rest of the party started to chat. The conversation was mostly about how they knew or knew of each other, and that, Mel realised, was through their work—which was, not surprisingly, all to do with finance, corporate stuff and the City in general.

She tucked into her roll and with half an ear listened to the chit-chat. With the other half she took the measure of the female whose intentions towards Nikos Parakis she was here to block.

Fiona Pellingham was very, very attractive, with her svelte, chic brunette looks enhanced by a clearly top-end designer evening dress in deep ruby-red. Mel had quickly assessed that Fiona was very much put out about her own presence.

The other two women present were not in Fiona's league looks-wise, but they were dressed elegantly for the evening and had the appearance of being long-time partners of the men they were with.

Everyone, Mel decided, seemed perfectly amiable members of their own class and background—which was about a thousand times more privileged than her own. But so what? She wasn't picking up hostility from anyone except Fiona, and she was being accepted for what she was: namely, Nikos Parakis's 'plus one' for the evening.

While the others chatted away in their well-bred tones, talking about the City, business and the financial world in general—which Mel found out of her league, but interesting for that very reason—she settled down to make the most of what was clearly going to be a gourmet meal.

A delicious-looking salmon terrine proved as smooth and light as she could want. It was washed down very nicely, she discovered, with the crisp, cold Chablis that was served with it.

She was just setting down her glass, enjoying the delicate bouquet, when she realised she was being directly addressed.

'So, what line are *you* in, Mel?'

It was the man sitting next to Fiona who had addressed her. The question had been politely asked, and Mel saw no reason not to answer in the same way. At her side, though, she could sense that Nikos had gone on the alert, ready to intervene. But she ignored him.

'FMCG,' she replied easily. 'Food retail. I've been

researching market segmentation and seasonal versus time-of-day product-matching against predicted demand.'

'Interesting,' her questioner responded. 'Are you with one of the big retail analysts?'

Mel shook her head. 'No, this is independent research—directly customer-facing.'

Beside her, she could swear she heard Nikos make a noise in his throat that sounded distinctly like a choke.

'What will you be doing with the data?' This from one of the others around the table.

'Oh, it will go to my client to support his expansion strategy,' she answered airily.

'And is that something that the Parakis Bank will be funding?'

Fiona's voice was superficially sweet, but Mel could hear the needles in it.

Before she could reply, though, Nikos's voice interceded. 'I'd have to wait until turnover reaches an appropriate level,' Mel heard him say. His voice was dry.

She turned to him, her eyes glinting. 'I'll hold you to that,' she said lightly.

Then, deciding that Sarrie's business expansion plans—let alone her own role in his business—had better not get any more probing right now from all these high-powered City folk who dealt in turnovers of millions of pounds, she changed the subject. Time to disarm Fiona…

'Nikos was telling me,' she said, directly addressing the other woman, 'what a rising star you are, and how much you've achieved.' She made her voice warm and her smile genuine.

A slightly startled, but gratified expression crossed

Fiona's face. 'Well, it's been hard work,' she acknowledged.

There was a definite thaw in her voice now—Mel was sure of it. She pressed on.

'How real is the glass ceiling in the City?' she asked, and widened her question to include the other two women there. 'You seem to be unhindered by it.' She went back to Fiona and let her approbation show in her face.

'It does take determination to break through it,' Fiona replied.

One of the other women nodded in agreement. 'And not having babies,' she exclaimed feelingly.

'The dreaded "mommy track".' Mel grimaced. 'It's still the ultimate dilemma, isn't it, for women? Career versus family.'

Just as she'd hoped, the conversation took off along the well-trodden path of whether high-flying women could have babies without jeopardising their careers and she left them to it. It was a vigorous debate, with one of the female guests strongly defensive about the 'mommy track', and Fiona and the other woman saying bluntly that families would just have to wait.

At Mel's side, she felt Nikos lean closer in to her.

'FMCG?' she heard him query heavily. One arched eyebrow was lifted interrogatively.

Mel turned to him and smiled sweetly. 'Fast-moving consumer goods—surely you know *that*, Nikos?'

His dark eyes glinted. 'And so do you, it seems.' His voice was dry now, with a hint of surprise in it.

Mel's gaze was limpid. 'Yes, the knowledge came courtesy of my degree in Business Studies,' she murmured. 'Oh, don't tell me you thought I was just a little blonde bimbo, Nikos, sweetie?' she mused.

The glint which was so becoming familiar to her showed in his eyes. 'Only if I feel like living dangerously,' he replied, the resigned humour in his voice audible.

Mel shot him a flashing smile of approval. 'Smart guy,' she said, with a quirk of her mouth.

'You know, I'm beginning to think I *am*. Inviting you tonight was the smartest thing I've done in quite a while,' Nikos replied, and there was something in his voice that told Mel he wasn't talking about her brainpower any more.

A tiny ripple of heat went down her veins.

Careful! The voice inside her head was sharp, and instant.

She was grateful to hear herself addressed by someone else. The question came from Fiona.

'And where do you stand yourself on the "mommy track"?'

Mel answered without hesitation. 'I'm afraid I'm pretty much indelibly focussed on personal goals and priorities at the moment,' she said, not elaborating to say that travel and globetrotting were those personal goals and priorities—not building a glittering career in FMCG data analysis. 'So right now,' she added feelingly, 'I'd definitely say I don't want a baby. Of course,' she allowed, 'I'm nowhere near your level, and never likely to be, so the whole "mommy track" thing wouldn't be the issue for me as it is for you.'

Again, her compliment on Fiona's high-powered career was well-received by its target. Mel could almost see her preening.

'Mind you,' she went on, 'there is another tricky issue that female high-flyers hit, which is the shortage of suitable partners for you in the first place. It's a pretty brutal truth that men "date down"—I mean, look at *me*. Here I am, a humble retail analyst, and I get to hang out with a guy whose family own a *bank*!'

'So how *did* you?' The needles were back in Fiona's voice.

Mel smiled disarmingly. 'Oh, Nikos can be so very… *persuasive* when he sets his mind to it,' she purred, in an outrageously over-the-top style, clearly meant to be humorous, that drew a laugh from the other guests.

Even Fiona smiled, and Mel was glad. She didn't blame the other woman for setting her sights on Nikos Parakis. She wouldn't have blamed *any* woman for doing so. With or without a bank in his family, Nikos was the kind of man that every female in town would make a beeline for.

And go weak at the knees over.

Like I'm doing?

The darting question—warning?—came before she could stop it.

At her side she could hear his deep tones take up the conversational baton.

'You've no idea how hard I had to work to get Mel here,' Nikos was saying lightly. 'In the end I think it was this venue that swung it for her.'

'It's certainly fabulous,' she agreed warmly, glancing around once more at the opulent ballroom.

'All the Viscari hotels have this level of cachet,' one of men commented. 'Something that sets them apart from the common run of luxury hotels.'

'Oh, yes, absolutely,' enthused his partner. 'I think my favourite so far has to be the one in Florence.'

The conversation moved into a lively discussion about just which of the ultra-luxurious Viscari hotels was the very best of all, and Mel left them to it.

The main course was being served, and she got stuck in with definite enthusiasm. The lamb melted in her mouth, and the Burgundy washed it down to perfection.

'To think I was going to turn this down,' she murmured sideways to Nikos.

He turned his head to glance down at her. 'Enjoying yourself?'

'Oh, yes,' she breathed. 'You know, I could definitely, *definitely* get used to this.'

Something flickered across his eyes. 'Well, enjoy...' he murmured, and reached for his wine glass.

Mel found she was lifting hers, too. There was a clink as the rims met together.

'To all my good ideas, Mel,' he murmured, and his eyes were like dark, melting chocolate.

Except that the melting sensation seemed to be inside her as he spoke.

She took a mouthful of the wine, hoping it would steady her, then got back to focussing on the gourmet food she was eating. That, at least, was a safe thing to do.

Beside her, Nikos's long lashed eyes rested on her averted face. There was speculation in his gaze. As if he were asking himself a question.

A question that had the dazzling beauty that was Mel Cooper at its heart.

Mel sighed luxuriously and leant her head back against the soft leather headrest of the car seat. 'This,' she announced extravagantly, 'has been the best evening *ever*.'

Nikos, sitting beside her in the back of the chauffeur-driven car, turned his head towards her and smiled. 'I'm glad you enjoyed yourself,' he replied.

'Definitely,' she assured him, turning towards him.

Their eyes met. Mel could see, even in the dim light of the car's interior as it made its way through the nearly deserted streets of London long after the midnight hour, that there was an expression in them that made half of her want to pull her own gaze away immediately, because that was the most prudent thing to do, and half of her want to go on letting her gaze entwine with his.

For a moment she almost let her gaze slide away—then didn't. The evening was going to end very soon now, and she was going to make the most of the short time left.

Make the most of Nikos.

He was just too damn gorgeous for her to do anything else.

It was a thought that had been forming all evening and now, with the end fast approaching, cocooned in the privacy of the car, she let herself indulge in the last luxury of gazing at him, drinking him in. She could feel the wine she had drunk with dinner filling her veins, could feel its effects upon her, but she didn't care. Right now it seemed good—*very* good—just to enjoy the moment.

'That's a pretty definite vote of approval,' Nikos said. His mouth quirked.

She tilted her head slightly. She must remind herself of just why Nikos had taken her with him this evening. Not for her own sake, but to serve as a foil against another woman's unwanted attentions. It would be sensible not to forget that. Especially when they were alone together in this confined space, with the driver behind his screen and the anonymous streets beyond.

'Do you think Fiona will try and pursue you again?' she asked.

The quirk deepened. 'Hopefully not.' The dark eyes were veiled as his long lashes swept down momentarily. 'Not now you've introduced her to Sven.'

Mel gave a gurgle of laughter. 'He's not called *Sven*,' she remonstrated. 'He's called Magnus—and anyway his name doesn't matter. Only that he's a Viking hunk and runs some trendy Nordic telecoms company, which means that Fiona can consider him dateable.'

'Let's hope he considers *her* dateable. It was *you* he was chatting up when you disappeared off to the powder room,' Nikos retorted.

There was, he realised as he spoke, a discernible bite in his voice. Seeing Mel walk back to their table with the 'Viking hunk' at her side had sent a primitive growl through him. Only when she'd made a point of introducing the Viking to Fiona and leaving them to it had the growl subsided.

'I let him—precisely because I wanted to hand him over to Fiona,' Mel riposted. 'I felt genuinely bad, cutting her out—she needed a consolation prize.'

'Well, I hope Sven keeps her busy—and away from *me*,' he replied.

'Happy to have been of use.' Mel smiled with exaggerated sweetness.

'And I'm *very* grateful to you, I assure you...'

There was a husk in Nikos's voice as he spoke—she could hear it. Could feel it vibrating deep within her. The humour of a moment ago was gone, and suddenly the breath was tight in Mel's lungs.

She knew she had to break that gaze holding her motionless like this, making her breathless, but it was impossible to move. Impossible to breathe. Impossible to do anything other than just sit there, her head turned towards Nikos, feeling him so close, so very, *very* close to her...

Then she realised something had changed. The car

had stopped moving. She jerked forward, jolting her gaze free to look out of the passenger seat window.

'We're here,' she said. Her voice sounded staccato.

Breaking that compelling, unbreakable gaze had freed her. Freed her to get out of the car, go back into Sarrie's sandwich bar and bid farewell to the evening. Farewell to Nikos Parakis.

A terrible sense of flatness assailed her. The evening was definitely, *definitely* over. The flatness was crushing. Her brief encounter with Nikos Parakis was at an end.

The chauffeur was opening the passenger door for her and, gathering her skirts, she made herself get out. The night air seemed chilly…sobering. As if all the fizz had gone out of everything. She knew that the alcohol in her bloodstream was exacerbating her reaction, but the knowledge didn't help counter it.

Nikos followed her out, giving a brief dismissive nod to the driver, who got back into his seat at the front of the car.

Mel painted a bright smile on her face. 'Thank you for a fabulous evening,' she said. 'I had the best time ever. I hope Fiona is now duly convinced that she doesn't stand a chance with you, and focusses on her Nordic telecoms hunk instead,' she rattled out.

In a moment the evening would truly be over. Nikos would bid her goodnight and she would get the sandwich bar keys out of her bag and go inside. Nikos would get back into his chauffeur-driven car, and go off to his fancy apartment, back to his glittering, luxurious life filled with tuxedos and five-star hotels and champagne.

She'd go back to making sandwiches. And to booking a flight on a budget airline, heading for the Spanish *costas*.

She waited for the customary little thrill of anticipation that always came when she thought about her future life—but it didn't come. Instead an unexpected chill of despondency sifted through her. How could something that only a few hours ago had been her sole burning ambition now seem so...*un*burning?

Because a few hours ago I hadn't spent the evening with Nikos Parakis!

Had she sighed? She couldn't tell. Could only tell that she was making herself stretch out her hand, as if for a brisk farewell handshake. A handshake to end the evening with before she walked back into her own life.

'Thank you,' she said again. 'And goodnight.'

She would do this neatly and briskly and they would go their separate ways. He to his world, she to hers. They had been ships that had bumped briefly into each other and were now back on course to their original destinations. And that was that.

You had fun—now it's over. Accept it. Accept it graciously and go indoors.

Right now.

And stop looking at him!

But she could not stop staring at him, or gazing into his ludicrously gorgeous face and imprinting it on to her memory.

She felt her hand taken. Steeled herself to give the brisk, brief handshake that was appropriate. Nikos Parakis wasn't a date—this whole evening had been a set-up...nothing more than that. She'd done what she'd been asked to do, had had a wonderful time herself, and now it was time to bow out.

So why did she feel so damn reluctant to do so?

She could feel the blood pulsing in her veins, feel her awareness of his searing masculinity, his ludicrous good looks, as she stood on the bleak bare London pavement at two in the morning, the night air crystal in her lungs. She seemed ultra-aware of the planes and contours of his face, the dark sable of his hair, the faint aromatic scent of his skin and the shadowed darkening of his jaw.

Why, oh, why was she just stuck here, unable to tear herself away, while she felt the warm, strong pressure of his hand taking hers? He was folding his other hand around hers as well, drawing her with effortless strength a little closer to him. Looking down at her, his long-lashed eyes holding hers just as effortlessly as she gazed helplessly up at him.

'Goodnight—and thank you for coming with me this evening.' There was a husk in his voice that belied the prosaic words.

Her hand was still enclosed in his and she was standing closer to him now. So close that she could feel her breasts straining, as if she wanted only to press forward, to bind herself against the strong column of his body. She longed to feel that sheathed muscled strength against the pliant wand of her own body, to lift her mouth to his and wind her fingers up into the base of his neck, draw that sculpted mouth down upon hers...

It shook her...the intensity of the urge to do so. Like a slow-motion film running inside her head, she felt her brain try to reason her way out of it. Out of the urge to reach for him, to kiss him...

It had been so, so long since she had kissed a man—any man at all. And longer still since she had given free rein to the physical impulse of intimacy. Jak had left for Africa long ago, and since then there had been only a few perfunctory dates, snatched before caring for her grandfather had become all-consuming.

And now here she was, gazing up at a man who was

the most achingly seductive man she'd ever encountered, wanting only to feel his mouth on hers, his arms
around her.

As if he heard her body call to him he bent his head
to catch her lips, and his mouth was as soft as velvet.
As sensuous as silk.

Dissolving her completely.

She moved against him and felt her breasts crushed
against his torso, that strong wall of steely muscle. Her
other hand lost its grip on her evening bag. It fell to the
ground, letting her freed hand do what it so wanted to
do—to slide beneath the fall of his tuxedo jacket, her
fingers gliding around his back, strong and smooth and
so, so warm to her touch.

Her eyes fluttered shut as she gave herself to a slow,
velvet kiss that seemed to lift her right off her feet, that
absorbed every part of her consciousness. Gave herself
to the sensuous caress of his lips on hers. Assured, expert, arousing…he knew exactly how to glide and tease
and coax her lips to part for his, to deepen the kiss with
skilled touch until he had everything of her he sought.

How long he kissed her for she didn't know. She
knew only that her fingers were pressing into his
back, holding him fast against her, and that her hand,
still crushed in his, was being held in the valley of
her breasts, whose peaks were taut against his chest
and beneath whose surface her heart was beating like
a soaring bird.

His mouth let hers go and he was looking down
at her—at her parted lips, her dazed eyes, her heated
cheeks. His face was unreadable, but there was a shadow
somewhere deep in the dark pools of his eyes… There
were words he wanted to speak—but he kept silent…

How long she stood there, just gazing at him, overwhelmed by his kiss, she couldn't tell. Something ran between them. She could not quite tell what, but she would not let herself read that wordless message. Would only, with a breathy little catch in her throat, step back from him, separating their bodies.

Then, with a jerky movement, she bent her knees and scooped up her evening bag, made her fingers open the clasp, extract her keys. She focussed on movement, focussed on stepping towards the door, unlocking it, opening it. When she was half inside, she turned.

He hadn't moved. He was still standing there, watching her. Behind him, his car purred silently at the kerb. It would take him back to his world and she would never see him again.

There was a sensation of tightness in her chest suddenly, as if breathing were impossible. Her eyes rested on his outline one last time.

'Goodbye, Nikos,' she heard her own voice say, softly now. Then she turned away, heading towards the back room.

The evening was over now. Quite over.

Outside on the bare pavement Nikos went on standing for a while, motionless. Then, with a sudden jerky movement of his body, he turned on his heel and got back into the car.

It moved off along the deserted road.

In his head, that wordless message hung.

It was a message he did not want to hear—never wanted to hear. Had spent his life blocking out.

A message that challenged all the precepts by which he lived his life.

CHAPTER FIVE

WITH A YAWN, Mel set the tap running to fill the hot water urn and started her routine preparations for opening up the sandwich bar. But her thoughts were a million miles away, remembering everything about the evening before. It filled her head as if she were there again, reliving it all. Reliving, most of all, that melting goodnight kiss from Nikos…

For a moment—just a moment—she experienced again that sense of questioning wonder she'd felt as they'd gazed into each other's eyes. Then, with an impatient shake of her head, she shook it from her. For three long years she'd had no romance in her life at all—no wonder she was feeling overwhelmed, having been kissed by an expert kisser like Nikos Parakis!

Her mouth gave a wry little twist. He'd have acquired that expertise by kissing scores of females in his time. Kissing, romancing and moving on. Keeping his romances simple—transient. Avoiding serious relationships.

Well, she could sympathise. Right now, with freedom beckoning, that was the way *she* saw things, too—no commitments, no complications. Just enjoying light-hearted, fun-time romance if it came her way…

She made a face as she set croissants to warm. Well,

it wasn't going to come her way courtesy of Nikos Parakis—that was for sure. He'd kissed her goodnight and headed back to his own life. He hadn't wanted anything more of her than that single evening.

She paused in the act of reaching for a packet of butter from the fridge.

What if he had? What if he'd asked for more?

Like feathers sifting through her mind, she felt again that moment when he'd finished kissing her—when they'd parted but had still simply been looking at each other, their eyes meeting. A message had passed between them…

A message she hadn't been able to read—*wouldn't* read.

She shook her head, clearing the memory. What did it matter anyway? Nikos was out of her life as swiftly as he'd come into it and she wasn't going to be seeing him again. That melting goodnight kiss was what she'd remember of him—the final icing on the *amuse-bouche* that had been the evening she'd spent with him.

And in the meantime she had a loaf of bread to butter.

Nikos was running. Running fast. But not fast enough. He upped the speed on the treadmill, his feet pounding more rapidly as his pace picked up. But he still could not outrun the memory in his head.

The memory of his kiss with Mel.

It kept replaying in his head…the feel of her mouth, soft and sensuous beneath his, that taste of heady sweetness in her lips…and it was still doing so now, back in Athens, over a week later. He was still remembering the words he had not spoken—the words he'd come so close, so very, *very* close to murmuring to her…

*Don't let the evening end now—come back with me—
come back and stay the night with me...*

But, as they'd drawn apart, as he'd finally relinquished her mouth, her soft, slender body still half embraced by his, she'd gazed up at him with that helpless, dazed expression in her beautiful eyes and the words had died on his lips. That wordless, unspoken message that had flowed between them had been silenced.

He knew why.

To have invited her to stay the night with him would not have been fair to her. He did not know her well enough to risk it—after such intimacy she might expect of him what he could not, *would* not give. He could not offer her anything other than a brief, fleeting romance.

Oh, he was no Lothario, getting a malign pleasure out of rejecting women after they'd fallen for him. He would far rather they *didn't* fall for him. Far rather they shared his terms of engagement. His short-term view.

Because the best relationships were short-term ones. He had ample personal evidence of that. His jaw tightened. And ample evidence that those who did not adhere to that view ended up in a mess. A mess that had fallout for others, as well.

Like children.

He knew only too well, with bitterly earned self-knowledge, that was why he did not risk long-term relationships. Because they could become a trap—a trap to be sprung, confining people in relationships that became prisons. Prisons they were incapable of leaving.

His expression darkened. That was what had happened to his parents. Locked in a destructive relationship that neither of them would or could relinquish. A macabre, vicious dance he'd had to watch as a boy. Still had to watch whenever he spent time with them and saw them gouging at each other like two wounded, snarling animals trapped in the same locked enclosure.

Why the hell they hadn't divorced years ago he could never fathom. Whenever he'd challenged either of them as to why they'd stuck together they'd both turned to him and said, 'But it was for *your* sake we stayed together. So you would have a stable home. There's nothing worse than a child growing up in a broken home.'

He gave a choke of bitter laughter now. If that had been their reasoning, he wasn't grateful for it. He'd headed for university in the USA with relief, then found his own apartment once he'd graduated and come back to take his place at the family bank.

He was still trying to avoid their recriminations about each other. He left them to it. Heard them out, but did not really listen. Got back to his own life as quickly as he could. Took up with women who would never be like his mother, would never turn him into a man like his father. Women who understood, right from the off, that while he spent time with them he would be devoted to them—but when that time ended he'd simply move on. When it came to the goodbye kiss, goodbye was what it meant.

Would Mel have understood that?

That was what he did not know—had not risked asking that night in London. Which was why he had to put that evening behind him, that kiss behind him—why he had to stop remembering it.

But that was what seemed so impossible, however hard he tried.

The treadmill slowed, coming to the end of its programme, and he stepped off, heading for the weights. But even as he pumped his muscles he could still feel the memory of Mel in his arms, feel the sensual power of that amazing kiss. It haunted him wherever he went, whatever he did.

Back at work, he made yet another determined effort to move on. Keeping busy must surely help. His diary for today was full, and tomorrow morning he was flying to Geneva. Then he was scheduled for Frankfurt, and after that there was some banking conference somewhere he was due to speak at. Where was it being held? Somewhere long-haul, he thought. New York? Atlanta? Toronto? Was that it?

But as he clicked on the link a completely different venue sprang up on his screen.

Bermuda.

An offshore banking haven, only a couple of hours' flight off the US East Coast, and best of all a subtropical paradise. He'd been before on business, but always on his own. The beautiful island just cried out for spending more time there, R&R—and not on his own…

The thought was in his head before he could stop it. Instantly he sought to eject it, delete it, but it was no good. It was there, indelible, right at the front of his mind. He knew exactly who should be with him on such a break—exactly who it was he wanted there.

Instantly he summoned all the arguments against it—the arguments that had stopped him whispering the words he'd wanted to whisper to Mel—but they were being drowned out. Drowned out by a cacophony of counterarguments.

She longs to go abroad—anywhere in the world. Bermuda would be perfect for her. It's not the kind of place she'd ever get to on her own—not the place for budget backpacking tourists—but with me it would be possible. I could show her a place she would otherwise never see.

It was a brilliant idea—just brilliant. And now it was in his head he could not obliterate it. It would not be silenced.

He stared out over his office, his thoughts churning. Overwhelming him with their power.

Why do I assume she would want more from me than a simple holiday romance? Why do I fear she would want something deeper, more lasting? Why not ask her and see? After all, she told me she wanted to see the world, travel everywhere—does that sound like a woman who wants to tie me down or get involved in a heavy relationship?

Even as he thought it alarm snatched at him. When had she said she was leaving London? Setting off on her travels? She might already be in Spain for all he knew.

The thought was like a blow. If she were gone, how would he ever find her?

She could disappear completely and I'd have no clue where she was!

Without realising it he'd reached for his phone. Urgency impelled him, overriding everything else. Only one thing filled his head—Mel, as she'd been that evening, so fantastically beautiful, so soft and ardent in his arms, the sweetness of her mouth, the honey of her lips.

I won't let her disappear from my life. Not without seeing whether I can't persuade her to come with me!

His secretary answered the phone instantly. Mood soaring, he gave her his instructions.

'Cancel Geneva and Frankfurt. Book me to London tomorrow instead.'

'Sarrie, here are the accounts for while you were away. I think they're looking quite good. I made a few tweaks to the menu, and tried out a few new things. I think they've worked.'

She'd added more boxed salads for diet-conscious customers, and sourced a scrumptious organic carrot cake for when they fell off their diets, keeping careful tabs on costs, sales and profits.

A sudden shaft of memory assailed her—of how she'd spun that impressive-sounding line about FMCG customer-facing research at that charity do, surrounded by all those high-flying career women. She hadn't meant it seriously...it had just been to amuse Nikos...

No. No thinking about Nikos.

No remembering that evening. And no remembering that devastating goodnight kiss.

This time tomorrow I'll be in Spain, and if I want romance I'll set my cap at some sultry Spaniard. That will take my mind off Nikos Parakis.

It had better.

Because so far nothing was taking her mind off him and everything was reminding her of him—even packing for Spain. When she'd refolded the evening gown she'd worn for him memories had rushed back into her head—memories of how he'd gazed at her when she'd glided up to him in the hotel, how he'd smiled at her, how at the end of that wonderful, fabulous evening he'd taken her into his arms to kiss her...

Stop it. Just...stop it. It's over, he's gone, and he's not coming back into your life.

That was what she had to remember. That was what she had to think about.

Not about the way he kissed me...turning me inside out and back again...

Most of all not wishing there had been more than just a single kiss...

If he'd kissed me again—swept me off my feet—if I'd gone with him—

No, she must not think of that—definitely, *definitely* not that!

And anyway—she dropped a clanging reality check down through her hectic thoughts—he *hadn't* kissed her again, had he? And there'd been no sweeping her off her feet, had there? No, he'd just kissed her goodnight and gone. The evening had ended and her brief, fleeting acquaintance with Nikos Parakis had ended, too.

Time for her to move on. To put Nikos Parakis out of her head for once and for all.

She heard the shop door open and, leaving Sarrie in the back room with the accounts and her packed suitcase, went through to serve their latest customer.

And froze.

'Hello, Mel,' said Nikos Parakis.

Emotions surged within her. Mixed emotions. Fighting each other. One emotion—the rational one that went with her head, that went with her packed suitcase, her airline ticket to Spain and her new life—was dismay. Just as she was finally on the point of leaving London, making a new start, putting him and their brief, intoxicating encounter behind her, *this* had to happen.

But that emotion didn't last. Couldn't last. It was flooded out by a far more vivid one.

Nikos was here—right here—just the other side of the counter, half a metre away and exactly as she remembered him. Tall, ludicrously, ridiculously good-looking, with his sable hair and his olive skin, and his eyes…oh, his eyes…all dark and velvety, with lashes you could sweep floors with. And the look in them was turning her stomach inside out.

The rush of emotion was unstoppable, palpable. Her face lit. She couldn't stop it.

'Nikos!'

The long lashes swept down over his dark, gold-flecked eyes. 'I'm glad you're still here,' he said.

She bit her lip. 'I'm flying off tomorrow morning,' she said. Did her voice sound breathless? She didn't know—didn't care. Knew only that her heart had started pounding, her pulse racing. Nikos Parakis—no longer just a memory of a fabulous evening, a goodnight kiss to remember all her life—was here, now, right in front of her in real, glorious flesh.

He smiled, and the tug of his mouth was doing things to Mel's stomach that it shouldn't—but did all the same.

'Then I've arrived just in time,' he said.

She stared. 'In time for what?' she asked automatically.

He changed his stance, became relaxed somehow. It made Mel aware all over again of the long, lean length of him, of the way the jacket of his suit fitted like a glove across his shoulders, the way his silver-buckled leather belt snaked around his narrow hips, the way the pristine white of his shirt moulded the strong wall of his chest. She felt the force of his physical impact on her assailing her senses like an onslaught of potent awareness...

'In time to ask you something,' he elucidated.

There was an expression in his face now that Mel could not read. Truth to tell, she could not do anything other than gaze at him, feeling her heart-rate soaring in her chest.

The intensity of emotion inside her kicked once more. He was speaking again. Saying something that knocked the breath out of her. Stilled her completely.

'Would you...?' Nikos said, the eyes resting on her veiled suddenly, she realised, even though they met hers. 'Would you consider a…detour…before you head for Spain?'

There was a husk in his voice as he put the question to her. The question he'd cancelled his engagements for, flown to London for. He'd driven straight here from Heathrow and walked into Sarrie's Sarnies to invite this fantastically beautiful woman, whom he could not get out of his head, to come to Bermuda with him.

Seeing her again, now, he wanted to hear only one answer to the question. Just seeing her in the flesh had slammed the truth of that into him with the full force of a tangible impact. He'd felt a kick go through him—a stab of exultation. Desire had coursed through him like a flash flood.

Would she accept what he was offering her? Share a few weeks with him, no more than that, before she headed off on her travels and they went their separate ways?

His eyes rested on her and his brow quirked. She was looking at him. Was it with a wary expression in her luminous blue eyes?

'I don't understand…' she said.

He elucidated. 'I'm due to speak at a conference in Bermuda next week. I was wondering…' his long lashes dipped over his eyes as he studied her reaction '…if you'd like to come with me?'

She didn't answer—not for a full second. She'd gone very still. Then her expression changed.

'Don't tell me Fiona Pellingham is going to the conference, as well?' she asked.

Mel's voice was dry. But her emotions, whirling around inside her, were not dry at all—they felt as if they were in a spin cycle, like turbulent laundry. Was

Nikos *really* standing there asking her to go to Bermuda with him?

He shook his head immediately. 'Nothing like that,' he assured her. His expression changed. 'This is just for you and me.'

She was staring at him still. 'Why?' she asked.

'Why?' he echoed. Then he smiled. 'Because, Mel Cooper, I can't get you out of my head—that's why. One kiss,' he told her, 'was not enough.' He paused. '*Will* you come with me?'

He could see her face working—see the emotions flitting through her gaze. He took a breath. Before this went further he had to speak—anything else would not be fair.

'A holiday, Mel—that's what I'm asking you to share with me. A holiday—fun, relaxation, good times. With each other. A few weeks in the sun. On a beautiful island which,' he said, 'I suspect is probably not on your itinerary but which, I do promise you, you *will* enjoy.' He paused. 'What do you say?' he asked.

She was silent still.

His voice changed. 'Mel, we can't deny the charge between us—it would be pointless to do so. So let's not deny it. Let's have some time with each other—a holiday—and then...' He took a breath. 'Then you go off on your travels, as you planned, and I... Well, I go back to banking. Nothing more demanding than that.'

He watched her take it in. It had been uncomfortable to spell it out, but he knew he'd had to. He wanted no deceit, no false expectations, no hope for anything more of himself than he could give her.

She'd gone very still again. She was resting her eyes on him, but not, he thought, really seeing him. It was as if she were absorbing what he'd said to her. What was behind what he'd said.

He fixed his eyes on her, waiting for her answer. Then she spoke. There was less strain in her voice now, but her tone was serious for all that.

She lifted her chin, looked right at him. 'Nikos… You gave me, without doubt, the most glamorous evening of my life. And you don't need me to tell you that that goodnight kiss would have won you a gold medal.'

The slightest tinge of humour infused her voice, and then it was gone again.

'But I really, *really* should say no to you now. It's the sensible thing to do. To say thanks, but I'm going to Spain tomorrow. I'm never going to see you again.' She closed her eyes for a moment, then opened them again. '*That's* what I've got to say to you.'

She meant it—meant every word. Of course she did. It was the only sensible thing to do. Nikos Parakis was temptation personified. How could he not be? But even with what he was offering her—a no-strings romance, a couple of weeks in the sun, in a place she'd never be likely to go to herself—she felt the ripple of danger go through her.

She'd melted like chocolate at a single kiss—what would she be like after a fortnight with him? And after a lot more than a kiss.

You melted because you haven't been kissed for years and the man who kissed you is a world champion kisser!

Her thoughts ran on…hectic, whirling around in her head…

Don't you deserve something like this? Something thrilling and wonderful and fantastic, with a man like Nikos? He's offering you exactly what you want now—a carefree, no-strings holiday romance. A few weeks of bliss and fun. Fabulous while it lasts—and unregret-ted when it's over.

His expression had changed. She didn't quite know how, but it had. He was looking at her still, but there was a glint in his eye—a gleam of humour and of ex-pectation.

'And are you?' he asked. His voice was limpid, his eyes lucent. '*Are* you going to say that? Say goodbye to me again?'

Mel looked at him. Heard the confidence in his voice and knew the reason for it. Knew, too, what the sensi-ble answer was—but why *should* she be sensible now? Her life was her own from now on—she could make decisions that maybe weren't sensible, but so what? *So what?*

A flutter of emotion went through her. She took it for excitement. Seized it. If a single evening with Nikos had been an *amuse-bouche* before the banquet that was to be her new life of freedom, and his melting kiss the icing on that *amuse-bouche*, then a holiday with him—and all that entailed—would be the most fabulous *entrée*.

The flutter of emotion came again. Oh, it was defi-nitely excitement. And why not?

Nikos was a gorgeously irresistible male—why should she resist him? They both wanted the same thing from each other—so why not take it?

He was quirking an eyebrow at her, waiting for her answer. A smile was curving his mouth…his eyes glinted in the sunlight.

She took a breath, lifted her chin. *Yes*, she would do it!

Her mouth split into a dazzling smile.

'So,' she said, 'when are we going?'

CHAPTER SIX

'I CAN SEE IT,' Mel's voice sounded excitedly. 'There— just coming into view!'

Nikos leant sideways in his seat, peering out of the porthole. 'So it is,' he said.

Mel gazed entranced as the deep cobalt sea beneath changed colour to a paler blue. The curving shoreline was fringed with a clear reef line, changing the colour of the sea yet again, turquoise in the lee of the little bays, with foam from the ocean swell catching on the rocks of the reef.

Could this really be happening? Could she really be gazing out over the western Atlantic, flying in a plane and descending to a subtropical, reef-fringed is- land far below?

She'd barely had time to say goodbye to Sarrie, her face flushed and her eyes as bright as sapphires with excitement as she'd seized what Nikos was offering her. And now here she was, Nikos beside her, as the plane descended to the tiny island below.

She could see houses and gardens and palm trees now, closer and closer, and then there was the tarmac of the runway and they were touching down.

'We're here!' she exclaimed.

Nikos grinned. She was reacting like a kid, but he

could see why. Hell, he was pretty damn ecstatic him-self. Here he was, his hopes utterly fulfilled, with Mel beside him, coming away on holiday with him—and she was everything he'd remembered about her. Even more beautiful… His gaze softened as it skimmed over her.

Deplaning was swift, and so was Immigration.

'It's so *British*,' exclaimed Mel, looking at the large portrait of the Queen that graced the immigration hall.

'It *is* British.' Nikos smiled. 'An Overseas Terri-tory—the last outpost of Empire. But most visitors are Americans, because it's so close to the Atlantic sea-board. You can get here from New York in a couple of hours—short enough for a weekend.'

When they left the small airport building a chauf-feured car was waiting for them. Mel spent the journey with her face pressed almost to the window, gazing at the scenery as they left the airport and started to head south.

'It will take a good forty minutes or so to reach the hotel, and we should get a good sunset there—the hotel is right on the beach,' Nikos told her.

He was thinking ahead rapidly. With jet lag, and Mel not being used to dealing with it, she would probably need an early night. He'd booked adjoining rooms at the hotel because he didn't want to rush her, or appear crass, and he knew—reluctantly—that a romantic eve-ning tonight might not be on the cards.

He continued with his tour-guide speech. 'We're by-passing the capital, Hamilton, although the old capital, St George's, is a must-see while we're here. It's one of the oldest European settlements in the New World. Most of the island south of Hamilton is covered by vil-las, as the land mass is so small here, but there are botanical gardens, and a few small agricultural plots. Of all things, Bermuda is famous for its onions.'

Mel laughed. 'It's all so incredibly *pretty*,' she said, gazing out over the stone-built houses, many of them painted in pastel shades of pink and pale green and yellow, set in lush tropical gardens with palm trees, hibiscus and vivid bougainvillaea. 'The houses have funny roofs—sort of stepped tiles.'

'It's to catch rainwater and channel it down into underground cisterns,' Nikos explained. 'There are no rivers here—the island is volcanic in origin, and the big harbours to the west are the remnants of an ancient caldera. So rainwater is essential. The island is lush, but the rainy season is only for a few months in the winter. Overall, the island is very fortunate. There are occasional hurricanes, but by and large it's clement all year round.'

Mel glanced back at him. 'Shakespeare is said to have used it as his inspiration for Prospero's magical island in *The Tempest*,' she said.

'Maybe he did. It was known to Europeans by then, and St George's was settled early in the seventeenth century. It was a dangerous place, though—the surrounding reefs are full of the wrecks of unfortunate ships.' He quirked an eyebrow at Mel. 'Do you fancy trying diving while we're here?'

Her eyes widened. '*Can* we?'

His smile warm and embracing. 'Mel, we can do anything and everything while we're here. This is our time together, and I really, *really* want you to have the time of your life.'

He did, too. It would be a joy and a pleasure to give her the holiday of her dreams—and he would take pleasure in *her* pleasure. Take pleasure—oh, such pleasure—in her altogether. Mel in his arms, his embrace, his bed...

Right now, life was very sweet indeed. This was set to be a great holiday—

'Oh, this is so *beautiful*.'

Mel's exclamation came from the heart. Sun was pouring over the breakfast terrace at the hotel, dazzling on the azure sea beyond. Palm trees waved in a deliciously light breeze, and canvas parasols shaded the breakfast tables.

Mel gazed about her, fizzing with excitement and wonder. Bermuda, the fabulous hotel, the glittering blue sea, the heat, the palm trees, the vivid exotic flowers tumbling everywhere over walls, the glimpse of a sparkling marble pool a few steps beyond the terrace—they were all real. No dream, no mere photo in a travel brochure, but all, *all* real.

And real, too, was the man standing beside her. Inside the fizzing champagne of excitement in her veins she felt her blood gave a kick, shooting adrenaline through her system.

Nikos was right here, beside her. She'd grabbed the strong, warm hand he'd held out to her and run off with him, winging across the wide Atlantic to land here, on this beautiful, gorgeous island in the sun.

She turned and grinned at him. 'It's just absolutely fantastic!' she exclaimed. 'I can't believe I'm really here.'

'Believe it,' Nikos assured her, his eyes smiling as they rested on her. Drinking her in.

Her long golden hair was caught back with a scarf, but the breeze was blowing it into a halo around her head, and her face was alight with pleasure as she gazed around, eyes wide. His breath caught at her beauty.

And the hotel was perfect—tucked away on a promontory overlooking the long, reef-fringed south shore beaches to the east and a calm, sheltered bay to the west, perfect for sailing. The accommodation was low-rise, pastel-painted cottage-style rooms, all with sea views.

'Is this where your banking conference is going to be?' she asked Nikos.

Nikos shook his head. 'No, that's taking place at one of the much larger, more modern hotels, closer to the airport.' He reached for the jug of chilled orange juice that a server had just placed on the table with a smile. 'I'll take a taxi there on the day I have to speak.' He glanced at Mel. 'Do you want to come along?'

She gave him a mischievous smile. 'I wouldn't miss it for the world,' she assured him. 'Seeing you in your natural environment.'

He made a slight face. 'My natural environment?' he echoed. 'Is that what you think?'

She looked at him. 'I don't know,' she answered. 'I don't know you well enough, Nikos.'

Her voice was sober suddenly, her expression uncertain. Did she *want* to know Nikos? Did it matter to her who he was? Wasn't he just a fantastic, gorgeous man whose company she enjoyed and who could melt her with a kiss? Wasn't that enough for her?

He reached across the table with his hand, just grazing her cheek with his fingers. The gesture was soft, fleeting. Reassuring.

'There is no rush,' he said. 'We're here to enjoy ourselves.'

The smile was in his eyes, on his lips. She nodded, relaxing now. He saw it, and was glad.

'Speaking of which…' He took a mouthful of freshly squeezed orange juice. 'What do you want to do after breakfast?'

Mel's answer was immediate. 'Hit the beach!' she enthused. 'I can't wait to get into that water. It's like something out of a travel brochure.'

'Great idea,' he agreed. 'The beach it is. We'll laze the morning away—and very possibly the afternoon, too.'

Which was exactly what they did.

After a leisurely breakfast, with Nikos regaling Mel with all he knew about Bermuda, they went back to their rooms to change into beach clothes. As she let herself into her room Mel knew she was grateful to Nikos for being sufficiently sensitive to the impulsive nature of their holiday together and reserving separate rooms.

Yes, she knew—oh, she most *certainly* knew—what she had committed herself to, but to have arrived last evening, jet-lagged as she'd been, and to have been thrust into the immediate intimacy of sharing a room— a bed—would have been too…too… Well, too awkward, really.

And definitely too rushed. When they came together—a little frisson of excitement shimmered through her at the thought—it would be when they were relaxed, comfortable with each other, and with a wonderful sense of anticipation having been built up during the day and heightened to heady passion in the evening…

Then he'll take me in his arms, kiss me as he kissed me before. But this time…oh, this time it will not be goodbye…it will be the very opposite.

Nikos and me, embracing, entwining, his mouth on

mine, his body clasped by mine, only passion and de-sire between us...

She gave her head a quick shake to clear the image.

Yes, well, that was for later. For now, she had to change into her new swimsuit, which would be christened in the turquoise waters of Bermuda.

Another little quiver of disbelief went through her as yet again the realisation of just where she was impacted. How absolutely gorgeous it all was.

Hurriedly she slipped into her swimsuit, pulling a long, loose, semi-transparent cover-up over her head and pushing her feet into flip-flops. She grabbed her beach bag and headed outdoors via the private patio, separated from Nikos's by a low grey stone wall that could be hopped over in a second.

Nikos was already waiting for her, lounging back in one of the terrace chairs at the little dining set provided. He got to his feet, and Mel's breath caught.

Board shorts in deep cobalt-blue hugged lean hips, and his torso was moulded by every square centimetre of a white short-sleeved top bearing a fashionable surfing logo. And he was sporting wrap-around sunglasses that made her want to drop her jaw gormlessly open and gaze at him.

It took a moment for her to realise that he was returning her stare. She couldn't see his eyes behind the opaque sunglasses, but that was just as well, part of her registered. The other part was trying hard to ignore the insistent fact that beneath the veiling of her cover-up and the sheer material of her swimsuit her breasts were shamelessly engorged, following an instinct that was as powerful as it was primeval...

I want him.

The stark, visceral words sounded in her head almost audibly as she stood, rooted to the spot.

'Ready for a hard day's beach-lounging?' Nikos smiled at her, the corners of his sculpted mouth crinkling.

Mel took a breath. 'All set,' she said with determined lightness, and they headed down the path that would take them to the beach below.

A line of white sunbeds had been set out along the pale sand that was already too hot to walk on. A beach steward ushered them to a pair with a little table in between them, a parasol overhead for shade, and towels draped over the foam mattresses, with more neatly folded at the end of each lounger. They settled themselves down, and the steward enquired if they would like refreshments from the beach bistro.

'OJ and sparkling mineral water, please.'

Mel smiled. How blissful just to give a request like that and know that two minutes later it would be served to her as she relaxed back on her lounger, gazing out over the sea, feeling the warmth of the day like a cocoon around her.

'This,' she announced feelingly, 'is absolute bliss.'

'No question,' agreed Nikos.

He reached across the space between their respective sunbeds and took her hand. It was an instinctive gesture, and he was hardly aware of doing it—except that the moment his fingers wound into her hers he knew it felt right.

Mel turned to look at him, then smiled. A warm, wide smile that seemed to encapsulate everything about what they had done—run off here, to this beautiful island in the sun, to have time to themselves, to have the affair that both of them wanted to have. He knew that with absolute certainty.

He gave a deep sigh of contentment and looked out to sea again. Beside him, Mel gave an echoing sigh— and then a wry little laugh.

'It's just so gorgeous,' she said, 'to lie here with absolutely nothing to do except relax on the beach. I feel utterly idle.'

Nikos turned his head to glance at her. 'That's the general idea of a holiday,' he said, amused.

She gave a semi-shrug. 'Well, I'm not used to holidays.' She glanced away, towards the brilliant azure sea glinting in the morning sunshine, then back to Nikos. 'I've waited just *so* long to start my real life—to travel as I've longed to do—that now I am I can't quite believe it. I keep feeling I should be working.'

The focus of Nikos's gaze sharpened slightly. 'Tell me,' he asked, 'why do you feel so strongly that you should be working all the time?'

He cocked an interrogative eyebrow at her, but his voice was merely mildly curious.

Mel's expression changed. Became thoughtful. But also, Nikos thought assessingly, became guarded.

'Habit, really, I suppose. Like I say, I'm not used to holidays. Not used to having time off.'

'I seem to remember you said you did waitressing in the evenings, after the sandwich bar had closed?' Nikos recalled. 'How long did you keep that kind of double shift going? It can burn you out in the end, you know.'

He sounded sympathetic, but Mel shook her head. 'Oh, no, that wasn't a problem. I was working for myself—building up my bank balance to fund my getaway. It was a joy to work, to be honest, in comparison with looking after my grandfather. *That* was—' She broke off, not finishing.

What word would describe that period of her life? Only one—*torment*. Absolute torment…

Torment to watch the grandfather she'd loved so much become more and more frail, in body and mind. Torment to be the only person who could look after him—the only person he wanted to look after him—so that she could never have a break or even the slightest amount of time to herself.

He was looking at her curiously now, and she wished she'd kept her mouth shut.

'Was he ill?' Nikos asked. Again, his voice was sympathetic.

'Yes,' she said tightly. 'His mind went.'

'Ah… Dementia can be very hard,' acknowledged Nikos.

A kind of choke sounded in Mel's voice as she answered. 'I was raised by my grandfather after my parents died when I was very little—they were killed in a car crash. My grandfather took me in to stop me going into care. That's why, when he needed care himself, it was my…my turn to look after *him*, really.'

Her voice was tight, suppressed. She didn't want to talk about this—didn't want to think about it, didn't want to remember.

Nikos was frowning. 'Surely you didn't have to cope single-handed? There must have been help available? Professional carers on call?'

Mel swallowed. Yes, there had been help—up to a point. That hadn't been the problem. It was hard to explain—and she didn't want to. Yet somehow, for some reason—maybe it was her release, finally, from the long years of caged confinement at her grandfather's side as he made the slow, dreadful descent into dementia and eventual death—she heard the words burst from her.

'He didn't want anyone else.'

Her voice was low, the stress in it audible to Nikos.

'He only ever wanted me—all the time. He couldn't even bear to let me out of his sight, and he used to follow me around or get distressed and agitated if I just went into another room, let alone tried to go out of the house. He'd wander around at night—and of course that meant that I couldn't sleep either…not with him awake and wandering like that…'

Her voice was shaking now, but still words poured out of her, after all the months and years of watching her grandfather sink lower and lower still.

'It's what the dementia did to him. He was lost in his dark, confused mind, and I was the only thing in it he recognised—the only thing he wanted, the only thing he clung to. If I tried to get a carer from an agency to sit with him he'd yell at her, and he'd only calm down when I was back in the room again. It was pitiful to see. So no matter how exhausting it was, I just couldn't abandon him—not to outside carers—nor put him into a nursing home. How *could* I? He was the only person in the world I loved—the only person in the world who loved *me*—and I was absolutely adamant I would take care of him to the end.'

Her expression was tormented.

Nikos's voice was quiet, sombre. 'But the end did come?' he said.

She swallowed the hard, painful lump in her throat. 'It went on for three years,' she said, her voice hollow. 'And by the time the end came he didn't know me— didn't know anyone. I could only be relieved—dreadful though it is to say it—that he was finally able to leave his stricken body and mind.'

She shut her eyes, guilt heavy in her heart.

'I'd started to long for the end to come—for his sake, and for mine, too. Because death would finally release him—' She swallowed again, her voice stretched like wire. 'And it would finally release me, too…let me claim my own life back again.'

She fell silent—horrified by what had poured out of her, shutting her eyes against the memory of it, haunted by the guilt that assailed her. And yet she remembered that terrible, silent cry of anguish at the captivity his illness had held her in.

She'd never said anything of her anguish before—never said anything of those heartbreakingly difficult, impossible years she'd spent as her grandfather's carer. And yet here she was, spilling her heart to a man who was little more than a stranger still…

Beside her, Nikos had stilled as he heard her out. Now, slowly, instinctively, he reached across for the hand that she was clenching and unclenching on her chest as she relived those tormented years she'd spent at her ailing grandfather's side. She felt his palm close over her fist, stilling her.

'You did your very best for him,' he said quietly. 'You stayed with him to the end.'

He took a breath, the tenor of his voice changing.

'And now you deserve this time of freedom from care and responsibility.' His voice warmed and he squeezed her hand lightly, then let it go. 'You deserve the most fantastic holiday I can give you.'

She felt her anguish ease, and took a long, deep breath before opening her eyes to look at him.

'Thank you,' she said, and her eyes were saying more than mere words could.

For a moment their gazes held, and then Nikos deliberately lightened the mood. He wanted to see her happy again.

'Tell me,' he said, 'would you like to take a boat out sometime?'

Her expression lit as she followed his cue. Glad to do so. Glad to move away from the long, dreadful years that were gone now. Her grandfather, she hoped, was in a far better place, reunited with his long-lost family. And she was free to live her own life, making her own way in the world, enjoying her precious, fleeting youth untrammelled by cares and responsibilities. Revelling in all the new experiences she could.

Like skimming across the brilliantly azure sea that lay before her.

'Yes, please! I've never been on a boat.'

His eyebrows rose. 'Never?'

She shook her head. 'No, never,' she confirmed. 'My grandfather didn't like the water. It was as much as he'd do to go on seaside holidays when I was a child. He would sit in his deckchair, in long trousers and a long-sleeved shirt, and wish he were elsewhere while I played, merrily building sandcastles and splashing around in the freezing cold English Channel.'

She spoke easily now, far preferring to remember happy times with her grandfather. Then her expression changed again.

'When I was older I used to gaze across the water and long to see what was on the other side.' She smiled. 'And now I know. It's *this*—this blissful, gorgeous place.'

Instinctively she reached for his hand, squeezing it lightly. 'Thank you,' she said. 'Thank you for bringing me here. I shall treasure the memory of this all my life!'

Nikos lifted her hand and grazed her knuckles lightly,

so lightly, with his mouth. Little flurries of electricity raced along her skin at his touch.

'It is my pleasure to bring you here,' he said, the husk audible in his voice.

Mel could feel desire pool in her stomach. Then, with a little laugh, she dropped his hand.

'I can't resist the water any more,' she cried, and got to her feet. She peeled off her cover-up and glanced down at Nikos. 'Last one in is a sissy!' she taunted wickedly, and hared across the hot sand to where the azure water was lapping at the beach.

She ran right into the water, which was blissfully warm to the skin, and plunged into its crystal-clear embrace. Behind her she heard a heavier splash, and then Nikos was there, too, grinning and diving into the deeper sea like a dolphin, surfacing again with his sable hair slicked back and water glistening like diamonds all over his broad muscled shoulders and torso.

'Not going to get your hair wet, then?'

It was his turn to taunt, and with a toss of her locks Mel mimicked his dive into the gently mounded swell and swam underwater, to emerge further out to sea, almost out of her depth. She trod water while Nikos caught up with her in two powerful strokes.

'This is glorious!' she cried exuberantly. 'The water's so warm it's like a bath!'

His grin answered hers and he dived again. Exuberance filled him as he surfaced for air some way yet further out. Mel swam to him and her eyelashes were glistening with diamond drops of water. Her slicked-back hair emphasised the perfection of her sculpted features. How incredibly beautiful she looked.

Without conscious thought, he caught her shoulders and pressed a swift, salty kiss on her mouth. Not with passion or desire, but simply because—well, because he wanted to. It lasted only a second and then he was away again, powering through the blue waters of the warm sea.

Mel came racing after him in the same exuberant mood. That sudden salty kiss had meant nothing—and everything. A joyous salutation to the playful pleasure of being in the warm, embracing sea, bathed in glorious bright sunshine, with fresh air and water spray and absolutely nothing to do except enjoy themselves. And enjoy each other...

The afternoon passed in as leisurely and lazy a fashion as the morning until, with the sun lowering, they made their way up the winding paths towards their rooms. Mel's skin felt warm and salty, and a sense of well-being filled her.

'A good first day?' Nikos asked.

'Oh, yes,' Mel assured him. She gave a sigh of happiness and went on walking. The day might be over but—a little thrill went through her—the night was only just beginning...

And what the night would bring was what she longed for: Nikos in her passionate embrace.

The little thrill went through her again.

The process of transforming herself from beach babe to evening goddess took Mel some considerable time.

'Take as long as you want,' Nikos had assured her, his eyes glinting. 'I know it will be worth the wait.'

Nearly ninety minutes later she checked herself out in front of the long mirror on the wardrobe door.

As she did so a memory fused in her head of the way she'd tried to inspect her appearance in Sarrie's back room, with nothing more than a hand mirror.

I had no idea that I'd be here only a couple of weeks later—here with the man I was meeting up with that night!

A sense of wonder went through her. And as she let her gaze settle on her reflection she felt wonder turn to gladness. She looked *good*.

She was wearing another find from her charity shop hunts—this time a sleeveless fine cotton ankle-length dress in a warm vermilion print, with a scoop neck that hinted at a décolletage without being obvious. Her jewellery was a simple gold chain, hoop earrings and a matching bangle, her footwear low-heeled strappy sandals comfortable to walk in but more elegant than flip-flops. She'd left her hair loose, held back off her face with a narrow hairband, so that it fell in waves around her shoulders. Her make-up was light, for she knew her face was flushed from the sun, protected though her skin had been all day.

Slipping her arms into the loose, evening jacket that went with the dress and picking up her bag, she headed out—ready for the evening ahead. Ready for all the evening would bring her—and the night that would follow...

When Nikos opened the door of his room to her soft knocking the blaze in his eyes told her that her efforts had been more than worthwhile, and she felt the blood surge in her veins. Her pulse quickened with her body's response to him as she gazed in appreciation at his tall, lean figure, clad now in long linen chinos and an open-necked cotton shirt.

He guided her forward through the warm, balmy night, along the oleander-bordered path up towards the main section of the hotel, where they would be dining, and she could catch the spiced warmth of his aftershave mingling with the floral tones of her own perfume, giving her a quivering awareness of his presence at her side.

The same awareness of him remained with her all through dinner, which was taken on the same terrace where they had breakfasted. The tables were now decked in linen, adorned with tropical flowers, with silverware catching the candlelight and the light from the torches set around the perimeter.

She felt as light as gossamer, floating in a haze of happiness to be here now, like this, with this man, in this gorgeous place, eating food that was as delicious as it was rare, beautifully arrayed on the plate, melting in her mouth, washed down with crisp, cold wine.

What they talked about she hardly knew. It was the same kind of easy, casual chat they had indulged in all day. About Bermuda, the sights they would see as they continued their stay, its history… They talked about films they had seen and enjoyed, about travel, all the places Nikos had been to that Mel was eager to hear about. Easy, relaxed, companionable. As if they had known each other for ever.

Yet underneath, beneath their relaxed conversation, Mel knew that a current was running between them. Another conversation was taking place and it was signalled to her in every raised beat of her heart, every swift mingling of their eyes, every movement of his strong, well-shaped hands as he ate or lifted his glass.

She knew she was keeping that conversation beneath the surface of her consciousness—knew that it was necessary to do so. For otherwise she would not be able to function in this social space. Yet the knowledge that it was shared with him, that just as she was constantly aware of *his* physical presence—the way his open-necked white shirt framed the strong column of his neck, the way his turned-back cuffs emphasised the leanness of his wrists—so he was aware of her, too—of *her* physical being. The way the candlelight hollowed the contours of her throat, caught the glint of gold in her earrings, burnished the echoing gold of her hair.

They were both aware of the courtship being conducted—silently, continually, seductively. Aware, with a growing, subtle assurance, of just how that courtship must find its completion…that night.

And so it did.

As they rose from the table eventually—the candles burnt low, almost the only couple left out on the terrace—without thinking she slipped her hand into Nikos's as they strolled back into the interior of the hotel. It seemed the right thing to do. The obvious thing.

His warm, strong fingers closed around hers and it felt right, so right, to let it happen. To walk beside him, closer this time, her shoulder sometimes brushing against his, her skirts fluttering around her legs, catching against him. From inside the hotel they could hear the low sound of a piano being played somewhere.

'Would you like another coffee? Or a drink in the lounge?'

'Only if you would,' she answered, glancing at him.

His eyes caught hers. 'You know what I want,' he murmured. 'And it isn't to be found in the piano lounge.'

There was humour in his expression, in his eyes. But his voice, when he spoke next, was serious.

'Is it what *you* want, Mel? Tell me truly. If it isn't, then you must say now. Because, to be honest…'

Now the humour was back again, and she could hear a touch of self-mockery, too, and was warmed by it.

'I'm not sure I've got the strength of mind or character to walk you back to your room and not come in with you—'

She glanced up at him, with a similar self-mocking wry humour in her own eyes. 'I'm not sure I've got the strength of mind or character to stop you coming in,' she told him. 'In fact...' She bit her lip. 'I strongly suspect I'd yank you inside my room even if you were being strong-minded—'

He gave a low laugh, and Mel could hear the relief in it. The satisfaction. She gave an answering laugh as they headed off through the gardens, back towards their rooms, towards what both of them knew would happen now...

There was a pool of darkness nearby, where the light of the low-set lamps that lined the stone pathway did not reach, and she felt him draw her into it with a swift, decisive movement. His hand tightened on hers and the other drew her round to face him. He was close... so close to her.

She felt her heart give a little leap and that electric current came again, sizzling through her body. She could not see his expression, but she knew what it was... what it must be...what hers must be. He was dim against the night, against the stars...

Unconsciously, instinctively, she lifted her face to his. His free hand slid to cup her throat, to tilt her face higher. She felt the smooth, gliding pressure of his fingers—their warmth, their sensuous touch. Felt her heart beating wildly now, her breath catch.

He was standing with his legs slightly apart, a dominating male stance, one hand still gripping hers, the other fastened to her with a strong, sensuous hold, the pad of his thumb on the delicate line of her jaw.

His long dark lashes dipped low over his eyes, glinting in the starlight. 'Well, if that's your attitude...' his voice was low and husky, and it made her bones weaken '...I'd better not disappoint you, had I?'

For a moment—just a moment—he delayed, and the pad of his thumb moved to her mouth, gliding leisurely across her lips. Her bones weakened further and her pulse quickened. With every fibre of her being she wanted him to kiss her...wanted to feel the warm pressure of his mouth...wanted the sweet taste of him...

'Nikos...'

She must have murmured his name, must have half closed her eyes, waiting, longing for his mouth to swoop and descend, to take hers in its silken touch.

His fingers wound in hers and his thumb slipped away now, his fingers touching at her throat, her jaw, gentling, caressing. And then finally...finally...his mouth descended to hers. Kissing her softly, sweetly, sensuously.

Endlessly.

She folded into him. A gesture as natural, as instinctive as the way her mouth opened to his. She wanted to feel the fullness of his kiss, the full bliss of it, as every part of her body dissolved into it.

Beneath the glint and glitter of the stars, in the soft, warm air, with the perfume of the night-scented flowers the susurration of the cicadas all around, his kiss went on and on. Claiming her, arousing her, calling forth from her all that she would bestow upon him that night, telling of all that he would give to her.

When his lips finally left hers she felt as if she was still in his embrace—as if she were floating inches off the ground and as if her heart were soaring around like a fluttering bird. He led her down the path to his room and then they were inside, in the cool, air-conditioned dimness. No light was needed—only the pale glow from the phosphorescence of the open sea beyond the windows.

He took her into his arms again, slipping his hands around her slender waist, cradling her supple spine as she leant into him, offering him her mouth…herself.

His kiss deepened, seeking all that it could find, and she offered all that she could give, her lips moving beneath his, her mouth opening to his in a rush of sweet, sensuous bliss. She could feel the blood surge in her veins, the heat fan out across her body, as she leant into him to taste, and take, and give, and yield.

She could feel him gliding the jacket from her shoulders, his warm hands slipping down her bared arms, and then she was pulling away from him slightly, and in a single fluid movement lifting the dress from her body, shaking her hair free of its band, giving a glorious, breathless laugh of pleasure, of anticipation.

As Nikos's eyes feasted on her she stood there, clad only in bra and panties, and a heady recklessness consumed her. Wordlessly she slipped the buttons of his shirt, easing her hands across the strong, warm column of his body. He caught her hands, his breath a rasp in his throat, and then he was folding her arms gently back, using the same movement to haul her against him, his mouth dipping to the soft, ripe swell of her breasts.

She gave a little gasp, feeling her nipples engorged against the straining satin of her bra. A low laugh came from him as his hands glided up the contour of her spine to unfasten the hooks that were keeping his mouth from what it sought to find. She felt her bra fall to the ground, felt his lips nuzzle at her bared breasts delicately, sensually, teasing and tasting until she gasped again in the sheer, trembling pleasure of it.

Her head fell back, her eyes fluttering closed, and an unconscious movement to lift her breasts to him over-whelmed her. A growl of satisfaction came from him and then he was scooping her up, lifting her as if she were a featherweight, carrying her across to the wide, waiting bed and lowering her down upon it.

She lay upon its surface, breasts still engorged and peaked, her eyes wide as she gazed up at him. Swiftly he discarded his own clothes, and then, with a groan, came down upon her. His weight crushed her, but she gloried in it—gloried in his questing mouth that now roamed her body, his hands likewise, exploring and ca-ressing and arousing such that if the world had caught fire that very hour she would have burned in the flames that were licking through her now.

Her breath quickened, her pulse racing as she clutched his strong, hard shoulders, feeling her body yielding to him, feeling his glorious, piercing posses-sion of her that felt so right, so incredibly, wonderfully right, nestling in the welcoming cradle of her hips. She felt the fire intensify within her, consuming her, until in a final conflagration she heard herself cry out, heard his answering cry, and felt a pleasure so intense it filled her entire being, shuddering through her, shaking and possessing her, on and on and on...

Until the quietness came.

Their bodies slaked, they held each other with slack-ened gentleness, beside each other, loose-limbed, em-bracing.

She sought his mouth. A gentle, peaceful kiss. He kissed her back, then grazed her forehead with a kiss, as well. His eyes were soft in the dim light.

There were no words—there did not need to be—only the gradual slowing of their racing hearts, their hectic pulse subsiding now. He drew her to him, his arms around her, hers around him, and with a little sigh she felt sleep take them.

CHAPTER SEVEN

'So, WHAT WOULD you like to do today? Anything on Bermuda you haven't seen yet?'

Nikos smiled encouragingly at Mel. They were breakfasting on Nikos's patio, gazing out over the aquamarine waters of the bay, as calm as a mill pond at this time of day. Breakfasting together like this had become the rule in the days since they'd arrived, after rising in a leisurely fashion, both of them having awoken to yet more arousal after a night of searing passion.

Hastily she reached for her coffee, hoping it might cool her suddenly heated cheeks. Time to focus on the day's activities—yet another wonderful, blissful day of self-indulgent holidaymaking.

In the week they'd already spent on Bermuda they'd covered nearly all the sights.

They'd toured the historic Nelson's Dockyard at the far west of the island, where British men-of-war had once dropped anchor, and which now welcomed massive cruise ships, disgorging their passengers to throng the myriad little cafés and craft shops.

They'd taken the ferry from the dockyard across to the island's bay-lapped capital, Hamilton, lunching on the sea front and exploring the shops. They'd gone to the old capital of St George's in the north of the island, with its white-painted little houses, art galleries, churches and museums.

And they'd been out to sea—Nikos had taken her sailing in the bay and further afield, and they'd enjoyed a sunset champagne dinner on a sleek motor yacht chartered to sail them around the island. He'd hired a dive boat, which had hovered over the reef for Nikos to dive with the instructor, leaving Mel content to snorkel on the surface, glimpsing long-sunk wrecks rich with darting fish, and the scary but thankfully harmless purple jellyfish that trailed long tentacles in the water deep below her.

Mel had wanted to see and do everything, had been excited and thrilled by even the simplest things— whether it was wandering through the beautiful gardens around the hotel, or pausing for coffee at a little Bermudian coffee shop overlooking one of the beautiful pink sand beaches. She was just revelling in being in this beautiful place, in the company of this fabulous man...

This is the most fantastic holiday romance that anyone could ever wish for.

Again she felt heat fan her cheeks. Nikos was so sensual and passionate a lover she was blown away by it. Never had she realised how incredible it could be when two people gave themselves to each other up to the very hilt of passion. How in the moment of union their bodies could pulse with an intensity, an explosion of sensual overload that wrung from her a response she had never felt before.

Jak had been a careful lover, and her memories of him were fond and grateful, but Nikos—ah, Nikos was

in a league of his own. All the promise…all the shim-
mering awareness of the irrepressible physical attraction
that had flared between them right from their first intemperate encounter…had exploded on their first night
together. And now, night after night, when he took her
in his arms, skilfully caressed her body to melting, she
felt transported to a level of sensual satiation she had
never known existed. And it was Nikos who took her
there…

Will there ever be anyone in my life like him again?

The question was in her head before she could stop
it. And so was the answer.

*How could there be? How could there be anyone
like him again—how could there be a time like this
ever again in her life?*

A little quiver went through her, but she silenced it.
She had come away with Nikos with her eyes open—
knowing he wanted only a brief, passionate affair and
nothing more. Knowing that that was exactly what she
wanted, too. A fabulous, gorgeous, breathtaking *entrée* in the feast of freedom that was to be her new independent life.

Nikos was for the wonderful, wonderful *now*, and
that was how she was going to enjoy him—how she
was going to enjoy their time together, night after night,
day after day.

Speaking of days…

'We still haven't done the Crystal Caves,' she said.
'Could we visit them today?'

'Why not?' Nikos answered with lazy complaisance.
'We can take the hotel launch around to Hamilton, do
a spot of shopping, have lunch and take a taxi on to
the caves.'

His eyes rested on her warmly. How right he'd been

not to let her fly off to Spain and disappear on her travels without him. Instead he'd brought her here, romanced her and made love to her, and he was with her day in, day out.

Satisfaction filled him—more than satisfaction.

Contentment.

He wondered at it. It just seemed to be so easy to be with Mel—so natural, so absolutely effortless. Conversation was easy with her. They still sparked off each other, just as they had right from the first, but now it was always humorous, easygoing, mutually teasing each other, but with a smile. And it was as easy *not* to talk as it was to talk. They could wander or lie on sun loungers or watch the sunset in happy silence.

Yes, being with Mel just seemed to…*work*. That was the only way he could explain it.

Not that he wanted to analyse it, or find words to describe being with her. No, all he wanted to do was enjoy this time with her. Enjoy it to the full. In bed and out.

And that gave him an idea—a very good one, now he came to think of it.

He glanced at his watch. 'I think the hotel launch leaves every hour to make the crossing to Hamilton. Do you want to make the next one? Or would you prefer to skip it and we could take an early siesta, maybe?'

He threw her an encouraging look.

Mel gave a splutter of laughter. She knew perfectly well what he meant. And sleep would *not* be involved!

'Early siesta? It's barely gone ten in the morning!' She got to her feet, stooping to whisper to him, 'You're insatiable—you know that? Honestly. Come on.' Her voice was bracing now. 'If we get going we can get the next launch.'

'So keen to go shopping in Hamilton?' It was Nikos's turn to sound teasing.

She gave another splutter of laughter. 'No. I don't need a thing—my bathroom's chock-full of complimentary toiletries.'

Nikos smiled indulgently. 'So easily pleased...' he said fondly.

'Well, I am!' Mel riposted. 'Everything...' she waved her arms expansively, taking in the whole resort and the island it was on '...is brilliant.' She turned a warm gaze on Nikos. 'And *you're* the most brilliant of all.'

He reached to stroke her sun-warmed bare arm. 'That's the right answer,' he laughed. 'I am *definitely* more brilliant than complimentary hotel toiletries,' he finished feelingly. 'And if you really, *really* insist...' he gave an exaggerated sigh '...I shall deprive myself of our...er...siesta...until after we get back from these Crystal Caves you're determined to drag me to.'

'Oh, you'll *love* them,' she assured him with a playful thump. 'They're a marvel of nature, the guidebook says. Limestone caves with pools and walkways all illuminated like something out of a fairy tale. What's more...' she glanced at him with a determined look in her eyes '...we won't need a taxi—you can get there by bus from Hamilton. I think we should do that—I'd love to see Nikos Parakis on a humble bus.'

He laughed, and they finished off their breakfast companionably, in harmony with each other and with the day ahead.

Gratitude for all that she had been given ran through Mel like circling water. So much. This fabulous place, this fabulous time—and this fabulous man who had given it to her and was sharing it with her.

* * *

The Crystal Caves were as breathtaking as she'd hoped from their description in the guidebook, and after their visit they headed back to their hotel and some time on the beach.

As the sun lowered, though, Nikos got to his feet.

'You stay on down here for a while,' he told her. 'I need to head back to my room—check over my speech for tomorrow.'

'Oh, my goodness—is it the conference already?' Mel asked, surprised.

'I'm afraid so. But, like I've said, I'm only putting in a single day there. Then we can get on with the remainder of our holiday.' He smiled.

Her eyes followed him as he made his way along the beach. A little frown furrowed her brow. Halfway— they were halfway through their holiday already. Nikos had said 'the remainder'—that was a word that had a tolling bell in it, pointing towards the end. The end of their time together. The end of their romance.

She felt a little clenching of her stomach.

The end.

Her gaze slipped away, over the sea beyond. Her frown deepened, shadowing her eyes. Theirs was a holiday romance—a brief, gorgeous fling—and holidays always came to an end. But it would also mean a start to her independent travels—her footloose, fancy-free wandering—going where she wanted, when she wanted, tied to no one and bound to nobody...

Not even Nikos.

It's what I want—what I've planned. What I've always intended.

The reminder sounded in her head—resolutely. Determinedly. Silencing anything else that might be trying to be heard.

* * *

The conference hall was packed with delegates in business suits, and Mel had to squeeze into a space at the rear. But from there she still had a good view of Nikos on the podium. But it wasn't his discourse on sovereign debt or optimal fiscal policy that held her gaze. Oh, no.

It was the way his bespoke tailored business suit moulded every long, lean line of his fit, hard body. The way his long-fingered hands gestured at the complex graphs displayed on the screen behind him. The way his expression—focussed, incisive, authoritative, as befitted a man who had responsibilities she could not dream of—would suddenly give a hint…just a hint…of the humour that could flash out so beguilingly.

So she sat and gazed, spellbound and riveted, until his Q&A session had ended and the audience was dispersing for lunch.

She didn't join him—this was his world, not hers—instead making her way to the poolside bistro. The area was busy, but after her lunch she found an empty sun lounger in the shade and settled down to leaf through a magazine, content to while away the afternoon until Nikos was finished with the conference.

A voice nearby interrupted her. 'Hi—didn't I see you in the conference hall before lunch?'

The American-accented voice was female, and friendly, and it came from the next lounger along. Mel looked towards the woman, taking in an attractive bikini-clad brunette, a few years older than her, with an extremely chic hairstyle and full eye make-up.

The woman smiled. 'Wasn't that last speaker something? The foreign guy with his own bank—total *dish*!' Her dark eyes sparkled appreciatively.

There was an air of shared conspiracy, an invitation to agree with her, and Mel found herself smiling in wry agreement.

Taking it as consent to keep chatting, the woman continued. 'Are you here as a delegate yourself? Or a spouse?'

'Well, not a spouse—just…um…a "plus one." I guess you'd call it,' she answered, not sure whether she should mention that she was the 'plus one' of the 'dish'… 'What about you?' she asked politely.

'Oh, my husband's a banker,' the woman said. 'John Friedman of Friedman Hoffhaus,' she added, looking expectantly at Mel.

Mel gave an apologetic shake of her head. 'I'm afraid I'm very ignorant of the banking world,' she answered.

'Oh—so who are you the "plus one" of?' the woman asked curiously.

Mel's expression changed again. 'Well, actually… um…it's the "dish",' she said apologetically.

Immediately the woman's eyes sparkled. 'No *way*! My, oh, my—you are one lucky, *lucky* lady! Mind you…' she nodded in tribute to Mel's blonde beauty '…I can see how you pulled him. The thing is, though,' she went on airily, 'how are you gonna *keep* him? Men that rich *and* young *and* good-looking are hard to hog-tie. You're going to have to have a watertight "get him to the altar" strategy to be his *permanent* "plus one"!'

Mel looked uncomfortable, not wanting to elaborate to a stranger on the fact that she and Nikos were simply here together on holiday and weren't an established couple—and that she was in no need of a strategy to 'hog-tie' him.

Not that Nikos was the kind of man to get hog-tied anyway.

For an instant so brief it wasn't measurable in time

a flicker of emotion went through her—but what that emotion was she could not tell. Did not want to…

The other woman was talking again. 'Maybe you'll find yourself pregnant,' she said, and now there was an openly conspiratorial look in her eye. 'That's what happened to me—worked like a dream.'

She glanced towards the shallow end of the pool, where Mel could see a preschooler splashing about, with a young woman—presumably his nanny—playing with him.

Mel was thankfully spared the necessity of responding to such an untoward comment by a server gliding by, offering coffee. She took one, and so did the woman, who now introduced herself as Nyree, eliciting a reciprocal if somewhat reluctant response from Mel.

She was relieved when Nyree Friedman changed the subject to that of shopping opportunities, for which she considered Bermuda inadequate, which led to her regaling Mel with the delights of New York for that purpose, and giving a little cry of disbelief when she discovered that Mel had never been there.

'Oh, but you *must*! Tell the dish you absolutely *have* to go from here,' she urged.

Not waiting for an answer, she chattered on, and Mel was happy enough to leave her to it. Nyree Friedman was chatty and convivial, but Mel had to conclude she was something of an airhead.

She didn't seem to be much of a devoted mother, either, for she was perfectly happy to leave her little boy's nanny to do all the entertaining of her son. Cynically, Mel presumed that the child had served his purpose in 'hog-tying' his wealthy banker father for Nyree. It was a depressing thought.

Their mostly one-sided chat about Nyree Friedman's

fashionable, affluent Manhattan lifestyle was finally brought to an end by the emergence of Nikos from the conference. He strolled up to Mel.

'There you are…' He smiled. Then his glance swept sideways to take in her partner in conversation, who had stopped mid-sentence, her eyes wide with open appreciation at the arrival of 'the dish.'

Her dark eyes sparkled. *'Hi…'* she said warmly, holding out a languid, perfectly manicured hand. 'I'm Nyree Friedman. I heard your presentation this morning—it was *fascinating*!' she breathed. Her expression was blatantly admiring.

There was a tug at the side of Nikos's mouth as he shook the extended hand—but briefly, Mel was glad to notice. No lingering contact with the attractive brunette…

'Well, I can only hope your husband was just as taken by it,' he replied drily.

Clearly, Mel realised, he knew perfectly well who Nyree Friedman's husband was—even if he'd never met his wife before.

Nyree's gaze was visibly eating Nikos up. Out of the blue Mel felt a dagger's blade of possessiveness go through her. Sharp and piercing. For an instant she wanted to grab Nikos and drag him away—and slap Nyree down at the same time, for daring to make eyes at him.

The intensity of the emotion shocked her. No *way* did she want to feel possessive about Nikos. Hadn't he told her right from the start that possessiveness was exactly what put him off a woman? The reason he'd asked her out that very first evening had been to ward off Fiona Pellingham's possessive intentions. No, possessiveness—from either of them—wasn't what their deliberately brief time together was about, she reminded herself sharply. Possessiveness had no place at all in a fun but fleeting holiday romance such as theirs was.

To her relief, Nikos's attention was back on her, and his eyes were sending a silent question that echoed his verbal one.

'I'm all done here now, Mel,' he told her. 'So if you're ready to go we can head off? Unless,' he went on politely, his glance taking in Nyree again, 'you want to stay longer?'

His tone was polite, but Mel knew he didn't want to stay on longer here at this huge, crowded hotel. He'd already told her he wasn't going to be attending the conference dinner that evening, and she'd been glad. She wasn't going to have him for much longer, and she didn't want to share him for any of that time if she didn't have to.

'No, I'm good to go,' she said. She looked across at Nyree, who was looking rueful. 'It was lovely to meet you,' she said brightly, getting to her feet.

'Well, we must meet up in New York!' Nyree said promptly. Her flirtatious gaze went back to Nikos, then changed as it moved past him. 'John,' she said imperiously, 'persuade this gorgeous man to bring his girlfriend to New York. She's never been—can you believe it?'

The man approaching was clad in a business suit, like Nikos, but he was a good twenty years older, thought Mel, and unlike Nikos very overweight.

He nodded at Nikos, then addressed Mel. 'Has my wife let you get a word in edgeways?' he asked with heavy humour. 'She does like to dominate the airwaves.'

It was said humorously, but Mel could detect underlying irritation at his wife's garrulity.

'It's been very...interesting,' Mel said politely.

John Friedman laughed again, a little too heavily, and then his attention was drawn to the small figure hurtling towards him.

'Dad! Dad!' he was calling out excitedly. 'Come in the pool!'

Mel watched him hug the pool-wet boy and ruffle his damp hair.

'I can't wait!' his father assured him. 'But I need to get changed first, OK?' His eyes went to his wife, who was still lounging back on the recliner. 'Will *you* spend any time with our son in the pool?'

There was a clear jibe in the question, and it drew an acid response from his wife.

'And wreck my hair? Don't be ridiculous. Besides, it's time for cocktails.'

'It's too early for cocktails—especially for *you*,' John Friedman said immediately. And pointedly.

Nyree's mouth thinned mutinously and it looked as if she was going to make an angry retort. To Mel's relief—for witnessing this marital acrimony was uncomfortable—Nyree's husband had turned to Nikos.

'You made a persuasive case in there,' he said, very much banker-to-banker now. 'Maybe we should discuss some potential mutual opportunities?'

'I'd be glad to,' Nikos said promptly.

'Good.' John Friedman nodded. 'Get in touch next time you're in New York.'

'Make it *soon*!' Nyree enthused, her gaze fastening greedily on Nikos again.

Nikos gave a non-committal smile and took Mel's hand, squeezing it meaningfully. He wanted out, she knew. And so did she. For all their superficial politeness, the atmosphere was uncomfortable, and the tension between Nyree and her husband was palpable. But they said goodbye politely, even though Mel could hear regret in Nyree's voice, and saw her eyes linger on Nikos.

As she and Nikos moved away Mel could hear Nyree start up. 'Oh, my God, John—your suit is soaking wet! Why do you let the boy maul you like that? It's ridiculous. You make far too much fuss of him.'

Her husband's voice cut across her. 'One of us needs to. You won't—so I do. I'm his father. And do you *have* to try and flirt with every man you see—even when they're obviously not interested in you?'

Mel grimaced as they got out of earshot, heading through the hotel grounds to pick up a taxi at the front. 'Eek—not a happy marriage, I think. Nor a great start for that little lad of theirs, I fear.'

There was an edge to Nikos's voice as he replied. 'No, indeed.' His expression was set. That barbed exchange they'd been witness to had been all too familiar. The sniping, the acid tones, the mutual accusations and complaints… He'd grown up with them. They weren't any easier to witness in other couples any more than between his own parents.

Mel cast him a curious, slightly guarded look. There'd been a lot in the suppressed way he'd said that.

He caught her glance and made a rueful face. 'Sorry, but they just remind me of my own parents. All smiles and bonhomie to others, but with each other constant tension and backbiting. Absolutely everything becomes a verbal skirmish.'

She gave him a sympathetic smile. 'It sounds very… wearing,' she said, trying to find a word that wasn't too intrusive into what was, she could tell, a sensitive issue for him.

He gave an unamused snort. 'That's one word for it,' he said. 'Two people locked together, hammering away at each other and making themselves and everyone else miserable.'

Mel looked concerned. 'Why on earth did they ever marry each other, your parents?' she asked.

'Would you believe it? They were infatuated with each other,' he said sardonically. 'My mother was the catch of the season—the belle of every ball—and every man was after her. She kept them all guessing, playing them off against each other, but my father ended up winning her because she was bowled over by him.'

His voice twisted.

'Then I came along and everything went pear-shaped.' He gave a hollow laugh that had no humour in it. 'My mother hated being pregnant—as she constantly tells me still—I ruined her figure, apparently. And my father stopped paying her the attention she craved. And then— worse—he felt jealous of the attention she gave me when I was little, so he started straying. That incensed my mother even more than his neglecting her, and the whole damn thing just spiralled downwards until they reached a point where they couldn't even be civil to each other.'

His mouth thinned to a tight, taut line.

'They still can't be civil to each other, all these years later. They've bad-mouthed each other for as long as I can remember. Not a good word to say about each other and expecting *me* to side with each of them. Yet they absolutely refuse to admit failure and divorce— it's beyond ghastly.'

Mel kept the sympathy in her voice. 'I used to feel very sorry for myself when I was young, not having parents, but who knows which is worse? No parents— or parents who make your life a misery growing up?'

'Yes, tough call,' acknowledged Nikos, terse now, after what he'd bitten out at length.

Where the hell had all that come from?

He found himself wondering why he'd made any reference to his bumpy childhood and warring family. It wasn't a subject he discussed with others. It was too deep, too personal. Too painful. But with Mel it had seemed...natural.

He sought for a reason for his embittered outburst.

Maybe it's because she didn't have it easy either, growing up with only a grandfather to look after her, missing a mother and father. Maybe that's why it's easy to talk to her about such things...

But he didn't want to think about his endlessly sparring parents and their utter insensitivity to anyone except themselves—their refusal to acknowledge the fact that their marriage was a failure and they should have ended it years ago. He'd washed his hands of both of them and left them to it.

Deliberately he took a deep breath to clear his clouded thoughts. He wouldn't spoil his time with Mel by thinking about his parents—let alone pouring it out to her again the way he just had. No, it was far more pleasant to know that he was here, with a woman like Mel at his side, making the most of this carefree time together.

With the conference over there was nothing more to do on the island except enjoy themselves. Revel in the passion that flamed between them and relish the absolute leisure and relaxation they had, day after golden day.

It doesn't get better than this...

The words shaped themselves inside his head and he knew them to be true. Had he ever enjoyed himself more in his life than he was doing now, with Mel? It was just so *good* being here with her. Oh, the sex was beyond fantastic—no doubt about that—and he'd always known it would be. But it was so, *so* much more than just the sex.

It's the being with her that's so good. Just every day—over meals, on the beach, sightseeing...just everything.

Right now, he thought, *I'm a happy man.*

It was a good feeling.

As they settled into the taxi, setting off for their own quiet hotel, Nikos gave a sigh of relief. 'I'm glad to get out of here,' he said. 'Now we can get back to the rest of our holiday.'

'A week to go,' said Mel lightly.

Her words drew a frown across Nikos's brow. A week—was that all? It would go by in a flash, as this last one had. His frown deepened. A week wasn't enough...

Rapidly, in his head, he ran through his diary. Was there anything critical the week after next? Offhand, he couldn't think of anything. And if there was nothing absolutely critical...

The idea that had struck him was obvious—and inspired, of all things, by the warring Friedmans.

He voiced it over dinner, having checked his online diary to confirm his assumption.

'Tell me,' he said as they settled down to their evening meal, which they were taking at the beach bistro, to refresh their spirits after the day's busyness, 'are you tempted at all by the idea of going to New York?'

Mel's face lightened. She'd been thinking along just those lines herself. Going to New York would surely be something to look forward to after this fabulous time with Nikos had ended, wouldn't it? And she needed something to look forward to...

'Oh, yes,' she said. 'It would make sense, being so close to Bermuda. If I can get a cheap flight, and find a cheap tourist hotel in Manhattan, then—'

Nikos interrupted her. 'What do you mean?' he demanded, his buoyant mood altering immediately.

There was an edge to his voice she found unaccountable. She looked at him, confused.

'Why do you talk about cheap flights and tourist hotels?' he went on, in the same frowning tone.

It was her turn to look confused. 'Well, I have to make my savings go as far as they can—'

'Not when you're with *me*,' he contradicted. His expression darkened. 'Unless for some reason you don't *want* to see New York with me?'

If she hadn't known better she might have read accusation in his voice. But accusation was so inexplicable it couldn't possibly be that.

'Nikos, that's a daft question,' she replied, in a rallying humorous tone.

But he was not mollified. 'Then what is making you talk of going there on your own?' he demanded.

She looked at him uncertainly. 'When you invited me to Bermuda, Nikos, you told me it would just be for a couple of weeks—around the conference,' she said.

He gave a dismissive shrug. 'So we make it longer. That's all. I've checked my diary and I can bring forward some meetings in New York scheduled for the following month. By extending our stay on Bermuda we can go straight from here to New York. Plus,' he finished, 'I could take up John Friedman's invitation—I dare say it would prove very useful to me.' He looked across the table. 'So, let's do it—shall we?'

His voice was expectant. But Mel's expression did not lighten in return.

'Nikos, I'm not sure it's a good idea—'

His brow darkened. 'Why?' His question was blunt.

Her eyes slid away, out over the dark expanse of water beyond the beach. She wanted to put into words her reluctance, and yet it was hard to do so. Hard because shooting through her, making a nonsense of reluctance, was an arrow of sheer exhilaration that seemed to be penetrating to her very core.

He wanted to stay longer on Bermuda, to take her to New York! Wanted to spend more time with her! Wanted not to kiss her goodbye and wave her off out of his life!

She felt the force of it—felt its power.

And it was that that gave her pause.

I came with him for a holiday romance—that's all. A couple of weeks with Nikos—a glorious, fantastic, fabulous entrée in the banquet of my new life of travelling, of freedom and self-indulgence—that was what this holiday was supposed to be. All that I planned it to be.

A holiday romance was something she could accommodate. Indeed, she'd envisaged fun-filled, light-hearted holiday romances as being an integral part of her new free life. Making up for the lost years of enforced celibacy, for the absolute lack of romance in her life while she'd cared for her grandfather.

But when did a holiday romance turn into something more?

If she let Nikos take her to New York what would come afterwards? He would still go back to Athens, wouldn't he? Still kiss her goodbye…

Her mind sheered away. She didn't want to think of that. Didn't want to think about anything except what she had now—their time together here in Bermuda. Their holiday romance…

Beautiful—and brief.

Her eyes swept back to him, found his resting on her, dark and stormy-looking.

'Why?' he asked again. 'Why is going to New York with me not a good idea?'

He would not let it go. Why was she saying such a thing? Weren't they having a fantastic time here in Bermuda? Why not keep going with it?

We're so good together.

That was what was in his head all the time. Simple, uncomplicated and true. There was no reason for her to be unenthusiastic about him going to New York with her. She wanted to go there—he wanted to go there with her. What was the problem?

He wanted her to answer so that he could dispose of her objections. But at that juncture the waiter arrived with their food, and as he left them Mel determinedly changed the subject.

He could see the ploy for what it was—a way to stop him grilling her—and he accepted it. There were more ways to persuade her than by out-arguing her...

That night, as he took her in his arms, he put into their lovemaking all the skill and expertise that lay within his command, deliberately drawing from her a consummation that left her shaking, trembling in his arms—left him shaking, trembling in hers.

Finally, sated and exhausted, they drew apart and lay beside each other, their bodies sheened with perspiration, their breathing hectic, the echoes of their shared ecstasy still burning between them. He levered himself up on his elbow, smoothing back her damp hair, gazing down into her wide eyes.

'Come to New York with me...' he whispered.

His lashes dropped over his eyes, his mouth dipped to graze her lips, parted and bee-stung from his passion.

'Come to New York with me…' he whispered again.

Surely she must be persuaded now? Surely she must not want what was between them to end before it needed to? And it did not need to—not yet. They did not have to part—they could keep going—keep going to New York and who knew how far beyond? Who knew how long this romance would last? All he knew was that he had no intention—none at all—of letting it go a single moment before he was ready.

But she didn't answer him—only let her eyes flutter shut and rolled herself into his waiting embrace. And he closed her against him, hugging her tight, so tight, against the wall of his chest.

In her head she could hear his voice—so low, so seductive, so tempting…

Come to New York with me…

In her body, deep in the core of her, she could feel the hectic pulse ebbing slowly, leaving only the incandescent afterglow of passion. She felt her breathing ease, her heated skin start to cool. But in her heart there was a tightening.

There was one thing she must say to him—only one thing. The sensible thing.

He was nuzzling at her ear, his breath warm, his touch sweet.

'Come to New York,' he murmured, coaxing and caressing. His mouth moved from the delicate lobe of her ear, grazing along the line of her jaw. 'Come to New York,' he said again.

She could feel his mouth break into a smile suddenly, and his arms tightened around her.

'Come to New York,' he said, and she could hear the

laugh in his voice. 'Because I'll go on asking you until you give in and say yes.'

He was kissing her eyelids now.

'Give in and say yes… Give in and say yes. You know you want to.'

He was laughing, and so was she, and suddenly, out of nowhere, she couldn't fight it any longer.

'*Yes!* OK—I give in! I'll come to New York with you!' Her capitulation was complete.

He gave a low, triumphant rumble and she was grinning, too, half shaking her head and then kissing him. Oh, what the hell? She hadn't been sensible at all. But she didn't care—couldn't care—not now…

Wrapping his warm, strong body against her, she wound herself tighter into his embrace. She felt a singing inside her. *She was going to New York with Nikos—* their holiday would be longer, their time together would be longer, there were still more glorious days to come.

CHAPTER EIGHT

'Is THAT YOU guzzling rum cake again?' Mel's voice was humorously indignant.

'Just testing it for quality,' Nikos assured her, licking his fingers after eating a slice of the cake that was the speciality of the island.

'Yes, well, if you test much more of it there'll be none left,' she riposted, removing the cake tin from him and placing the lid firmly back on top. 'I'll keep this in *my* room, I think.'

Nikos laughed. 'We can always go to Nelson's Harbour and restock.'

'We'll need to if you keep eating it like that.'

She dropped a kiss on his head before stepping over the dividing wall between their patios and heading indoors. Emerging again, she saw Nikos was pulling on his shirt. Despite the rum cake, his pecs and abs were still spectacularly honed.

Mel felt a ripple of desire go through her. But this wasn't the time to indulge in a siesta—not least because it was only just after breakfast and they were about to head to the beach.

As they stretched themselves out on their beach loungers, just above the tide line so that the spray from the waves breaking exuberantly into airy foam on the soft pale gold sand could cool their sun-heated bodies, lying on the beach seemed especially blissful.

But that, she knew with a squeezing of her heart, was because their days here were finally running out…

Then they'd be off to New York—for their last, final few days together.

And then goodbye…

Finally, goodbye.

Despite the heat of the beach a sudden draught of cold air seemed to be playing around her body. She fought it back.

But it's not the end of the holiday yet! I've still got time with Nikos.

And yet it was precisely the fact that she'd felt that cold draught that caused her concern.

I shouldn't be so eager to stay with him—I shouldn't be clinging to our time together like this. It isn't what I intended at all. I should be excited at the prospect of going on to see the rest of America—exploring all the places I've only ever read about or seen on films or TV. I shouldn't be wanting to go on being with Nikos all the time—I shouldn't…

But the problem was she *did* just want to go on being with Nikos. Here on Bermuda. In New York. And beyond…

For a moment she tried to force herself to imagine exploring the USA on her own—but her mind had gone blank. Beyond New York there seemed to be nothing at all…

Dismay filled her. This was not good—not good at all. For so long she'd thought and dreamt of nothing but being footloose and fancy-free, going where she wanted, when she wanted, making her own way across the world, free as a bird... Yet now there seemed to be only a blank ahead of her.

The time would soon come when they would go their separate ways—she to see the rest of America, he to head back to Athens, to his life. Their holiday together over.

The chilly draught came again.

She didn't want to think about it—didn't want to face it. Didn't want to think that in just a few days' time it would all be ending.

But what—what will be ending?

That was the question she shied away from answering.

'Mel—bad news.'

She turned abruptly, halting in the action of fastening her packed suitcase. Nikos was standing in the open French windows of her room. He was frowning, phone in hand.

'What's happened?' she asked, alarmed.

Their extended time on Bermuda had finally ended, and now they were due to head off to New York.

Mel could not deny that she'd given up on those ambivalent feelings she'd had about his determination to take her to America for a final few days together—she didn't even try. There was no point. They were going there now, and that was that. They were booked and packed. Any moment now their bags would be collected and the hotel car would take them to the airport for their late-morning flight to New York. So it was too late to question why she was so uneasy about it all—wasn't it?

'I'm going to have to change our plans,' Nikos said, his voice short. 'We have to head back to Europe. Something's cropped up and I can't get out of it—I'm really sorry.' He gave an annoyed sigh. 'New York is off the cards—I'm getting us booked on the evening flight direct to London, and then we'll need to drop down to Athens straight away...'

She was staring at him. Just staring.

He came up to her, slid his phone away and put his arms loosely around her waist.

'I'm really sorry,' he said again, apology in his eyes. 'But on the other hand...' he dropped a light kiss on her nose '...you'll get to see Athens instead of New York.'

She stepped away from him.

'Nikos—'

There was something in her voice that made him look at her.

Emotions were shooting through her like bullets. What had she just been thinking? That it was too late to be so uneasy about extending her time with Nikos yet further? Her expression twisted. Suddenly out of the blue, with a phone call that had changed.

'Nikos, I can't come to Athens with you.' The words fell from her lips.

It was his turn to stare. 'Why not?' There was blank incomprehension in his voice.

'Because...because I'm going to New York. Because seeing the USA is what I've planned to do.' She swallowed. 'I know you were going to be with me for a couple more days in New York, but I'm...I'm going on, Nikos. The way I planned.'

His face was taut. 'Change your plans. See Athens instead. Didn't you say you wanted to go "everywhere"?' he challenged. 'You haven't even set foot in Europe yet.'

She shut her eyes. She could hear a kind of drumming in her ears.

I thought I'd have a few more days with him...just a few more days...

But that wasn't going to happen. It was over—right now.

Because of course she couldn't go to Europe with him—it was out of the question. Just out of the question.

'Nikos—no. I can't.'

'You can't *what*?' he said, the words cutting into the space between them.

He could feel emotion starting to build in him, but he didn't know what it was. Knew only that the woman he wanted with him was saying she couldn't be with him...

'I can't just...just tag along with you to Athens. What *as*, for heaven's sake? Here, we've been on holiday, but if you go back to your home city—well...what will I be doing there with you? What *am* I to you there?'

How can I have nothing more than a holiday romance with you if we're not on holiday?

He was staring at her, his eyes dark, his expression darker.

She had to make him understand.

Something had changed in his eyes. 'What had you in mind?' he said.

His voice was dry. As dry as the sand in a desert.

It was her turn to stare, not understanding what he was saying—why he was saying it. Emotion was churning away inside her and she felt a sense of shock—shock that the moment she'd thought would be deferred for a few more days was upon her. Right now.

Then he was speaking.

'Mel, I was clear with you from the start, wasn't I?' she heard him say. 'Before we came here? I never fed you a line—you knew the score with me from the start. Don't expect anything more than that.'

His voice was flat, unemotional. Had she read more than he'd intended into his saying they needed to head for Athens? He hoped not—he really hoped not.

Because 'anything more' is not how I live my life. I've seen where 'more' can take people—how it can screw things up...screw people up...

His mind sheered away from familiar thoughts, familiar reactions. Things he didn't want to associate with Mel—not Mel.

I just want what we have now—because it's good... so good—and I want it to go on just the way it is. I don't see why it can't, but why can't she see that, too? Why can't we just go on the way we are? Not question things the way she's doing now?

Mel's face worked. 'Nikos, I don't expect anything more of you than what we've been having.' She swallowed, making her voice lighter. 'Which is the most fantastic holiday that anyone could ever imagine. A holiday that...' She swallowed again, and this time there seemed to be something in her throat as she did so, though she didn't know what. 'That is over,' she finished.

The expression in his eyes changed. Had she seen a flash of emotion? And if she had, what had it been?

For a moment she thought it might have been relief.

Or had it been regret?

Well, whatever it was, it didn't matter. All that mattered now was...was...

A strange, hollow sense of emptiness stretched inside her.

All that matters now is saying goodbye...

She made herself move—walk up to him, loop her arms around his neck. He was standing stock-still, all muscles tensed.

'Nikos, I have had the most fantastic time with you,'

she told him, steeling herself to say what must be said right now—days before she'd thought she would be saying it. She smiled at him, made herself smile, because smiling at this moment was suddenly very necessary to her. 'But…'

She let him go, stepped away again. She took a breath. It was painful, somehow, to draw breath in and out of her lungs, but she had to do it. Had to say goodbye to him.

'It's come to an end, Nikos,' she said. 'I'm sorry we're not getting our…our bonus time in New York, but… well…' she gave a little shrug with muscles that did not want to move '…there it is. All holidays end. So has ours.'

That was all the time they'd planned to have with each other—nothing more. So why was he glowering at her the way he was, his expression rejecting what she was saying to him?

She bit her lip, hating what was happening but knowing there was no alternative.

This has come too fast—I'm not ready…not prepared—

Out of nowhere panic boiled up in her chest, suffocating her. She had to fight it down. Had to make herself speak to him in a tone of voice that sounded reasonable.

'I'm sorry this has just happened so fast like this— but, oh, Nikos, we always knew this moment would come. Whether now or in a couple of days in New York it doesn't matter much. We mustn't make a big deal of it—it *isn't* a big deal and it mustn't become one.'

There was a plea in her voice now—even she could hear it. But who was she pleading with? Him—or herself? Well, she mustn't think about that. Mustn't think about anything except making herself reach for her nearby handbag, clutch it to her.

He was still standing there, motionless. His face was frozen, as if turned to stone.

Why is it like this? Why? It shouldn't be hard to say goodbye and get on with my own life. It just shouldn't!

'Nikos, I'm going to take the hotel shuttle to the airport—make that New York flight on my own. I know the London flight isn't till this evening, so there's no point you setting off now. And…and I don't want to say goodbye at an airport…'

I don't want to say goodbye at all.

The words were wrung from inside her, but she ignored them—she had to.

'I don't believe you're doing this.'

That deep, accented voice. But no longer flat. No longer edged. Just—harsh.

'It's for the best. It really is,' she heard herself say.

She picked up the handle of her suitcase, backing towards the door. As she yanked it open she paused. Looked at him one last time.

For some strange, inexplicable reason he looked out of focus. Blurred.

She blinked, trying to clear her vision. Trying to keep her voice the way it had to be—the only way it could be when a holiday romance came to an end. 'Have a good flight back,' she said.

She smiled. Or thought she did. She wasn't sure.

She wasn't sure of anything at all except that she had to manoeuvre her suitcase out onto the path that ran along the back of their rooms. A hotel buggy was waiting there, ready to take both of them up to the hotel for the airport shuttle. Now it would only take her.

She let her suitcase be hefted up, clambered onto the seat herself. Nerveless…numb. Her chest was bound with steel bands, her vision still blurred. The afternoon heat pressed down on her like a crushing weight.

The buggy glided off, taking her away.

In Mel's room Nikos stood very still.

The room was empty. Quite empty.

Emotion sliced through him. He stopped it. Meshed himself together again. Made himself walk towards the house phone and pick it up, speak to the front desk to request, in tones that were curter than he would normally use to a member of hotel staff, that he be booked on the London flight that evening. Then he put the phone down. Stared about him.

She'd gone. Mel had gone. That was the only thought in his head. She'd waved him goodbye and walked out.

And he couldn't believe it. Just could…not…believe it.

In the space of a few minutes he'd gone from having Mel with him to not having her.

She walked out on me. She just walked out on me!

The slicing emotion came again—vertically from the top of his head right down to his feet. Slicing him in half, as if each side of his body would keel over separately. Destroying him.

Breath ravaged his lungs as he drew air into them, hauling the two sides of his body back together again by raw strength of will. He was in shock, he knew. Recognised it with the part of his mind that was still capable of functioning, which was somewhere deep inside him, somewhere very remote, it seemed. Shock was all there was to him right now. And the disbelief that went hand in hand with it.

The ringing of the house phone made him jolt. Automatically he picked it up, listened as he was told his flight had been booked, automatically gave his mono-syllabic thanks before hanging up.

He walked out through the French windows he'd walked in through only minutes earlier. When his world had been completely different…

When Mel had been in it.

But now Mel was gone.

Oh, God, she's gone.

The emotion came again, like a sweeping knife, head to foot—and this time it severed him in two completely…

Mel was standing in bright sunlight, heat beating down on her bare head. The view was beyond all imagining.

The great chasm in the earth a few metres beyond her was a full ten miles wide at this point, she knew—one of the greatest natural wonders of the earth. But as she stood at the rim of the Grand Canyon she could not feel its grandeur, nor its wonder. All around her tourists were milling, exclaiming, taking photos, grouping and regrouping, but still she stood, gazing out over the contorted rocks that cascaded down into the belly of the earth, where far below the Colorado River snaked along the almost subterranean base of the canyon.

She was taking part in an organised day tour from Las Vegas, having flown in from Washington, where she'd gone after New York. She'd assiduously visited every landmark on the tourist trail, determined to miss absolutely nothing.

Determined to fill every moment of the day with occupation. With busyness and fulfilment.

Determined to show that she was living her life to the full, seeing the world and all its wonders as she had planned and hoped so much to do.

Determined *not* to let herself remember the brief, glorious introduction to that new life of hers that she had had courtesy of Nikos.

It had been good—brilliant—fantastic—fabulous. But it had only ever been supposed be a glittering, gorgeous introduction to her new life of hedonistic freedom after long servitude. Travelling on her own, going where she wanted when she wanted, footloose and fancy-free, answerable only to herself—that was what her new life was supposed to be about.

So she must not stand here and think of Nikos. Must not stand here and see only him in her mind's vision, not the jaw-dropping stupendous splendour of the Canyon.

And above all she must not—must not, *must not*—let that most dangerous and fatal thought creep into her head: *If only he were here with me, standing beside me now, and we were seeing all this together... If only he were seeing everything with me...*

Seeing everything with her...

If only he'd been with her in New York, seeing the sights with her as they'd planned. The Statue of Liberty, Central Park, the Empire State Building. And then in Washington, seeing all the historic monuments there, and then—oh, then the complete contrast of Las Vegas...so gaudy and garish and such ridiculous tacky *fun*!

In her head she could hear him laughing with her, murmuring to her, could feel him sweeping her into his arms, kissing her senseless and carrying her off to their bed to find passionate, burning rapture in each other's arms.

Oh, the longing for him was palpable, the yearning all-consuming. There was an ache inside her...she wanted him with her so much...

But he wasn't with her. Would never be with her again. They would never stand beside each other seeing the wonders that the world had to offer. Never sweep each other into their arms again.

So she must get used to it. Must accept it. Must simply stop letting thoughts like that into her head. Such uselessly tormenting thoughts...

She must simply go on standing there, staring blindly, vacantly out over this chasm in the earth. While inside her there seemed to be a chasm almost as vast.

CHAPTER NINE

'So, how was Bermuda?'

It was a casually asked question, and not one that should have made Nikos tense instantly. He made himself return an equitable reply.

'Not a bad conference,' he said.

'Nice venue, too.' His acquaintance smiled. 'Did you manage to add on any holiday time?'

Somehow Nikos managed an answer, and then ruthlessly switched the subject. Whatever he talked about, it wasn't going to be his time in Bermuda. It wasn't even something he wanted to *think* about.

That desire was, of course, completely fruitless. He thought about Bermuda all the time.

And Mel. Always Mel.

Mel laughing, head thrown back, glorious blonde hair rippling. Mel gazing at him with that expression of amusement, interest—desire. Mel melting into his arms, her mouth warm and inviting, her body clinging to his, ardent and eager...

Then he would slam down the guillotine and make himself think about something else. Anything else. Anything at all.

Work was what he mainly thought about. Lived and breathed. He'd become a powerhouse of focussed, relentless dedication to the business of the bank. Deal after deal after deal. Tireless and non-stop. Rising early and working late.

He was back to working out a lot, too. Muscle mass glistened…heart and lungs purred like the engine of a high-performance car. Sinews were lean and supple like a honed athlete. It was essential to keep his body occupied.

Because his body had a mind of its own. A mind he could not allow to function—not in the slightest. A mind that made every cell in his honed, taut body crave another body—a body that was soft and satin-smooth and sensuous as silk. Flesh to his flesh…

He still wanted her.

The irony of the situation was not lost on him. He was the one who'd wanted nothing more than a temporary affair. Had wanted only a holiday romance with Mel.

But no one had said how long the holiday had to be, had they? No, they hadn't. Or *where* it had to be. It could just as easily have been here in Greece. Mel had never seen Greece, and showing her the glories of the ancient ruins, the beauty of the islands and mountains, would have entranced her.

But she'd turned it down. Turned down spending more time with him. Gone off on her travels just the way she'd always planned to.

That was what was so galling now. That the very thing that had once reassured him that she would accept the temporary nature of her romance with him was now twisting back to bite him!

Bite him hard.

The door of his office swung open and his father

JULIA JAMES 141

strode in from his adjoining office, his expression angry, as it so often was, Nikos thought with a silent sigh.

'Do you know what your mother has done now?' his father demanded. 'She's taken herself off to Milan. She says it's because she's out of clothes—*ha!* That woman could open a fashion store with her wardrobe. But I know better. She's in a ridiculously unnecessary sulk—just because she's taken it into her stupid head that I'm having an affair with another woman.'

Nikos's mouth tightened. *Oh, great, that was all he needed.* His father sounding off to him about the latest behaviour of his wife and how it irritated him.

'And are you?' he replied bluntly.

His father waved a hand impatiently. 'Do you blame me?' he demanded, his voice aggrieved. 'Your mother's impossible! Completely impossible! She's taken off at just the most inconvenient time. We are *supposed* to be joining Demetrius Astarchis and his wife on their yacht tomorrow! Now what am I supposed to do?'

'Take your mistress instead?' his son suggested acidly.

'Don't be absurd. They're expecting your mother and me. She should be there—Demetrius and I do a valuable amount of business with each other. If nothing else, your mother should realise that the only reason she can run riot in couture houses is because of the effort I put in to keep the coffers full. She owes me *some* loyalty!'

Nikos forbore from pointing out the obvious—that loyalty was a two-way street, and keeping a mistress was not the way for his father to win his wife's. But he also knew, with weary resignation, that his mother's poisonous tongue couldn't have done a better job of driving away her husband than if she'd changed the locks on the house.

He'd never heard a conversation between them that didn't involve his mother making vicious little digs at his father all the time...or sweeping sabre strokes of bitter accusation.

He looked at his father now, standing there angrily, filled with self-righteous indignation at his wife's errant behaviour, and felt an immense exasperated irritation with them both.

'Is that what you came in to tell me?' he asked tightly, having no intention of being drawn into witnessing any further diatribes by his father against his mother.

'I wanted to check over the Hong Kong trip with you,' his father said, still ill-humoured, 'and warn you that if your mother hasn't deigned to return before you go I'll have to go and fetch her home. I'm not having her roaming around Europe, bad-mouthing me to everyone she knows. And I'm not leaving her in Milan on her own too long either—catching the eye of some predatory male!'

He gave his son a withering look.

'Not that your mother has any looks left—she's not aged well,' he said sourly. 'Which is another reason,' he finished defiantly, 'for me to find something more agreeable to look at than her crow's feet.'

Nikos forbore to add oil to burning waters by reminding his father that his mother was equally and vocally critical of her husband's jowly features and increasing paunch. Instead, all he said was, 'I've got the meetings in Hong Kong all set up. Take a look.'

He found he was glad he had a trip to the Far East coming up—it might help take his mind off his own miseries. Though it didn't do him any good to realise that he was already thinking how much he'd have loved to show Hong Kong to Mel.

We could have flown down to Malaysia after-
wards, Thailand, too, and Bali—even on to Australia,
maybe.

And from Australia they could have taken in New
Zealand—and beyond that the verdant jewels of the
South Pacific islands…

He tore his mind away. Why torment himself? Why
think about holidays he would never have with Mel?
All she'd wanted from him was a brief few weeks on a
single island. Nothing more than that…

'Good,' his father was saying now. He glanced at his
watch. 'I must go—I'm having lunch with Adela.' He
paused. 'I might not be back afterwards…'

Again, Nikos deliberately said nothing.

Not even as his father headed back to his own office, adding, 'And for God's sake don't tell your mother.
That's all I need.'

What you need, thought Nikos grimly, *is a divorce.*

But that wouldn't happen, he knew. His parents were
locked in their bitter, destructive dance, circling round
each other like snarling dogs, biting at each other constantly.

That's why I've stayed clear of long-term relation-
ships. So I'll never get trapped in an ugly, destructive
relationship the way my parents have.

Moodily, he jackknifed out of his chair, striding
across the office to stare out over the streets of Athens
below. Thoughts, dark and turbid, swirled in his mind.

He didn't want to be here, staring out over the city
of his birth, working himself senseless, just to block his
mind from thinking about what he *did* want—which
was to be somewhere utterly different.

With Mel.

He shut his eyes, swearing fluently and silently inside his head. He was off again, thinking about Mel— wanting her…wanting her so badly it was a physical pain.

But she was gone—gone, gone, *gone*. She had walked out on him and she'd been *right* to walk out on him—that was what was so unbearable for him to face. Mel had done exactly what would have happened anyway, a few days later—ended their affair. It had been just as he had planned it to be—transient, temporary, impermanent.

Safe.

Safe from the danger he'd always feared. That one fine day he'd find himself doing what his father had just done—walking in and snapping and snarling, berating and bad-mouthing the woman he was married to.

His eyes opened again, a bleak expression in them. He could hear his father's condemnation of his mother still ringing in his ears. Together or apart, they still laid into each other, still tore each other to pieces. The venom and hostility and the sheer bloody nastiness of it all…

They couldn't be more different from the way Mel and I were together…

Into his head thronged a thousand memories—Mel laughing, smiling, teasing him with an amused, affectionate glint in her eye at his foibles—him teasing her back in the same vein,—both of them at ease with each other, companionable, comfortable, contented…

Contented.

The word shaped itself in his head. He'd used it in Bermuda—trying to find the right word to match his feelings then.

Contented.

That had been the word—the right word…

Me and Mel. Mel and me.

Because it wasn't just the passion that had seared between them—incandescent though that had been—it was more, oh, so much more than that.

His mind went to his parents. They were always complaining about each other, with lines of discontent, displeasure, disapproval around their mouths, with vicious expressions in their eyes when they spoke to each other, spoke of each other to him.

Nothing, *nothing* like the way he and Mel had been.

He felt his body tense, every honed muscle engaging, as he stared out of the window—not seeing what was beyond the glass, not seeing anything except a vision of Mel's face. Beautiful beyond all dreams, but with an expression that was far, far beyond beauty to him. She was smiling at him, with a softness in her eyes, a warmth—an affection that reached out to him and made him want to reach out to her. To cup her face and drop a kiss on the tip of her nose, then tuck her hand in his, warm and secure, and stroll with her, side by side, along the beach, chatting about this or that or nothing at all, easy and happy, *contented*, towards the setting sun...

All the days of my life...

And into his head, into his consciousness, slowly, like a swimmer emerging from a deep, deep sea, the realisation came to him.

It doesn't have to be like my parents' relationship. I don't have to think that will happen. Mel and I aren't like that. We're nothing like that. Nothing!

He could feel the thoughts shaping inside his head, borne up on the emotion rising within him. If that were so, then he could take the risk—*should* take the risk— the risk he had always feared to take. Because never had he met a woman who could take that fear from him.

As if a fog had cleared from his head, taking away the occluding mist that had clouded his vision all his life, he felt the realisation pierce him.

Mel can—Mel can lift that fear from me.

That was what he had to trust. That was what he had to believe in.

What we had was too good—far too good to let go of. Far too good to cut short, fearing what it might become in years to come. I refuse to believe that she and I would ever become like my parents. I refuse to believe that the time we had together—that brief, inadequate time—couldn't go on for much longer. Not weeks, or months—but years...

His breath seemed to still in his lungs.

All my days...

For one long, breathless moment he stood there, every muscle poised, and then, as if throwing a switch, he whirled around, turned on his heel and strode back to his desk. His eyes were alight—fired with determination, with revelation, with self-knowledge.

She might not want him—she might be halfway around the world by now—she might turn him down and spurn him, go on her laughing, footloose way, but not before he found her again and put to her the question that was searing in his head now. The question he had to know the answer to...

Snatching up the phone on his desk, he spoke to his secretary.

'Get me our security agency, please—I need to start an investigation. I need—' he took a hectic breath '—to find someone.'

The plane banked as it started its descent into Heathrow. Mel felt herself tilting, and again the sensation of nausea rose inside her. She damped it down. It had started when they'd hit a pocket of turbulence mid-Atlantic, but they would be on the tarmac soon—then she'd feel better.

Physically, at least.

Mentally, she didn't feel good in the slightest. She felt as if a pair of snakes were writhing, fighting within her—two opposing emotions, twisting and tormenting her. Her face tightened. Her features pulled taut and stark. She had an ordeal in front of her. An ordeal she didn't want but had to endure. Had to face.

This wasn't the way it was supposed to be.

A holiday romance—that was all she'd ever intended Nikos to be. A brief, glorious fling—then off on her travels as she'd planned for so long. Happy and carefree. On her own.

Travels had turned out to be nothing—to be ashes— without Nikos at her side to share them with.

It wasn't supposed to have been like that...

Missing him so much...

Missing him...missing him all the time—wherever she went, wherever she'd gone. Just wanting to be with him again. Anywhere in the world...so long as it was with him...

How could she have been so unbearably stupid as to walk out on him? He'd asked her to go with him to Athens and she'd refused.

I could have had more time...more time with him...

Yet even as the cry came silently and cruelly within her she heard her own voice answer the one inside her head—even more cruel.

How much more time? A week? A month? And then what? When the holiday romance burned itself out? When he finally didn't want you any more because all he wanted was an affair...? Nothing permanent. Nothing binding between them.

She heard again in her head his warning to her that horrible, horrible morning in Bermuda when she'd walked out and gone to the airport to fly to New York alone.

'What had you in mind? I made it clear, right from the start, that I was only talking about a few weeks together at the most...'

A hideous, hollow laugh sounded inside her. A few weeks? Oh, dear God, now she had the means to be with him, to keep him in her life, for far longer than a few weeks...

A permanent, perpetual bond between them.

Her features twisted.

No, it wasn't supposed to have been like this at all.

I wasn't supposed to fall for him.

She swallowed the nausea rising in her throat again.

I wasn't supposed to get pregnant...

CHAPTER TEN

NIKOS EXITED THE brand-new office building, heading for the car that waited for him at the kerb. He glanced up at the sky between the tall serried ranks of modern office blocks in downtown Hong Kong. The clouds had massed even more, and the humid air had a distinct chill to it. The wind was clearly rising. The local TV channel had been full of news of an impending typhoon, speculating on whether it would hit the island or not.

Back at his hotel, he noticed that the typhoon warning notice had gone up a level. His mouth set. He still had more meetings lined up, but they might have to be postponed if the weather worsened. Once a typhoon hit in force the streets would be cleared of traffic, the subway shut down and the population kept indoors until it was safe to go out again.

From his suite at the top of the towering hotel, with its view over the harbour, he could see the grey water, choppy and restless, and watched frowningly as ocean-going ships came in from the open sea beyond to seek shelter from the ferocious winds that were starting to build. The way things were going, it was more than likely his flight back to London would be cancelled.

Frustration bit at him. The last thing he wanted

was to be stuck here in Hong Kong with a typhoon threatening!

He forced himself to be rational. He'd set the security agency he used for personal protection to the task of tracking down the woman he *had* to locate—and that would take time. Even as he thought this a memory darted with piquant power—the memory of his first evening with Mel, bantering with her about how she should take a bodyguard with her on her travels to keep all predatory males away from her...

How long ago that seemed—and yet also as if it were only yesterday...

Automatically, he checked his mobile and email—still nothing from the agency. With a vocal rasp, he got stuck back into his work yet again.

Patience—that was what he needed. But he wasn't in the mood to be patient. Not in the slightest.

The tube train taking Mel into the City, towards the London offices of the Parakis Bank, was crowded and airless. She felt claustrophobic after the wide-open spaces of America, and she was dreading the ordeal that lay in front of her.

She should have phoned first, she knew, but she hadn't been able to face it. Nikos probably wasn't even in London now—why should he be? But maybe she could talk to his PA, find out where he was, how best to get in touch with him. At worst she could leave the painfully written letter she'd got in her bag. Telling him what she had to tell him...

She'd written it last night, rewriting it over and over again, trying to find the right words to tell him. The right words to tell him the wrong thing. That their holiday romance had ended in a way that neither of them could possibly have foreseen. That neither could possibly have wanted.

Yet even as she thought it she could feel emotion rising up in her—feel the conflict that had tormented her since her first shocked and disbelieving discovery of what had happened. Conflict that had never abated since—that was going round and round and round in her head, day and night.

What am I going to do? What am I going to do?

The train glided to a halt at another station and the doors slid open. More people got off. Then the doors slid shut and the train started forward again, out of the lighted platform area and back into yet another tunnel. Stop, start, stop again, start again—over and over. And still the words went round and round in her head.

What am I going to do? What am I going to do?

She was pregnant, with an unplanned baby, by a man who had only been a holiday romance. That was the stark truth of it.

It was the very last thing she had ever thought would happen.

She heard her own words, spoken so casually, so confidently, at the charity dinner Nikos had taken her to—their very first date.

'Right now, a baby is definitely not on my agenda.'

All she'd wanted was the freedom to indulge her wanderlust—finally, after so many years of looking after her grandfather. She hadn't wanted more ties, more responsibilities.

Other words cut into her mind. Not hers this time. Nikos—talking as they'd walked away from that mismatched couple at the conference hotel. Telling her bitterly how his parents had become warring enemies.

'When I came along everything went pear-shaped.'

That was what he had said. Showing her his scars—his fears. His determination never to risk what had happened to his parents happening to him.

And now, thanks to her, that was what was facing him.

Her features twisted and emotion stabbed at her like a knife...a tormenting, toxic mix of dismay, fear, doubt and fierce, primitive protectiveness...

What am I going to do? What am I going to do?

Round and round the question circled in her tired, exhausted brain, with no answer at all.

The train pulled into yet another station, and with a start Mel realised she should have changed lines at the previous one. Hastily she pushed her way off, pausing on the platform to look around for directions to the line she needed. As she was staring about the large lettering on the advert plastered to the curved wall in front of her suddenly caught her eye.

Pregnant? Unsure?
Overwhelmed? Confused?

Her gaze focussed instantly, and the words below resolved themselves into sense in her brain.

Talk to us in complete confidence for help to find your way forward.

Beneath was the name of a charity she had been vaguely familiar with in her student days, but had never had need to pay any attention to.

Until now.

She stared, repeating the words of the advert inside her head. *Unsure...overwhelmed...confused?* Dear God, she was all of those, all right. Her eyes drifted to the address given on the advert, registering that it was nearby.

Her grip tightened on her suitcase and with a jerk she started to head towards the escalators.

Oblivious of the quietly dressed man doing likewise a little way behind her...

Fifteen minutes later she was seated, hands clenched with tension, in a consulting room at the charity's walk-in offices.

'You really should take longer to think this through.' The woman talking to Mel spoke with a warm, sympathetic, but cautious tone.

'I *have* thought it through—I've thought it through over and over again...ever since I found out I was pregnant. It's the only thing I've been thinking about.'

Mel's voice was stressed. She had poured everything out, tumbled and conflicted and anguished, and the trained counsellor had listened quietly and attentively. Then she had spelt out to Mel the options that were available—the choices she could make.

As Mel had listened she had felt her heart grow heavier and heavier at the answer to the question that was tormenting her—that had tormented her ever since she had stared, disbelieving, at the blue line on the pregnancy test kit.

She looked across at the counsellor, her expression strained, but there was a resolve in her eyes that had not been there before.

'My mind is made up,' she said. 'That's my decision. My baby—my responsibility for what happens.'

She got to her feet. Once more a slight wave of nausea bit at her, and she swallowed it down.

The counsellor had stood up, too.

'I am always here,' she said, her voice kind, 'if you

feel you want to discuss this further…talk things through again.'

But Mel shook her head. 'Thank you—but, no. I know what I'm going to do.' She gave a difficult smile. 'Thank you for your time. It's been…' she took a breath '…invaluable. You've helped me to reach the answer I needed to find.'

She held out a hand, shook the counsellor's briefly and made her way back out on to the street. Her pace, as she headed off, was determined. Resolute. But her tread felt as heavy as her heart.

As she headed back to the tube station she got out the letter she'd written so painfully the night before. Tearing it in two, she dropped it in a litter bin. Then she went back down into the Underground. This time taking the direction away from the City.

Away from Nikos's offices.

There was nothing to tell him now. Nothing at all.

Her mind was clear on that.

Finally the writhing snakes that had tormented her had ceased their endless conflict.

Her baby was hers and hers alone.

And as she sat carefully down on a seat in the tube train her hand crept to her abdomen, spreading across gently. Protectively.

Nikos threw himself into his first-class seat on the plane as they boarded in Hong Kong, relief filling him. Finally he was on his way back to Europe. The typhoon had hit, just as he'd feared, and all flights had been cancelled. Now, though, the delayed flights were resuming and he was headed for London.

But he still didn't know where Mel was. His investigators had drawn a blank—and in a way he wasn't surprised. Because how *did* you locate someone who was one of thousands of tourists?

He'd told the agency about the sandwich bar she'd worked in, in case that might help. Maybe her former employer could shed some light on where she was right now? Hadn't Mel said that Sarrie was the uncle of a friend of hers?

And there was a possibility that she might be traceable by checking out the former address details of anyone with her surname who had died the previous year in North London, to see if they could locate the address of her late grandfather's house. If they could, then maybe the estate agents handling the tenancy had contact details for Mel?

With a shake of his head, Nikos waved away the glass of champagne being proffered by the stewardess in First Class, oblivious of the admiring look the attractive brunette had thrown his way. He was oblivious to all females now. Only one in the world mattered to him—the one he was trying to find—the one who was somewhere…wandering the face of the earth…

What if she's met someone else by now?

That was the fear that bit at him—gnawed at him in the night, when his body ached for Mel to be in his arms…

But he wouldn't let himself think like that—he wouldn't. He would hang on to the purpose he'd set for himself: he would find her and put to her the one thing he needed to say.

The one thing it was most vital to him that she knew.

Some twelve hours later Nikos strode out of the long-haul terminal at Heathrow. His car was humming at the kerb and he threw himself in, barely greeting his driver. Flicking open his laptop, he loaded his emails.

A surge of triumph welled in him—there was the email he'd been longing to see.

It was from his investigators and it was headed with the magic words: Subject located.

Yes! He all but punched the air even as his finger jabbed at the screen, opening the email. His eyes seized on the words and he started to read.

And then, inside his head, all hell broke loose.

Mel stepped out on to the pavement, hefting her suitcase out over the doorstop of the flat she had been staying in. It felt heavier than it had used to feel. Maybe the weakness she felt was to do with early pregnancy? Her mind was a blank—it was the only way she could keep going.

She'd booked a flight from Luton to Malaga, and now she had to get to Luton. But first she had a medical appointment. At a clinic that the counsellor at the pregnancy advisory charity had recommended to her and then made an appointment with.

The appointment letter was in her hand and she stared at the address again, trying to decide whether to take a bus or make for the Underground. The bus would be slower, but it would avoid her having to lug her suitcase down the tube station escalators.

She opted for the bus—she'd have enough suitcase-lugging to do once she got to the airport, and then at the other end in Malaga. She'd have to find somewhere to stay the night there…maybe a few days…until she could sort out accommodation and get her head around the new life she was going to make for herself.

One that was going to be so very, *very* different from what she had thought it was going to be.

But her mind was made up. There was no changing it now.

My baby—my decision. The only way it can be.

The heavy stone was still in her stomach, weighing her down, pushing the ever-present sense of nausea into her gullet. But it wasn't the physical impact of her pregnancy that was making her feel like this—feel as if she was being crushed to the ground…

She turned to start walking along the pavement towards the bus stop at the end of the road. Her feet dragged as if she was wearing shoes of lead.

The car braking sharply as it slewed towards the kerb made her head whip round. Recognition drew a gasp of disbelief from her. And then dismay.

Raw, shattering dismay.

Nikos was leaping from the car, charging up to her.

Dismay exploded in a million fragments—shot to pieces by the tidal wave of an utterly different emotion that surged across every synapse in her brain, flooding it with its totality.

Nikos! Nikos—here—in the flesh—in front of her—alive and well and *real*!

Not the hopeless memory in her head that was all he'd been these last endless weeks since she had walked away from him in Bermuda.

But real—oh, so real. How he'd suddenly appeared on the street like this she didn't know—didn't care. She knew only that a searing flash of joy was going through her.

Then that searing flash of joy was gone—shot to pieces in its turn.

Her arms were clamped in steel. His voice speared into her in fury.

'You're *not* doing it. Do you understand me? You're not doing it. I'll never let you do it. I don't care what the law says—I will *never* let you do that!'

Rage was boiling from him, burning in his eyes, and his face was twisted with anger as his words struck into her. She could only stare at him, not understanding...

Nikos saw the incomprehension in her face, layered over her shock at seeing him, and it maddened him yet more.

'How could you even *think* of it? How *could* you?'

The paper in her hand fluttered from her fingers to the ground. Automatically she tried to bend her knees to pick it up, but Nikos was still pinioning her and she couldn't move. He saw her movement and his eyes went to the letter on the ground. With a snarl he seized it himself, staring at it. His face whitened.

'*Thee mou...*' His voice was hollow. 'You're going there now—aren't you? *Aren't you?*'

From somewhere—she didn't know where—she found her voice. It was strained, as if it was being pulled unbearably tight.

'I didn't want you to know,' she said.

But it was too late now—the written proof of her medical appointment had revealed everything to him.

Another snarl broke from him. 'No! You were going ahead with it without even telling me, weren't you?'

Greek words burst from him—ugly and accusing. She didn't know what he was saying—only that it contained fury. Sickness rose in her. Dear God, she had been right in her decision not to tell him.

She made herself speak again as he stood there, the betraying letter in his hand, his face contorted with fury.

'It...it seemed the best thing to do, Nikos. I...I didn't want to involve you in any of this...'

'*Involve* me?'

He stared at her as if she'd spoken in an alien tongue.

Then a sudden, sickening realisation hit him. His hand, which had been still clamped around her arm, dropped away. He took a step back.

'Is it mine?'

Three little words—but in them a wealth of accusation. She paled, and he heard his voice going on, cutting at her with slashing words.

'It's a reasonable question to ask. After all, I picked you up easily enough, didn't I? Maybe you got a similar offer when you went off to New York without me? Maybe *he's* the guy who got you pregnant?'

She gasped as if he had struck her. *'No!'* she cried, the word tearing from her in rejection.

Emotion leapt in his eyes. 'So you admit it's mine? You admit it—and yet here you are, with the evidence of your damnable intentions in your hand, and you were going to say nothing to me—*nothing*!'

She shut her eyes, misery overwhelming her. 'I told you—I thought it would be for the best. It wasn't an easy decision, Nikos—truly it wasn't.'

More Greek broke from him, dark and furious. 'You never wanted to be pregnant, did you? Don't tell me otherwise, because I won't believe it.'

Her features convulsed. 'No—I didn't want to be pregnant,' she said, the words torn from her. 'When I realised it seemed…it seemed…'

Nikos supplied the words. 'An end to your freedom?' His voice was heavy, crushing.

'Yes. Pregnancy seemed…seemed the last thing I wanted…' She spoke faintly, as if the words could barely be spoken.

He turned her appointment letter over in his hand, his eyes never leaving her. 'And so you decided to regain your freedom,' he said, and now his words were not just heavy and crushing—they were swords, stabbing into her, strike after strike, pitiless and condemning. 'You decided to end the pregnancy.'

He saw her whiten like a sheet. The blood drained from her face. Inside him, unbearable fury lashed. Fury and something so much more.

All she wants is to get rid of the baby we created between us. It means nothing to her but a burden, a curb on her freedom!

And that was why she had bolted. Because surely she must have known that the moment he knew she was carrying his child there could be only one outcome?

For a second—just a fraction of a second—he felt his heart leap within him.

Mel—back with him. Back with him and bringing with her a gift even more precious than herself.

He felt his lungs squeezed, the air crushed from them.

But she didn't want that—didn't want him. And she had never wanted his baby.

Instead she wanted what she was set on doing now. What that starkly condemning report had told him. The report that had informed him she had been spotted entering a high street charity for a walk-in consultation.

The comment in parentheses had been unemotional.

We would advise our client that this particular charity is supportive of pro-choice options for women with unplanned pregnancies.

In a single sentence he had read heaven—and hell.

She was staring at him now, still as white as a sheet. She felt the words he'd thrown at her sear into her brain like a burning brand of accusation. Her mouth opened.

Words were desperate to take shape, to fly across the gaping space between them, to counter the dreadful accusation he had hurled at her.

'Nikos! It isn't like that. It—'

But he was cutting right across her, stopping her speaking.

'Don't try and defend it. You can call it what you like, but we both know the truth of what you are planning to do.'

The terrible words were like knives, slashing at her. She could not bear to hear them. She gave a cry, backing away as if he had struck her physically. Features convulsing, she thrust past him, out into the roadway.

She had to get away—oh, dear God, she had to get away.

There was a screech of brakes, a hideous sound of squealing rubber. And then, as if in some horror movie slow-motion, Nikos saw the car hit her…saw her frail, fragile body crumple like paper and fall to the tarmac.

CHAPTER ELEVEN

HE WAS THERE in an instant—a heartbeat. The space of time between living and dying. He was yelling—he could hear himself yelling—but it was as if it were someone else. Someone else yelling as he saw that fragile figure crumple to the ground. Someone else yelling like a madman for an ambulance.

Because he was on his knees beside her, horror in his face, his eyes, in his whole being.

Let her be alive! Dear God in heaven, let her be alive. It's all I ask—all I beg! Anything else—anything else at all—I can bear. But not that—oh, not that!

It was all that consumed him in the eternity it took for the ambulance to arrive.

She had a pulse—it was his only desperate source of hope—but she was unconscious, inert, scarcely breathing, still as white as a sheet.

I did this to her. I did it. The punishing accusation went on and on in his head.

The paramedics tended her, phoning ahead to the hospital that they were bringing her in, checking the car's driver for shock and whiplash.

Nikos piled into the ambulance with her. 'Is she going to be all right? Please God, tell me.'

But the ambulance crew were adept at tragedy, and

only gave platitudes to him. There could be no answer to that question until she was in A&E...

Time stopped...time raced. Time blurred.

When the ambulance arrived at the hospital the emergency team fell to work. Nikos hung on to the doorjamb of the resuscitation bay and prayed—prayed with all his strength.

'Just *tell* me!' He was beyond coherence.

One of the doctors looked up. 'Looks like only bruising, lacerations—no sign of internal damage...no lung damage,' he reeled off. 'One cracked rib so far. No skull trauma. Spine and limbs seem OK, though she'll need a scan to check thoroughly.

'And she's coming round...'

Nikos swayed, Greek words breaking from him in a paean of gratitude. Mel's eyes were flickering, and a low groan sounded in her throat as consciousness returned. Then, as her eyes opened fully, Nikos could see her expression change to one of anguish when she saw all the medics clustered around her.

'My baby,' she cried. '*My baby!* Oh, please—please don't let my baby be gone. Please, no—*please, no!*'

Immediately the doctor responded, laying a calming hand on her arm.

'There's no sign of a bleed,' he said. 'But we'll get you up to Obs and Gynae the moment you've had your scan and they'll check you out thoroughly. OK?'

He smiled down reassuringly and Mel's stricken gaze clung to him. Then, before Nikos's eyes, she burst into crying. 'Thank God. Oh, thank God,' he heard her say.

Over and over again...

And inside him it felt as if the world had just changed for ever.

'Thank God,' he echoed. 'Thank God.'

But it was more than the life of his unborn child he was thanking God for—so, *so* much more…

Then the emergency team were dispersing, and a nurse was left to instruct that Mel be wheeled off for a scan and then up to Obs and Gynae. Once again Nikos was prevented from accompanying her, and frustration raged within him. He needed to be with her—needed her to be with *him*.

After an age—an eternity—he was finally told that she was in Obs and Gynae and that her scans, thankfully, had all been clear. Again, Nikos gave thanks—gave thanks with all his being.

He rushed up to the obstetrics and gynaecology department, heart pounding…

There were more delays there—more being kept waiting, pacing up and down. He focussed on one thing, and one thing only—getting to Mel. And then finally—finally—he was allowed to see her.

She was in a side ward, blessedly on her own. She was conscious still, but her face was pale—apart from the grazing on her cheek from where she'd collapsed on the tarmac after the impact. Her face whitened yet more as the nurse showed him in.

He rushed up to her—then stopped dead.

The expression on her face had stopped him in his tracks. She was looking…*stricken*.

He felt a hollowing out inside him. Horror washed through him again as he saw in his head that nightmare moment when the car had struck her and she'd crumpled like paper.

Then another emotion seared through his head.

His eyes fastened on her, desperate to read in her gaze what he absolutely, totally *had* to know. He heard in his head her terrified cries down in A&E.

'My baby,' she'd cried—and he could hear her cry still. *'My baby! Oh, please—please don't let my baby be gone. Please, no—please, no!'*

Relief, profound and infinitely grateful, had ripped through him that at that moment—at that moment of extreme danger to her baby—she had realised she wanted it. Realised how precious it was. How precious *she* was.

'I nearly lost you—I nearly killed you...'

He took a jerking step towards her. Saw her expression change.

'Oh, God, Mel—I'm sorry. I'm so sorry.' The words burst from him.

Words shaped themselves on her lips. Were uttered with difficulty and strain and a terrible emptiness. 'You thought I wanted to kill my baby.'

It wasn't an accusation, only a statement. But it came from a place he didn't want to exist.

He swallowed. 'I know—I know you don't. I heard you, Mel. I heard your terror when you came round—you were terrified for your baby.'

He saw her hand move slightly, unconsciously, to lie across her abdomen. Sheltering. Protective.

Emotion stabbed within him. 'Mel, I—'

His voice was jerky, but hers cut right across it.

'How could you think that, Nikos? How *could* you?' Her eyes were piercing—accusing. Horrified.

A rasp sounded in his throat. 'You said yourself that you didn't want to be pregnant. That it would be an end to your freedom.' He took a ragged breath, memory searing through him. 'And I kept remembering how you told Fiona Pellingham that you didn't want a baby now—'

Her face worked. She acknowledged the truth of what

he'd just said—knew she had to face it. 'That was my first reaction, yes—but it wasn't the only one, Nikos. Truly it wasn't. But it was so…so complicated.'

Complicated… Such a weak, pathetic word to describe the searing clash of emotions that had consumed her as she'd stared at that thin blue line on the pregnancy testing kit.

They were there still, consuming her. Anguish churned inside her that Nikos should think…should think…

He was staring at her. 'You were on your way to an abortion clinic—I saw the appointment letter.'

Her face contorted. 'It was an antenatal appointment. That's all it was! To have a check-up before I fly to Spain tonight. How could you think it was for anything else? How *could* you?'

She took a shuddering breath.

'My old GP is miles away, and I'd have had to wait days for an appointment. So the woman at the charity made an appointment for me at a mother and baby clinic.'

He was staring at her still. Still not making sense of things. 'It's a pro-choice charity,' he said, his voice hollow. 'They arrange abortions for women who have pregnancies they don't want.'

Her features were screwed up. 'Yes, they do, Nikos. But they also help with all the other alternatives, as well. Like single-parenting—raising a baby alone.' Her expression changed again. 'How do you know I went to that charity?'

He took a deep breath. This wasn't the way he'd thought it was going to be—this moment of finding her again. Shock still reverberated through him—shock upon shock. He remembered the terror as he'd read the report that had totally changed everything—for ever. It had given him the most wonderful gift he could imagine—and threatened to tear it from him in the same moment.

Mel—carrying his child.

Mel—wanting to destroy their child…

Mel—crumpling to the ground as the car hit her, nearly destroyed by his accusation.

Cold snaked down his spine like iced water as he realised how hideously close he'd come to losing everything—everything he was most desperate to keep.

'I…I've been trying to find you. I sent investigators to search for you. They found you, finally, where you were staying—and they saw you there. I only just got their findings now—when I landed at Heathrow. I've been in Hong Kong. There was a typhoon.'

His jerky, staccato words ground to a halt.

'I've been trying to find you,' he said again.

It was, he knew, the only thing he had to say to her. Nothing else mattered—nothing at all.

Except that I've found her. That she's alive, that she carries my child!

Emotion flooded through him.

Our child—she bears our child.

Wonder and gratitude soared in him. He felt weak with it.

She was staring at him.

'You were trying to find me?' Her voice was faint.

'*Yes!* Mel—Mel, I—'

But she cut across him. 'Oh, dear God, I wish with all my heart you hadn't. I wish you'd never found me.' Her face buckled. 'Never found me and never found out about the baby.'

Her voice was anguished. Inside her that same impossible conflict of emotions was still warring, tearing her apart.

Oh, dear God, what a mess this is—what an unholy, impossible mess!

She felt again that stabbing wound, the lashing blow that she'd felt when she'd heard the full import of his words—the cruel accusation he'd hurled at her that had made her want to run, to flee straight into the path of the car that had nearly killed her—nearly killed her baby.

Nikos's baby—that I didn't want him to know about— Because if he did...

'I never meant to involve you in this, Nikos,' she said, her voice twisted, her eyes pleading.

He was staring at her again. 'What do you mean, *"involve"* me? Mel, this is *our* child. Our baby!'

How could she talk like this? Say she hadn't wanted him to know?

Words she had said earlier now registered with him— something about going to Spain, taking a flight that day...

The cold snaked down his spine again.

Had he not sent his investigators to find her she would have disappeared again.

And I'd never have known—never have known she was carrying my baby—our baby!

Fear at what had so very nearly happened gouged at him.

She was answering him—her voice low, strained.

'It doesn't have to be, Nikos. It can just be *my* baby. That's why I went to that pregnancy charity—I needed someone to talk to about not telling you about the baby. She...she helped me make my mind up. And then she went through the practicalities of raising a child single-handed, without paternal involvement, taking all the responsibility on myself.'

'*Thee mou*—why? *Why?* Why even *think* like that?' The words broke from him.

She didn't answer—couldn't. Could only press her hand against her abdomen again, feeling…needing the reassurance that her baby was safe—*safe*. The baby she would raise on her own, as she had come to realise she must. Because anything else was…impossible. Just impossible…

She felt her throat tighten. To see Nikos again—here…so real—but for him to be as far away from her as he could be…

He saw the emotion on her face. Realised what it must mean. She hadn't wanted him to know she was pregnant because she didn't want him *involved*.

Didn't want him in her life.

After all his hopes…all the hopes that had soared within him as he'd stood in his office in Athens…when he'd realised that he and Mel were nothing, *nothing* like his parents. That what they had between them could never descend into the bitter farce that was his parents' marriage.

But now his hopes were ashes in his mouth. Heaviness filled him.

She wants her freedom—the freedom she's craved for so long—the freedom she left me for and still wants.

The freedom he could not take from her—*must* not take from her.

Not even for the sake of the child she carried—*their* child. The child she wanted to raise on her own—free of him.

He sought for what he must say now. Letting go of

his hopes…letting them fall to the ground, dashed to pieces…

'You must have known…' he said, and his voice was hollow, but so, *so* careful. 'You must have known that I would…stand by you, Mel.'

He was picking his words with infinite care. All that she had said to him while they'd been together, about how precious her newly gained life of freedom was to her, came back to him like blows.

It was why she left me—to safeguard her freedom.
Why she walked out on me when I wanted more of her than she wanted to give.

He would let her keep that freedom—he must. He would not try to chain her to his side in a life she did not want. If she wanted to raise their child herself he must let her—he *must*.

Whatever it cost him.

He came towards her now, took the hard chair that was near the bed and sat himself down on it. Took a deep, steadying breath in order to say what he must say now that she'd made it crystal clear that she'd never wanted to tell him about her pregnancy. Never wanted him *'involved.'* The word twisted inside him like snakes.

'You know I'll stand by you, Mel. There'll be no money worries. I'll see to everything. Look after you, whatever you choose. So you can live wherever you want—well, anywhere child-safe, obviously.'

She heard him speak, and each word was like an arrow in her. But with each word she knew irrefutably that after all her anguish and turmoil, her longings and her fears from the very moment she had seen that thin blue line on the pregnancy test, that she had done what had proved the right thing to have done. She knew she had made the right decision in determining to head for Spain, not to tell Nikos about being pregnant, not to burden him with it…

But it was too late now—he knew she carried their child. And now she would have to take the consequences of his knowledge. Protect herself from them as much as she could.

A pang went through her…

He made as if to reach for her hand, then stopped, drew back. Then he spoke again.

'I know how vital your freedom is to you, Mel. I'll protect that for you as much as I can—make as few demands on you as I can. So long as from time to time you let me…let me—'

He stopped, unable to continue.

Let me see my baby—my child. Let me see you, Mel—let me be a part of your life, however small…

He swallowed, forced himself to keep going, to keep his voice studiedly, doggedly neutral—impossible though it was to do so, when inside he was holding down with brute force what was burning inside him.

'But please, Mel, don't disappear without my knowing—that's all I ask. I have…responsibilities…for you… for the baby…'

The word tolled in her brain. *'Responsibilities…'* Yes, that was all it could be to him. He'd been angry—furious—and understandably so, when he'd thought she wanted a termination. But now that he'd realised she wanted this baby—how terrified she'd been when she'd thought she might lose it—now it was just a question of…*responsibilities*.

Responsibilities she would—*must*—keep as light as possible for him. She must assure him of that.

'I won't…impose on you, Nikos. Financially I'll be

all right. I have the rental income from my grandfather's house, and until the baby is born I can work. I'm
going to base myself in Spain, probably, because I can
live cheaply there. There are various child benefits I'm
entitled to claim as well—that woman at the charity explained it all to me.'

'Impose?' he echoed. 'Mel, this is *my* baby you're
talking about. It goes without question that I'll take
care of everything.'

She shook her head violently. It hurt, but she didn't
care.

'Oh, Nikos, that's why I wish to God you'd never
found out. I know how scarred you are by your parents
chaining themselves to each other. That you never want
to run such a risk yourself. That's why you only wanted
a brief romance with me. The last thing you want is to
be trapped—trapped as you are now—trapped by unplanned, unwanted fatherhood. And that's why I was
never going to tell you about the baby. So *you* could
be free.'

Her voice was anguished, no more than a whisper
now.

'If you'd never known about the baby we could both
have been free of each other…'

For a moment…for an eternity…there was silence.

Then… 'Free of each other?' Nikos's echo of her
words dropped like lead into the silence.

Abruptly, he let go of her hands. Pushed the chair
back roughly. Got to his feet. Paced about the narrow
room. Turned back to look at her. Tension radiated from
him.

'Your freedom to roam the world after all those years
looking after your grandfather—mine to avoid any

kind of repetition of the snake pit that is my parents' marriage—is that it?'

There was something strange in his voice—something that made her stare at him. Not understanding. Not comprehending.

He didn't wait for an answer—just ploughed on. That same strange note was in his voice, the same strangeness in his face…his eyes.

'All my life I've run scared,' he said. 'Scared and, yes, *scarred*. Scarred by what I've had to witness between my warring, snarling parents. Tearing each other apart…tearing their marriage apart. And I dreaded, *dreaded* that I might end up doing the same.'

He took a breath—a shuddering breath.

'I vowed I would never run that risk. And I vowed I would never get involved with any woman who could endanger that vow. I only ever wanted temporary relationships. Nothing…deeper. Nothing…longer. Nothing longer than a holiday romance.'

There was a twist in his voice now, and it was heavy with irony. Bitter self-mockery.

'Just the way you did.' He took another breath, felt it razoring his lungs. 'We were so well suited, weren't we, Mel? In our own different ways we wanted the same thing—our freedom.'

He gazed at her—at the way she lay there, at her golden hair, her beautiful face—and a thousand memories came rushing to his head of those glorious days they'd had together—so good…so *good*.

So *right*.

And in the golden wash of those memories came knowledge, pouring like a fountain through him. Confirming—in a tidal wave of emotion—what had swept over him when he'd set out to find Mel again—to beg her to stay in his life.

He stilled. Thrust his hands deep into his trouser pockets. Stood there immobile, unreadable. Then something changed in his expression. He seemed to stand straighter—taller.

He looked at her lying there, her body ripening with their baby...their child-to-be.

'I want a new freedom,' he said. His voice was different now—resolute, adamant. 'The freedom not to be scarred by my parents' marriage—not to be fearful of repeating their mistakes. The freedom, Mel, to say finally what I have crushed down up to now, because I don't want to put on you what you do not want. You want your freedom—honoured and preserved—and I won't try and hamper you, or constrain you, or curtail you in any way. I know how hard-earned it is, how well deserved it is. You have your scars, too, Mel, but for all that I still want a new freedom.'

He paused, took a razor-edged breath. Then spoke again.

'I want the freedom to say this, Mel.' He took another breath, just as sharp, and absolutely vital to his existence. 'You said if I hadn't known about the baby we could have been free of each other.'

Between them, the silence stretched. Mel could not speak, could say nothing at all, for suddenly there was no breath in her lungs—no breath at all—and still the silence stretched between them.

Then... 'I don't want to be free of you.' Nikos's voice seared into the silence. 'When I saw that car hit you— oh, God, I thought you were dead. I thought you were *dead*! That I'd lost you for ever. And it was the worst moment of my life.'

It felt as if his heart was being impaled, speared again by the terror he'd felt as he'd watched her crumple to the ground. He relived that moment of absolute nightmare, knowing with grovelling gratitude to all the powers-that-be that he'd been spared. Knowing with a blaze in his head, in his heart, that he could not go on without speaking.

He surged on. It was too late to stop now—far, far too late.

'I want you to come back to me so much. I can't help hoping…hoping against hope…that despite everything—despite all that you've ever said to me—you might just—just…' He took a final ragged breath. 'Just want to come back to me. That you might just,' he said, and his eyes could not leave hers…not for a second, not for an instant, 'want to make your life with me.'

He had said it. Finally he had said it.

His heart was bared now, and it was beating for her and her alone. And if she spurned it—if she looked at him with pity, with rejection, after hearing words that had only made her want to flee from him the more—then he would bear it. But if he didn't put his words out there, then she might never know…never guess…just what he felt for her.

'I don't want to be free of you, Mel. I *can't* be free of you. You're in my head, and in my thoughts, and in my blood. You're in my *heart*, Mel…'

His eyes were blazing…the blood was roaring in his veins.

'There's only one freedom I want, Mel. I want to be free to love you.'

There was silence—absolute silence.

Nikos's gaze lasered down at her, willing her to speak. To say something—anything. But she simply lay there, her face as white as ice. Then he saw slow, thick tears start to ooze from beneath her eyelids.

He was at her side in an instant—a fraction of a second. Seizing her hands, clutching them to him.

'Mel! Don't cry—oh, my darling one, don't cry. I'm sorry—I'm sorry that I said all that to you. I should never have burdened you with it.'

But she only wept more, and he had to scoop his arm around her shoulders and cradle her against him. She wept into him—tears and tears and more tears. He soothed her hair and held her close, and closer still. And then, somewhere at his shoulder, he heard her speak. Muffled and tearful.

Carefully, mindful of how fragile her body was, he lowered her back upon the pillows. But she clung to his hand still. Her eyes swam with tears.

'I want that freedom, too. Oh, Nikos, I want it more than anything in the world!' Her face crumpled again. 'I want to be free to love you, free to *tell* you that I love you. And to love you the way I do.'

She wept again, and he held her again, and she was as light as a feather. For all the world weighed nothing now—nothing at all.

'I missed you so much,' she sobbed. 'I tried so hard not to miss you, but I did. All the time in America I missed you. I missed you wherever I went. Everywhere without you was...*awful*. I wanted you with me. On the Staten Island Ferry, at the top of the Empire State Building... I wanted to laugh with you in Las Vegas, revel in all its gaudy garishness. And I wanted you to stand beside me at the rim of the Grand Canyon and look down a mile deep into the earth. I wanted you everywhere I went. And you weren't there, Nikos, because

I'd walked out on you—and I'd walked out on you because…because…'

The sobbing came again, and once again he was
soothing her, stroking her hair, clasping her hand tight,
so tight.

'Because I knew that if I didn't go then, I'd never go.
And I *had* to go—it was a holiday romance we had—
only that. That was all you wanted—and all I wanted—
all I thought it would ever be. But it wasn't, Nikos—it
wasn't, it *wasn't*… But it had never been *supposed* to be
anything more than a holiday romance because I wanted
to be free—free like I've wanted to be for so, *so* long.'

She pulled away from him, her face working, full
of anguish.

'When I first found out I was pregnant I…I was
distraught. I was terrified that I'd be plunged back
into having to take care of another human being just
when I'd got my own life back. But at the same time
I felt my heart leap with joy. I had a *baby* growing inside me—a wondrous new life—and it was *your* baby,
Nikos. Yours. And I realised…I realised…' her eyes
were clinging to his and her hands were clinging to
him '…I realised, Nikos, that all I wanted on this earth
was to be free to love my baby—free to want my baby
more than anything else in all the world. And because
of that…because of that—'

She broke off, tears welling again, her voice choked
with emotion, with discovery.

'Because all I wanted was to love my baby I knew…I
knew—oh, Nikos—I knew it meant I was free to love.
Free to love *you*. Love you the way I wanted to. The way
I'd feared to because it was loving my poor grandfather
that kept me by his side so long. I feared love would be

a tie. And I thought all I wanted was to be free of all ties. Free of all bonds.'

Tears flowed down her cheeks and she felt her heart must surely overflow with the emotion now pouring through her.

'But to love *you*, Nikos, is to be free.'

He moved to sweep her to him, but she held him back, fear leaping in her eyes.

'But *am* I free to love you, Nikos? Am I? You talked of standing by me and "responsibilities". And—'

'Mel, my darling one, I said that only because I didn't want to burden you with my wanting you the way I do. With my wanting, more than anything in this life, to be your husband—your devoted, loving husband—the father to our beloved child—with you, my beloved wife.'

She gave a little choke of laughter and of tears. Of happiness and bliss.

'What fools we've been. Denying what we both craved.'

'Each other!' Nikos finished, and then he swept her to him, wanting no more pointless words, no more unnecessary doubts, no more fleeting fears.

He was free, finally, to hold her, to embrace her, to kiss her—to love her. As she was free to love him in return. And they were both free to love the child she carried.

Free to be happy with each other—all their lives.

A cough sounded from the doorway. They sprang apart. The nurse took in Mel's tear-stained face and frowned slightly.

'Happy tears or sad tears?' she asked enquiringly, with a lift of her eyebrow.

'Happy,' said Mel and Nikos in unison.

The nurse's gaze went to their fast-clasped hands,

and she nodded. 'Not too much emotion,' she advised, with another nod and a smile. 'Not good for baby.'

She picked up the notes from the foot of the bed, glancing at them. 'Overnight stay for observation,' she confirmed. Then she glanced at Nikos. 'I'm sorry to tell you this, but it's not actually visiting hours at the moment. It's only because your—'

'Wife-to-be,' Nikos inserted, throwing a glance at Mel.

'Your wife-to-be,' echoed the nurse dutifully, 'has come up here from A&E.' She looked again at the pair of them. 'It's visiting hours at six, so come back then. In the meantime…' her mouth twitched, and her expression was sympathetic now '…you've got five more minutes.' She whisked out.

Nikos turned to Mel. His heart was soaring. Soaring like a bird in flight.

'Will five minutes do it?' he asked her, his brow lifting questioningly.

Mel shook her head. She was floating somewhere above the surface of the hospital bed—she didn't know where. Didn't care.

Had it been so simple? Had a holiday romance been the real thing all along?

I wanted freedom, but my freedom is here—here with Nikos. Here with our child, waiting to be born.

She felt her heart constrict. Whatever names Nikos might want, one she knew. If their baby was a boy it would be named for her grandfather. The grandfather she had loved so much. Not the stricken husk he had become, but the loving, protective grandfather she remembered so clearly.

Oh, Gramps—you wanted me to find a good man— and now I have. I have!

'OK,' said Nikos. 'Well, if five minutes won't do it…' his eyes softened as he gazed down at her, the woman he had claimed the freedom to love '…how about fifty years?'

Her face lit. 'Sounds good to me,' she said. 'Sounds *very* good!'

He bent to kiss her. 'To our Golden Wedding Anniversary, then, and all the golden years between.'

'To our golden years together,' echoed Mel, and kissed him back.

EPILOGUE

THE CHRISTENING PARTY at Nikos and Mel's newly acquired family-sized villa on the coast outside Athens
was crowded with guests. Mel sat in almost regal splendour on the sofa, and young Nikos Stephanos Albert—
already known as Nicky—lay on her lap, resplendent
in his christening gown, fast asleep, oblivious to all the
admiring comments that came his way.

The vast majority of those came from his doting parents, and Nikos, standing beside the sofa, was gazing
down at his newborn son with an expression little short
of besotted, accepting all the homage as nothing more
than perfectly right and reasonable. Their son *was* the
most amazing baby ever, and no other could *possibly*
be even a fraction as wonderful.

They were not alone in this view, for Nikos's parents
shared it with them.

'Hah!' exclaimed Stephanos Parakis proudly, gazing
benignly down at his grandson.

'He looks like you,' said his wife fondly. His *new* wife.

Nikos's eyes tore themselves away from his infant
son and settled with approval on Adela Parakis. Even
if she hadn't turned out to be a very calm and level-
headed divorcee of forty-plus, rather than the sultry
mistress he'd assumed, Nikos would have approved of

her. For she had been the catalyst that had finally trig-gered his parents' decision to call time on their tor-mented marriage.

One of the catalysts, Nikos acknowledged.

The other was the elegant silver-haired man at the side of Nikos's mother—the new Principessa Falesi. The widowed Principe had met her at a party in Milan, and such had been his admiration for her that his mother had received with equanimity the news that her hus-band wished to remarry.

Now, as Principessa, she was enjoying a new lease of life—and of beauty. For as her son's eyes perused her they could see that his mother had clearly under-gone a facelift, chosen a dramatically more flattering hairstyle and, if he were not mistaken, had a few addi-tional discreet nips and tucks, as well.

He was glad for her—glad for both his parents. Glad for their late happiness with other partners, and glad that their respective remarriages had enabled them—fi-nally—to be civil to each other…especially when they now had a common fascination with their grandson.

'He has my eyes,' observed the Principessa with complacent satisfaction, approaching with her new husband.

'He does,' Mel smiled. Nikos's mother was being very gracious towards her, and Mel wanted to keep her that way. So she didn't point out that *all* newborns had blue eyes.

Nikos refrained from telling his mother that, actu-ally, his son had his wife's eyes—which just happened to be the most beautiful eyes in the world…

Memory struck through him—how Mel had flashed her sapphire eyes at him in that very first encounter, and how they had pierced him like Cupid's proverbial arrow.

Happiness drenched through him. And disbelief.

A holiday romance? How could he *ever* have been idiotic enough to think Mel—wonderful, fabulous, adorable, beloved Mel—could be nothing more than a holiday romance? She was the most precious person in the world to him.

Along with Nicky, of course.

Instinctively he lifted Mel's free hand in his and wound his fingers warmly into hers. She shifted her gaze to look at him, love shining in her eyes.

'A daughter next, I would recommend,' the Principessa said to Mel.

'Oh, yes,' agreed Mel. 'That would be ideal.'

'But you must watch your figure, my dear,' her mother-in-law reminded her.

'I fully intend to aspire to be as elegant as *you* in that respect,' Mel assured her, and nodded admiringly.

The Principessa gave a little laugh, and bestowed a careful smile of approval on her daughter-in-law. 'You must visit us in Milan, my dear, when my grandson is old enough to travel,' she said, catching her new husband's arm.

'Oh, that would be *lovely*!' enthused Mel. She glanced up at Nikos. 'Wouldn't it?'

'Yes, indeed,' he said hurriedly. 'Are you leaving already?' he asked.

'Alas, we must. We are flying home this evening.'

The guests were starting to disperse, and shortly after his mother's departure Nikos's father left as well, informing his son as he did so that Mel, Nicky and he were also invited to visit himself and Adela whenever they liked.

Nikos thanked him heartily, and saw them both to their car. As he came back into the villa Mel was in the hallway, cradling Nicky, who was now wide awake.

'He needs a change,' she said cheerfully. 'Want to help?'

'I wouldn't miss it for the world.' Nikos grinned. 'Do you mean a nappy-change? Or a change out of that metre-long silk embroidered concoction he's wearing?'

'Both,' said Mel. 'And then, if you won't think me a bad mother, I'll hand him over to Nanny, and you and I can sneak off to dinner before he needs his next feed.'

She gave a wry little smile of gratitude. It was amazing, she acknowledged, just how easy motherhood was when there was a nanny on hand. And when the baby's father was as devoted and willing as Nikos was.

'Great idea,' Nikos said with enthusiasm. 'It's more than time I had you to myself again.'

As they headed upstairs to the lavishly decorated suite that was Nicky's nursery Nikos said, 'By the way, we've been invited to a wedding—'

'Oh? Whose?' asked Mel interestedly.

Nikos gave a glinting smile. 'Would you believe Fiona Pellingham—and Sven?'

Mel gave her gurgle of laughter. 'His name's Magnus,' she said. 'But it's lovely news. I'm so glad for her.'

'Well, you were the matchmaker there,' Nikos reminded her.

Mel smiled fondly at her husband. 'And she was ours in a way, too, if you think about it. If she hadn't been pursuing you, you'd never have asked me out.'

Nikos put his arm around her shoulder. 'I'd have found another reason,' he answered. 'There was no way I could ever get you out of my head.'

She paused at the top of the stairs to kiss his cheek.

Her eyes were soft with love. 'Nor me you,' she assured him.

The dark eyes glinted with wicked humour. 'Love at first sight, was it?'

She spluttered, remembering their intemperate sparring at that first prickly encounter in the sandwich shop. 'We got all the aggro out of the way,' she told him firmly. 'Oh, and on the subject of sandwich shops—I heard that the Sarrie's Sarnies franchise is going great guns. Thanks to your business loan.'

'Well, didn't I promise that if his turnover increased I'd consider funding his expansion?' Nikos reminded her as they gained Nicky's bathroom and got to work on the delicate task of parting him from his ornate christening robe.

'He's very grateful,' Mel assured him. 'And so,' she added, 'is Joe. For sponsoring that new homeless shelter he's in, and the medics for addiction and alcoholism treatment.'

'Well, I'm grateful to Joe in return,' Nikos riposted. 'When I showered him with all those damn pound coins you'd dumped on me in your splenetic rage...' he ducked as Mel swung him a playful thump of objection, then lifted Nicky free of his gown '...I realised you were right about more than just how the booze was killing him—that you were *entitled* to be put out about the way I behaved to you. And that I owed you flowers to make amends.'

Mel gently laid their infant son down on his changing mat. 'Well,' she said, throwing another wicked glance at her husband, 'you can go on making amends.' She stepped aside. 'Go on—your turn for the nappy-change.'

'I couldn't just hand you the clean nappy, could I?' Nikos asked hopefully.

'Nope,' said his wife sternly.

Her husband dropped a resigned kiss on her forehead. 'It's a price I'll pay willingly for a happy marriage,' he told her.

Mel reached up to him with her mouth. 'Correction,' she told him. 'For the happiest marriage in the world.'

She took a wad of cotton wool, holding it at the ready for Nikos, talcum powder in her other hand.

Nikos grinned. 'Right, as always,' he agreed.

Then, with a squaring of his shoulders, he got to work to prove to the woman he loved just how much he loved her...

And beneath their joint ministrations the child who had brought them back together gazed cherubically up at the two people who loved only him more than they loved each other.

* * * * *

MILLS & BOON®

It's Got to be Perfect

When Ellie Rigby throws her three-carat engagement ring into the gutter, she is certain of only one thing. She has yet to know true love!

Fed up with disastrous internet dates and conflicting advice from her friends, Ellie decides to take matters into her own hands. Starting a dating agency, Ellie becomes an expert in love. Well, that is until a match with one of her clients, charming, infuriating Nick, has her questioning everything she's ever thought about love…

Order yours today at
www.millsandboon.co.uk